"Buckley describes vividly the difficulties of
people living and competing with each other in
Elizabethan England."
—*Kirkus Reviews*

High Praise for Fiona Buckley's
Ursula Blanchard Mysteries

A PAWN FOR A QUEEN

"Jam-packed with action, suspense, and court intrigue. . . .
Cleverly plotted. . . . Buckley adeptly captures the spirit
and the drama of the Elizabethan Age."

—*Booklist*

"Ursula continues to tack as skillfully as ever between
loyalties to her ruler and her family—a dramatic
strength this sixth dose of Elizabethan realpolitik brings
into especially sharp focus."

—*Kirkus Reviews*

QUEEN OF AMBITION

"Engrossing. . . . Suspenseful. . . . The challenging plot
and winning heroine will satisfy existing historical fans
and should attract new ones."

—*Publishers Weekly*

QUEEN'S RANSOM

"Buckley's amusingly modern characters mesh successfully with the well-researched plot, and readers will be wrapped up in the sixteenth-century thrill of pitfalls lurking around every corner."

—*Publishers Weekly*

"Now is a nice time for Tudor fans to light a flambeau, reach for some sweetmeats, and curl up with *Queen's Ransom.*"

—*USA Today*

"Quick pacing, a sympathetic and modern heroine, and political intrigue make this sixteenth-century mystery series as complicated and charming as an Elizabethan knot garden."

—*The Tampa Tribune*

"*Queen's Ransom* is a fantastic historical fiction novel filled with royal intrigue. Renowned for her characterizations, Fiona Buckley is a creative storyteller who makes the Elizabethan era fun to read about."

—*Midwest Book Review*

"Satisfying and thought-provoking. Buckley well demonstrates the political and emotional tension between Protestant England and the Catholic states in the early sixteenth century."

—*Over My Dead Body! The Mystery Magazine Online*

THE DOUBLET AFFAIR

"An intricate tale rich in period detail and vivid characters. Among writers of historical mysteries, Buckley stands out for the attention and skill she brings not only to suspenseful plotting but to the setting that supports it."

—*Publishers Weekly*

"Buckley's grasp of period detail and politics, coupled with Ursula's wit and intelligence, make the story doubly satisfying."

—*The Orlando Sentinal* (FL)

"A delectable novel that is must reading."

—*Midwest Book Review*

TO SHIELD THE QUEEN

"The debut of Ursula Blanchard, young, widowed lady of the Presence Chamber at Elizabeth I's court, combines assured storytelling and historical detail. A terrific tale most accessibly told."

—*The Poisoned Pen*

"A lively debut that's filled with vivid characters, religious conflict, subplots and power plays. Ursula is the essence of iron cloaked in velvet—a heroine to reckon with."

—*Kirkus Reviews*

"Buckley's tantalizing re-creation of Elizabethan life and manners is told with intelligence and gentle wit. A noteworthy debut."

—*Library Journal*

ALSO BY FIONA BUCKLEY

A PAWN
for a
QUEEN

FIONA BUCKLEY

POCKET BOOKS
New York London Toronto Sydney Singapore

POCKET BOOKS, a division of Simon & Schuster, Inc.
1230 Avenue of the Americas, New York, NY 10020

Copyright © 2002 by Fiona Buckley

Originally published in hardcover in 2002 by Scribner

All rights reserved, including the right to reproduce
this book or portions thereof in any form whatsoever.
For information address Scribner, 1230 Avenue of
the Americas, New York, NY 10020

ISBN: 0-7434-1031-9

First Pocket Books printing November 2003

10 9 8 7 6 5 4 3 2 1

POCKET and colophon are registered trademarks of
Simon & Schuster, Inc.

Cover design by Min Choi
Front cover illustration by Harry Bliss

Manufactured in the United States of America

For information regarding special discounts for bulk purchases,
please contact Simon & Schuster Special Sales at 1-800-456-6798
or business@simonandschuster.com

This book is for my East Anglian family:
Godfrey, Sandra, David, and Judy

Prologue

It is my wedding day.

I think I have made the right decision. I hope I have. My dear Fran Dale, who has been my devoted (and often harassed and exhausted) tirewoman for so many years, doesn't think so. Nor does her husband, Roger Brockley, my equally devoted though often critical manservant. They both wish I had chosen someone for whom I could feel deeply, as I did for my previous husbands, Matthew de la Roche and Gerald Blanchard.

As for old Gladys, the most ancient member of my household and certainly the most maddening, she has presented me with a love potion that she said, with a fanged leer, might be a help to my bridegroom, in case of any difficulty, mistress.

But Matthew and Gerald are both in their graves and I have had enough of passion. I will trade it gladly for a life that is safe and settled. Yes, even now, though this is the month of May, and the air is full of birdsong and blowing blossom. Passion is beautiful but dangerous. There are many other things that I can share with my new partner in life, many tranquil interests that we have in common. I have made my choice and hope to be content with it.

I am dressed, brocade skirts gleaming, my hair brushed to a dark gloss and folded into waves in front of a white cap edged with beads of gold and crystal. I have put on the rope of pearls that is my bridegroom's gift to me. He awaits me now, and the minstrels are ready to play for us as soon as we emerge from the church, and to escort us back to Withysham House, where the feast is laid.

Am I doing the right thing or the wrong thing?

I once told my friend Rob Henderson that I loved the call of wild geese as they flew. He replied, not altogether approvingly, that I had just said something about my nature. Just as I have said farewell to passion, I must also part with the wild side of my nature, now.

And about time, too. I'm so thankful.

I think.

1

In the Dark of the Morning

At half past seven on a January morning, the dawn should have been breaking, but the sky was so overcast that to all intents and purposes, it was still dark and I had half a dozen servants standing about with flambeaux so that our little party could see to mount the horses.

Malton, the elderly former steward who had been called out of retirement to look after Withysham while the present steward, Roger Brockley, accompanied me on my journey, held one of the torches and another was in the unsteady grasp of ancient Gladys, who was even older than Malton and shouldn't be out in this bitter northeasterly but had insisted all the same.

Gladys wasn't exactly a servant, more a responsibility. She did what she could about the house and was good at doctoring hurts and fevers and also at milking cows, but I didn't employ her. She had attached herself to me, and Gladys, bless her acid tongue and good heart, was fond of me.

The chill wind, flowing over the downs of Sussex, carried a threat of snow. The breaths of people and horses alike smoked visibly in the torchlight. Brockley, who was also an experienced groom, had made sure that all the horses had warm saddlecloths, but as I mounted, I could tell by the droop of my gelding's head that he would rather have stayed in his nice snug stall. I sympathized. I too was well clad but my teeth would have chattered if I'd let them. My tirewoman, Fran Dale, already in her saddle, was less restrained than I was, and her teeth really were chattering, audibly. My nine-year-old daughter, Meg, perched on her sturdy pony, was just a small, hunched shape beneath her stout cloak and felt hat, and her nurse, Bridget, waiting on the pillion of Brockley's cob, Speckle, was a weird spectacle because she was a fat woman to start with and her defense against the weather consisted of a vast hooded mantle that Bridget had constructed herself using old blankets, because she said that they were thicker than conventional materials. As a result, Speckle looked as though he had a she-bear on his crupper.

I settled myself, gathering up my reins and gazing wistfully back at my house. Withysham Abbey was not modern. My home had no white plaster and black timbering, no tall ornamental chimneys or elegant imitation battlements. It had once been an abbey of nuns, until King Henry the Eighth dissolved the monasteries and sold off their buildings and lands, and even now, Withysham's quiet gray stone walls, its low, pointed doorways and slender leaded windows, had an out-dated, ecclesiastical air.

But it was homely, too. The candlelight within the flawed medieval panes spoke of comfort indoors. At this moment, I wished with all my heart that I were back in the friendly shelter of those lit rooms. My earlier willingness for this errand had completely evaporated. I shouldn't be doing this, I thought. I didn't *want* to do it. The seventeenth of January, with snow in the wind, was no time to start a journey that would take me at least to Northumberland and might even compel me over the border into Scotland. Besides, I was worried about Meg.

As if she had heard me thinking, Meg edged her pony over to me. "Mother?"

"We'll be on the move in a moment, darling. I hope you're warm enough."

"Yes, thank you. Only, I wanted to ask . . ."

"Yes, sweetheart?" I said, larding my words with endearments because I was so very anxious about her and so reluctant to face the separation that was now only a day away.

"Will it be all right? Will the Hendersons let me stay with them?"

"What makes you think they won't, darling? They've always made you welcome before."

"I know, but . . . once or twice, I've heard you talking to Dale and Brockley . . . I wasn't listening on purpose. I just heard you."

"Did you, indeed, little Mistress Bigears?" I said, trying to sound amused.

"Yes. I'm sorry, Mother. But—will it be all right?"

"I hope so!" I said.

Brockley was swinging into his saddle and checking his girth. Dale was muttering dismally that this was terrible, that she never could abide riding long distances and in cold weather like this . . . !

"Let be, Fran," said Brockley. I still called my tire-woman Dale because that was her name when she entered my service but since then, she and Brockley had married. Strictly speaking, she was Mistress Brockley now, which was often an advantage because Brockley could sometimes check her habit of complaining, which I rarely managed to do.

"We're on our way now, and that's that," Brockley said firmly. "You wouldn't want to stay behind and neither the mistress nor I would want that, either. Madam?"

"Yes, Brockley," I said. "We're on our way."

And so, calling good-byes to the shivering servants, we started out. As we reached the gates, I glanced back once more and noticed wryly that they had plunged back into the warmth of the house before we had fairly left the premises. The flambeaux were gone. Only the faint glimmer of candlelit windows remained. How long, I wondered, before I would see my home again?

I should never have agreed to this, but it was too late now.

My family, the Faldenes, had old-fashioned attitudes, and in more ways than one. They clung to the old Catholic religion despite Queen Elizabeth's legislation against it, and their domestic life was similarly behind the times. In modern households, it was now customary for the family to dine in private, separately from their servants. At my family home of Faldene House, where I was brought up, everyone dined together and the great hall was still the center of the household, just as it had been in medieval times.

It was also still decorated with the swords and pikes of bygone Faldenes who had fought at Agincourt and Crécy. According to my mother, when she came home in disgrace from the court of King Henry the Eighth, with child by a court gallant whom she would not name—presumably because he was married—her outraged parents and her brother, Herbert, marched her around the hall, pointing at these relics of heroism, and accused her of betraying them. Which was most unfair because many of the family's bygone heroes had had careers that were as lively off the battlefield as on it, and we had plenty of unofficial relatives in Faldene village and beyond it, too, in the neighboring hamlet of Westwater and in the village attached to my present home of Withysham, five miles away.

I, Ursula Faldene, was the daughter born to my mother after her return home. When my grandparents died, the responsibility for my mother and for me passed to Uncle Herbert and his thin, sour wife, Aunt Tabitha. They discharged it dutifully, I suppose. We weren't turned out to beg for our bread. That much, I admit.

I was even allowed to share their children's tutor, and thus I did receive an education, though it was a grudging one. What I did not receive, however, except from my mother, was kindness. When I was sixteen, she too died, I think worn-out by life in a constant atmosphere of disapproval. I might well have ended my days as unpaid dogsbody to my aunt and accounts clerk to my uncle (who eventually realized that an educated Ursula could be of more use than an illiterate one), except that I caught the eye of Gerald Blanchard, son of a neighbor.

Unfortunately, Gerald was betrothed to my well-dowered cousin Mary, daughter of Uncle Herbert and Aunt Tabitha. I suppose it was natural for our respective families to be enraged when we eloped.

We never regretted it, though. With Gerald, I traveled to Antwerp, where he worked for the queen's financier, Sir Thomas Gresham, and it was Gerald who gave me my dark-haired daughter, Meg. When he died of small-pox, Meg and I came home to England and an uncertain future, because neither the Faldenes nor the Blanchards were willing to help us. Mercifully, we had other friends, including Gresham, who were more generous. Strings were pulled; arrangements were made. Foster parents were found for Meg, and Ursula Blanchard, impoverished widow, became a Lady of the Queen's Presence Chamber, and after a time, married again, this time to a Frenchman, Matthew de la Roche.

That was a passionate union but a doomed one, for he was Elizabeth's enemy, working against her, which too often drove us apart. Now Matthew too was dead, of a summer plague, and I was widowed once more, but by this time I was well provided for. I was the chatelaine of Withysham, dignified and comfortable, with profitable land attached to it. I had expected to live there, retired from court life and united with my daughter at last, and—well, yes—to enjoy the chagrin of Uncle Herbert and Aunt Tabitha at having their despised and baseborn niece as a well-off, well-respected, and extremely well-dressed neighbor.

What I didn't expect was to be hunted up by a distracted Aunt Tabitha and dragged, not by coercion but by pleading, back to Faldene and put in the position of one who could be their savior, if only I would let bygones be bygones and agree.

2

The Cry of the Wild Geese

It had happened so quickly. Only twenty-four hours before that dismal dawn start, I had woken to what I thought would be an ordinary day at home. Before midday, I had been confronted in my own parlor by an Aunt Tabitha I hardly recognized, dressed in an old cloak that she must have snatched up without looking at, and with her gray hair escaping from a cap that didn't even look clean and a desperate expression. Asked what the matter was, she said: "We need your help. Our son . . . your cousin Edward . . . he has gone to Scotland and . . . I think he's gone to do something . . . something that people might say is wrong . . ."

"To do with Mary Stuart?" I asked sharply. Mary Stuart was Queen Elizabeth's rival for the throne of England and she was in Scotland. And the Faldenes had conspired on her behalf on a previous occasion.

"Yes. Yes! He's been before. Your uncle and I have been worried for a long time. I wanted to ask your advice in the summer, before you went off to court, but I didn't know what to say. I didn't think I could trust you. Not after what you did to my husband. Only now . . . we're all frightened. His wife is frightened too and . . . Ursula, you're the only person now that we *dare* trust. You're family. We want you to go after him and bring him back and . . . stop him before it's too late! It would be in the interests of the queen . . . yes, I know we're Catholics, but we can't let Edward risk himself like this . . . young people can be so passionate . . . Ursula, please help us!"

I asked her to tell me what she meant. "If it's in Elizabeth's interest," I said, "I will help you if I can."

"It *would* be to the queen's advantage," said Aunt Tabitha earnestly. "We want Edward to stop what he's doing—stop completely. Ursula, come back to Faldene with me. Your uncle's there, and Helene, Edward's wife. They want to talk to you too. Come *now*," Aunt Tabitha implored me. "Then I won't have to explain it all twice."

An hour later, I was in Faldene House, sitting by the hearth in the great hall. The fire was well made up against the cold and on a nearby table stood glasses and a wine jug, meat pies, and sweet cakes. A hovering servant girl was ready to refill glasses and offer the dishes.

Aunt Tabitha set great store by the social niceties. Her servants were so well trained that they were sometimes attentive to irritation point, and my aunt would always proffer refreshment to a visitor, no matter how odd or harassing the circumstances. When the Faldenes went in for conspiracy before, Uncle Herbert had been arrested, and according to my kitchenmaids, who had kinfolk in service at Faldene, she had even offered food and drink to the men who came to do the arresting.

My uncle owed that unhappy experience to me. When I was at court, I had done rather more than walk, dance, and ride with Queen Elizabeth, and occasionally, as a privilege, carry her prayer book and hand it to her in chapel. I had also undertaken a number of confidential and sometimes dangerous tasks for her Secretary of State, Sir William Cecil. Withysham had been granted to me in payment for one of those tasks. It was my success in another that had led to Uncle Herbert's removal, for several months, to the Tower of London.

In other words, I had first stolen his daughter's betrothed and then sent my uncle himself to jail. It was hardly surprising that he detested me. Nevertheless, it was through the episode of the Tower that he and my aunt had learned of my secret other life. Now I sat sipping their wine and thinking that all this had an ironic side to it. In this hall, I had been shouted at and bullied and even beaten; in this hall I had wept with pain, trembled with fear, and seethed with rage that I dared not express. Now I was the one with the power. Today, they were in such desperation that they wanted to call on my services themselves.

It was plain enough, of course, that my cousin Edward was in some way breaking the law. That gave me a qualm, but if whatever was required of me really was in Queen Elizabeth's interests, then surely I could do it, and keep my family's counsel as well. For one thing, although in the past I had suffered unkindness at their hands, I had not actually *wanted* to send my uncle to the Tower and certainly didn't wish to do so again. Whatever pain he and my aunt had caused me in my childhood, I had already done them more than enough harm to outweigh it.

Also, like it or not, Aunt Tabitha was right: the Faldenes were family, and as I had never known my father, they were the only family I had. Big, fleshy Herbert Faldene, with his inborn stinginess and his gout, was nevertheless my uncle, my mother's brother, and his son Edward, Helene's husband, was still my cousin. Anyway, there were children involved.

When the rest of the family had joined me by the fire, Helene was the first to speak.

"You have come to see us at my mother-in-law's plea. Does that mean you will help us? I beg you that you will, madame." Helene had been brought up in France and had retained French mannerisms. Marriage, indeed, hadn't changed her at all as far as I could see. She was still the same lanky young woman I had first met three years ago, with the same pale complexion, mousy hair, and round shoulders. "I have two little girls," she said. "If anything befalls Edward, they will be fatherless." She also retained the high-pitched and self-righteous voice that had always set my teeth on edge.

"It is a dreadful thing for children to be deprived of a father," said Aunt Tabitha.

"He would be a martyr," said Helene, "and that is noble—but . . ."

I couldn't quite resist letting them know that old

hurts still rankled. "You feel that the substance might be better than even the most admirable shadow?" I said caustically. I turned to Aunt Tabitha. "I had no father," I said. "And my daughter, Meg, lost hers and much you cared."

"Please, Ursula." It was extraordinary to hear that tone of appeal in my aunt's voice.

My uncle was less restrained. "Your mother was always gentle in her manners, I'll grant her that. You must take after your father—whoever he was," he said. He leaned toward me as he spoke, his stiff, heavily padded red doublet creasing across his ample stomach. His right foot, sliding forward, bumped into the table leg. He yelped. "Damnable gout! It's the curse of my life. Despite the fact that we didn't know who on earth your father was, my wench, we gave you a home and an education. You owe us something. Without a good upbringing, you would not have been acceptable at court. Do you forget that?"

"Herbert, I beg you!" Aunt Tabitha protested, and Helene, taking out a handkerchief, wiped tears from her eyes. Her distress was obviously real, and in spite of myself, I felt sorry for her.

"You are our only hope," she said tearfully. "Please don't fail us!"

"I spoke my mind," I said. "I admit I have a sharp tongue." My second husband's nickname for me had been Saltspoon. My saltiness was part of my attraction for him, although from the moment we were wed, he did his best to make me sweeter. Poor Matthew.

I would never hear him call me Saltspoon again.

No use to think of Matthew now. "Tell me the full

story," I said. "My cousin Edward, I take it, has been dabbling in . . ." I was going to say *treason* but checked myself ". . . in politics."

"As did your French husband, Matthew de la Roche," said Uncle Herbert. "In fact, they were in touch, working together."

The story came out, told by first one and then another. Being Catholic, my family did not regard Queen Elizabeth as the rightful monarch since their Church didn't acknowledge that her parents, King Henry the Eighth and his second wife, Anne Boleyn, were ever lawfully married. For Catholics, the true queen was Mary Stuart of Scotland, an undoubtedly legitimate descendant of King Henry the Seventh.

"As you well know," said Uncle Herbert grimly, "I was imprisoned for the crime of helping to gather money for her and collecting information about English households willing to support her claim. Ah, that Tower! The cold! I confess it—when I was freed, I feared to go on with the work, but my son Edward volunteered in my stead and his contact was Matthew de la Roche."

"I was so proud of him," said Helene mournfully. "But . . ."

"I knew that Matthew was engaged in dealings of this kind," I said. "But we never discussed them and I had no idea that he was still in touch with Faldene."

"As part of his work," said Uncle Herbert, "your husband compiled a list of households friendly to Mary and sent it to Scotland. Edward was one of his informants, one of many, of course. When the civil war broke out in France, the work virtually came to a halt, but last year, after the war had ended, Edward went to France."

"He didn't go on . . . on political business, not at first," said Helene. "His purpose, madame, was to sell my property there. We hoped to use the money to buy a house here."

"Edward, as you know," said Uncle Herbert, "is not our eldest son. Faldene will eventually go to his elder brother, Francis. Edward and his family are welcome here while we live, but they cannot stay here forever."

"Edward managed the sale and brought the money home," said Helene. "But while he was in France, he also called upon your husband, the Seigneur de la Roche."

"Did he? I had no idea." I spoke bleakly, thinking with sorrow how much Matthew and I had had to conceal from each other. "I suppose I had come back to England by then," I added.

Matthew and I had lived together in France for a while, and my visit to England the previous spring should only have been a brief absence from him, to deal with a family matter. But first one thing and then another had intervened to keep me on this side of the Channel, and then the plague had come and taken Matthew's life.

"I expect so," said Helene. "It was in May." I nodded. "Anyway, your husband was pleased to see Edward. Seigneur de la Roche wished to set the work going again and to prepare a new, up-to-date list."

"The list would certainly have altered during the interruption of the civil war. Some people would have died and others would have changed sides," said Uncle Herbert. "Very often," he added sourly, "those are the ones who are living in what used to be abbeys. They are afraid that if Mary Stuart were to come to power, she would want to restore the stolen buildings to the Church. I daresay you understand, Ursula. After all, Withysham was once an abbey."

Aunt Tabitha rolled her eyes and I found myself giving her a reassuring smile. "It's all right," I said. "I am not going to take offense. Please go on."

Edward had apparently agreed to communicate with some of Matthew's sources of information in England. He would write to some and visit others personally. He had been educated in Northumberland and was acquainted with a number of the said sources in that district. He had agreed to visit these himself in order to coax worthwhile offers of support out of them. Having obtained as much information and as many promises as he could, he would send a report to Matthew, who would meanwhile have collected extra details from various other people with whom he was directly in touch. He would complete the updated list and dispatch it to Mary. "For the time being, we put off looking for a house of our own," said Helene. "Edward had much to do. He had many letters to write and he had to take great care in choosing trustworthy messengers."

"He dismissed his valet," said Aunt Tabitha. "He found the man reading his correspondence and suspected that the man was a government spy. A shocking thing. Such a betrayal of trust."

"There is more than one kind of treachery," I said, and saw them flinch. "What happened next?" I asked.

"I became frightened, because of the valet," said

Helene. "It looked as though Edward might be under suspicion . . ."

"To begin with," said Aunt Tabitha, "Edward didn't tell us of his meeting with your husband in France. We didn't at first know that he had begun the work again or realize why he had sent the valet away." She beckoned to the hovering servant girl. "The wine jug needs refilling. And go and make sure that my guest's manservant has had proper refreshment."

"Please, madam, do you wish for any further cakes or pasties?"

"Yes, yes, by all means." Aunt Tabitha waved the girl impatiently away. "What was I saying? Just after the valet was dismissed, Edward traveled north to see his contacts there in person as he had promised to do. He told *us*—his parents—that he was simply going to see old acquaintances in Northumberland. But while he was away, we saw that Helene was very anxious over something. She was pregnant at the time and she was so worried that it made her ill."

"I kept fainting," said Helene miserably. "And weeping."

"At length," said Aunt Tabitha, "we persuaded her to tell us what was wrong and then we learned why he had really gone to Northumberland and also that he intended to visit Scotland as well—and that before he left, he had had reason to think that his valet was spying on him. We agreed with Helene that this must mean that someone somewhere suspected Edward. We were greatly alarmed. That was when we first considered coming to you—except that we were afraid to trust you."

"I had never been easy in my mind about Edward's work for Mary Stuart," said Uncle Herbert. "But he was so eager . . ."

"And I encouraged him," said Helene, sniffing. "As I said, I was so proud of him. But not after the business with the valet! I tried to dissuade him from going north and I was so thankful when he came safely back. I implored him to take no more risks. He said he wouldn't. He said that he had learned some very useful facts. He had only to put them together with the reports he had asked for, from other people in different parts of the country, and then he could prepare his final document for Matthew and his task would be done. The other reports had mostly come while he was away, so he was able to get on with that without delay. And then . . ."

I interrupted. "How did Edward communicate with my husband? Or indeed, with his contacts elsewhere in the country?"

"We have reliable servants here," said Uncle Herbert. "They carry messages within the country. For keeping in touch with Matthew de la Roche, in France, we used Matthew's own couriers. There were two regular ones. They even kept to their normal schedule throughout the time of the civil war. They traveled back and forth between France and Scotland. One was an itinerant tooth-drawer and the other was a peddler. The tooth-drawer went on foot; the peddler had a mule. They were excellent couriers because they were so ordinary. They were the sort of folk no one ever notices."

I said nothing but inwardly I sighed. Matthew and I

had disagreed about so much, but I had truly loved him, and curiously, one of the most endearing things about him had been a kind of innocence. Matthew genuinely believed that Mary Stuart ought to be queen of England, and that if she became so she could simply tell the English to return to what he called the true faith, and that would be that. The truth was that Mary would never gain the throne without a vicious and gory civil war, and if she won it, then England would be wide open to emissaries of the Inquisition with all its attendant horrors. I could never make Matthew see it. When I tried to point these things out, it was as though my words just slid off from him, turning away like beggars from a closed front door.

Now, I thought, my uncle and his family were displaying the same streak of innocence. From working with Sir William Cecil, I knew very well that ordinary men making commonplace but frequent journeys were the likeliest bearers of treasonable messages and that they were far from unnoticed. Cecil had a payroll on which literally hundreds of harbormasters, innkeepers, and ships' captains were listed, and they kept him informed of who traveled on what routes and how often. I had no doubt that the journeys of the tooth-drawer and the peddler had been noted long since. What Helene said as she resumed the story confirmed it.

"I was afraid that Edward would be angry when he knew that I had told his parents what he was about, but when he came home, he just shrugged and said that he had expected them to guess, anyway, since he had used Faldene servants to carry messages back and forth," she said. "He made his report—it was in the form of a list of families and what each family had offered—and waited for one or the other of your husband's couriers to arrive. The peddler usually came back from Scotland in early August and the tooth-drawer perhaps a week or two later. But they didn't come, and then a messenger brought word of your husband's death to Withysham, and as a matter of family courtesy, the news was passed to us by your steward, Malton. Edward was upset. He didn't know what to do. He had no idea who had replaced Matthew de la Roche, if indeed anyone had! But soon after that, another messenger, a stranger from London, came to tell us that the tooth-drawer and the peddler had both been seized on their way south and were in prison in London. And then . . . then . . ."

"Edward became so anxious about his new list," said Aunt Tabitha. "De la Roche had intended the information eventually for Mary Stuart in Scotland—in Edinburgh—but De la Roche was dead . . ."

"And Edward decided not to worry about the extra items of information that Matthew had collected and to take his own list to Scotland himself," I said helpfully. "Am I right?"

"The man from London refused to carry it," said my uncle. "He said it was too dangerous, that the arrest of the other two couriers showed that too much was known. But Edward left yesterday, despite all the pleading of his womenfolk."

"Father-in-law, you yourself begged him not to go!" said Helene.

I glanced toward the tall windows that looked out

to the front of the house. The sky beyond was iron gray, and the ride from Withysham had been bitter. "Why so much haste? If it's as cold as this in Sussex, the snow in the north is probably six feet deep."

"It wasn't haste, precisely. He didn't mean to travel *ventre à terre*," said Helene. "He said that if the weather slowed him down, it couldn't be helped, but go he would, just the same, simply to be done with it. He promised to take care, and to call on his friends in the north, as before, as though he were just making social visits . . ."

"Such a likely thing to do, in January!" snorted Aunt Tabitha.

". . . and just make a brief visit across the border, deliver the list, and come back," Helene finished. "But . . ."

"The valet," said Aunt Tabitha, "and the two couriers who were arrested, all this has made us sure that Edward is most likely being watched, has perhaps been followed. We did indeed argue against it, but he wouldn't listen and set off yesterday, as your uncle says. We were up most of last night, fretting and worrying, and in the end, we decided. Someone must go after him, catch him before he crosses the Scottish border if possible—and make him see that it's too perilous; he must come back and . . ."

"Tear the list up," I said. "That is my price. On that, I insist. If necessary, I'll steal the list and tear it up myself. I'll probably have to. If he won't listen to you, why should he listen to me?"

"He knows what you did to me in the past, for Queen Elizabeth's sake. You can threaten him," said my uncle candidly. "None of us can because he knows we would never carry the threat out. You, on the other hand, might. You might also be better than any of us at such things as stealing lists. You're our only chance, anyway. I can't go. My gout won't let me. My elder son, Francis, as Edward once did, is gaining experience of the world in an ambassador's entourage and is in Austria. I can't even inform him, let alone call on him for help. Your aunt isn't strong enough and Helene has her children to care for."

"One barely a year and a half old and little Catherine not yet three months!" said Helene. "If anything happens to Edward now, they won't even be able to remember their father! Madame, he is not, as I told you, traveling in great haste, and he means to linger a day or two with more than one household in Northumberland. If you tried, we think you might be able to catch him up. Will you try? Will you?"

"It's your kind of task, isn't it, Ursula?" my uncle said. "I never thought I'd see the day when I had to ask you to use your curious and frankly, in my opinion, your dubious skills for us . . ."

"Herbert!" wailed Aunt Tabitha.

I looked out of the window. The winter dusk was already gathering. I said: "Today is nearly over. But I can leave at first light tomorrow morning."

I had better reasons for agreeing than they knew. I knew a good deal about the current political situation. A young man called Henry Lord Darnley, a Tudor descendant and a cousin of both Queen Elizabeth and Queen Mary, was due at any moment to start out for Scotland, ostensibly to see his father, who was visiting the family estates there, but in reality to present himself to Queen Mary as a potential husband.

He was being allowed to go only because he was a slightly less lethal prospect than a marriage between Mary and some Catholic prince with armies at his command. Even so, a Mary Stuart reinforced by a Tudor-bred consort could be very interested indeed in having up-to-date details of people who might help her to raise an army on English soil. It was my duty to get my hands on that list if I could and destroy it.

And I had another reason for agreeing. I didn't say yes simply because it was my duty or even because Edward was family (though I did have a glow of satisfaction over my own good-heartedness).

It was the excitement that drew me. I did not have the kind of nature that could be satisfied forever with well-planned dinners and linen rooms full of faultlessly folded sheets interleaved with dried lavender. Plenty of people considered that wrong in a woman—there were times, indeed, when I thought so as well—but it was the way I was made. Queen Elizabeth and Cecil had recognized it and made use of it.

This particular opportunity had come to me in a time of grief and loneliness like a summons back to life. It was like the call of the wild geese in the cold, wide sky, a sound that I loved.

Or so it seemed when I was sitting by the hearth at Faldene. The mood didn't last through the cold early start next morning. Then, as I rode reluctantly through the gatehouse arch of Withysham, I wondered at myself. On more than one occasion in the past, I had determined to give up my perilous way of life. Every time I made such a resolution, I seemed to break it five minutes later. A new task, a new set of challenges, would call to me, like the siren voices of the wild geese. It seemed that I would just never learn.

3

Lying to a Friend

"I can give you money," said my uncle Herbert. "A hundred and fifty pounds in sovereigns."

An anguished spasm, which had nothing to do with gout, crossed his face as he spoke. My uncle hated broaching his coffers. His anxiety about Edward must be intense. "A horse could go lame," he explained. "You might need to buy another. Or you might get into some kind of trouble and . . . need to bribe someone."

Edward, annoyed at being pursued and alarmed at being threatened, might arrange for me to get into trouble, he meant. We both knew it but neither of us spelled it out.

"I'll take it and return what I don't need." I was thinking rapidly. "I'll have to make arrangements for Meg," I said. Aunt Tabitha started to say that Meg could come to Faldene but I looked at her, and she fell silent.

She knew that I would never consign Meg or any other child to her.

"What I do need," I said, "is all the information you have. *All*. Everything that you can tell me about Edward's journey and the people he intends to visit in Northumberland and Scotland."

My cousin, it appeared, had not been indifferent to the risk he was running. His sense of duty had sent him northward but he too had been alarmed by the incident of the valet and the fate of the two couriers. His decision not to travel fast was partly because he wanted to be unobtrusive. For the same reason, he was riding his own horse rather than attempting to hire as he went along.

"Hiring makes a traveler more noticeable. He didn't want that," Helene said. A strand of mousy hair slipped out of her cap and she pushed it aside with a tremulous hand. "He'll have to be careful even in Scotland itself! Queen Mary's right-hand man is her half brother James Stewart—the Earl of Moray—and they say he's a Protestant! He may not be in sympathy with this business—with his sister collecting the names of English supporters, I mean. Edward might not be safe even in Edinburgh!"

I gathered that Edward intended to stay at inns as he journeyed through England. "Until he reaches Northumberland," said my uncle. "Once there, as we've told you, he'll stay with his various friends."

Northumberland was a Catholic stronghold, which was why Edward and his brother Francis had been educated for a while in a Northumbrian home. The family concerned was gone now. The older generation had

died and their son had left the county. They had however had a social circle in their district, and Edward
and Francis had of course made acquaintances among
the neighboring families.

Edward was apparently going to call on four households between the Northumbrian town of Newcastle
and Scotland. There were the Elkinthorpes, who lived
in Newcastle, and the Wrights, whose home was about
ten miles farther north. Two others, the Bycroft and the
Thursby families, lived close to the border, and within
nine miles of each other.

"He knows the Thursbys very well," Helene said.
"Or so he told me. The Bycrofts are the ones he knows
least—he only met them through the Thursbys last
summer. They and the Thursbys are friends. He means
to visit both, though. He said that the Bycrofts live a
mile to the west of a hamlet called Grimstone. They
have the same name as their house—Bycroft. The
Thursbys live somewhere called St. Margaret's."

I asked for writing materials and took notes busily.
"Tell me," I said, "in case I have to chase him right across
the border, where exactly is he going in Edinburgh? To
the court? Does he have an entrée there?"

"Not directly," said Aunt Tabitha. "Your husband's
original messengers, the peddler and the tooth-drawer,
were humble folk and they passed messages to Queen
Mary through intermediaries. Edward means to use
the same intermediaries. He knows them—he met
them when he went to Scotland last year. There are two
of them. Dear God, I would go after him myself but I
cannot ride far or fast any longer. Age tells."

For the first time ever, it struck me that Aunt

Tabitha was indeed looking older. She gazed at me out of tired eyes. "Helene knows their names," she said.

"Yes," said Helene. She frowned, putting her fingers to her temples. "If I can remember aright. I made him tell me, before he went. He didn't want to—I think in case suspicion pointed to this house and we were questioned. But I said I had to know where he was going and who he meant to see; I had to!" Her voice rose, with a hysterical edge. "So in the end, he did, though he didn't write them down and said I mustn't, either. One of them is a man called Sir Brian Dormbois. He is in the service of an uncle of Queen Mary—I think he controls the retainers. But he has a house of his own outside Edinburgh. The other's a woman—a widow, related in some way to one of the queen's maids of honor. There are four of them, all called Marie. This woman's name is Simone . . . Lady Simone Something." She massaged her temples fiercely. "Lady . . . Lady Simone Dougal, that's it. But I can't tell you how to find her." She looked at my rapidly moving pen. "I don't think you really ought to write down names."

"I'll be careful," I said. "But this is information I must have and though my memory is good I dare not risk a lapse. I'll carry this note folded small and squashed into my stays."

Uncle Herbert said anxiously: "You should be able to catch him up. You will be trying to hurry, while he isn't. But you must go properly attended, for safety and propriety. Take those two servants of yours with you, but don't let them slow you down. I advise you to use your own horses, as Edward is doing."

"I agree," I said, thinking that Dale would hate all

this. She was a poor rider and apt to tire quickly. I really ought not to take her, but I must have Roger Brockley and there were good reasons why, in that case, I couldn't leave Dale behind. My best chance of overtaking Edward before the Scottish border probably depended on the visits he meant to make in Northumberland. They would halt him for a few days, and with just a little luck, I would catch up with him there. I had better not use my favorite mare, Bay Star, because with her Arabian blood and delicate legs, she wouldn't be strong enough to cope with long distances in what might well be terrible northern weather.

"Leave quickly, for the love of God!" Aunt Tabitha implored me.

"Yes, as soon as you can! You must, you *must* overtake him in time!" cried Helene.

Roger Brockley had come with us to Faldene and was waiting to escort me home. On the way, I told him what I had undertaken. As always, I was frank with him. Roger Brockley was a countryman approaching fifty, a stocky, dignified figure with a high, polished forehead strewn with gold freckles and steady blue-gray eyes. His calm voice had a country burr and he was as reliable as granite. I could trust him with my life. Indeed, in the past, I had. We were friends, no more, but no less, either. I knew what he would say to this and he duly said it.

"Oh, madam!" he said, and shook his head at me reprovingly, as though I were an erring child. "Setting out for Scotland in January!"

"Edward's my cousin," I said firmly, "and I have to get him back before he runs into real danger. I have no choice. Nor, I'm afraid, have you—or Dale. I know," I said, "that in her own favorite phrase, she just can't abide long-distance riding, but it will be that or stay behind at Withysham and she won't agree to that, I know."

"Nor should she," Brockley agreed.

We didn't enlarge. We understood each other well enough. There had been a time—a very brief time—when the friendship between me and Roger Brockley had slid perilously close to love, and Dale had known it. We had drawn back from the brink, and Dale had nothing now to fear. The decision we had taken was forever. Nevertheless, I knew quite well that Dale would rather die in the saddle than stay at Withysham while Roger and I rode for Scotland without her.

Once I was home, what seemed like half a hundred things had to be settled at top speed. Dale, predictably, set up a wail at the prospect of such a journey in such a rush—"and oh, Mistress Blanchard, in *January,* oh dear, oh dear . . . !" But when told to pack she did as she was bidden and packed for herself as well, without further ado.

The most difficult matter to deal with was that of Meg. Her small face drooped when I told her. "But, Mother, I thought you were going to stay here and that we were going to study together."

I put my arms around her. Meg would be ten years old next June, and every day she seemed to grow more like my first husband, Gerald. Lately, perhaps because she and I had been together more than we had been for years, I had noticed the resemblance more. At times it was so strong that it even sent me to my mirror to look at myself, to notice that in this way or that I was like my mother—and then to wonder which characteristics came from my unknown father, and wish, more strongly than ever before, that I knew who he was and what he had been like.

Meg was so much her father's child. Her hair was rook's wing dark, and her eyes were brown, just like Gerald's. My own dark hair had a faint reddish tinge and my eyes were hazel. Her face was shaped like his, too, with a square chin, quite unlike my pointed one. In Meg, I saw Gerald again, and despite all that had happened since I lost him, I would never forget him. I was glad to have Meg as a living testimony to that happy, stolen first marriage of mine.

I had enjoyed teaching her. She was an apt pupil, neat-fingered at her embroidery and on the virginals, but sharp-minded too, so that instructing her in Latin was a delight, like filling a bright glass with good wine. "It's only for a short while," I told her. "Perhaps a month. It might be less if the weather is kind. In the meantime, you can stay with Mistress Henderson at Thamesbank. You know you like it there. Why, it's your second home! You spent years there when I was at court—and in France."

"Yes, Mother," said Meg with a sigh, and not until we were actually setting off did she tacitly admit that she knew that the Hendersons and I were no longer the friends we had once been because she had heard me talking to the Brockleys.

I didn't have secrets from either of them and it was true that I had talked to them about my rift with the Hendersons. It was not a rift with Mattie, but with her husband. He too was an agent in Cecil's employ. The previous year, we had worked together on the same task, seeking out the truth of a dangerous plot in East Anglia and delving into the life of a curious and far from amusing family with the unsuitable surname of Jester. I had been more successful than Henderson, and he had resented it.

All the same, I hoped the Hendersons wouldn't refuse to take care of Meg for me. She would be better off at their home, Thamesbank, than here with only her nurse, Bridget, to look after her. At Thamesbank, she would have the company of the Henderson children, and could study with their tutor.

I decided that we would carry saddlebags and shoulder satchels and dispense with a packhorse, although it would limit the amount of spare clothing we could carry. To Uncle Herbert's sovereigns, worth thirty shillings each, I added the same amount from my own coffers, including some coinage of smaller value. The total was heavy in weight, but divided among the three of us, it was manageable.

As an agent of Sir William Cecil, I also had a habit of wearing an open overskirt with secret pouches hidden inside them, in which I could carry a dagger and a set of lockpicks (this had often proved useful). I added a few extra sovereigns as well.

Our first day's journey brought us to Thamesbank, to

the west of London, near Hampton, just as dusk was falling. The porter sent his son running ahead of us from the gatehouse to alert the household, and as we rode into the courtyard, to the usual greeting of barking dogs and cackling geese, Mattie Henderson came out to meet us. "Ursula! The boy said it was Mistress Blanchard, with her daughter, but I could hardly believe . . . you sent no word in advance and I didn't expect . . . !"

"No, I suppose you didn't," I agreed. "I didn't have time to forewarn you. But we're here now, and the reason why we've come is important. Can we shelter here for the night?"

"Of course you can. Get down and come inside!"

Presently, I joined Mattie in her parlor, where a fire was burning, candles were lit, and hot food was already waiting. Bridget and Meg had gone to the nursery and Dale had withdrawn to eat with Brockley in the kitchen. "But they'll have the same as us and there's hot milk for Meg, as well," said Mattie. "I didn't think you'd want to wait for supper. You must be perished. Rob isn't here. He's at court. Now, sit down, and tell me what I can do for you."

I sat opposite my friend, and in the light of the candles, we studied each other's face.

"I've missed you," said Mattie. "It's a long time since we have even exchanged letters. How are you? I was so sorry to learn about Matthew's death."

"Thank you."

"I never thought it was a wise marriage for you," said Mattie honestly, "but you loved him and I know what that's like, too. I have thought of you often and prayed for you. Please believe me."

"I do. How is your new baby? Well, she's some months old by now, of course. You called her Elizabeth, didn't you?"

"Yes. You shall see her presently. She's a bonny child, though she was so small when she was born that we feared for her. They feared for me, too, but I came through safely though forty is late for childbearing."

"I prayed for you," I told her. "Rob was very worried about you, you know."

Mattie nodded. She had changed, I thought. The Mattie I had known had been bubbly and slightly irreverent, but now her face was grave and her dark blue woolen gown and plum-colored kirtle were a sober choice of colors for her. The beginning of an extra chin was propped on her neat white ruff.

"Mattie?" I said.

"Oh, Ursula. I'm so glad to see you again! I just wish things were not so . . . so difficult."

It was time to be frank. "Last year," I said, "I accidentally offended Rob. I did nothing that I am ashamed of; it was just—accident, as I said. I only hope that it won't keep you from helping me now."

"In what way?" Mattie gestured toward the food, and I reached out to help myself.

"I want to leave Meg and Bridget here with you," I said, as I loaded a trencher. "I have to take an unexpected journey."

"Oh? Where are you going?"

I had been afraid that she would ask that. In the eyes of the court, in the eyes of Queen Elizabeth, and Sir William Cecil, and also of Rob Henderson, my mission to rescue Edward was thoroughly illicit. To them he would be a traitor. Since I was setting out to stop him from performing a treasonous errand, I was not actually breaking the law. It is not a criminal offense to stop someone else from committing one. Nevertheless, as a Lady of the Queen's Presence Chamber, I should not be going on a journey that might lead me into Scotland unless I had official sanction, and I could not seek such sanction because for one thing I didn't have time, and for another, I couldn't do so without betraying my own family. This meant that I could not confide in Rob's wife either. Rob was a courtier.

However, I had had time to think of a story. I took a mouthful of food to hearten myself and said: "It's a family matter. You know that my cousin Edward Faldene married a girl called Helene, who was brought up in France—she was a connection of my first husband."

"Yes. I recall that," said Mattie cautiously.

"Since then, Edward has visited France and sold some of her property but a mistake of some kind was made and he also sold some jewelry which she wanted to keep. It was her mother's and is of great sentimental value to her. It's gone to a family in Northumberland. I am going to try to get it back from them. Edward himself is . . . is too busy to go just now."

"It must be of very great value, sentimental or otherwise, if you're setting off in such a hurry and in the depths of winter," said Mattie.

"There's been a death in the family concerned and the property may be distributed round various relatives," I said, lying smoothly. "So yes, it's urgent." That was true, anyhow! "I'm trying to mend relations with my family," I said. "We've been too long estranged.

Families shouldn't be divided. And, Mattie—nor should friends."

Mattie looked at me and then away, and sighed. "No. There I agree. And you want to leave Meg with me? That's all?"

"I can't leave her at Faldene. Family feeling doesn't go that far! But at Withysham I still haven't got the kind of people I need before Meg can stay there without me. She needs a gentlewoman as a companion and a proper tutor and I haven't found them yet."

"Meg is welcome at any time. You should know that, Ursula. Well, I suppose you did know it, or you wouldn't be here. Rob would agree, I feel sure. However cross he is with you, he would never turn against a young child who has nothing to do with the dispute."

Cautiously, for the sake of courtesy, I said: "How is he?"

"Well enough when he left here. The fever he caught in Cambridge came back during the autumn but passed off in a few days." Mattie smiled ruefully. "It hindered his work in Cambridge, didn't it? That led to some of the trouble between you. I'm sorry. Yes, of course Meg and Bridget can stay here and I will care for them just as usual. Please don't worry. But, Ursula . . ."

"Yes?"

"Are you sure," said Mattie, "that this journey north is wise? Forgive me, but—is there more to it than just the recovery of some jewelry?"

I shook my head. "No, indeed."

"You know your own business best," said Mattie.

I had an uneasy feeling that she didn't believe me.

4

Cuckoos and Ravens

The skies cleared as we journeyed north, but the cold did not abate. Morning after morning was frosty, with stiff white grass and frozen pools and a cruel little wind that made our noses run and our eyes water. Still, it dried the trackways, and at first we made fair speed. By starting early, taking regular breaks, and judging our pace carefully, we sometimes covered as much as thirty miles a day. We inquired about Edward at the various hostelries that we visited, and once or twice we heard news of him. Soon it was clear that although a lone horseman usually has the advantage of a party, we were catching up. Originally, he had had two days' start, but by the time we got to York, on Thursday the 25th January, we were only a day behind him.

If the weather held, we would catch him before he reached Northumberland, but as we rode out of the city of York, I realized that it wouldn't. The sky was clouding over and the cold was intensifying, gripping our very bones. It was the kind of iron cold that is like a climatic migraine. Migraine, to which I am subject, rarely subsides until I've been miserably sick, and that type of bitter cold rarely gives way until it has climaxed with a snowfall.

At one point I tried to encourage our spirits by suggesting that we should sing, but every song that occurred to us seemed to have spring or summer in it, and when I tried to lead us in declaring that "Summer Is A-Coming In; Loud Sing Cuckoo," Brockley actually became annoyed.

"It's not the season for cuckoos, madam. At least," he added meaningly, "not ones with wings."

"You mean us?" I said. "I take your point, but we've also taken on this task. We shall just have to get on with it."

"It'll be worse before it's better," said Brockley. I told him to give over croaking like an old raven, but I had an unpleasant feeling that he was right.

The road we were on avoided the bleak hills to the west and made for Newcastle through lower country, where there were a few farms and hamlets. They were widely scattered, though, and their inhabitants seemed to be staying at home, like squirrels curling up in their drays to let the winter pass. Once the city was behind us, the road was lonely. A lone farmer driving a mule cart crossed the track and called a greeting in an incomprehensible accent, and once we overtook a shepherd with a flock, but that was all.

Then, quietly and inexorably, the first flakes came.

They were small and few to begin with, but soon they were bigger and falling more and more thickly, until we were riding with heads down into a silent, blinding blizzard of flakes the size of half crowns.

In minutes, the grass verges of the track were vanishing beneath a layer of snow and we could see no farther than a couple of yards ahead. Brockley pulled down the scarf that he had wrapped around his mouth and nose as a defense against the cold, and said grimly: "I knew this would happen."

"I wonder how far it is to the next house?" I said. "Or should we turn back to York?"

"But we're three hours out from York!" Dale moaned. She fished a napkin out of her sleeve and blew her nose. "And we haven't passed through a hamlet for two hours at least."

"Before this started, I saw chimney smoke somewhere ahead," Brockley said. "The chief risk is that in this, we'll ride straight past it!"

"We just mustn't," I said. "How far away was it?"

"A mile or so, I'd say," said Brockley. "We won't miss it if we're careful. It'll be beside the track or else there'll be a track leading off to it. We must keep a sharp lookout."

We rode on, keeping together, our pace held down to a walk. Glancing at Dale as she rode beside me, I saw that her features were pinched with the cold and her nostrils bright pink, while the pockmarks that were a legacy from an attack of smallpox long ago were standing out as they always did when she was unhappy or out of sorts. She caught my eye and tried bravely to smile, but her blue eyes were miserable.

"It's all right," I said. "We shall find shelter soon."

I didn't say that I had never ridden through weather such as this before. Dale wasn't very strong, and as I shook the settling flakes off the backs of my gauntlets, I wondered how long my own strength would hold out in these conditions.

Brockley was riding in a kind of forward crouch, scanning the ground. "If only the earth wasn't disappearing under the snow," he grumbled. "Hoofprints and footmarks might tell us when we were getting near dwellings, but now we can't see them."

"There's a track off to the left!" Dale exclaimed.

We pulled up. "The only thing is," said Brockley, "we don't know if it leads toward the chimney smoke I saw, or whether it's just a path to a farmer's fields."

"We've got to try," I said, shivering.

We were fortunate. We had guessed right. A few minutes later we were in quite a sizable hamlet and pulling up under an inn sign depicting a rather comical blue boar with big tusks at one end but a sweetly curling tail at the other. Then there were grooms to take the horses and unload the saddlebags, and an aproned landlord to greet us and tell us in a broad northern accent just how lucky we'd been.

"If thee'd not turned in at t'reet place, thee'd have had ten mile or more to ride to find another. T'big house where t'folk live that own the land burnt down afore Christmas and they've all gone to live in Leeds."

Brockley, as ever, went with the grooms to see that the horses were properly tended. He never trusted strange grooms with our animals. Dale and I, however, were shown to a parlor where a fire was burning. "In this weather, we keep every hearth in the place alight," the landlord said. "Thee can freeze solid within doors if not." He took our wet cloaks and gauntlets and disappeared, saying that he would put them to dry in the kitchen and then bring us some mulled wine, and we stood by the fire to thaw out. "Ma'am," said Dale wanly, "it's not my place or Brockley's to tell you this, but do you know what we both wish?"

"Yes, Dale. That I would stop gallivanting about on one adventure after another and settle down to a quiet domestic life as a well-behaved widowed gentlewoman. Now what is it?" Dale was looking at me with a curious expression, as though she were in some way weighing me up, but not sure whether or not to tell me her conclusions. "If you have something to say, then say it," I told her.

"I'm a fair bit older than you, ma'am, past forty-five, to tell the truth, but I remember what it was like to be a young woman. No one wants you to be lonely . . ." She bit her lip, hesitating again.

"Say it. Whatever it is," I said.

"Well, ma'am, I don't know that living as a widow'ud be the best thing for you, but a quiet life, yes. What I think—what Roger and I think—is that after a while, you ought to get married again, to some nice English husband who'd help you run Withysham and be company for you and help you look after your land and your house. Someone who'd be kind to Meg, of course, I mean. Well, that's what young widows do, mostly, isn't it?"

"Yes, I know. I'm not offended. You may be quite right."

"A young woman like you, ma'am, shouldn't be alone. That's what we feel."

I couldn't say: *and then you wouldn't have to ride with me, here, there, and everywhere, hating every moment of it, so as to guard Brockley from my attractions.* Nor could I say: *you have nothing to fear. He doesn't need to be guarded because he's in no danger from me, nor I from him.* The thing had, in the past, been put into words but it must not be spoken again because some scars hurt so much when touched, and even if words are the truth, how is one to prove it?

"I know it will be hard to put the memory of Master de la Roche behind you, ma'am," Dale said. "But others do it and are glad they did."

"I know. In any case, I last saw my husband nearly a year ago. It's quite a long time." I smiled at her. "When we're back at Withysham, I will think your advice over, seriously."

"How long will that be, I wonder?" Dale remarked.

"No longer than I can help," I told her.

I glanced at the window. Nothing could be seen but a curtain of steadily falling snow. The landlord, returning with the mulled wine, remarked that it had come on sudden-like and that a party of gentlemen who had stayed at the Blue Boar the night before us and seemed to be in a hurry would probably have got as far as the next hostelry along the road but would be fair tearing their hair by this time, because likely enough, they'd be stuck there for days. "I hope thee's not in any haste."

"We are in a way," I said. "At least, we're trying to catch someone up—a . . . a relative of mine who's gone north and is needed back at home, urgently. His name is Edward Faldene. Has he been through here?"

"Master Faldene? Oh aye, I mind on him. Slept here the night before last. Left early yesterday, but thee's not that far behind him."

We were too far behind him to please me, for it sounded as though he had gained on us again. I itched to press on farther but knew it was impossible. Still, if we couldn't move forward then probably he couldn't either, and if we didn't after all catch him up before he reached Northumberland, we would surely come up with him while he was paying his various visits there. When we did . . .

I hadn't yet given much thought to how I would deal with Edward when we finally found him. How would I persuade him to give up his errand when even his wife and parents couldn't, when even the argument that his children needed him had had no power? Uncle Herbert had suggested that I use threats. Very typical of Uncle Herbert! But Edward, as a lad, had despised his base-born cousin Ursula, and I did not know how much his father had really told him about the life I was now leading. Would threats from me really weigh with him?

I had said that, if need be, I would steal his list and I might perhaps manage to go through his luggage, but what if he was carrying it on his person and sleeping with it under his pillow? I would be left with only one other alternative, which was somehow or other to incapacitate him. If I could get hold of the ingredients, I supposed I could make a purge and slip it into a glass of wine and hope that once he was forced to take to his bed, I would get a chance to examine his discarded clothing. It was a repellent prospect.

Once again, with all my heart, I wished I hadn't come.

Once again, uselessly, I longed for Matthew to be alive once more, so that I could return to our home on the Loire and be Madame de la Roche, and never go adventuring again.

We were stuck at the Sign of the Blue Boar for three days. We could only hope that wherever Edward was, he was similarly trapped. Eventually, the cold eased and a shower of rain in the night made the tracks passable again. Our horses had at least had a rest. We set out once more.

The state of the road was discouraging. The rain had only partly cleared the snow. The tracks were full of slush, hock-deep in places, and here and there snowdrifts still spilled across our path. Brockley had picked out the sturdiest and most surefooted animals in the Withysham stable, but in these conditions, the finest horses in the realm would have slipped and slithered, just as ours did, and balked at fording streams full of racing, icy meltwater.

By sheer determination (which meant nagging on my part and what I admit was an unkind blindness to Dale's drawn face), we kept going, but from the Blue Boar to Newcastle took six days altogether.

In Newcastle, we heard further news of Edward, and learned that he was still two nights ahead.

"If only I had wings!" I groaned.

＊ ＊ ＊

The next news of Edward came from the Elkinthorpe family, who lived in Newcastle and had been the first set of friends on whom Edward had proposed to call. They were wool merchants, well-to-do on the proceeds of fleeces from Cheviot sheep and openly Catholic, as many households were in the north of England, with a chaplain and a small family chapel.

While dealing with Edward's friends, I thought it best to say that although in England I was known as Mistress Blanchard, I was actually the widow of Matthew de la Roche, a Catholic Frenchman. I was therefore accepted at once as a fellow Catholic, and learned that Master and Mistress Elkinthorpe and their unmarried daughter showed their faces at the local Anglican church once a month, and had found that if they did so, no one molested them.

Edward had stayed with them, but only for one night.

"As though we were an inn," said Master Elkinthorpe disapprovingly as he showed us into his hall. Here, as at Faldene, the life of the household was still lived in communal fashion in one big, raftered chamber going the height of the house. Elkinthorpe was a large man with a bulging middle and his quilted winter doublet made him look enormous. "It isn't the way we expect our guests to behave," he said, in tones of hurt self-importance.

"But he did say he wanted to get on as fast as he could." Mistress Elkinthorpe had a plump figure but not the placid countenance that so often goes with it.

She was very lined and had an air of enduring patience. I suspected that she spent a good deal of time and effort in soothing a husband who took offense too easily. "He was weary of the road and wanted to put it behind him, and he was on an errand of some importance, I believe," she said anxiously.

"And wouldn't say what it was even when I asked him outright. In my day, young men showed more courtesy to their elders," said Master Elkinthorpe. "You need to get him back, you say?"

"Yes. A family matter in Sussex," I said.

"And the family sent you, instead of a proper courier?"

"I have an errand to the north as well," I improvised hastily, and although his thick white eyebrows rose inquiringly, I didn't enlarge, leaving him to surmise that I wasn't going to explain my purpose any more than Edward had, and take offense at me as well, if he chose.

I think he did choose, because he then became very silent, not to say huffy. The hospitality at the Elkinthorpes' was good in a fashion, with plenty of food on the table, and comfortable bedchambers, but it couldn't be called an agreeable visit and we piled on further offense when we expressed a wish to leave the very next day.

"But it's a Sunday. You can't possibly travel on the Sabbath," said Mistress Elkinthorpe, scandalized. "You'll surely want to join us in our chapel!" Master Elkinthorpe also made it clear that in his view, it was unthinkable for us to leave. I got the impression that he was almost prepared to bar his gates to stop us. I was passionately against delay, and then, to my exasperation, found that Brockley supported Master Elkinthorpe, though not for the same reason.

"The horses are very weary again, madam. We're pushing them too hard. We might be wise to give them a day's rest."

"But we'll lose ground!"

"Master Edward must have a tired horse too, madam. Very likely, when he reaches friends who are— er—more easygoing than this household is, he will give his animal a rest as well. It may not make that much difference."

"That's nothing but guesswork!"

"You could call it experience, madam!"

"Oh, for God's sake!"

But I knew Brockley in this mood, and for all my impatience, I also knew that he was highly skilled in the care of horses and that his advice shouldn't be ignored. Reluctantly, therefore, I yielded, but slept badly that night. We had lost our chance of catching Edward up before he got to Northumberland; and now I was beginning to fear that even our chances of coming up with him before he crossed the Scottish border were melting faster than snow in rain.

"I just hope his Edinburgh contacts are all away from home!" I said snappily to Brockley. "Because if he gets to them before we get to him, I've wasted my journey!"

I asked Mistress Elkinthorpe, whom I rather liked, how far it was to the Scottish border. "Oh, no more than fifty miles," she said.

We would leave at first light on the Monday, I said.

❋ ❋ ❋

The Wright family were Edward's next objective. Helene had told me that they lived at a place called Holtby House. When we inquired the way at an inn, however, we learned that the house was empty. The Wrights apparently had another home in the Midlands and had gone south for the winter. Edward could not have stopped there.

The landlord was an active, well-informed man, though rough in his speech, and was at least able to give us some information about the whereabouts of Grimstone hamlet and Bycroft House, and also of St. Margaret's, the home of the Thursbys. What he told me gave me an idea.

As we journeyed on the next day, I said: "We could reach the Bycrofts tomorrow, but I think we should pass them by. It would mean turning aside from the direct road—there's a left fork, apparently—and going about three miles out of our way. We'd do better to go on to the Thursbys at St. Margaret's. Just past the fork, there's supposed to be an inn called the Holly Tree where we could get midday food, and we might well reach as far as St. Margaret's tomorrow afternoon. If Edward has gone roundabout to see the Bycrofts, we might arrive at St. Margaret's the same time, or even find him there!"

"Oh, I do hope so!" said Dale wistfully.

I glanced at Brockley, who was riding beside me, while Dale, who had the quietest horse, was lagging behind. His face was impassive as a rule, but glancing at him, I saw that he was looking worried. "Traveling in such weather isn't good for Fran," he remarked in a low voice.

I didn't answer. I felt guilty about Dale myself. I nodded, pulled my hat farther down over my ears to protect them from what was now a sharp east wind, and rode on.

We had stayed at inns of varying standard in the course of our journey, but I have to say that the one where we spent the next night was easily the nastiest of them all, being dirty and drafty with a landlord who seemed to be permanently drunk, and whose slattern of a wife produced dreadful food. Dale and I, after repeated demands for hot water, obtained a pailful that was more or less warm and washed some underlinen, but the sorry fire in our bedchamber hadn't dried it by morning and we had to pack it still damp and ignore the fact that the linen we were wearing now smelled. We asked about Edward, but he hadn't been there. "Too much sense," muttered Brockley.

That morning, we also woke to find ourselves in the midst of an interesting new weather phenomenon: fast-flowing fog.

Fogs are frequent enough in the south, of course, but they usually go with windless weather. Here however we were evidently amid cloud blowing in from the North Sea. We set off determinedly enough, scarves around our faces to keep out the clammy mist. "We've got to watch for the fork," Brockley said. "We need the right-hand road. Take heart, Fran. Even at this sluggard's pace we should reach the Holly Tree in less than three hours and perhaps we'll find a good fire there."

Keeping a lookout was harder than it sounded. The

fog was as blinding as the blizzard. As far as we could tell, we were riding over bleak uplands, along a track edged with heather and coarse grass, but even the verges kept on fading into the vapors. "We ought to have found this place the Holly Tree by now, surely," Brockley said, when rather too much time had gone by.

We pulled up and listened. There was no sound but the hiss of the wind. We rode on a little way and then stopped again, also in vain. Not until the third halt, when we were all becoming very worried, did a faint clank come to our ears. "Ah!" said Brockley, and spurred on. A moment later, the blowing mists parted enough to show us a cluster of cottages. They were miserable places, made of gray stone, which seemed to be piled up rather than built, and roofed with a mixture of slate and thatch. They seemed to be huddling together for protection from the elements, like a flock of sheep. There was a well in front of them, and this was the source of the clanking, for a couple of shawl-wrapped women were hauling up water. Brockley urged his horse forward and hailed them.

Communication was difficult because they spoke in such broad northern voices that he could barely understand them, while his southern voice was just as bewildering to them, but he managed in the end and rode back to us, shaking his head. "I asked where the Holly Tree was," he said. "But it seems that we missed the fork and took the left branch without knowing it. This is Grimstone. Either we go on to Bycroft, which is another mile, or else go back."

"Can't we go on to Bycroft?" pleaded Dale.

"No," I said firmly. "We go back."

What happened next was not Dale's fault. She could not possibly have engineered the accident when her gelding stepped into a pothole, almost fell, and threw her over its head, and then, when we had picked Dale up and made sure she wasn't really hurt, turned out to be lame.

"It's Bycroft for us, madam," said Brockley, feeling the animal's foreleg. "This poor beast can't be asked to limp farther than that. I'll have to lead it and Dale must ride behind me."

I swore, realized that this was pointless, and tried to make light of the disaster. "It's fate. Some unknown providence doesn't want us to catch Edward up. Did you know, Brockley, that the ancient Greeks saw fate as a woman spinning the inescapable pattern of our lives on a loom?"

"My education didn't have the Greeks in it," said Brockley. "I was taught my letters and numbers and a tiny bit of Latin by the vicar in the village where I was born and that was it. I don't see fate as a woman with a loom, madam. I see it as an unshaven fellow with uncut hair, wearing patched brown fustian, and crouching in ambush with a crossbow."

When Brockley made jokes he nearly always did it with an expressionless face. This was a perfect example. As usual, there was a brief pause while I worked out that he was jesting. Then I laughed and saw the answering glimmer in his eyes. And then I saw Dale's face.

I could have kicked myself. I was always doing it. No, *we* were always doing it. We so easily let ourselves slip into these moments of intimacy, when we shared an allusion, a joke, that Dale hadn't grasped, shutting her out, hurting her, poor Dale, who loved us both and would never never have hurt us in return.

Dale had said I should marry again. I had said I would think about it, but the truth was that even Gerald's memory had not quite ceased to haunt me and Matthew was alive in me still. But Dale was right. Sooner or later, I must face it. Oh, dear God, if only Matthew were still alive, so that I could go back to him and leave the Brockleys in peace together at Withysham.

"Very well," I said resignedly. "Come along, then. Bycroft it is."

The fog was clearing when we arrived at Bycroft. It was a harsh-looking place, for like most border manor houses it was built for defense, with a lookout tower at one end, complete with arrow slits, and a stout encircling wall. When the gatehouse porter led us into the cobbled courtyard, we saw that the living quarters of the house were on an upper floor, for a flight of steps led up to the main entrance. The ground floor, to judge by the wisps of hay blowing around its one low door, was an undercroft used for storing fodder and probably for housing livestock as well.

Our welcome was friendly enough, though formal. As we dismounted, the door at the top of the steps opened, and a steward in black velvet livery, with a gold chain of office, came down to meet us, to bow in respectful greeting and ask our names. He recognized mine and his stiff manner unbent somewhat.

"Madame de la Roche will certainly be most welcome in this house. Master Bycroft is with his bailiff at the moment but will join you shortly as will the mistress when she has finished hearing her chaplain's daily reading from a devotional work. Mistress Bycroft is a most pious lady and ours is a pious household, but we are also hospitable as you will find. Here are the grooms to see to your horses. Come in!"

5

"Our Daughter Was Beautiful"

The steward no doubt thought he was telling the truth when he said that Bycroft was hospitable. So it was, in a way. Dale and I were shown to a bedchamber with a crimson-hung four-poster bed, and a maidservant came to conjure a fire into life for us. There were, however, no fur or sheepskin rugs to welcome one's toes on freezing mornings, as I had at Withysham and Mattie had at Thamesbank. Even the Elkinthorpes had had rugs. Here, there was just the floor, with an old-fashioned strewing of rushes.

The ceiling was ornate, with painted and gilded crisscross beams, but the walls were bare gray stone, unadorned except for one small wall hanging depicting the Last Supper. A plain toilet stand held a simple earthenware set of basin and ewer. Far more noticeable—beautifully carved, in fact—was the prie-dieu for private devotions. The housekeeper who showed me and Dale to the room pointed it out immediately, as something that I would most certainly wish to use.

"The mistress spends perhaps three hours a day at hers, madam."

"Most admirable," I said, and was thankful that Dale, who was ardently Protestant, had the self-restraint not to make any acid remarks about popish practices until the housekeeper had gone.

"I do say private prayers sometimes, Dale," I said mildly. "You know that."

"You do it decently, ma'am; just a few quiet prayers, kneeling by your bed as a Christian should. Not making a show of it like this."

"Well, we must keep up the pretense. We were told that this was a pious household. I can trust you, I hope."

"Yes, ma'am," said Dale, and I knew she would keep her word. In France, failing to guard her tongue had once landed her in a dungeon and she had never forgotten it.

Hot washing water was brought and Dale, after going to investigate, found a drying room where our damp linen could be aired. Brockley reported that the stabling was satisfactory, that the horses were being properly rubbed down and fed, and that he had been offered adequate accommodation among the other grooms in the stable loft. "You'd best stay with the mistress tonight, Fran, but I shan't sleep cold, don't worry."

The hospitality, in fact, was there, but it had an austere tinge. The steward's statement that this was a pious household, though, was entirely true. Piety suffused the place. The prie-dieu and Mistress Bycroft's hours at it were merely details in a bigger pattern.

We dined an hour after our arrival, in a hall with more bare stone walls, except for some coats of arms and one large crucifix. Master Bycroft, tall, dark-bearded, and grave of mien, presided at one end of the table. At the other end sat his wife. Her hair was hidden under a matronly cap but her pale complexion and huge gray eyes suggested that she was probably fair. She had a disconcerting habit of fixing you with those great eyes when she spoke to you, as though she were trying to read your soul.

Not that there was much conversation over dinner, which was shared by the three children of the house, a boy of perhaps fifteen and two girls, somewhat younger. They, like their elders, were very quiet. The person most in evidence was the chaplain the steward had mentioned, though he wasn't dining with us. Instead, he stood at a small lectern in a corner of the hall, from which, before the meal began, he recited a lengthy grace, which included a prayer for Mary Stuart of Scotland—"the poor beleaguered lassie, harassed by that devil's emissary John Knox and his noble followers, who style themselves the Lords of the Congregation and should know better and will rue their evil-doing for all eternity when they come at last to the fires of hell."

I had heard of John Knox from Cecil, and I was aware that he was more or less the founder of the Protestant movement in Scotland and was famous for being a fanatic. It was disturbing, though, to hear the hatred in the chaplain's voice and the fervent way in which Master and Mistress Bycroft said *amen*.

After this inflammatory grace, we were able to sit down to our meal, but conversation still didn't flourish, for the chaplain read to us throughout most of dinner, from the works of St. Augustine, and even when he stopped, shortly before the end, the only conversation consisted of Mistress Bycroft catechizing her son and daughters to make sure they had paid attention to the chaplain.

When dinner was over, I sent Dale, who though not really hurt had received some bruising when she fell and was in any case obviously worn-out, to rest. Meanwhile, I allowed Mistress Bycroft to take me to her parlor, where I seized the chance to explain that I was anxious to resume my journey because we were trying to catch up with my cousin Edward and recall him to Sussex. "Has he been here, by any chance?"

"Why, yes," said my hostess. "He slept here the night before last and left early yesterday morning. He was going on to the Thursbys."

So we were now only a day and a half behind him. "We wanted to go straight on to the Thursbys in the hope of finding him there," I said, "but one of our horses has gone lame." I had been thinking. "I would like to see my manservant," I said. "He's looking after it."

Brockley, duly summoned to speak to me, said that the horse was improving. "There is a cut but not, I think, a wrench. I've dressed it and I fancy that we'll be able to continue tomorrow."

"I'd like to see for myself," I said, staring hard at Brockley to indicate that I meant I wanted a little private conversation.

"Of course, madam." Brockley picked up the signal. "If you will come with me to the stable . . ."

Presently, stooping over the gelding's foreleg in the stall, I said: "There's no chance that we could get on our way to the Thursbys this afternoon, is there, Brockley? If Dale rests for an hour . . ."

"Dale needs longer than that, madam, and so does this horse. Besides, dark would come down on us before we could get so far. It's nine miles or thereabout, or so you told me."

"I know. But we're close behind Edward now and I don't want him to get to Scotland ahead of us after all. And this place! I'm afraid all the time that either Dale or I will say the wrong thing and give ourselves away. This house isn't just pious, it's . . . it's . . ."

I could hardly find the words to express it. I did not myself know how genuinely I believed in God. He was supposed to be a God of love but I had seen too many horrors to be convinced of that. When not traveling or otherwise prevented, I attended church once a week, as most people did, and in times of trouble, as Dale knew, I might say a private prayer or two. Mostly, though, I left religion out of my thoughts and conversation alike. The Bycroft obsession with it seemed to me like a distortion of the mind, and the savage attitude of the chaplain was frightening.

"I didn't see you at dinner," I said to Brockley. "I hope you've eaten. But if you'd been there, you would have heard the chaplain more or less damning the Protestant leader in Scotland to hellfire!"

"I daresay," said Brockley, and as he replaced the dressing on the gelding's fetlock, he gave his rare chuckle. "I've been hearing from the other grooms how the lady of the house goes down into Grimstone with comforts for the poor and to help the wives with their lyings-in and instructs them in the true religion practically without stopping. Some of them tell lies about when their babies are expected, so as to get it all over before she arrives to harangue them when they've other things to think about! But I think we'll have to put up with it until tomorrow."

There was nothing for it. "Very well," I said, and went back to Mistress Bycroft, who sympathized with my anxiety to find my cousin and took me to her own room, so that we could both kneel down by her prie-dieu and offer prayers for a happy conclusion to my errand. The process, believe it or not, lasted three quarters of an hour.

We got away from Bycroft the next morning without anyone saying anything disastrous, and for a change, the weather was kind to us. The ride to the Thursbys at St. Margaret's took us through some wild and barren hill country, but it went smoothly. Dale's gelding was walking sound again, Dale was rested, and I felt hopeful. According to Helene, Edward knew the Thursbys well. He must have reached them the day before yesterday, but if he made a stay of any length anywhere, it would be with them. Once again, I was full of hope.

However, by the time we reached St. Margaret's, just before noon, Dale was drooping again and her horse was once more showing signs of lameness. I was relieved that our ride was over. Like Bycroft, St. Margaret's was defended, with an encircling moat and a curtain wall topped by battlements. It was a further reminder that the Scottish border was close. The Scots had a wild reputation. Cecil had once traveled to Edinburgh and he had told me something of the north. Their border had always been liable to trouble; it was a state of affairs that went back for centuries. Raiders still from time to time swooped across into England to seize sheep or cattle. The English pastures, on the whole, were lusher than the Scottish ones and the stock correspondingly fatter.

Once past the gatehouse and the frowning wall we discovered that St. Margaret's, though it didn't greatly resemble Withysham, was obviously a former abbey. I supposed that this explained its name. It was built around three sides of a cloistered courtyard, and adjacent to it was a chapel nearly as big as the house. I wondered gloomily whether the Thursbys were as pious as the Bycrofts.

But they were not. Euphemia and John Thursby turned out to be older than the Bycrofts but much sprightlier. They were a pair of small, jolly, rotund people, red-cheeked and bright-eyed, Robin and Robina Goodfellow in the flesh. (Aunt Tabitha did not believe in such things and once beat me for even mentioning them, but at Faldene, the servants had believed in Robin Goodfellow, the mischievous fairy who could either wreak havoc or confer blessings. They regularly placated him by leaving dishes of milk out for him at night, which the cats usually drank.)

The Thursbys were amazingly alike, even to the point that when they smiled, each revealed a gap to the left of their upper front teeth. I was not surprised to learn when, after washing and changing I rejoined them in the parlor, that they were second cousins and had had to get a dispensation to marry.

They chatted merrily about themselves and seemed to enjoy their resemblance to each other, for it even extended to their clothes. His doublet and her gown were made of the same deep green velvet with yellow flowers embroidered on it.

Their home was a delight, its stern outer walls a complete contradiction to the comfort within. I had been shown at once to a bedchamber, as though it were taken for granted that I would stay the night, and it was a delightful room, the walls elegantly paneled and hung with pleasing tapestries, and gracious mullioned windows overlooking the cloisters and the knot garden. All the hearths that I saw looked as though they had been enlarged to accommodate welcoming fires instead of the meager affairs that were in keeping with vows of poverty. The knot garden was exquisitely laid out with low box hedges to outline the beds, and even the stable-yard had a couple of apple trees.

"The horses eat the windfalls," Mistress Thursby said. "And so do the stableboys, and why not?"

They obviously loved their house and enjoyed showing it off to guests. They were apologetic even over a mild delay in serving dinner. "Our steward is not here just now. He is a Scotsman with family over the border—as indeed we ourselves have—and went off yesterday, to see a kinsman who's been ill or had an accident or some such thing," Mistress Thursby said. "Our household isn't being overseen as well as it is when Hamish is here. He'll be back soon, of course, but he's missed, I assure you! He is so attentive to detail. We have a fair amount of company, even in this lonely place. We breed horses and people come to buy our stock at times, and now and then, of course, groups of traveling players come by, or a stray peddler or merchant. I am expecting an uncle of mine soon— he comes each year to stay for a few weeks. And of course, we often see our neighbors the Bycrofts. Although to tell you the truth, the Bycrofts . . ."

And then we all looked at each other and laughed, and Master Thursby said solemnly: "But they are excellent people in their way, and Mistress Bycroft never ceases from good works. She often goes to Grimstone to take charity to the poor villagers and her husband sees to it that their cottages are kept in good repair. Nor do they neglect to tend the souls of their tenants. No one can fault them."

Whereupon, we all chuckled again. A servant brought in some wine and poured it, and as I sipped mine, I remarked that St. Margaret's must have been altered a good deal since the days when it was an abbey. "I know," I said, "because my own house was once an abbey and that, too, had to be much adapted before it became a real home."

I paused, and then, catching at a chance to establish my Catholic credentials, I added gravely: "If the true religion should ever be restored in England, I suppose the Church might reclaim Withysham from me. I should be sorry, although I know in my heart that it would be right."

There was a sudden hush. All the puckishness went

out of Mistress Thursby's face. She actually put up a
hand to brush tears from the corners of her eyes. "Oh,
dear," she said miserably.

Easygoing as the Thursbys seemed to be, I had accidentally touched a tender spot. "What is it?" I asked.

"Now, don't you go making too much of it, my
dear," said Master Thursby to his wife. "The fact is,"
he added to me, "that we love St. Margaret's too much
and can't help but hope we will never lose it."

"It would break my heart if we did," said Mistress
Thursby.

"Yes, well, that's as may be. But if it's ever God's will
that our religion be restored in England, well, as
Madame de la Roche says, it's a sacrifice we might have
to make."

"The heartache would be so terrible," said his wife
sadly.

"Yes, it would," her husband agreed somberly. "But
as yet, it hasn't come to pass. So let us talk of something else."

I obliged by asking about Edward, hoping against
hope that he might be somewhere on the premises,
but I was disappointed. He was not.

"Oh yes, he's been here," Master Thursby said.
"But . . ."

"I take it he's gone on to Edinburgh," I said heavily.
"I know that he meant to. When did he leave?"

"The day before yesterday, after dinner. He'll likely
be there by now. He didn't even spend a night here,
for all we invited him," Mistress Thursby said.
Silently, I cursed. "He seemed so impatient to finish
his journey," said my hostess. "He spoke of you once,

you know—when he was here last summer. Not that he said much, except that it was you that went with his wife's guardian to bring his bride out of France. But we knew he had a cousin Ursula."

It had never occurred to me that Edward might have talked about me. I thanked providence he hadn't said more. According to Uncle Herbert, he knew that it was I who had got my uncle, Edward's father, clapped into the Tower. I certainly didn't want any of Edward's friends to know *that*. Perhaps the talkative Thursbys had interrupted him too soon! (The Bycrofts were probably too busy praying to listen, anyhow.)

"I need to find him as soon as I can," I said. They regarded me with expectant interest and I added primly: "It concerns his family at home—it is a private thing, which I'm not at liberty to discuss—but it really is serious. You gave me a charming bedchamber in which to change my dress and I suspect that you would be happy for me to stay here overnight . . ."

"Indeed, we expect you to stay!" Euphemia exclaimed.

I shook my head. "I think we should travel on after dinner and try again to catch Edward up. We could cover a few more miles before nightfall. Can you advise us about the route and where we can stay overnight? What inns are there along the way?"

The Thursbys at once began to shake with mirth. The brief distress over their fear of losing their home had passed and now they resembled nothing so much as a pair of merry gnomes. I looked at them in astonishment.

"You're almost into Scotland," said Mistress

Thursby, "and there are no hostelries in Scotland. Drinking places, yes, but not places to stay."

"There are traditions of hospitality, though," said her husband. "Nobles stay in each other's castles and houses; ordinary folk look for lodgings in cottages and farmhouses and so on. There are a couple of places along the way where you'll get beds for the night and supper, of a simple kind, and I can give you some addresses in Edinburgh where you can find lodgings. I know where Edward was probably going to stay; I can tell you that as well."

"I'd be grateful," I said, and added politely: "You know Scotland well?"

Once more, their cheerful countenances clouded. "Oh yes," said Mistress Thursby, "we have relatives there, as I said. More cousins. We share Scottish forebears, John and I."

I must have looked inquiring, for Master Thursby said: "We used to visit them at times, but the last such time was a sad business for us. We never dreamt . . ."

"We're not so very young," said Euphemia, "and our children are grown. Our son is wed and lives on the farm that was his wife's dower—maybe thirty miles from here. But our daughter, our dearest Jane . . ."

"We took her with us to visit our cousins, nearly four years ago it was," said Master Thursby. "Our cousins are well-to-do people in Edinburgh, merchants in cloth and spices and well acquainted with all the fine folk. They got us invitations to a banquet given by a noble who had a castle to the west of Stirling, the town at the head of the Firth. We rode out and stayed a night there, and while we were there, one of our host's sons fell in love with our daughter."

"She was sixteen," said Euphemia in a trembling voice. "And she was just growing up. She'd been quite an ordinary-looking child, and then, just before we went to Scotland, almost overnight, she bloomed. It was as if she went to bed one night as just a lass, awkward, with a few spots, and woke the next day as though a good fairy had kissed her in the night. Suddenly she was beautiful. Our daughter was beautiful . . ."

Her voice faltered. John Thursby said: "Our host's son talked to her at dinner and danced with her after, and came to us the very next morning, before we left, asking for her hand. But we didn't care for him . . ."

". . . and nor did Jane," said Euphemia. "All of us thought him rough and crude and how right we were. We said no to the proposal, and went back to Edinburgh. But when we set out for home a week later, we were held up on the road by armed men—under the command of this young noble. Our daughter was taken from us. We didn't realize at first who had done it, but we soon found out. He took her back to his father's castle and his father, who was no better than his son, saw nothing strange in it. We rushed back to our cousins, but before we could even begin trying to make inquiries or lodge a complaint with the authorities, would you believe it, we were openly invited to the castle to visit our daughter and our new *son-in-law*— that's what the invitation said: *son-in-law*—as though it had all been a normal marriage. Jane was raped the moment she reached the castle and then told that in Scottish law this made her the wife of the man who had ravished her!"

"It isn't true," said Master Thursby. "But Jane was too innocent to know that. She believed what she was told, and when she was offered what her ravisher called the consolation of religion, meaning a lawful marriage by a Catholic priest—these wretched nobles were Catholics, as we are, and more shame to them—then she agreed. Before we could get to her, she was truly married and there was nothing we could do to save her. We told her we could get it annulled, but she was a virtual prisoner in the castle and ten thousand annulments wouldn't have got her person out of the hands of those . . . those . . ."

"What of Jane now?" I asked.

"She died," said Master Thursby shortly. "Of homesickness and ague in that vile, cold castle, and probably of ill usage too. She had a black eye when we saw her on that visit. It wasn't a long one. It was made plain to us that we weren't welcome to stay more than a day or two. We were only asked, I think, to have it made clear to us that we had no power to help Jane."

"When we had to go away and leave her there, she cried and cried. I shall never forget it," said Mistress Thursby.

"We tried to find a way to make the authorities act, but all we got from anyone was that she was lawfully married and nothing could be done," said her husband. "It was before Queen Mary came back to Scotland. Perhaps she would have had pity. We found no pity anywhere. She was dead in six months. They sent her belongings back to us and told us that she had had Christian burial. God have mercy on her soul, and a curse on the soul of the man who seized her."

"But—is that a commonplace in Scotland?" I asked, staggered.

"It's very different from England, believe me," said Master Thursby with feeling. "Yes, such things happen now and then. When Queen Mary herself first arrived from France, there were a couple of plots to seize her and marry her forcibly to this noble or that. The great Gordon clan were involved in one of them, and young John Gordon, who had presumed to her hand, was executed for it. The plots all came to nothing, but no, there was nothing remarkable about them. Not in Scotland. It is a wild place with little rule of law." He eyed me with unwonted gravity. "You're a good-looking young woman and you have property in the south, have you not? Edward told us that. You ought to take care."

"I shall not be in Scotland long," I said. "Or so I trust. I only want to catch up with Edward and I hope to have his company coming back."

Master Thursby rose to his feet. "I'll give you a note of places to seek shelter, on the way to Edinburgh and in it, and how to find the house where Edward is probably staying. Our friends who educated him— they died of lung congestion during a bad winter a few years back, as no doubt you know, poor souls—owned some houses in Edinburgh and the couple Edward's most likely staying with were their tenants. Macnab their name is. The property was sold in the end, when our friends died, but the Macnabs stayed put. Master Macnab is one of the head gardeners at Holyrood Palace, the queen's residence. They'll not have much room, though. They might not be able to take you in as well. You'd best ask our cousins for shelter while you're in the city. Their name is Keith. I'll write you some lines of introduction."

I said: "Can we borrow a horse from you? One of ours has gone lame. Otherwise Dale will have to ride on Brockley's pillion."

"Oh, my dear," exclaimed Mistress Thursby, "we told you—we breed them! Did you bring your own horses all the way from Sussex? The poor things must be nearly foundered. Well, our grooms will take care of them. Paul Bisselthwaite is very good at doctoring lame animals."

"Especially if you slip him a few pennies extra for his trouble," observed her husband dryly.

"Well, and why not, after all? He does *take* the trouble," said Euphemia. "Leave them here and take fresh ones all round. Keep ours as long as you need them and pick up your own on your way back south again."

6

The Open Window

After taking dinner with them, we bade good-bye—
with some regret—to the hospitable and voluble
Thursbys, and on new mounts set out across the miles
of wild moorland that lay between us and Edinburgh.

We spent one night more on the road, in a little cottage. I was by now attuning my ears to the change in
accent, and although our hosts spoke broad Scots, I
was able, just about, to converse with them. They tried
to make us comfortable but hadn't much wherewithal
to do it with. The horses shared a byre with some goats,
and with the cottagers we shared a supper of salt bacon
and rye bread. Then we slept as best we could, wrapped
in fleeces, on the floor by the fire, and had thin ale,
goat's cheese, and porridge for breakfast. The porridge
was made of good oatmeal but lacked the raisins and
sugar that usually accompany porridge in the south.
Instead, it was served with salt.

Between that and the previous evening's bacon, we set off next day feeling rather thirsty and when, during the morning, we came across a tavern in a small village, Brockley insisted on stopping for ale all around. "There wasn't enough at breakfast and if I don't have a proper drink I'll never get the taste of salt out of my mouth, madam, and I daresay you and Fran are no better."

We reached Edinburgh in a winter twilight. We rode through a frowning gate in a city wall, and looking up, saw the towering bulk of the castle on its hill, with candlelit windows here and there. We ourselves were in a long street, mostly full of people who seemed to be clearing market stalls away. Tall houses soared up on either side, with upper floors overhanging the road and little alleyways between, dark mouths under arched entrances. As with most city streets, there was a smell of rubbish and ordure, but there was a wind, too, with a sea smell in it.

Even I was too tired to seek Edward out that night. "The morning will do," I said. "Let's find these Thursby cousins."

We found someone whose accent we could understand and who was able to direct us. We were already in the right street, a thoroughfare that we gathered was a main route between the castle at one end of the town and the queen's chief residence of Holyrood at the other. The Keiths' home was in a small close almost opposite the High Kirk of St. Giles, and there was no missing that, for it was as dignified and majestic a church as I ever saw anywhere. Within a few minutes after making our inquiry, we had found our destination.

Only to discover that we weren't entirely welcome.

The master of the house, apparently, had fallen ill with an apoplexy.

But the laws of hospitality held good. There was stabling at the rear for our horses, and we were provided with supper, a good one this time, and warm if crowded beds. I shared one with the two grown-up Keith daughters, while in the next room Dale shared a mattress on the floor with the three maidservants, and Brockley, as so often, slept over the stable with the grooms.

Being a place of anxiety, the household was astir early. We broke our fast by candlelight, with good fresh bread, fried bacon, and a sufficiency of ale. Our hostess was too concerned about her husband to join us, but her daughters deputized for her, and when asked if they knew where the Macnabs lived, they said yes.

They gave us directions willingly and if, no doubt on their mother's instructions, they also gave us directions to a stable that would look after our horses and an address that might give us lodgings henceforth, I could understand why. I apologized for having descended on the family at such a difficult time, hoped that their father would recover and promised to pray for him, and set off with Dale and Brockley just as the sun was rising.

The city was still quiet. We hadn't far to go, no more than a little way back along the street to where the houses, though tall, were narrower than the Keiths' roomy residence; cramped timber-fronted affairs with doors opening almost straight onto the road, although there was a stretch of fencing just in front where we could tether the horses. Brockley was pleased, as he didn't want to stay outside and hold them. "It would be best if I came in with you and Fran, madam. So that you look properly attended and in case Master Faldene is, well, difficult."

"He's not likely to attack us, Brockley, and we're not proposing to wrest the list from him by force if he doesn't want to hand it over. It will have to be persuasion at first and, after that, cunning! That is, if he hasn't passed the list on already. If only we could have traveled a little faster or he'd gone a little slower!"

"Let us hope for the best, madam. But I still feel . . ."

"So do I, really. Yes, come inside with us, Brockley."

I did wonder if perhaps we had arrived too soon and would find the household still not fully up, but the door was opened to us promptly enough, although the youthful maidservant who opened it couldn't make out a word we said and we couldn't understand her, either. The attuning of my ears hadn't gone far enough to cope with a dialect as broad as hers.

However, she called Mistress Macnab, and the lady of the house, fortunately, was able to talk to us. She was a small, busy, businesslike person, fully dressed for the day, with her sleeves rolled up for kitchen work. Aye, Master Faldene was in her house, had been for the last two nights, and this morning was still in his chamber, for all the day was well begun, and yesterday he'd been just as slow getting up, complaining that he wasn't well. But in her view, it was high time he showed himself, and if we'd step inside, her husband would call him, as Macnab had not yet left for his day's work though he was up and active. The gardeners at Holyrood started later in winter but Macnab was in a position of responsibility, and made sure he was always there first, and rose betimes accordingly. Mistress Macnab was clearly proud of her husband. Equally clearly, she disapproved of slugabeds.

Two nights, I thought. Edward had been one whole day in Edinburgh. "What was wrong with my cousin?" I said, as Mistress Macnab stepped aside to let us in. "Did you see him at all yesterday? Did he go out?"

"I never saw hide nor hair of him, and I dinna know what his trouble was, for he wouldna say. We only spoke through his door. Whether he went out or not, I wouldna know, for I was out myself half the day, at the marketing. Some good cheap fish there was for sale, and a ship in with oranges, a treat for the bairns and with my man being such a good provider, and letting our attic room as well, we can afford such things now and then. This way . . ."

She showed us through a small entrance hall to a back room, where we were presented to Master Macnab, a stocky, sandy fellow, who was just coming in at the back door accompanied by a serving lad, both of them carrying big baskets of firewood. Macnab had a dour face but was obliging enough and had a fairly lucid accent. Dumping his load on the floor and telling the boy to get on with filling the hearthside baskets, he turned to a staircase that came down into the corner of the room. Over his shoulder, he said: "Best come up with me. I'll shout to him to be sure he's fit to be seen, and then if ye've private matters to discuss, ye can talk in his room."

We followed him up the stairs. They led up through a bedchamber where the maidservant was working half in and half out of what I at first took to be a large cupboard. Only as I passed close to it did I realize that it was actually a double bed, and that whoever used it must be shutting themselves in at night like walled-up anchorites. The very idea made me choke. Macnab, however, was leading us on up a farther flight, through another bedchamber (with two bed-cupboards in it), and finally to a tiny top-floor landing where it ended abruptly at an attic door, presumably the attic that Mistress Macnab had mentioned.

"We've nae other room to spare, but Master Faldene's stayed here before and said he was happy enough with it," Macnab said, rather defensively, as though we had criticized the accommodation.

I murmured something to the effect that I was sure of it and Macnab rapped on the door. There was no answer, and he clicked his tongue in annoyance. "Master Faldene! There's folk here to see ye and it's past time for breakfast!"

Still, there was no reply. Macnab lifted the latch and pushed the door ajar.

The hoarse yell he let out must have shaken the whole house. He plunged forward into the room and we plunged after him. When it was too late, he stopped and turned to us, gasping, "Dinna come in!" but we already had, all three of us. We could see what he had seen.

Dale screamed. I did not, because I clapped my hands to my mouth just in time. Brockley drew in his breath with a horrified hiss.

The room was cold, with bitter air sweeping through it from the one small window, which was swinging open. The bed was not a cupboard one but a small four-poster, its curtains pulled open. Edward lay sprawled amid a disordered pile of sheets and rugs. He had been stabbed through the chest, probably with a broad-bladed sword. He had not died at once. He had struggled and hemorrhaged from mouth and nose before the end. His mouth was open in a rictus of pain and terror. His face, his nightgown, the bedding, the curtains, and the lime-washed wall behind the bed were all splashed and hideous with dark, dried blood.

His gown was torn away from one shoulder and there were black bruises on his arm, and when, shuddering, I stepped forward to look at him closely, I saw that there was a lump on his jaw and more bruises under the blood around his mouth, where powerful hands had held him down and struck him half-senseless and then stopped his mouth until there was no longer any need to restrain him.

There were bloody footprints on the floor and a length of sheet that had been pulled out from under Edward's body bore red-brown smears, as though the murderer had used it to wipe blood off himself. It was easy enough to see how the assassin had got in. The attic floor was smaller than the rest of the house. Under the window was the roof of the story below and from there it was not a very long drop to the wall that divided the Macnabs' house from an alleyway running alongside on the left, leading from the High Street to some other street to the rear. From alleyway to wall to roof to attic window would be an easy progression for an active man, and the return journey just as easy. Furthermore, it was clear that someone had made it, for the bloodstained footprints led to the window and there were other traces of blood on the attic windowsill and on the roof below.

I had caught up with my cousin Edward but somebody else had got there first.

7

Dissolving into Chaos

The Macnab household dissolved into chaos. Dale rushed downstairs, shouted an incoherent explanation to Mistress Macnab, who was on her way up to investigate the outcry, and then fled to the back door to be sick out of it. The little maidservant who had been making a bed stopped making it, and without knowing what had happened but sensing that some terrible disaster had struck the house, started to wail.

Shivering and swallowing, I began to follow Dale down the stairs and encountered a bewildered Mistress Macnab in the first-floor bedchamber, where she was trying to quiet the maidservant. I managed to explain matters more clearly than Dale had, although this was hardly useful at first, since the maidservant only wailed the louder while Mistress Macnab, after listening to me with her mouth open, lost her businesslike air in an even noisier outburst of wild and tearful lamentations.

However, some sort of order was presently restored. Mistress Macnab regained a white-faced but resolute command of herself, hushed the maidservant at last, and led her down to the kitchen. Brockley shut Edward's door and stood guard outside it, while Dale, my dear Dale, who was so frail in some ways but so gallant in others, also pulled herself together, went to the kitchen to cleanse her mouth with a beaker of the well water, which was apparently kept there in a clean pail, and then sensibly suggested that the maid should occupy herself by mulling some ale for everyone. This proved a bigger task than expected, involving rather a lot of ale, because the screams and lamentations had been heard by the neighbors and half a dozen people had by now arrived at the door to ask what was amiss.

Master Macnab, though, had kept his head. The Thursbys had talked as though Scotland were a nightmare of anarchy, but of course, it was not. Edinburgh was a city of renown with a provost, a town council, a constable, and a sturdy band of law enforcement officers. Macnab, after asking one of his neighbors to go up to Holyrood and explain why he would not be at work that day, dispatched his serving lad to fetch authority to the scene.

Before it arrived, however, and while Mistress Macnab was in the kitchen dispensing mulled ale to her uninvited guests, I slipped upstairs again and said to Brockley: "Quick. I want to look at Edward's things, to see if I can find anything that looks like a list. It might be in cipher."

Had I not had a harsh experience of life over the last few years, I couldn't have made that search, in that room where Edward's body lay. I could do it—just—only because I had seen civil war in France and murder in my own land too. I had been hardened, perhaps more than a young woman with a daughter to bring up should ever be hardened. Even so, it took all my courage to enter that chamber again, and when I did, I stopped short, trembling, because Edward was lying with his face toward me. The sight of the distorted, bloodstained mouth and staring eyes was almost too much for me.

Brockley, however, had come in with me, and there were times when he had an instinctive, not to say uncanny, knowledge of what was going on in my mind. Stepping quickly past me, he caught up the stained sheet that had been pulled out of the bed and tossed it over Edward's face. "We need not work with him staring at us like that," he said. "Now, where do we start?"

We made a rapid but thorough search of my cousin's belongings. It didn't take long because, just as we had done, he had traveled with only such things as he could carry in a couple of saddlebags and a satchel for his back. Apart from his nightgown and the clothes he had been wearing yesterday, he had a spare pair of shoes, a couple of shirts, some underlinen, a fustian doublet and hose for riding, and one decent doublet and hose for use when dining in good houses.

This last outfit was obviously costly, as though he had expected to be entertained at some very good houses indeed. The material was black velvet, the hose embellished with thin stripes of silver thread and the doublet embroidered with a scattered pattern of small silver stars. It was fastened with matching buttons, each covered in black with a silver star on it.

The doublet had seen some wear. I noticed, as I handled it, that a couple of buttons were missing from the front, one at the bottom, at waistline level, and one halfway up. Their absence wouldn't be noticeable, though. A belt would obscure the waistline one and a well-placed pendant would hide the other. This was still a fine garment fit for formal use. It was probably his best one. Had Edward, I wondered, hoped to find his way into Queen Mary's court after all?

All his things had been carefully unpacked and arranged in the clothes press and the chest that were part of the room's furnishings. He also had a belt pouch of money, a silver cross on a chain—just the right length for concealing that missing button, I saw—and a leather bag containing soap and razor. "Whoever attacked him wasn't interested in plain robbery," Brockley observed.

What Edward did not have, however, in any form, enciphered or otherwise, was anything resembling a list of names. We not only searched his saddlebags and satchel, but also felt each item of clothing in case a paper had been stitched into it. We investigated both the press and the chest with care, and Brockley, without comment, performed for me the grim task of feeling under the stained pillow and the mattress, and then, as a last resort, examined the nightgown.

He did it carefully, so that the constable's men should see the scene as it had been when we found it. He also did it in vain. Straightening up at last, he shook his head. "There's nowhere more to look," he said.

Just as he turned away from the bed, however,

he stooped and picked something up from the floor.

"Being jammed into saddlebags doesn't do fine clothes much good, madam. I reckon this is a button off his doublet."

I took the little black and silver thing and then paused, looking around me again. Then I swore.

"Madam?" said Brockley, faintly disapproving.

"I wonder if he delivered that list before he was killed, Brockley. From what Mistress Macnab said, it didn't sound as though he went out yesterday but he might have done. She didn't really know. Because I think he's worn that black velvet doublet since he's been here, and that means a formal call of some kind. Look. His saddlebags and satchel are on the floor over in that far corner and the press is on one side of them and the chest on the other. If the button came off during unpacking, it would most likely be over there, not here by the bed. He must have lost it when he was dressing or undressing." I shrugged wearily. "Well, we tried, but that's probably the end of it. Anyway, our other reason for coming after him was to get him home again before he came to any harm and . . ."

"Quite. I think," said Brockley, "that we should leave this room now. I'm sorry you should ever have seen what's under that sheet."

We went out. Brockley resumed his vigil outside the door and I went back to the kitchen. No one asked where I had been but I said, by way of explanation: "I felt unwell," and I know I looked it. I accepted some mulled ale and asked for some to be taken to Brockley. Five minutes after that, the constable's men arrived, cold-faced and efficient.

The next few days were busy and frightening. The body was removed. The Macnabs, shuddering, set about cleaning the attic. I was given permission to gather up my cousin's belongings to send to his wife in Sussex. I was also permitted to arrange his funeral and see him buried.

It was a strange feeling, to stand in a cold, wet wind by a graveside in Edinburgh, watching the coffin that contained my cousin Edward as it was lowered into the earth.

Edward and I were about the same age. He had been twelve when he was sent to Northumberland to complete his education and I had been glad to see the last of him. For my taste, he was far too much like Uncle Herbert, his father, by which I mean that he was overweight but remarkably soft-footed in spite of it and liked nothing so much as stealing up on servants—or his illegitimate cousin Ursula, who lived at Faldene only through his father's charity—to catch them doing something amiss. Then he would gleefully report the matter to his parents and enjoy the result.

At twelve years old, I hadn't liked Edward at all. Nevertheless, the image of him lying dead in his room was stamped into my brain and it had outraged me. When they put him in the ground, just as though he had been beloved and would be sorely missed, I cried.

But after that, of course, inevitably, came an inquiry, which in England we would have called an inquest. And that was the point at which the entire business followed the example of the Macnab household at the beginning, and chaos took command.

8

Muddy Waters

The inquiry should properly have preceded the burial, but we gathered, through Master Macnab, who had an acquaintance on the town council, that there had been confusion over setting up an inquest because of a matter that was nothing whatever to do with Edward himself.

The Burgh Court had begun to make the arrangements but it happened that the Burgh Court was at loggerheads with the provost just then, because the provost suspected that a recent Burgh Court verdict had been swayed by bribery. The provost and the town council therefore demanded to take this new case over themselves. The wrangling looked at first as though it would go on for a long time, which was why I was allowed to lay my cousin to rest.

The day after that, however, an edict came from Holyrood House, from the queen's representatives there, to say that this unsavory business must be investigated at once, no matter who undertook it, and the provost seized the initiative. A proclamation was read at the Cross of St. Giles, announcing that the provost himself would preside and that the inquiry would open on Wednesday the fourteenth day of February and that all concerned were required to present themselves at somewhere called the Tolbooth at ten of the clock on that morning.

Which we duly did, feeling nervous.

By *we*, I mean Brockley, Dale, myself, and the Macnabs. We all felt that suspicion had gathered around us, the Macnabs in whose house Edward had died, and the cousin who had descended on Edward in such haste. We had all been forbidden to leave the city and, indeed, I think we came within a hairsbreadth of being actually arrested.

I worried over what to wear, for although the one good dress I had brought was appropriately black, as became a lady recently widowed, it had no farthingale and had suffered, like Edward's clothing, from being squashed into a traveling bag, not to mention acquiring stains from being worn at several dinner tables.

However, while the town council and the Burgh Court were arguing, I reduced some of the heavy weight of coinage I had brought with me, by buying some materials. I found a tailor willing to accept an urgent commission, thus acquiring a black velvet overgown with an ash-colored satin kirtle and a fresh, black-edged ruff. For Dale, I had a new gown made in dark blue. It was as well, for the proceedings began in a fashion both somber and formal.

The Tolbooth turned out to be a civic building like a small castle, next to the High Kirk of St. Giles. We went in through an intimidatingly massive entrance, and the gatekeeper shut the door after us so quickly that the tunnel-like passage beyond was in near-darkness. As we followed him through it, I became uncomfortably aware that prisoners were kept in this building. Somewhere, faintly, I could hear raucous shouting, and a woman crying, and, most unpleasantly, someone hammering on a door and hoarsely bellowing that he didn't want to hang; he didn't want to die, in God's name he was innocent! It made the gooseflesh rise on my arms.

The gatekeeper, who could apparently see in the dark, brought us out of the tunnel and handed us over to an usher at the door of the hall, and once we were inside the ugly sounds faded. The hall was impressive. There was a pulpit at one corner and the usher told us that the room was used as a chapel for the prisoners, and that the famous Reformist leader John Knox sometimes came to preach. Today, the pulpit was empty. Instead, a thronelike chair and a table with a gavel had been set upon a dais, and beside the dais was a long bench.

Presently a jury of twelve dark-clad men came in and stood in a line beside the bench, and then the provost, in a black, floor-length clerical gown, arrived with his clerks and six guards and took his place on the dais.

I never learned his name. He was addressed throughout the proceedings as My Lord Provost. I can see him in my mind's eye, though: a small, fussy man with flyaway white hair under his cap, and a pink, purse-lipped face. I was surprised that this murder, which on the face of it was a squalid killing in an unimportant household, was being taken so seriously that Holyrood had intervened, but I soon learned why.

Whether or not Edward had meant to go to Queen Mary's court in person, Queen Mary apparently had heard of him. In his opening speech, the provost stated that the death in such circumstances of one whose name was known to Queen Mary and whose family, by repute, was well regarded by her, was a most shocking event. It was as well, he said, that Her Majesty was absent from Edinburgh on a Progress to Fife on the far side of the firth, since her good and gracious spirit would be most grieved to think of such a heinous crime occurring to such a man in her capital city.

Interestingly, he then announced that an illustrious visitor from England, the queen's cousin Henry Lord Darnley, was now in Edinburgh and being entertained at the palace of Holyrood. What a poor impression of Scotland this disgraceful business would give him! said the provost in shocked tones. So Darnley had arrived, I thought, and even if the general public didn't know it, they must know at Holyrood that he was here to court the Scottish queen. No wonder the authorities were on edge.

The provost was now declaring that all present should ask for the guidance of God in illuminating the truth and reaching a true verdict. Having delivered himself of these pious sentiments, and having led us briefly in prayer, he signed to the jury to be seated on their bench, and then got on with the inquiry briskly enough.

It began conventionally with testimonies from Mistress Keith, the Macnabs, the officers who had investigated, myself, and various supporting witnesses. To my relief, it was soon established that the Brockleys and I had all been in the company of others throughout the night of the killing. Mistress Keith herself, representing her husband, who, apparently, was recovering from his illness though still unable to bear witness in person, declared that since I and my servants were strangers, none of us could have got out of her house at night without rousing the guard dogs, whose baying would have wakened the whole district.

As for the Macnabs, who had been letting their attic to paying guests for years, no one could advance any reason why they should suddenly have turned on one of the said guests and murdered him. The usual motive in such cases was robbery, but Master Faldene had not been robbed and the Macnabs were known to be perfectly solvent.

The open window and the trail of bloodstained marks were in any case plain evidence that the killer or killers had come from outside. The trail led over the roof of the lower story to the wall and down into the alley, where it stopped. The alley, which the constable's men called a wynd, led from the High Street to a less important street called Cockburn Street, emerging into both through narrow arches where miscreants could have lurked in the shadows until they were sure it was safe to step out.

"Verra likely," said the officer who presented the report, "an accomplice, or more than one maybe, was waiting in the wynd with clean footwear and cloaks.

Looking commonplace enough and leaving no further trail, the killers could have escaped into the town where, nae doot, they went to ground."

I now learned, however, that as a stranger, I was still required to give an account of my purpose in Edinburgh. I was called to explain myself.

I was careful in what I said. From the moment when the constable's men first questioned me, on the day that we found Edward's body, I had been appalled at the prospect of getting into the deep and muddy waters of political relations between England and Scotland, let alone the question of possible schemes against Elizabeth. I had decided, quite simply, that I wasn't going to.

On the other hand, I had to tell them a certain amount. I had already briefly confirmed to the inquiry that I was Edward Faldene's cousin, Madame de la Roche, widow, who had come to Edinburgh to see him on family business. Urged to enlarge on the said family business, I told them that Edward's wife and parents had sent me to fetch him back because they were worried about his safety. Thereafter, I pleaded ignorance.

"I don't know why he came to Scotland because they wouldn't tell me what it was all about," I said, as firmly as I could. "They only insisted that they were worried about him. I asked why, of course, but they just shook their heads."

They had pleaded with me to come after him, I explained, because they hoped that a family member would have more chance of persuading him to come back than an ordinary messenger, and I was used to traveling, as I had in the past journeyed to Antwerp with my first husband, and later lived in France with

Matthew de la Roche. I had also for a time been attached to the court of Queen Elizabeth and gone on Progress with her.

I mentioned my link with Queen Elizabeth in the hope that it would be some sort of protection, and I think it was. To me, my story sounded thin. I didn't think I would be believed when I said I didn't know Edward's business in Scotland, and I expected to be pressed hard on the subject, but I was not. After I had stood down, however, there was a surprise.

The proclamation that summoned us to the inquiry had also required any who had knowledge bearing on this horrid murder to tell the authorities forthwith. A tavern keeper by the name of Master Furness was now called and came forward to say that an Englishman named Edward Faldene had been caught up in a quarrel in his tavern, though not on the eve of his death, but on the previous night.

It transpired that the other party to the quarrel was present, and he too was called forward. He emerged from the crowd, a dark, hirsute fellow with a scowling face. To my English eyes, the plaid that he wore belted around him gave him a wild appearance, though it was no doubt a good protection against the penetrating cold. There was a hearth in the hall and the fire was lit, but in a chamber of that size, it made little difference.

He gave his testimony straightforwardly. Despite his permanent scowl, he had a certain dignity. What he had to say, though, was hardly helpful. He identified himself as Adam Ericks, son of Johann Ericks, a soldier domiciled in Scotland but born in Norway, and Jessie Ericks, who had been born Jessie Gordon and was actually a distant cousin of the current head of the Gordon clan. Adam was a skilled practitioner with the claymore—I gathered that this was the form of broadsword used in Scotland—and made his living as one of the retainers of a nobleman called Patrick Lord Lindsay, who was a Protestant and an associate of James Stewart, the Earl of Moray.

Around the court, heads nodded, mine included, as I recognized the name that Helene had mentioned, that of Queen Mary's powerful Protestant half brother by one of her father's many mistresses. That he was his sister's chief aide, and that she had other ardently Protestant nobles in her entourage, was certainly one of the more piquant features of the Scottish court.

"I ought to have gone with the Progress to Fife, but I was sick and couldn't," Ericks said. On shaking off his illness, however, he had celebrated his return to health with an evening in Master Furness's tavern. While he was there, Edward Faldene had come in and Ericks had noticed that Edward wore a cross.

"I'm of the Reformed persuasion, sir, like my master. I follow the preacher John Knox, whose house is close to this very building. I have often heard him speak . . ."

"Aye!" broke in a loud, harsh voice from the back of the room. "And so the man has, for he is often among my congregation here in this verra Kirrk of St. Giles and I am here today at his plea!"

The voice had an astonishing resonance. Everyone turned around. At the back of the court, a thickset, dark-clad, pale-faced man in middle age had risen to his feet. He now launched into a harangue.

"I've spoken with this man Erricks!" The r's rolled like thunder. "Many a time he has asked me godly questions. He is passionate for the Prrrotestant faith but he is honest and in my hearing, none shall say he is a murrrderer of men in the night and not be challenged!"

The provost, his pursed lips jutting out, was bristling with indignation. Clearly he considered that after defeating the Burgh Court, interference from any other quarter was the last thing he had expected.

"Master Knox! If you wish to testify, then you may do so, but after we have finished with Master Ericks, if you please!"

So the famous John Knox, the virtual founder of the present Protestant movement in Scotland, had agreed to interest himself in this matter, on behalf of Adam Ericks. I peered across the room at him, intrigued, for this was the man against whom the Bycrofts' chaplain had railed, the preacher who had caused the Bycrofts to refer to Queen Mary as a poor beleaguered lassie.

With a sense of depression, I recognized his breed. This was a bigot or I had never seen one. I had to my own discomfort crossed the path of a similar individual in the rival encampment, so to speak. Matthew had once had a passionately, not to say murderously, Catholic acquaintance called Dr. Wilkins. Knox, the ardent Protestant, was remarkably like Wilkins. Even their voices, thick and deep, were similar.

"Continue with your testimony," said the provost, in a steely voice, to Adam Ericks.

Heads reluctantly turned again, away from the

famous Knox to the possibly infamous Adam Ericks. "Aye. Well, I don't like these popish symbols. If folk want to follow the pope, they ought to be a bit decent and discreet about it, to my mind. Or better still, not follow him at all."

Once more, an officer spoke up, this time to inform the court that just after Her Majesty Queen Mary first arrived in Scotland, Ericks's employer, Patrick Lord Lindsay, had led a violent protest when she attempted to hold a mass at Holyrood House. Master Ericks had been one of the crowd trying to storm the chapel, shouting and brandishing weapons. Only a determined stand by the Earl of Moray, who had on this occasion chosen to defend his half sister rather than his religion, and had personally stood in the chapel doorway to defy the mob, had kept it out.

I wondered what the young queen's good and gracious spirit had thought of a scene like that. At that moment, a new commotion broke out around Knox, causing the officer to falter and stop speaking. Knox, brushing other people out of the way, was marching toward the empty pulpit. Reaching it, he climbed the steps, faced the hall, and began to declare loudly that it was a grievous day when the idolatrous mass was allowed to be heard in the very chapel of the queen, in the palace where he himself had once been a royal chaplain.

"Master Knox! This is not the time or the place! Be good enough to leave the pulpit immediately!" shouted the provost.

A couple of men, both well dressed, who seemed to be Knox's friends, pushed their way to the foot of the pulpit and began trying to persuade him to come down. Knox continued to declaim, booming that on that day at Holyrood, Ericks had been only one of many other honest men outrraged by this blasphemy, and had in fact been loyally following his lorrd, who was in turn one of Knox's own followers. The provost, his face now red instead of pink, picked up his gavel and pounded the table in front of him in fury. One of the men climbed into the pulpit and took Knox's arm. Knox resisted; the other man pulled, and the two of them lurched about and then came down the pulpit steps in a stumble that was just short of a fall.

The near-accident produced a few snorts of laughter, but Knox, shaking his friend off, drowned them out by thundering: "For Patrick Lindsay is one of the Lorrrds of the Congrrregation whose shepherd and pastor I have the honor to be . . ."

The crowd had turned to him again and he was on the verge of mounting the pulpit once more, no doubt in the hope of taking over the entire proceedings. By raising his voice once more and using the gavel as though he wanted to smash the table to pieces, the provost regained control, but I could feel that the balance of power in the room was slipping. For the moment, Knox was forced into silence, and his friends held him back from the pulpit, but we all felt that at any moment he might burst out again.

Ericks, asked for his side of the story about the interrupted mass, coolly agreed that it was true and added, with apparent pride, that he had personally snatched an altar candle from a servant who was carrying it to the chapel and thrown the thing on the ground and stamped on it. There were various murmurs in the court, by the sound of them mostly of agreement by people who already knew about the exciting first Sabbath of Queen Mary's reign in Scotland and had probably taken part in the uproar. They assuredly were not expressions of surprise.

Standing there with Brockley and Dale, I realized that, after all, the Thursbys had been partly right. Prompt though the officers of the law had been to investigate my cousin's death, nevertheless, this was a violent land where a mob trying to interfere with the private worship of their sovereign was not thought strange or even particularly wrong, and a respectable minister with great lords in his following might encourage such a thing.

Ericks, once allowed to resume his testimony, said, quite openly, that with a few tankards of ale inside him, he was apt to be free with his fists and had let himself be provoked by the sight of Edward's cross and had "told the popish fellow to put it out of sight." Edward had indignantly refused, and words had been exchanged.

"I asked him who he was, prinking about wearing silver crosses, and he told me his name and said he was a supporter of Queen Mary, but I didnae like his mincing southron voice, so I threw a punch," said Master Ericks casually.

Edward had hit back, and with bystanders cheering the two of them on, there had been a lively display of fisticuffs until the tavern keeper pushed his way through the crowd to yank the pair apart and tell them to go and settle their quarrel outside.

"But the mincing white-livered craven gave me the slip and dodged off into the night," said Ericks in disgust.

He had tried to pursue his quarry, but not for long, because he was still a wee bit short of breath after his illness. No, he had not followed Edward home and had no notion where he was staying. He had given up the chase and been back in the tavern within a few minutes, and there were those there who knew him and could say so. The tavern keeper, recalled, bore this out. He also said that he had heard most of the exchange between the two men and no, Edward had not said where he was lodged.

"So I don't think Ericks could have known. Besides, it makes no sense. It was just a squabble. They're always happening, especially with Ericks. I've had to order him out a couple of times before. That sort of thing doesn't lead to *this*."

By *this*, he meant assassins who crept in at windows in the small hours of the morning, more than twenty-four hours after an argument in a tavern, and stabbed people in their sleep, and he was right. Everyone knew it, and if they hadn't known it, John Knox, interrupting the proceedings for the third time, and this time wresting control from the provost so forcefully that even though he was not in the pulpit, he nevertheless became to all intents and purposes the presiding authority, proceeded to tell them.

Ericks, he declared resoundingly, was a good man, zealous for the Reformed faith, and he, Knox, would testify to Ericks's charrracter at any time and in any fashion it pleased the prrovost or any other authority to require. To suppose that Ericks had gone on to spend the day after the argument in creating a tangled scheme of stealthy murrder, and one, at that, which most likely needed at least one accomplice, was madness, and to believe it was to believe the whispering of demons. If Ericks had encountered Edward again, likely enough he would have offered rrighteous blows but as for crrreeping in at windows with a blade in his hand . . . !

"If this poor honest man Adam Erricks is named as the murrderer?" roared Knox, "it will be over my dead body and so I tell you!"

Loud cheers broke out from the people around him, and standing on tiptoe to see over the crowd, I realized that, in fact, quite a number of men were gathered around him now and that some of them, judging from their rich furred cloaks, were some of his Lords of the Congregation.

And no doubt they had retainers with them.

Whether or not Knox and his supporters swayed the verdict, I can't be sure, but I would wager that they did. Confronted with the possibility of mayhem and further bloodshed, the provost and his jury did what Knox plainly wanted them to do and eliminated Ericks as a suspect. The provost was visibly simmering with anger but he was helpless, his court's verdict decided by outside influence just as the Burgh Court's verdict had been on an earlier occasion.

Not that the verdict was itself unfair. I did not myself think that Adam Ericks was guilty. It was true enough, I thought, that as the verdict said, Edward Faldene, visitor on unknown business from England, had been murdered by a person or persons unknown.

Then I realized with infinite relief that it was over and

we were free to go. Thankfully, we made our way out through a crowd of townsfolk, hindered only by a crippled lady who was being carried in a chair, and who gave us a sweet, apologetic smile as we stopped to let her be borne out of the hall ahead of us.

The Macnabs had not had room for us—unless we used the attic, which we certainly didn't want to do. We had taken the lodgings recommended by the Keiths. They were not far from the Macnabs' house, in another narrow, timber-fronted building, and they were chilly, cramped, and poor.

Our landlady, who had a plump face and a comfortable figure but eyes as cold as slate, kept one room free, she said, so that she could get some money for letting it to folk visiting Edinburgh, even if it meant her children sleeping on the floor in their parents' chamber. One glance at the room showed that it was not only free of the children but practically free of furnishings as well. All it contained was a very small hearth for which we had to buy our own coal and firewood, a plain table with a bench on each side, a mattress to go on the bare floor and some blankets to cover it, and some more bedding inside a tall built-in cupboard, similar to the one I had seen at the Macnabs.

I gathered that I was expected to take the box bed while my servants shared the mattress, but although I was accustomed to curtained four-posters, the idea of sleeping in a pitch-dark cupboard appalled me. I told Brockley and Dale that if they could stand it, they could have it. I would prefer the floor. They said the box bed was quite warm and comfortable, and I must say that my solitary mattress was neither, but I preferred piling cloaks on top of me to changing places with the Brockleys.

We couldn't find any alternative lodgings, though. The pending inquiry had made people suspicious. Our cold-eyed landlady had only let us in because, she said, she knew the Keiths and trusted them. "But ony trouble," she warned us, "and ye're oot. So tak that as a warning."

She was kind enough to say, when we returned from the inquiry, that she was glad it was all over and that our names were clear. She then spoiled the effect by asking delicately how long we would be staying.

Brockley started to say that we would be leaving almost at once but I checked him. "I may have some business to complete in Edinburgh," I said. "Do you really object if we stay on for a few days? Have we given you any cause for complaint?"

Grudgingly, she admitted that the answer was no. "Truly," I said, "we have just been caught up in this tragedy by chance. And it is a tragedy. I am grieving for my cousin and dreading the news I must carry back to his wife."

"I'll grant that you've been no bother as yet. Well, as long as that continues . . ."

"It will," I said, and led my companions upstairs to our room. I closed the door firmly behind us. Brockley and Dale regarded me questioningly.

"Are we not to leave Edinburgh at once, then, madam?" Brockley asked. "But—why?"

"When I gave evidence," I said, "I didn't tell the court of inquiry everything."

"No, madam," Brockley agreed. "You didn't mention the list."

"That wasn't all I didn't mention," I said. "Listen, both of you. I was given leave to pack up my cousin's things and I did so. I did it myself. Brockley, do you remember that on the day when we found him, you found a button from his black velvet doublet lying on the floor by the bed?"

"Yes, madam. But what of it?"

"I looked at his doublet when I was packing it," I said, "and there were two buttons missing, right enough, but when I looked again at the one you found, I saw that it wasn't one of them. The stars embroidered on the black doublet and its buttons are proper five-sided stars with the outlines filled in with silver stitchery while the one we found on the floor has a crisscross pattern in silver thread. It's similar at a casual glance but not when you really look at it. It doesn't resemble buttons on any other item of his clothing, either."

"But . . ." said Dale, puzzled, and then stopped.

"I showed it to Mistress Macnab and asked if it had come from the clothing of anyone in the house," I said. "I didn't say where I'd found it—just that I'd picked it up off the floor. She looked at it and said no, it didn't belong to anyone in her house and I believe her."

"So, what are you saying, madam?" Brockley asked.

"I thought when we found it," I said, "that it was evidence that Edward had gone out wearing his best doublet, which might mean he had gone to see one or other of his contacts, Sir Brian Dormbois or Lady Simone Dougal. They sound like the sort of people one wouldn't normally visit in travel-stained riding clothes. While I was talking to Mistress Macnab, I asked her to tell me as much as she could about anything

Edward had said or done after he arrived. I said his wife would want to know."

They nodded.

"It seems," I said, "that although Mistress Macnab doesn't know whether or not he went out on the day after he arrived, he did indeed go out the previous evening—that would have been to the tavern—and was only wearing his brown riding clothes then. She said he wasn't gone all that long. Now, if you remember, at the inquiry, Adam Ericks said that while he himself was in the tavern, Edward came in, wearing a cross, and by the sound of it, their argument broke out almost at once."

"Yes, Ericks did say that," Brockley agreed. "And he asked your cousin who he was, and Master Faldene told him his name. There's no doubt that Master Faldene was the man Ericks quarreled with."

"Yes. When Edward came back, Mistress Macnab let him in, but she didn't see him clearly because of course it was after dark and she only had a candle. She didn't know until the inquiry that he'd been in a fight. He didn't tell her. What he did tell her, next day, was that he wasn't feeling well and he spoke through the attic door—he wouldn't show her his face. Mistress Macnab may not know whether or not he did go out that day, but the maidservant thinks not. I spoke to her as well. He had all three meals—breakfast, dinner, and supper—in his room. He was called for each of them, but every time he said he was unwell and asked for the food to be left outside his door. I suspect that he stayed indoors all that day, and it does look as though he didn't want anyone to see his face—didn't want to be seen with the marks of a fight on him, in fact."

"That lump on his jaw, madam," said Brockley. "We thought it was part of—of what his murderer did to him, but it might have been done by Adam Ericks."

"Very probably," I said. "But do you see what I'm saying? When he went out to the tavern, he apparently wasn't gone long, so I doubt if he went anywhere else first, and in any case he wasn't dressed for visiting. When he got into the tavern, Adam Ericks accosted him at once, so he didn't have much of a chance to speak to anyone else then, either. The next day, he almost certainly stayed in. What all this means is that he had no opportunity to get in touch with either of his contacts. And in that case—where's the list?"

There was a silence.

At length, I said: "I was afraid to speak of that list to the provost or in the court. I didn't know where it might lead. Religious feelings quite obviously run high in Scotland, and when I heard that story about the attack on the chapel when Queen Mary was hearing mass, I was sure I was right to be afraid. I could have found myself under suspicion of spying! It would be said that no innocent person ought to know anything about a thing like that list. I feel contaminated because I *do* know of it!"

I paused, but they were silent, guessing, I think, what was going to come next.

"From the first," I told them, "although I came without their knowledge or consent, I knew that I had a responsibility to Sir William Cecil and the queen, as far as that list is concerned. I agreed to chase Edward and get it back if I could, for their sake as well as my family's. I wanted to destroy it. Only, I have to find it first."

"And also," I added, after I had paused again and neither Brockley nor Dale had replied, "Edward Faldene, however misguided, was my cousin. He has been murdered. Well, I want to know who did it, and it seems to me that the list and the murder could be connected."

"And you intend, madam, to make your own inquiries?" said Brockley, finding his tongue at last.

"Yes, Brockley."

The pockmarks were standing out on Dale's face, a sure sign that she was horrified. Brockley was shaking his head. "It would have been better," he said, "to give full information to the provost and let him do it."

"I told you. I thought it would be dangerous for me and perhaps for you."

"And this," said Brockley, "a private inquiry of your own—*isn't?*"

9

Delightful Enemy

Although I thought it most unlikely that he had seen
them, the obvious place to start was nevertheless with
Edward's contacts.

"Apart from a button with a silver crisscross pattern
on it, they're the only leads I have," I said to Dale and
Brockley. "I suppose it's *just* possible that he saw one of
them when he first arrived in Edinburgh, before he
came to the Macnabs—or that he sent the list to one of
them by a messenger. At least, they may know something about any other acquaintances, or business, or
enemies that Edward had in Edinburgh. I must start
somewhere."

The problem was to find them. Helene had given
me their names but she hadn't known where Lady
Simone lived, and what she knew about Dormbois
wasn't too helpful, either. He had a house outside Edinburgh, apparently, but was in the service of one of the

queen's uncles. I supposed that he had accompanied the royal Progress.

"We might inquire about them at Holyrood," I said. "Someone there might know."

Brockley, however, once he had wearily accepted that I meant what I said, offered an idea of his own. "The minister at the Kirk of St. Giles might have heard of them, even if they're not members of his own flock. I fancy he would know something about all the foremost people of Edinburgh. If you wish, I'll go and ask him."

"Please do," I said. I looked out of the window. The day had started bright but the sky was darkening. "Meanwhile," I said, "Dale and I must buy ourselves some clogs. I think the streets will soon be muddy."

When we returned to the lodgings, carrying the clogs in a bag, Brockley was waiting for us. In fact, he was gossiping in the kitchen with our landlady's maidservant and her spitboy, but he heard our voices at the door and came out to meet us.

"I've been scraping acquaintance with the household, madam. You never know when you might hear something useful."

"Did you see the minister?" I asked him.

Brockley's normally impassive face broke into its rare smile. "I did, madam. He knew both Dormbois and Lady Simone. He is not sure, but supposes that Dormbois is with the court, as you thought. Lady Simone Dougal however is here in the city, in fact farther up this very street, nearer to Holyrood. Her home is called Pieris House. It's just past St. Mary's Street, the minister said. Not that I need have troubled him, not on account of Lady Simone."

"What do you mean?" I asked him.

"I mean, madam, that one of her servants has been here with a letter for you." He held it out. "I rather think, from what the man said, that Lady Simone is as anxious to see you as you are to see her."

I broke the seal and read the letter aloud. The Lady Simone Dougal would be most grateful if Madame de la Roche, widow of Matthew de la Roche, would be kind enough to call on her on the morrow, after dinner, at the hour of three.

I looked at Brockley. "The hand of fate," I said.

The smile had gone from his face. "I hope not in ambush," he said.

"Oh, come now, Brockley!"

"As you were reading that letter out, madam, I was thinking of what we saw in Master Faldene's room. I am not easy about this. I wish we were leaving at once. One of these days, madam," said Brockley grimly, "you will end up in a dungeon or dead, and us with you!"

Dale looked frightened. "Brockley," I said, "all three of us have been in dungeons before now, and I grant you that we've come near to being dead as well. But I don't think a social visit to a well-bred Edinburgh lady is likely to have such drastic results."

"We've visited at least one well-bred lady before, with *very* drastic results," said Brockley grimly.

He was referring, as I well knew, to a journey we had once made to Wales, to a castle with a most remarkable chatelaine.

"I'm quite sure," I said bracingly, "that there can't be two Lady Thomasines!"

* * *

It poured with rain that night, turning the streets to quagmires, just as I had feared, with rivulets of water running down every slope. I had spent money on clogs, but if you wish to make a good impression on a lady of title, it isn't advisable to arrive at her door mud-splashed and clumping along in clogs. I therefore sent Brockley for our horses and we did it in style, in the saddle.

Pieris House was handsome. Built of gray stone, it was tall, as so many buildings in Edinburgh seemed to be; and looked quite modern, with its elegant windows and its ornamental towers and chimneys. It stood behind the protection of a gatehouse and courtyard, but the gate was invitingly open, and when the porter learned who I was, it was only moments before we were shown into the courtyard, where grooms came to take our horses, and a butler, dressed as formally as the provost had been, came down the steps from the main door to escort us inside.

Brockley, as was his habit, went off with the horses, but Dale and I were led up a wide, shallow flight of oaken stairs that rose through three stories, before we were taken through a curtained door into a most delightful parlor. Tall windows, set in deep embrasures with cushioned seats, gave a view out to the sea, and the fire in the hearth smelled of applewood. Underfoot the boards were spread with rushes, as at Bycroft, but sprigs of sweet rosemary were scattered among them to refresh the air, and the walls were hung with tapestries. Rich mulberry velvet curtains kept drafts from stealing through the doors at each end of the room. There was a shelf of books, several carved settles strewn with more bright cushions, and a table spread with white damask, on which wine and cakes stood waiting.

And on a couch near the fireside, with an embroidery frame in her hands and a glossy rug of dark fur drawn over her, lay the crippled lady who had smiled at us when we were leaving the inquiry.

"You are Lady Simone Dougal?" I said in surprise.

Remembering my manners, I dropped quickly into a curtsy, but our hostess had put her work aside and was stretching out a hand to me. "No formality, if you please." She spoke good English but her accent was French. "My dear Madame de la Roche, I am glad that you could come. Seat yourself and take some refreshment, yes, and your woman too. This is an hospitable house, I hope!"

She was as delightful as her parlor, a fragile little lady with a white, paper-thin skin, and eyes, which though sunken with time and ill-health, were still a beautiful summer blue. Her white cap was set on the back of her head and the soft hair in front of it was halfway between gold and white. She smiled at me once more.

"Forgive me for not rising. I had an illness some years ago, a fever like so many other fevers, but when I recovered, I found I had lost the use of my legs."

"I am sorry. Would you prefer it," I said, "if we talked in French? I speak the language well."

The blue eyes lit up. "What a pleasure," she said in her native language. "I would, indeed. I came from

France, you know, a quarter of a century ago, when the present queen's mother, Mary of Guise, came over to marry the Scottish king. I and one of my cousins were among her maids of honor. We both married here in Scotland, and my cousin's daughter now serves Queen Mary. Robert and I had no children, alas. If we had, I would have made sure they grew up knowing French. Take some wine, my dear. That too is French, from the vineyards of the Loire Valley, which I believe you know so well."

"Indeed," I said, and signed to Dale to pour for us. "Wine for you, Lady Simone?"

"A little, yes. I thank you." Though she was ailing and well past her youth, she was as fresh and feminine as a primrose. "Chérie," she said tenderly, "if I may call you so, I asked you here for a reason and not a happy one. But I was so distressed to learn of the shocking death of your cousin Edward Faldene, and it seemed to me, when I went to the inquiry, that perhaps you were not saying all you guessed at. You came to Scotland at the behest of his family, did you not, because they feared he was running into danger. But what kind of danger? Do you know more than you said when you bore witness? Do you have any idea who killed him?"

I regarded her sadly. "Lady Simone," I said, "if you had not sent for me, I would have come anyway. To ask you the same question."

We studied each other for several moments, sipping the excellent wine and considering what to say next. At length, I said: "One thing I wished to ask was whether or not Edward came to see you or in any way got in touch with you before he . . . before he was killed. He was out in the town two evenings before, that much we know."

Lady Simone shook her head. "No, he did not. How is it, by the way, that you knew, before I wrote to you, that he and I were acquainted?"

"His wife, Helene, gave me your name and said that he meant to call on you," I said cautiously.

"Did she say why?"

I hesitated. Then I said: "It is true that I was wary when I bore witness at the inquiry. In fact, I believe that he may have had a message for Queen Mary, which he wished to pass to her through you. As well as wishing, very much, to find out who murdered my cousin, I would also like to know whether that message reached its destination safely. You see," I added confidingly, and with regret, because she was so very sweet and I was deceiving her, "I think it possible that he was carrying the message, whatever it was, on behalf of my husband, Matthew de la Roche. You evidently know that my husband is dead, since your invitation to me described me as his widow. Had you met him?"

"I didn't know he was dead until the inquiry, when you declared yourself as his widow, chérie. I never met him, but I had heard of Matthew de la Roche, yes, for his name is known at Queen Mary's court and my young cousin sometimes visits me and talks of court affairs. I must offer you my condolences. My own Robert passed away only two years ago and I have not yet ceased from weeping. You, of course, wish to see that whatever business your husband had in hand was completed. You are a Faldene by birth, I imagine, and you married De la Roche, so that must make you a Catholic too."

"But naturally," I said, and was thankful that as we were speaking in French, Dale probably hadn't followed this. She spoke a little of the language but not well. If she had understood, she probably wouldn't have been able to stop herself from looking scandalized.

Lady Simone sighed. "I wish I could help but I cannot. Edward Faldene did not come to me or send any message to me. Was it written down or carried in his head? You found nothing among his belongings?"

"No, nothing. Most certainly, I looked. Lady Simone . . ."

"Yes, my dear?"

"He had another possible contact, a man called Sir Brian Dormbois. I believe he is with the court. If you happen to know anything about him . . ."

"Dormbois? I can't tell you where he is just now but very likely with the court, yes. He has charge of some of the retainers of the queen's uncle Rene. The court is on Progress, though expected back in Edinburgh soon—at the end of next week, I believe. They were going to Fife, on the far side of the firth. Let me see . . . *Liz-zie!*" Startlingly, the flowerlike Lady Simone raised her voice and emitted a musical but extremely carrying call, and from beyond the mulberry curtain at the far end of the room a maidservant appeared. Lady Simone rapped out something in very broad Scots and the girl, with a curtsy, disappeared, to return a moment later with a small wooden box. Lady Simone opened it, rummaged in it, and produced a piece of paper.

"My young cousin—Mary Seton, she is called—gave me this in case I should want to write to her while she is away on the Progress. It is a list of the places the queen intends to visit and the dates, as near as possible. The weather may interfere, of course; it often does. Ah, yes. I think the court will be at Wemyss Castle now, on the way back, and yes, should return to Edinburgh on Saturday week. Sir Brian Dormbois will come with it."

"I think," I said, "that I would like to present myself at the court when it returns—except, of course, that I am not sure if I'll be able to enter it. I realize that my husband's name was known there, but it is a fact, as you will have heard at the inquiry, Lady Simone, that I have also served Queen Elizabeth. Perhaps I would not be permitted entrance."

"Ah. Now there I can help you. A letter of introduction from me will smooth your way. *Liz-zie!*" The simple device of the handbell was apparently not known at Pieris House, but Lady Simone somehow managed to let out these commanding calls without losing one whit of her grace. The maidservant reappeared and was sent off to fetch writing materials. "And what about clothes?" said Lady Simone. "Did you come provided with dresses suitable for court?"

"I . . . no. I have this black gown, and another which is not in a good state after all my traveling, and that's all. But if I have a week in hand, something can be done about that."

"Yes, that would be wise. My dear," said Lady Simone, "one thing about you confuses me. From what you said when you spoke at the inquiry, it seemed that you have been living in England, close to your family of birth. But Matthew de la Roche, your husband, was in France, was he not? How did this come about? Were you living apart?"

"No," I said, relieved that here at least I could tell the truth. "We were both living at his home in France, but I have a daughter by a previous marriage and she was being fostered in England. I left her there during the civil war in France, but last year I came to England to collect her and take her back to France."

"Ah. But you did not do so?"

"No, because Matthew wrote to me and said that plague had broken out near Blanchepierre, his château, and that I should stay in England till the danger had passed. Then I heard that—it had taken him."

"And you chose to remain in England? Living where? Actually with your family?"

"No. I . . . I have a house of my own about five miles from theirs," I said. There was no need to go into how and why Queen Elizabeth had presented it to me. "It's called Withysham," I said. "It was once an abbey, as so many houses in England used to be."

I was speaking casually, making conversation, wishing to appear quite at ease, but Lady Simone pounced, just like a sweet and pretty cat that has seen a careless sparrow.

"And is that a worry to you?" she asked. "In case, one day, our queen should become yours?"

"I have never thought about it," I said, fairly honestly, since I did not see Mary ever superseding Elizabeth and therefore had had no need to think about Withysham's future if she did. "But I have met people who do worry about it, yes." I was thinking, of course, of the Thursbys.

Unexpectedly, Lady Simone said: "My husband once owned one of those old abbeys—in the English Midlands. It was left to him by an English uncle. Robert sold it just before his own death, though. It was leased to tenants and we never lived there, but he visited it occasionally, to make sure it was kept in good order. On his last visit, he was approached by some emissary or other of Queen Elizabeth and asked if he would give an oath that he would back Elizabeth if ever there should be a war between England and Scotland. They told him that he might lose the former abbey if a Catholic ruler ever took the throne. He didn't believe that. He said he was sure that our Queen Mary would never reward faithful followers by taking their homes away from them, and that this was nothing but a ploy, a cruel pretense of Elizabeth's. But he decided that he was not easy in his conscience, owning a house which ought to belong to God, and sold it."

I wasn't sure what to say in reply, and after a longish pause, inquired mundanely if Sir Robert had got a good price.

"Oh yes. He gave some of it to the Church," said Lady Simone. "Though not all. We are all human!" Her smile was enchanting.

The maid came back with the writing materials and the Lady Simone wrote the letter of introduction for me. Then we talked for a while of other, harmless things, such as the winter weather and the embroidery she was doing, until I felt that it was the right moment to leave.

"Chérie," she said, as I rose, "I am sorry that you could not tell me what I wanted to know, and that in turn I could not help you, either. I am also sorry that a young woman like you should be involved in this unsavory business. Take my advice. It is no doubt a grief to you that Matthew is gone, and it is good of you to attempt to finish his work—but it would be wise to lose no time in marrying again. If you wish me to look about for a suitable *parti* for you, I will gladly do so."

For her parting comments, she had reverted to English. Out of the corner of my eye, I saw Dale give a tiny, probably involuntary, nod. The pair of them, I thought indignantly, were like a couple of well-meaning sheepdogs, trying to shepherd me like a wayward ewe into a nice safe pen called Matrimony. Gravely, I said: "Thank you, Lady Simone. But it is too soon as yet."

"Ah well. You know your business best." Lady Simone put out her hand to take one of mine. "I will pray for you, chérie, and that God may send you a man worthy of you. I will pray too that Sir Brian Dormbois has received and passed on the message that Edward was bringing, thus releasing you from the errand. Your husband and your cousin both longed for the day, my dear, when our sweet Queen Mary should be recognized as the true heir not only of Scotland but of England too, and for the moment when with her to lead the way, England will return to the true faith."

"It may never come about, you know," I said gently. "There are many in England who would stoutly resist. From all I have heard, Queen Mary has much work to do for the faith here in Scotland. She has John Knox to oppose her."

Lady Simone sighed. "Indeed, she has had to tread carefully since she came here. You have seen for yourself what John Knox is like." The frail fingers tightened around mine. "But all will be well," she said earnestly. "God will guide us and bring our countries back to Him. Do your best, chérie, and trust in Him."

I had seen the religious civil war in France; I had been obliged, once, to listen while Uncle Herbert and Aunt Tabitha described a burning to me, in detail. I looked at Lady Simone kindly, seeing once again that innocence that had been so much a part of Matthew and was even part of my family at Faldene.

"I will always do my best," I said obliquely, and kissed her in farewell.

Brockley was ready with the horses. As we rode back toward our lodgings, I said to Dale: "That was difficult. She is so delightful. Who wants delightful enemies?"

"Better than nasty ones, perhaps," said Dale, with some asperity. "Less dangerous, ma'am!"

"I'm not so sure about that," I said. "One can so easily begin to feel sorry for them."

Some time later, when Brockley, having stabled the horses again, rejoined us in the lodging, he and Dale came together to my chamber.

"Brockley has something to tell you, ma'am," said Dale, her eyes sparkling.

"I didn't waste my time while I was waiting for you at Pieris House, madam," Brockley said. "I did a bit of chatting with her servants, same as I've done here. It seems that her butler drinks in the same tavern where that fellow Ericks and your cousin had their fight. He saw it!"

"Yes?" I was suddenly alert. "What did he have to say about it?"

"Well, it was much as Ericks said, only according to Lady Simone's butler, there were some strangers there, men he'd not seen in that place before, though by their dress, he thought they were someone's retainers, like Ericks himself. You remember that it came out at the inquiry that some of the bystanders were encouraging the fight?"

"Yes, I do."

"Well, the butler said that that was mostly these strangers. He said they were urging Ericks on for the most part, shouting things like *Go on, hit the popish bastard!* and the like." Brockley disliked strong language but came out with his quotation in valiant fashion.

"You mean," I said, "that someone was trying to . . . do what? Stir up trouble for Edward? Or for Ericks? What are you saying?"

"I'm not sure," said Brockley frankly. "But it struck me as just interesting and worth telling you. Suppose they'd been out for your cousin's blood and thought of using Ericks? Getting him excited and hotheaded, and then, later on, bribing him to go further? And offering to help—to be the accomplices?"

I surveyed Brockley thoughtfully. "I'm impressed. Brockley, you're amazing. You disapprove of the way I live and yesterday you made it plain that you wished I would leave all this to the provost, and yet . . ."

Brockley's rare smile appeared. "Perhaps, at heart,

madam, I respect your feeling for your cousin, and your desire to see justice done," he said.

"Or perhaps," I suggested, "when it comes to the point, you're as much of a hunter as I am a huntress."

Brockley smiled once more. And then, as in the past, I saw Dale's stiff face.

We had done it again, Brockley and I. Once again, we had shared something that Dale did not. We were always doing it: private jokes, tacit declarations of partnership. Hurting her by accident.

It must end. I did not think I could simply go and marry again, but I could find another lady's maid and another personal manservant, and so release Dale to devote herself to Brockley, and Brockley to be the steward of Withysham. I would put distance between us and lay the past to rest.

Once I had found Edward's killers and tracked down that list.

We were all thankful to do no more traveling for a while. I was sleeping badly, in any case, constantly troubled by a nightmare in which I lay helpless in my bed, staring at a window and watching while a faceless figure with murderous intentions forced a way in and came toward me, at which point I would awaken, crying out.

During the day, I was busy. Dale and I spent the following week obtaining new clothes, suitable for me to wear at Queen Mary's court. I provided myself with several outfits, the finest being a silvery gray brocade overdress and sleeves, with kirtle and slashings of a shot silk in which silvery gray and pale violet were subtly mingled. This would do for any formal occasion.

When I had taken delivery of the new clothes, I made a small addition of my own to my new overgowns. It was an addition that already existed in the gowns I had brought with me from home. Inside each of the new open skirts, I sewed my usual hidden pouches. To carry, as before, some money, a set of lockpicks, and a small but very sharp dagger. And the black and silver button.

During that week I also visited a number of tailors to show them the black button with the silver crisscross pattern on it, which we had found in Edward's room. I thought that one of them might recognize it, might be able to say yes, I supplied a doublet with buttons of that pattern to such and such a man.

None of them, however, had ever seen it before.

On Monday the twenty-sixth of February, Queen Mary having been back in Edinburgh for two days, I armed myself with the letter of introduction from Lady Simone and rode to Holyrood Palace through a misty gray morning. The mullioned casements and many-windowed towers of the palace reminded me painfully of Château Blanchepierre, where I had lived with Matthew and which I would never see again. My eyes stung. Ah well, let them. After all, I was here as Matthew's widow, Madame de la Roche, anxious to pay my respects to the queen he had served so loyally.

10

Elegance and Ice Water

I am recounting this tale this many years later, looking back across time. I was born before Mary Stuart but I have long outlived her. She died in her mid-forties, on the block in the great hall of Fotheringhay. By then, she had become one of Elizabeth's most dangerous enemies, and although she went to her death declaring that she was a martyr for her religion, she was actually condemned for plotting herself cross-eyed in an effort to get Elizabeth assassinated. I know. I know.

But I have never found it easy to think of someone I have met and talked to meeting a violent end, and besides, whenever I think of Mary Stuart, I find myself remembering her as she was when I was shown into her presence at Holyrood.

She took me completely by surprise. Here, against all expectation, was yet another delightful enemy.

While Dale and I waited for my letter of introduction to be taken in ahead of me, I had passed the time in wondering what Mary would be like, for I had heard little good of her. She was said to believe herself to be the rightful queen of England, on the grounds that King Henry had not been legally married to Elizabeth's mother, and the English courtiers, outraged that someone who was already a queen in both Scotland and France could want any more crowns, usually referred to her as a greedy little brat.

Then, when at length a page came to say that she would receive me, we were led through an anteroom where some of her Scottish nobles were standing about, talking to each other, and my first impression of the Scottish court was not exactly one of civilized elegance. They all seemed to be bulky men with beards, and most of them were draped in thick, belted plaids or fur-edged cloaks. Like Bridget on Brockley's pillion when we set out from Withysham, they reminded me of bears. They made Dale nervous, and as we passed them, she kept close to me.

Greedy brat. Anteroom full of hirsute males. Unlikely visions danced in my head. But Mary Stuart was a grown woman and had been reared at the sophisticated court of France. She couldn't be either hairy or furry, and surely she wouldn't have a blatant resemblance to a grasping child. No. She would be intensely dignified and formal. After all, she *was* a queen. My first encounter with Elizabeth had been very formal indeed.

But instead of showing us into an audience chamber to meet a bejeweled lady enthroned on a dais, the page led us into a pleasant parlor, with padded stools and window seats, and cushions everywhere. The only fur was in the form of the rugs on the floor. A good fire sent waves of heat through the room, and Mary herself, seated at a little distance from it, was embroidering and talking quietly in company with a couple of young women, while two men—one small and ugly, with a grotesquely big nose and large dark eyes under heavy lids, the other tall and handsome, but both beautifully dressed—stood nearby, tuning lutes.

A group of other men, also much better dressed than the gathering in the anteroom, stood by a window, looking out over the town and talking and the words *hawking party* drifted toward me as I entered.

"Madame de la Roche!" announced the page. Dale and I both curtsied, but Mary had risen at once, handed her embroidery to the young girl on her right, and was advancing with hands outstretched.

"Madame! I am most happy to see you!" She spoke to me in French. "No, no, please get up!" She raised me to my feet. She was far taller than I was but as graceful and pliant as a sapling; she didn't tower over people but leaned benevolently down to them. Turning her head, she addressed the second young woman, who had very sparkling eyes and was by far the livelier-looking of the two girls. Still in French, she said: "Mary, take Madame de la Roche's maid to the women's chamber and see that she is looked after. Madame, come and sit beside me. This is such a pleasure."

It was genuine. There was no doubt about it. She really was glad to see me; my arrival really was a pleasure. I was handed into a seat and I sat down bemusedly, because if all this unaffected charm had come as a surprise, Mary Stuart's appearance was an even bigger one.

I had not thought she would have a family resemblance to her cousin Elizabeth.

It was mainly a resemblance of coloring, for she had far more inches than Elizabeth, and she lacked the long, pointed chin that made Elizabeth's face look so much like a shield, behind which whatever Elizabeth was thinking could be concealed. Mary's childlike oval features, on the contrary, offered all her moods and thoughts openly for inspection.

But like me, Mary was a widow and she was wearing black, which threw the clear pallor of her complexion into contrast. That fine pale skin was just like Elizabeth's. So was the light red hair arranged in bright waves in front of the lace-edged cap, and if Elizabeth's eyes were not so markedly almond-shaped, they were exactly the same shade of golden brown.

I hadn't expected any of that. No, indeed. Feeling as though the breath had been knocked clean out of me, I tried to be attentive as introductions were made, in a curious mingling of French and Scots-cum-English. The girl to whom she had passed her embroidery was her dear friend Mary Seton, who, I realized, was Lady Simone's kinswoman. The other young lady, the lively one with the sparkling eyes, who had taken Dale off with her, was Mary Livingstone.

"Who is to be married next month, the first of my dear Maries to wed," said Mary Stuart, as merrily and confidingly as any girl hoping to dance at the nuptials of a friend. "I have four Maries altogether," she added, "at least, in Scots and English they are all called Mary, like myself, but in French we say Marie, and here in Scotland, the word Marie means a maid of honor. So I call my dear girls my four Maries. It is a play on words. Mary Fleming is at a music lesson and Mary Beaton is at my behest taking medicine and soup to a sick guest. These northern winters cause so many agues and fevers."

She held out her hand to one of the men with the lutes, the handsome one. "This young gentleman is a visitor from England, Henry Lord Darnley, a cousin of mine and most welcome to my court." She wasn't using the royal plural, I noticed. Darnley, bowing to me with a delightful smile, said: "This is such a pleasure, madam," and I rose to make a correct curtsy to him. I had glimpsed him before at Elizabeth's court, when he came there with his mother, Lady Lennox, who was not only a cousin of Elizabeth's but also had the reputation of being the most ambitious woman in England. She had long harbored dreams of marrying him to Mary Stuart if she could. Now, the English government had decided to let him have his chance.

I wondered what Mary had made of him so far. He was elegantly tailored, his blue velvet doublet fitting across his broad shoulders with the perfection of a skin, not a wrinkle to be seen. His manners were polished, but now that I saw him at close quarters, I noticed that his good looks had one flaw. His ears were so pointed that they gave him an oddly pagan appearance, as though he were a faun out of Greek legend. I found it difficult not to stare at those ears.

They didn't seem to worry Mary. However, as yet, she appeared to regard him as just a straightforward visitor. Her gaze didn't linger on him, but moved on at once to the small, ugly man, whom she introduced as David Riccio, new to her court, her recently appointed

secretary for French correspondence and already one of
her favorite musicians. Riccio also bowed over my hand
and greeted me in a marked Italian accent. Well, Mary
had spent most of her life in Europe and European
influence was to be expected in her circle.

The men by the window then came over and I
found myself being greeted by James Stewart, otherwise known as Lord Moray, and Lord Robert Stewart,
both of them Mary's half brothers. I learned later that
they spelled their surname differently from hers due to
a complex family history. Just how complex Scottish
family histories could be, I hadn't yet discovered.

My final introduction was to a short, dark, strong-
featured man whose name was James Hepburn, Earl of
Bothwell. Wine and sweetmeats were brought and
handed around. Then a slight but marked hiatus in the
general conversation told me that I was now supposed to
state my purpose in this visit. I assembled my thoughts
into what I hoped would be the right order and turned
to Mary.

"Madam, you must be wondering why I have presented myself to you." I used English, knowing that as
long as I spoke fairly slowly, most of the Scottish
courtiers would probably follow it. "I have no very special purpose. I simply felt that since I was here, and
since I believe that you have . . . have heard of my late
husband, I should come to offer my respects. My husband greatly admired you."

"And worked for my interests," Mary said gently,
also now in English, though with a heavy Scots bias. "I
never met the Seigneur de la Roche but I knew of his
work and was most grateful." She smiled at me. I think

the secret of her charm lay in the fact that when she was talking to you, she always made you feel that her mind was wholly on you, that you were the most important person and interesting person in the world.

"I am being remiss," she said. "Since I returned to Edinburgh, I have received a report on events here during my absence and I know that as well as losing your husband lately, you have now suffered a further dreadful loss. You arrived in the city to find that your cousin had been murdered and you were among those who discovered his body. That must have been a terrible thing. I can only offer you my condolences, knowing that in such a case, words are of little use."

"We also heard," said Moray, in a level voice, "that you had come to Edinburgh in the first place in the attempt to persuade your cousin to return to England—that for some reason you and the rest of his family feared that he might be running into danger. Yet you could not tell the court of inquiry what kind of danger you feared, or from whom you feared it."

He was a tall, brown-haired man, considerably older than Mary, with a face as watchful as hers was open, and his manner toward me was guarded rather than friendly.

"Yes," I said. "That's true. I didn't—I still don't—know what his family meant by danger. His parents and his wife wanted me to come after him because they thought only a family member would have any influence with him. I agreed because his wife in particular was much distressed. She has two small children." Out of the corner of my eye, I saw Mary nod sympathetically and knew that with her at least I had struck a chord. "But none of them," I said, "altogether trusted me, because although I was married to Matthew de la Roche, I have also served Queen Elizabeth."

"Yet you are a Catholic?" said Moray, who, as I well knew, was not.

"But English born," I said. "Many English Catholics are loyal to Queen Elizabeth and so am I. Matthew was not, of course. But I feel I owe loyalty to the sovereign of my country and, as I said, I have served her at court." I wondered as I said it why I sounded in my own ears like a complete hypocrite, even though I was telling the precise truth.

Mary, however, was nodding. "You spoke at the inquiry of your service at the court of England. You see how well informed I am! I understand your point of view. It is to be respected."

"Did your attachment to Elizabeth not—er—complicate matters with your husband?" inquired Moray, while his half brother, with an air of neutrality, offered me sweetmeats.

"In marriage," I said sententiously, accepting some marchpane, "it is sometimes best if the parties simply do not discuss matters on which they disagree. After all, there are so many other things to talk about and share."

I regret to say that at this point Darnley grinned and winked at me and Bothwell uttered a snort of what I can only call ribald amusement.

Mary, ignoring them, laughed and said: "How wise." She turned to Mary Livingstone, who had rejoined us. "You must talk with Madame de la Roche before your wedding, my Marie. She has wise counsel for you."

"Madam," I said, "I did have one small, personal purpose in coming to your court. If I may speak of it . . . ?"

"But of course! Tell me!"

"It was a terrible shock to find my cousin as I did. I have had nightmares since then. I did know that there were people in Edinburgh that he hoped to see. One of them was Lady Simone Dougal, whose letter of introduction smoothed my path to you. Alas, she had not seen him. I hoped she had—so that I could talk to someone who had spoken with him lately, and take back to his family any news I could of how he was during his last days on earth. But I haven't yet found the other person. His name is Sir Brian Dormbois and I believe he may be here at your court. If so, is there a chance that I might have just a few words with him?"

Of course I could. Mary was as eager to please as though I were the queen and she the supplicant. For the first time I took in how young she was, much younger than I. I did a rapid calculation in my head and worked out that she was only twenty-two, to my thirty.

But *certainement,* said Mary, switching back to the French tongue, she knew Brian Dormbois. He was a Scottish noble in the service of her uncle Rene and they were both at Holyrood and should be somewhere about. Someone should be sent to find Dormbois and send him to me.

"I will go, madame!" said David Riccio and Henry Darnley simultaneously and Mary laughed at them.

"Are you vying to do my errands? You shall both go,

in different directions, and so Dormbois may be found the sooner. Riccio, seek for him indoors and Henri"—she gave Darnley's name its Gallic pronunciation—"try the courtyards and stables and the mews. He is as likely to be found there as anywhere."

She picked up her embroidery again and sat there, sweetly amused as they bowed their way out and departed. Then a shaft of sunlight fell across her work, and she glanced up at the window.

"The sun is out! At last! How the gray weather of this land depresses my spirits at times. I have had no exercise today. I will take a turn in the gardens. Come, my Maries. Will you join us, Madame de la Roche? Dormbois can come to you there as well as anywhere."

With Elizabeth, it would have been an order, while with Mary, it was a request. I chose, however, to interpret it as a command, and accompanied her as she led the way out, beckoning to me to walk beside her. Moray walked on her other side, while Mary Seton and Mary Livingstone followed close behind. I had the impression that these two, although they were not in the least alike, were united in one thing: their deep affection for their mistress.

It was real, that affection, and in time I learned that the other two Maries, whom I had not yet seen, shared it too. Mary Stuart was one of those who engender love. They can do it even while they scheme and plot. She even did it to me. I don't like to think of that scene of butchery at Fotheringhay. Even the hardened men who carried out the execution can't have found it easy.

Meanwhile, it was still 1565, long before the happy sunshine was darkened by the shadow of the block. Mary, her strides long and brisk, swept us all down a stair and out into the open. On the way, people appeared with cloaks, which we all hastily donned, because the sun, for all its brilliance, had no warmth.

"Where are you lodged, madame?" Mary asked me as we paced through a formal knot garden, where there would be primroses before long and patches of turned earth were awaiting seedlings. "I hope you are comfortable."

I began to describe my lodgings, but she interrupted me. "Oh, I know those buildings. But they are mean affairs—they are not for a lady of my royal cousin's court! There are rooms to spare here; you must lodge at Holyrood while you are in Edinburgh. Have you horses?"

"Yes, madam, three of them. They are at a stable in the town. They . . ."

"There are stalls unused in my stables, too. James!"

"As you will," said Moray, though not with great enthusiasm. "I will pass on your orders to the steward."

"Stalls for three horses—and there's an empty suite in the north tower. You know the one," Mary said. "Bid him have it prepared for guests. As queen of Scotland, I must uphold the Scottish tradition of hospitality. You shall move in this very evening, Madame de la Roche. What servants have you apart from your woman?"

"Just a manservant, who is also my groom, madam. He is the husband of my tirewoman, though. If there is room in the suite . . ."

"Oh, indeed. There are three rooms there. You shall stay for Mary Livingstone's marriage, for there is only a week to go. Mary, you must show Madame de la Roche your wedding gown."

"Queen Mary is giving me my gown," said bright-eyed Mary Livingstone, "and my banquet, and my dowry."

Robert Stewart and the Earl of Bothwell had followed us out to the garden, though at a more leisurely pace, but now caught us up and drew Mary's attention away from me with talk of the hawking party, which they had been discussing when I arrived. I fell slightly behind, looking about me and taking in my surroundings.

Holyrood was indeed a very beautiful palace, well suited to Mary, and unlike anything I had expected to find in Scotland. A number of people had emerged from it to do as we were doing and seize a chance of walking in the sun; others were hurrying on errands which no doubt they had put off until the outdoor world was pleasanter. Since I knew he was employed by one of Mary's nobles, I should not have been taken aback to come face-to-face with Adam Ericks, but I was.

I hadn't suspected him during the court inquiry but Brockley's discoveries had most decidedly aroused my doubts. The sight of him instantly brought back the all too vivid memory of that room in the Macnabs' house, of Edward's dead body, with its stretched mouth and staring eyes and the blood.

I stopped short and I know I turned pale. Adam had recognized me, as well. His eyes flicked over my face, and hardened. He went past without speaking and I stood still, while Mary Stuart and her companions walked on ahead.

On impulse, I fumbled in my hidden pouch and found the button. Stooping, I made believe to pick something up from the verge of a flowerbed and then, turning, I called: "Master Ericks!"

He halted, looking over his shoulder.

"I think you dropped this," I said, holding up the button, and walking back toward him. I held the button out on my palm. "I thought I saw something fall as you passed me."

He looked at it and then at me, his mouth curling in dislike. "That's none of mine. I've lost nothing."

I stared at him, and he stared inimically back. I supposed he had reason to find me objectionable. He knew nothing of Brockley's probing, but at the inquiry he had nearly been accused of murdering Edward, and whether he was innocent or guilty, it was bound to annoy him.

I shrugged. Either he had seen the trap and avoided it, or he genuinely didn't recognize the button. I opened my mouth to say I was sorry to have troubled him, but he got in first, his voice raised in anger.

"I take it that ye want to pin some blood-guilt on me. I'll hae none of it! Aye, Master Knox is in the right of it! Wummen shouldnae hold rule over men, nor poke their noses into affairs that are none o' theirs!"

Now I was the one who was annoyed. "I merely asked if you had dropped this! If you think I am trying to pin blood-guilt, as you call it, on you, then you must have it seriously on your mind! For my part, I only want to find the one who murdered my cousin, and since he *was* my cousin, don't try to tell me that his death is none of my business!"

"I do tell ye! I'd not lower mysel' to go creepin' in at windows in the night, even to rid the earth of a papist. Even to rid it of the pope himself! And now I'll be on my way and I'll thank ye not to accost me again in this manner."

"And Madame de la Roche will nae doot thank you to use more courtesy toward her," said a voice beside me and I turned quickly, to find an unknown gentleman standing there. Unlike most of the Scotsmen I had seen, he was clean-shaven, and his hair, dark except for a little early silvering (for he was surely under forty) at the temples, was cut neatly short. He was as well tailored as Darnley, his mulberry-colored doublet a flawless fit, and topped by a narrow, open ruff of snowy linen. Despite the cold, he was carrying his cloak tossed carelessly over his shoulder.

"I am Sir Brian Dormbois," he said. "You were seeking me, I hear. Is this fellow troubling you?"

I opened my mouth to say no, it was just a misunderstanding, but Dormbois didn't wait for me to answer. "I rather think he is," he remarked, and without more ado, he caught hold of Ericks, spun him around, and landed a kick on his rear. I exclaimed in protest and Ericks swore at him over his shoulder, but Dormbois stepped forward and Ericks took himself off, though not entirely without dignity, even managing an ironic sketch of a bow to me before walking away. Dormbois picked up his cloak, which he had dropped, and became once more the fashionable gentleman of a moment ago.

"That really wasn't necessary!" I said, considerably startled. "I irritated him, though I didn't mean to."

"I know about him, and you," said Dormbois. "I knew your cousin Edward. I've heard all about the inquiry. Do you think he did it?"

"I don't know. I wish I did."

"Quite. He and Edward Faldene had had an altercation, so it looks possible. Edward hadn't been in Edinburgh long enough to quarrel with many people." His voice was clipped and Scottish but also educated, the accent mild compared to that of Ericks. "You wanted to see me?" he said. "That long lad Darnley came to fetch me to you."

"I did want to see you, yes. I knew that Edward knew you. I wanted to ask . . . if you saw him before he died." Carefully, as with Mary Stuart, I trotted out my excuse for asking. "I want to tell his wife as much as I can about the last days of his life."

Dormbois was shaking his head. "I'd help and gladly if I could, but no, I didnae see him, though maybe I would have, if I'd been in the city at the time."

"You were with the court in Fife?" I asked.

"Och, no," said Dormbois, to my surprise. "I'm in command of Rene of Elboeuf's retainers but I'm not always with the court. I'm often at my home. I've good captains under me. I descend on them now and then and put the fear of God into them, but for the most part my life's my own. I'm no' dependent on my pay, anyhow."

He grinned in a disconcerting fashion. He had thick black eyebrows and eyes that were not merely hazel-green like my own but a cold, clear green. When he was amused, they glinted like ice water in sunlight, and he had the kind of grin that slides right up the sides of the face and presents you with a view of its owner's molars. His teeth were in superb condition. He was extremely attractive and somehow, alarming as well. He also gave me an odd feeling that I had seen him somewhere before, though I couldn't think when or where.

He sobered. "My home's outside of Edinburgh, between here and Stirling, and as it chances, I had something to call me back there not long since. My land agent, Jamie Fraser, had a brother to visit him. I wanted a look at the brother. Jamie's been lame since he fell into a gully while he was stalking deer and broke his leg. I wondered if the brother would make a replacement, if I could get him away from his present folk. But no, Hamish Fraser is just an indoor steward and has no wish to change. Och well. Jamie has good men under him and he knows his business. He can still ride a horse. I'll make do with him for a while yet."

"Hamish?" I said. "That reminds me of something— he wouldn't be steward to a family called Thursby, at St. Margaret's, just south of the Scots border?"

"Aye, that'd be him. You know the Thursbys?"

"I stayed with them on the way north," I said. "You know them also?"

"Och, all the families of any standing know each other, here and in Northumberland. That's the way it is up here in the north. I warn you, if you go to any banquet or gathering here, be careful what you say. Ask who a pretty girl is, and you'll likely find the person you're talking to comes from a family that's got a feud with the lass's father. And beware of sharp answers, even to a fellow who's been impertinent, in case you find that on the other side of you, you've got his brother-in-law or his second cousin twice removed. Till you know who's married to who, and who's feuding with who, better keep a still tongue."

"Can I talk about the weather?"

Dormbois laughed, giving me another magnificent view of his teeth. "Aye. Yes, that's safe enough."

I said suddenly: "I would like to know a great deal more about Adam Ericks but I don't know how best to find out. Can you advise me?"

"Ah." The glinting eyes fastened on me with a keen interest. "I guessed right, then."

I was nonplussed. "You guessed . . . ?"

"It's not just a tale of your cousin's last days that you're after, is it? Not just a matter of a few word pictures of him to put into his wife's mind to comfort her. You want to know who killed him. You've a feud with his murderer and you're out to hunt him down. Mostly men's work, that would be, but you wouldn't be the first woman to set out on such a quest for want of a man to do it for you. Am I right?"

More disconcerted than ever, I answered him truthfully. "Yes."

"Well, and why not? You'd make a good Scotswoman, my lass. You think the way any of us would. I know nothing of Ericks, but I can find out more for you, I daresay. If you think it'll help."

"I can't tell, not until the knowledge is in my hands."

"I'll try," said Dormbois briskly. "I'll see what I can learn this very day. There's a hawking party tomorrow morning. Queen Mary's fond of falconry. I'm invited and free to bring a guest. You'll join it and ride with me? While we ride, I can tell you what I've learned."

"Well . . ." The thought of a morning's sport appealed to me, but I wasn't altogether sure I wished to be Dormbois's guest. "Would I need Queen Mary's permission? After all, if she is to be present . . ."

"She'll not object. Darnley said she had taken to you. And I take leave to say, Madame de la Roche, so have I."

I blinked. The gaze that Sir Brian Dormbois had now fixed on me had become bold and searching, as though he were wondering what I looked like beneath my cloak and my black velvet.

I took an involuntary step backward. I had been right to find this man alarming. This sounded ominously like a complication, of a sort that I decidedly didn't want.

"There will be no objection either, I trust," I said modestly, "if I come attended? It is my custom to have my groom always nearby when I ride out."

The ice-water eyes glinted again. "Pretty ways, very becoming! But I shoot straight for my target, lassie; I don't believe in havering and nor do you, I fancy. If you did, you'd not be setting out to hunt a murderer. I like you fine already and I'll know you better before long or my name's not Dormbois. What's a groom? We can always lose him!"

11

Falconry and Fever

For purposes of unraveling the mystery of Edward's death or the fate of his list, the hawking party was useless. It wasn't even enjoyable just as an outing, not as far as I was concerned, anyway.

With Dale and Brockley, I had moved into Holyrood the previous evening. Queen Mary herself had come to see if I was comfortable and reiterated that I must stay for Mary Livingstone's wedding, which was to take place a week later. "And I hope you will stay longer. Be with us for two weeks, at least. It is such a pleasure to welcome congenial guests," said Mary engagingly.

Our new quarters were certainly an improvement on the lodgings down in the town. We had three rooms, not overlarge but very comfortable, and Brockley approved the stabling for our horses. He had our mounts saddled and ready in good time for the hawking party.

When, attended by Brockley, I joined it in the courtyard, Queen Mary was already there, dashingly attired like a man in breeches, doublet, and a hat with a feather in it a good twelve inches long (the effect, oddly enough, was not masculine but enchantingly female). With her were Mary Seton, the earls of Moray and Bothwell, Henry Darnley, and half a dozen lesser gentry. Dormbois came out of the palace last, accompanied by a short, red-faced priest, with whom he seemed to be arguing. Catching sight of me, he raised a hand in recognition and turned to the priest and visibly snapped at him, at which the man's face turned a deeper shade of red and he retreated—or rather, scuttled—back indoors.

"That was my secretary, Father Bell," Dormbois said, coming up to me. "He ministers to all the Catholic souls at my home but comes with me when I travel, since I'm no great hand at the reading and writing. He is forever forgetting his place and reminding me that I should arrange this or write a letter about that. Are we no' ready to go?" he added restively, putting a foot in his stirrup and swinging himself astride. "Ah. Here is my falconer." He smoothed the leather glove on his right hand and leaned down to take his bird, a beautiful female peregrine, onto it. "Let us hope for good sport."

Brockley helped me into the saddle, and then mounted his own horse and positioned himself behind me as we moved off. I had neither hawk nor falcon, but I was ready to take pleasure in this outing across the heathery hills outside the city. The skies were gray but the cloud was high, and beneath it the weather was dry and there was a silvery winter light in which one could see for miles.

Except that from the very beginning, Sir Brian Dormbois rode close beside me, and the first thing he said to me was: "I am sorry, lassie, but the time has been too short and I havenae discovered anything aboot Adam Ericks. I'm for my home tomorrow, but I'll be back two days before Mistress Livingstone's wedding, and maybe then I can do some prying for you. We shall meet at the festivities."

"Thank you," I said, and wished that he were not riding so very close that his right knee was almost brushing my left one. I was glad that Brockley was at hand.

"You should ride astride for this kind of sport," Dormbois remarked. "As Queen Mary does."

"I'm used to the sidesaddle."

"You ride verra well," he conceded.

"Thank you," I said, wondering doubtfully just what form Dormbois's prying, as he called it, was likely to take. Looking at the thick, dark eyebrows and the glinting eyes and teeth, I thought that if ever there was a man who was not of a tactful or dissembling nature, Dormbois was that man. Changing the subject, I said civilly: "You say you have to go home for a few days. You have a family there? You have a wife?"

"Two," said Dormbois with a sigh, and I turned to stare at him, before recovering myself and saying in tones of scientific inquiry: "You follow the Muhammedan faith, then?"

"No," said Dormbois, acknowledging the hit with another ice-water glint. "They're in the churchyard, poor souls, and I didnae have them both at the same time. There was Jeannie, when I was no more than a lad, and a richt sweet wee thing she was. But she was young—too young, verra like, and she died in child-bed and the baby with her. Then I went to France, to visit kinsmen there and to serve Queen Mary—Queen of France as she was then. My father was French, a younger son of a good family. He liked to travel, came to Scotland, and fell for my mother, who was her father's only child, and heiress to our keep and our land. He wed her and stayed. I look all Scots, like her, but I wished to see France and my father—he died only last year—arranged it for me. It was there I met my lord Rene of Elboeuf and entered his employ. It was also there that I met my second wife, Marguerite."

"That's a pretty name," I said.

"She was a pretty lass. But when we all came back to Scotland with Queen Mary, well, the climate of Scotland is raw and harsh compared to France and it didnae agree with her."

"Queen Mary spoke yesterday of a guest who had fallen sick at Holyrood," I said. "She put it down to the northern winter."

"Verra likely! Scotland is fine for those that are bred there. My mother loved it; it was some malady from badly cured meat that was her death, not the climate. But poor Marguerite never even survived one winter. Also, my home of Roderix Fort is a rough place com-pared to the châteaux of France. I brought her here in August but she shivered even then, and she pined in Roderix as though it were a prison. She fell ill as soon as the cold set in, and I spent that Christmas in mourning. I believe that ye've also been wed twice, Madame de la Roche? Edward did not speak of you to me, but it is known here at court that Matthew de la Roche wed a young widow."

I found myself obliged to tell him something of my history, of my runaway marriage with Gerald Blanchard, of the birth of our daughter Meg and Gerald's death in Antwerp from smallpox, and of my second marriage, only a few months later, to Matthew de la Roche, who was then a visitor at Elizabeth's court.

As I talked about Matthew, however, I grew extremely uncomfortable. The main reason was the simple fact that Dormbois and I were on a hawking party. For it was on a hawking expedition, though admittedly on a hot day in Richmond Park rather than a cold one in Scotland, that I had first met Matthew. Like Dormbois, he was half French, and he had talked to me and asked me about myself just as Dormbois was doing now. At that time, I had been still grieving for Gerald, who was only a few months buried; now, in the same way, I was suffering from the loss of Matthew, also only a few months dead.

This ride with Dormbois was too much like an echo of that long-ago ride with Matthew. I had known very quickly that Matthew was interested in me and now I was sure I could see the same signs in Dormbois. When a man like Dormbois canters at a woman's side with his eyes fixed on her, talking to her continually, and listening attentively to every word she says, it only means one thing.

When Matthew began to court me, though, I knew

from the first that I was drawn to him, and I was not drawn to Dormbois in the same way. With Matthew, thinking that it was too soon, I had tried to resist a temptation. Dormbois was different. He too was attractive in his way, but I did not find him a temptation, but somehow or other, a threat.

I was glad when a shout from Bothwell told us that the business of flying hawks at game had started. The party scattered over the hillside. Dormbois unhooded his falcon, which roused her feathers and showed immediate interest in the world. Then he threw her up and she soared away, to hover and glide above us, awaiting a glimpse of prey, and we broke off our conversation in order to attend to her.

Over the next half hour, our hawks brought down a few small birds and rabbits, and I got away from Dormbois, to exchange brief, laughing remarks with Mary Seton and Darnley. But then there was another hiatus and once more, there was Dormbois at my side, expressing triumph because his peregrine had caught a brace of rabbits, and asking me to tell him about my daughter and my home in the south.

I found his intent gaze worrisome and looked ahead between my horse's ears while, politely, I talked about Meg and described Withysham. Withysham interested him.

"It must be verra different from Roderix. Now, Roderix is a plain Scottish fortress, somewhat in need of civilizing—aye, I'll admit that, much as I love the place—but my lands are wide and the soil is good, too. I care for my lands and let nothing go to waste."

He paused so that I instinctively looked at him.

Once again, I encountered that bold and searching gaze that had made me uneasy in the garden at Holyrood. To my annoyance, I felt myself redden, and the maddening Dormbois promptly gave me the full benefit of that glittering grin. "I don't like to see a woman like you go to waste, either, lassie," he observed.

I didn't answer, mainly because I couldn't think of an answer. The grin intensified. "There's one thing that both Jeannie and Marguerite would have said of me," he declared. "I'm a damned good lover."

I could hardly believe my ears. The man was impossible. Another shout, from Moray this time, gave me an excuse to spur my horse and gallop away from Dormbois, and a furious signal with my arm brought Brockley up beside me in his stead.

"Stay there," I said to Brockley. "Don't leave my side."

"Has that man been offering you impertinence, madam?"

"You could say that, yes. And when he first proposed this outing and I said I'd have my groom with me, he said we could always lose a groom. Don't you dare let yourself get lost!"

"Don't worry, madam," said Brockley grimly.

But of course, there was still the matter of finding out more about Adam Ericks. Throughout the rest of the outing I kept my distance from Dormbois as far as I could, but I several times caught glimpses of that disconcerting smile, and when we all bunched up together to ride back through Edinburgh, he once more edged alongside me to say: "If I have news of Ericks, madam, I will tell you at the wedding."

"Thank you," I said wearily, wishing I hadn't tried to make him my deputy for my inquiries about Ericks. I wanted no more to do with him. He hadn't seen Edward. He hadn't got the list. There was no point in pursuing this acquaintance and some very good reasons for ending it.

The image of Edward in death was still savagely vivid, crying out for justice. But for that, I thought, I would leave Holyrood the very next day and set out for home.

As it was, I knew I could not. I must consult with Brockley and see what new ways there were by which we might make inquiries. I could not give up searching for Edward's killer until all possibilities had been tried and had failed. Even if it meant giving Dormbois a chance to obtain some information.

When I returned to my quarters, I found that I could not have left Holyrood on the morrow in any case, for to my distress, I was confronted with a tottering Dale, whose face was very white, except for an ominous, orange-tinged patch of color on each cheekbone, and whose first attempt to speak to me was lost in a volley of sneezes. "I'm sorry, ma'am," she said huskily when the sneezing was over, "but I seem to have a fever. I think I may have caught cold."

12

Confrontations

In this crisis, even the pursuit of Edward's slayers had to wait. Dale needed care. Except for my occasional attacks of migraine, I had the sound Faldene health, and Brockley was as tough as a ship's timber, but Dale was vulnerable. With Dale, even a cold could never be disregarded as trivial, and this was more than a cold. Like Sir Brian Dormbois's hapless second wife, and the unknown guest at present being cosseted at Holyrood, she had fallen victim to the northern climate, probably exacerbated by the exhaustion of our long journey (not to mention the horror at the end of it).

In the few days before the Livingstone marriage, Brockley and I had our hands full with her.

However, the warmth and comfort of our suite and the nursing we gave her did their work, aided (which touched me) by a kindly message from Queen Mary, who had heard of Dale's illness and sent along a page not only with her good wishes but also with a draft to encourage sleep.

"Her Majesty says to tell you it is made of some foreign poppy and will help a sick person to sleep if sore throat or headache are keeping them awake. Good sleep is part of healing, she says," the page repeated.

Whether the sleep that the poppy draft did indeed induce made any difference, I don't know. But after three days of fever and sneezing, Dale began slowly to recover, and our own efforts with balsam inhalations and doses of horehound stopped the cold from attacking her lungs. By the day of the wedding, she was still pale and visibly weak, but she said in firm if nasal tones that she couldn't abide the thought of asking anyone else to help me dress for the occasion. Valiantly, and oblivious to my assurances that she need not, she got onto her feet, saw to my hair, and fastened me into my silver-gray and violet gown.

I thanked her sincerely and went to the wedding in a cheerful mood, looking forward to it as a treat after the worry of Dale's illness, and a day's holiday from the matter of Edward. Mary Livingstone was marrying for love, and the celebrations should therefore be full of happy potential, like the launching of a ship or the laying of a foundation stone.

I was more at home in Holyrood by then. It can be lonely, attending a function when you know hardly anybody there, but although, while looking after Dale, I had never left the palace, I had still had a few brief intervals in which to learn more about the court and make some new acquaintances, and I had seized my opportunities. The more I knew about this Scottish world, the better my chances of tracking down Edward's killer, and as an extra, I could now expect friendly greetings at the wedding and partners for the dancing.

Admittedly, my efforts to learn more about the touchy and much-intermarried Scottish nobility hadn't all been successful. Their pedigrees were so entangled that they resembled knitting that has been got at by a playful kitten, and their feuds were nearly as bad. It would be a long time before I had all that off by heart.

On the other hand though, I had now met Mary Livingstone's bridegroom, John Sempill, a well-born young Englishman who was one of the best dancers at the court, and I had learned that one of the other Maries, Mary Fleming, was being courted by the queen's Secretary for English Correspondence, a middle-aged man called William Maitland, whom I had also met.

I had had conversations too with the little Italian David Riccio, and with a somewhat curious individual called Christopher Rokeby, who was part of the English ambassador's permanent staff in Scotland but seemed to be more often about the court than attending to his ambassador, making himself useful and, I suspected, prying.

He was a round-shouldered man of goodness knows what age, with dull clothes and a grayish face and a knack of being unobtrusive. I saw him sometimes hovering where he could overhear conversations between people who had clearly failed to notice him. I suspected that he was in the same line of business as myself, by which I mean one of Cecil's agents. He got into conversation with me several times, and I thought gloomily that if my presence in Scotland wasn't reported to Cecil by anyone else, it probably would be by means of Christopher Rokeby.

I did once or twice think of asking his help, but he also had a knack of fading away just as I had almost worked around to asking him, as though he had sensed my intention and wished to avoid it.

In addition, I had been approached, when taking a short turn in the formal garden, by the queen's uncle Rene of Elboeuf, who insisted on walking with me for a while. Since he was Dormbois's employer, I decided that I could at least ask a few questions about Dormbois and did so, to be told that he was a most trustworthy and valiant soldier, willing to do anything his lord commanded.

I tried to probe further into this intriguing testimonial but Elboeuf, a gallant Frenchman to his very bone marrow, changed the subject and started paying me compliments, obliging me to remember that Dale was due for another dose of horehound, which I must hurry off and give to her.

I had done my best with the week, I said to myself. Dale had recovered her health and I had learned a little, though it didn't include anything that pointed to Edward's killers or the fate of his list. I wondered whether Dormbois really would appear at the wedding and whether, if he did, he would have any news for me. I would have to be glad, now, of help from anyone, for the scent was growing colder every day.

It was done. Amid wafts of incense and much feminine cooing, and sumptuously dressed at Queen

Mary's expense, Mary Livingstone had become Mary Sempill, and no one had tried to burst in and disrupt the nuptial mass, either. Largesse had been distributed to the beggars of Edinburgh. With the three remaining Maries and a number of other ladies, I had gone to the bridal chamber to strew dried rosemary and other sweet herbs and little fresh flowers across the coverlet of the bed, so that the couple could be bedded amid fragrant scents and the symbols of spring and fertility.

Before that, however, came the banquet and the dancing.

There were two top tables on the dais at the banquet, one for the couple and their families; the other for Queen Mary and her immediate circle: her uncle Elboeuf, her half brothers, their wives, her honored guest Darnley (very fashionable in black velvet, which set off his fair hair), and two of her Maries, Seton and Beaton.

I saw the Earl of Bothwell sitting just below the dais with some other men and women of rank, including one exquisitely dressed lady with strong, dark good looks, whom someone pointed out to me as Bothwell's sister, Lady Janet Hepburn. Also at the Bothwell table, with an air of having been squeezed in because no one knew quite where to put him, was the ugly little secretary, David Riccio. I was a little lower down, at a parallel table, my wide silvery-gray farthingale bumping the even wider one of Mary Fleming's splendid blue velvet. She was off-duty, and opposite to her sat her would-be lover, the middle-aged William Maitland.

The room was big, with a gloriously painted ceiling and tall, mullioned windows, but it was also crammed and extremely noisy. The Earl of Bothwell had been drinking deep and was arguing with someone, thumping his goblet on the board for emphasis and declaring his point of view in a resounding bass voice. At my table, a trio of noblemen whom I didn't know, all with arm muscles bulging through their embroidered sleeves and red, drunken faces, were exchanging coarse jokes and guffawing loudly, and somewhere behind me someone kept emitting loud, hoarse belches, like a raven with indigestion.

Looking about me, I could not see whether Dormbois was present or not, but Maitland had noticed that I kept on turning my head to gaze about me and put his own interpretation on it.

"Amusing, is it not?" He was a Scotsman, but he was both educated and traveled and could look on his fellow countrymen with an objective eye. He was also a trifle pedantic and enjoyed instructing people. "Two cultures in collision. Queen Mary brought France with her when she came here, and now you see it laid over our rough ways like very thin gold leaf over a slab of Hibernian rock."

"Really?" I turned to him in surprise.

"Were ye not thinking the same thing?"

"I expect Madame de la Roche would not have put it so poetically," said Mary Fleming, smiling warmly into his eyes.

Not wanting to reveal an interest in Dormbois, I flinched at the sound of another frightful belch from behind me and said: "Yes, you mean *that,* I suppose. And that," I added, as renewed guffaws burst out a few feet away. "I hadn't thought of it quite as you put it, but of course, you're right. And there are plaids and fur edgings all mixed up with the brocades and satins . . ."

"And offerings of blood pudding amid the confections of spun sugar," said Maitland. "Scotland and France will never mix, any more than our whiskey mixes with good wine and God knows there are some men mixing those as well." He looked around disapprovingly as one of the guffaws turned into a retch and one of the red faces turned a delicate shade of green. Two of the ribald trio quickly got up, hoisted their friend's arms around their shoulders, and steered him out of the room, at speed.

"I observe," said Maitland dryly, "that the Earl of Bothwell and that golden-haired English lad Darnley have already been overcome."

I hadn't noticed when it happened, but Bothwell's argumentative voice had stopped. I looked around and saw that he was missing and that Darnley, too, had quitted his place. Queen Mary was looking at his empty seat quite regretfully, evidently sorry that he had gone.

"And there goes Elboeuf as well," said Maitland as the queen's uncle got to his feet. "Provision will have been made," he added reassuringly. "Just outside. At these affairs, there are always a great many such disasters, and many beautiful garments ruined beyond hope. It all means profits for the merchants and tailors, not to mention the laundresses. Some more wine, Madame de la Roche?"

"Thank you, no, I have had enough." The wine was very strong and I didn't wish to be among those needing the facilities so helpfully arranged. There was no sign that Bothwell or any of the others were returning. But as I scanned the room in a casual search for them, I saw the face I had looked for earlier. Dormbois was there after all. As my gaze lit on him, he looked my way and raised a goblet in salute to me. I would speak to him, I thought, when the dancing began.

The ball was held in an adjacent room. Streamers embroidered with words of well-wishing and garlands of evergreens and paper flowers spanned the room; crossed banners bearing the devices of Sempill and Livingstone adorned the wall above the canopied throne provided for the new-wed pair. Not that they occupied it for long, for when we all crowded into the room on the heels of the principals, the musicians were already in their place in the gallery overlooking the floor. Within moments, they had begun a galliard melody, and John Sempill was on his feet, holding out his hand to his bride and leading her out to open the dance.

They had the floor to themselves for a short while, and then Queen Mary herself, partnered by Moray, rose to join in, and that was the signal for everyone to follow her example. At that moment, Dormbois appeared at my side, offering me his arm. "Will you partner me, madam? Your mourning state does not prevent you?"

"Not today. I note that the queen is dancing too, and I have no wish to be a death's-head at the feast," I said, and went with him onto the floor.

As well as not wishing to cast a blight over the merriment, of course, I also wished to speak to him in something like privacy. At the edge of the floor, I had been standing in a crowd of others. Now, as Dormbois and I faced each other to exchange bow and curtsy before beginning to dance, I said in a low voice: "You have news for me?"

"Iphm," said Dormbois irritatingly. "Maybe. But you are too businesslike too soon. First, let us dance."

We did. He was an excellent performer, I must say: surefooted, agile, with an air of having a perfectly fit body under complete control. He was wearing mulberry again, which suited him, and a number of very fine rings, which flashed in the light from the tall windows as he held my hand aloft. The days were lengthening and it was not yet time for candles.

When the galliard was over, he handed me back to my place and then, to my annoyance, left me without a word in order to claim the hand of another lady for a pavane. He did not return to me for an hour. The dances grew livelier, well-bred galliards and dignified pavanes giving place to spirited reels and hilarious round dances. Queen Mary, obviously enjoying herself immensely, took part in most of them, with a variety of partners, although they didn't include Darnley, who seemed to have disappeared for good, along with Elboeuf and Bothwell.

Anxious to talk to Dormbois again, I tried to avoid dancing too much and declined offers from Riccio and the depressing Rokeby, although I took the floor once with Maitland and joined in with a round dance, for which partners were not needed.

Dusk drew on at last, early, for the day was overcast. There was an interval, during which people could get their breath back and the musicians could take some refreshment, and a steward announced that a supper had been laid in the dining hall. The candles were lit. As the music started up again, I began to wonder if Dormbois had left the festivities like Darnley and the others, but then he was back, once again offering his arm. I accepted, and at once found that we were parading, not onto the floor, but through the door to the supper room.

Here too, there were candles but fewer than in the dancing chamber and there were pools of shadow along the walls. As yet, only two or three people were there, standing with their backs to us as they chose cold meat and cheeses from the table. Dormbois, after pausing for a wary moment in the doorway, gripped my elbow and steered us quickly across a corner of the room. He whisked us out through a side door, down a staircase, along a short passage lit by a couple of flickering flambeaux in wall sconces, and into a small stone-floored chamber. This was lit by two more flambeaux, but the window embrasures were caves of gray shadow. He led me to one of them and sat us down on the padded window seat.

"Well," I said, "if anyone finds us here alone together like this, my reputation won't be worth a penny."

"Who is going to find us, lassie? I made sure no one in the supper room noticed us. My apologies for leaving you so brusquely earlier, but I didnae want to draw any attention to us. Not that they'd be interested, anyhow. They'll be too busy thinking up rude jokes to make at the bedding. I was sorry not to dance with you longer for you dance like a dream come true. As I told you the day we met, I like you fine."

"Thank you. You dance well, too. But, Sir Brian . . ."

"Oh, lassie!" He shook his head at me and put a heavy arm around my shoulder. I thought it politic not to remove myself, but I could not help stiffening and he gently shook me. "Och, now, I'm not an ogre, am I? And nor are you a timid virgin. Twice-married should mean seasoned."

"I am not a dish of venison, either," I said tightly. "Sir Brian, I must ask your pardon if I seem lacking in response, but I am lately widowed and I have no wish to . . . to involve myself with any other man as yet." Even as I said it, I was conscious of the warmth of his hand, which lay on my upper arm. It had been a long time since I said good-bye to Matthew, a long time since I felt a warm, loving male hand on me.

I said primly: "I am only here with you because I hope you have something to tell me. I think you know that. Please, if you have found out anything that bears on my cousin's death, let me know what it is."

"Businesslike, businesslike." He shook his head again, and a stray flicker of light from one of the torches made his silver temples gleam.

"Sir Brian, please!"

He withdrew his arm, and no, I did *not* regret the removal of that warm, strong hand. I told myself so, with vigor. "I've news, surely, lassie," he said. "Not the name of the fellow who crept in at your cousin's window and put the blade in his chest. Maybe it was Ericks and maybe it wasn't. Who knows? But I can tell you this: Master Furness, the tavern keeper, who told the inquiry of the quarrel between Ericks and Edward Faldene, didna come forward of choice. He is not a man to get entangled in an affair like murder, unless he had to. Someone laid information with the authorities, and it was the constable's men who went to him and questioned him and required his testimony. And I know who laid that information."

"Who?" I turned eagerly toward him. Too eagerly. His right hand was behind my head and his mouth was on mine on the instant. I froze, keeping my lips closed, and after a moment he sat back with a sigh.

"You're a hard conquest, lassie. Well, the harder the nut the sweeter the kernel; that's what I've always thought."

"Sir Brian, you were saying . . ."

"Aye, I was. But for the moment, I think I'll say no more."

"What?"

"I could have you, you know," he said thoughtfully. "Here on the floor of this very room. We're here alone and I'm stronger than you are."

"This palace is full of servants." I sat still however, knowing by instinct that it was the safest thing to do. The more you waggle a piece of string, the more readily will a kitten pounce after it; dogs chase rabbits—or cats—mainly because they run. I have seen a dog completely disconcerted by a cat that sat down in its path and stared at it. "I'm sure," I said icily, "that a few loud screams would attract attention."

"I daresay they would. And in fact, I have no intent to force you. That's no way to make love. A man's needs must be desperate to do such a thing and desperate in these matters I have never been," said Dormbois complacently. "But sometimes, when a lassie is especially charming, a little persuasion may be in order, to convince her where her own best interests and happiness may lie. You want the name of the man that gave Ericks's name to the authorities. I will tell you, sweeting, as your morning gift, when you wake on a pillow with your head next to mine . . ."

"How dare you? It would appear," I said, standing up and shaking my skirts angrily, "that I shall be forced to discover what I want to know by myself. I made a grave mistake in asking for your help."

"Och, not so fast, lassie." Out shot that strong hand again, and it closed on my wrist. "I said I had no mind to force you, but I've told you a little, have I not? Will you no' give me a kiss, a real, loving kiss, by way of payment? Is that too much to ask? You might enjoy it! Why not try?"

"There's someone in the passage! Let me go at once. I am not prepared to be discovered in your arms!"

I spoke so sharply that his grip actually did slacken and, jerking myself free, I stepped quickly away from him. It was just as well, for the sounds in the passage were coming nearer and an instant later the door was thrust open. Three men blundered into the room, disputing.

"Thisisanoutrage!" One of them was extremely drunk and slurring all his words together. As they stumbled into the circle of light from the torch above the door, I saw tousled fair hair above black velvet. "You have no right, no rightatall . . . !"

"I've every right, you damned young fool." One of the men grasping him also had fair hair, though his was a deeper shade, and as I stood transfixed, I recognized his voice. "You were sent here for a purpose and I was sent here to see you did your best at it, and no, I will not look on while you throw it all to the winds . . . !"

"Lemme alone, I tell you!" This was accompanied by a surge of movement, as of violent resistance, followed by an ominous *"Aaaaurgh!"*

"Oh, Gawd, he's goin' to throw up again," said the third man. He was dressed, as far as I could see, in soldierly brown, and his voice, which was also familiar to me, was that of a Londoner.

"I woanallowit . . . not a child. Getchahandsoffme! Wouldn't treat Bos . . . Bot . . . Bothwell or Elbif . . . Elboeuf like this-ohGod—*urgh!*"

"Rene of Elboeuf and the Earl of Bothwell aren't courting Scotland, and if you're being treated like a child it's your own fault! You'll bloody well get sobered up and you'll go back up there and dance with Her Majesty . . . oh, bring it up on the floor, damn you! Throw it up and throw it out and let's hope you've brought nothing back from that whorehouse that's harder to be rid of than bad wine . . ."

"Aaaaurgh . . . gh!"

"Tut tut," said Dormbois reprovingly from behind me. The soldierly Londoner had grabbed the head of the drunk and was holding him steady while Henry Lord Darnley, wooer of Queen Mary Stuart, Lady Lennox's precious son and hope of future power, emptied his system onto the flagstones. The man with the dark gold hair jumped out of the way with a muttered oath and found himself staring straight at me. "Dear heaven, what's this? We don't seem to be as private as we thought . . . who are you? And who's that in the window behind you? Come into the light!"

"Good evening, Master Henderson," I said, to my friend Mattie's husband, Rob, with whom I had, to my regret, quarreled when we had worked together the previous year. "This is Sir Brian Dormbois, who has been trying to obtain some information for me. Dear Rob . . ." The endearment was a sop, an attempt to reawaken our old friendship, though I could see, even in the shaky torchlight, that there was no friendship in his face. "Dear Rob, what on earth are you doing in Scotland?"

13

Links in a Chain

Rob appeared to know Dormbois already. He cut short my attempts to introduce my unwanted suitor more fully but requisitioned his services immediately to help his man take Darnley away to be sobered up by the fastest means possible and then returned—preferably chastened—to the wedding festivities and the ballroom and the company of Queen Mary Stuart. Rob then sank down onto the window seat vacated by Dormbois, wiped his brow, and said: "I could kill that wantwit Darnley." Unexpectedly, his tone was almost amiable.

"Rob, what's going on? I thought you were at court in Whitehall."

"I was, but I was given an assignment which brought me north."

"Looking after Darnley?"

"Exactly. And it takes some doing, I can tell you."

"I don't understand," I said. I sat down at the other

end of the window seat. "I knew that policy had changed—that Queen Elizabeth and Cecil had decided that a marriage between Mary and Darnley wasn't, after all, the worst thing that could happen, even if they are both Tudor descendants. But you're talking as though they actually want the marriage so much that they've sent someone—you—along to promote it."

"They do and they have. I'm the someone. Oh, Darnley was hardly their first choice. What Cecil really hoped," said Rob, "was that Robert Dudley could be married off to Mary. *He* hasn't got any Tudor ancestors and he's a good sound Protestant . . ."

"I wouldn't trust too far to that," I said, remembering an occasion when Elizabeth's good-looking Master of Horse had harbored serious hopes of marrying her, despite widespread disapproval, and been quite prepared to change his religion if Philip of Spain would promise to lend him an army with which to put down any indignant rebellions.

"No, nor would I, to tell you the truth. But he really does have affection for Elizabeth and I fancy they looked on that as a safeguard. Anyway, it came to nothing. He didn't want Mary, and even though Elizabeth made him Earl of Leicester last autumn, Mary still doesn't want to marry the man that she calls the Queen of England's horsemaster. In the tone of voice you'd use to say *a mere groom.*"

"That sounds coarse, for Mary Stuart," I said, amused. "She's so charming. Has she really said that?"

"I've heard her." Rob did not share my amusement. He said soberly: "Mary is on the marriage market. You know all this, Ursula! If we don't stop her, she is likely to marry into one of the European Catholic royal families—Spanish if she can manage it—but anyway, someone willing to back her claim to Elizabeth's throne through force of arms. Compared to that, Darnley has considerable advantages, just because he *is* of Tudor descent. A son from such a marriage would be a sound heir for England, and by the look of it, Elizabeth is never going to produce one of her own. And he's not likely to be dangerous to England himself, because firstly, he doesn't have an army at his beck and call, and secondly, we have his mother in England. One threatening move on Darnley's part, and Lady Lennox will be in the Tower. She's our hostage, in other words."

"Er—how much does Darnley know about all this?"

"It hasn't occurred to him that his mother's our hostage, no. He knows that the marriage is thought politically sound and that he's expected to do his best to bring it about, and that his reward will be to be King of Scotland and father of England's heir. The trouble," said Rob glumly, "is that our golden-haired lad—the long lad the Scots call him, because of his height—is as vain as a peacock and likes the company of roisterers like Bothwell and Elboeuf. I saw them leave the banquet together and followed. Along with my man Barker . . ."

"So that's who it was! I thought I knew his voice."

"Yes, Geoffrey Barker. He's one of my best men. He came with me when we went after Darnley and helped me get him out of the whorehouse that the Earl of Bothwell and the Queen of Scotland's irresponsible uncle took him into. It was an expensive place," said Rob fairly. "The clients are offered a choice of wines and a dish of oatcakes and a chance to talk to the girls before they pick one and proceed to business. The wines are cheap and the oatcakes are underdone and the girls talk such broad Scots that it might as well be Chinese, but never mind. I didn't want to create a disturbance, so I had to pause to explain myself to the madam. That delayed me and I didn't get at Darnley before he'd passed the refreshment stage. I just hope the girl was clean!"

"How do you know the wine was bad?" I asked with interest.

"You haven't changed, have you, Ursula?" said Rob, and now the unfriendliness was back. "Trust you to ask a sharp, nasty question. For your information, the madam gave me some, but one sip was enough. It was horrible. But Darnley probably drank all of his and he'd already had a skinful at the banquet. He's had a good education," said Rob disdainfully, "but he has no taste. In any sense of the word."

"I didn't intend to be sharp or nasty," I said.

"I daresay. You never do, but it seems to be part of your nature."

"Rob, please!" There was a pause. Then I said: "Why is it I haven't seen you about the court before? I've seen Darnley often enough."

"I've been ill. That damned marsh ague I caught in East Anglia last year is recurrent."

Studying him in the wavering light of torch and candle, I saw that his handsome face was somewhat drawn, as though with recent sickness. It made him look older. "Queen Mary told me she had a guest who was ill. That must have been you," I said. "Mattie said you'd had an attack, before Christmas. I'm sorry."

"Are you? It got me out of your way last year, if I recall."

"I needed your help and couldn't have it," I said in conciliatory tones. "Rob, I didn't cause you to have the marsh ague and I didn't want you to have it. Why do you blame me?"

"I don't."

"Then—why are you so angry?"

"You make me angry because you continually interfere in things that are not your concern and you gained advantage, intentionally or no, from my sickness. Now you turn up in Scotland, where you have no right to be, without Queen Elizabeth's permission. Or do you have it?"

"No. I wanted to catch up with my cousin Edward Faldene, but he was murdered before I could reach him. I suppose you know about that."

"Oh yes. Most of Edinburgh knows about the killing of a man called Faldene, and I have seen a report of the inquiry." He paused, as if he were trying to cool his annoyance and choose his words before deciding what to say next. "You amaze me, Ursula," he said at length. "You set out—in January!—to ride the length of England to bring Edward Faldene home. Why? What was he to you? You used to talk to me and Mattie about your childhood, and you said that when you were both children at Faldene, you hated him."

"I did. He was spiteful and a bully," I said. "But he was still my cousin. Also, he has children. They haven't done me any harm. Edward's parents and wife thought he was running into danger and I came, at least partly, to get the children's father back for them. And now that

I'm here, I take a poor view of finding a cousin of mine stabbed to death in his bed. Even a disagreeable cousin."

"Oh, my God," said Rob exasperatedly. "Are you on one of your quests?"

There was a silence. Then I said: "Yes, I suppose so. I want to know who killed him. I want justice for him. Wouldn't you?"

"If I were a young woman, I wouldn't set about it personally. The authorities are the proper people."

"So far, they haven't had much success! And anyway, there's something else."

"And what might that be?"

"Edward was bringing something with him," I said. "I can tell you because he's dead now and beyond harm." Briefly, I explained about the list. "I wanted to get hold of it before it reached Mary Stuart," I told him.

"I see." Rob considered. "And your understanding is that this is a list of English families willing to support Mary if ever she should invade England, by offering men, money, accommodation, and arms?"

"Yes. Did you already know about it?"

"I knew that such a list existed, certainly. Its earliest version was discovered some years ago, among Mary's private documents here in Holyrood. Have you come across a man called Rokeby?"

"Christopher Rokeby?" I said in surprise. "Why, yes."

"He's one of ours. He has done a little bribing of clerks in the Scottish secretariat. He found that first list, copied it, and sent it to Cecil. I have a copy of that one myself. I keep it in my own document box and it's here with me."

"I wish I knew if Edward did get the new version to her," I said. "He wasn't intending to go to her direct, and anyway, if he had, I think she would have mentioned it to me. She knows I am his cousin. He had two contacts, and both say they didn't see him before he was killed, but one of them might be lying." I hoped Lady Simone wasn't. I had liked her so much. But Dormbois, I thought wryly, was capable of anything. "Or," I added, "he might have handed the list to someone else that I don't know about. It certainly wasn't among his possessions."

"So," said Rob, "you want to know what became of the list, and you want to know who killed Edward."

"The two things are probably connected," I said. "I have a feeling that they are—like links in a chain."

"I daresay. But you shouldn't be investigating them. Oh, in God's name!" He ran a hand over his brow again, and studying him anew, I concluded that the drawn look on his face was not only due to recent illness but to genuine anxiety.

"Rob," I said. "I *have* to investigate."

"No, you do not! I'm serious, Ursula. Let me try to explain. You think I resent you and yes, in East Anglia I was very bitter against you, but it wasn't simple jealousy. I was angry because you couldn't see that you were harming yourself as well as me. I don't wish harm to either of us! It's the very opposite!"

"I don't altogether follow."

"Yes, you do! Don't be obstructive! I'm speaking, and it's time you realized it, as a friend!"

"I'd like to think so," I said. "We used to be friends, and I would like to think that in spite of last year, we still are." I had known Rob for many years. We had worked together, helped each other. In all that time, curiously, although he was a very good-looking man and I was not ugly, we had never been more than friends, but it had hurt me when I thought we had become less. I wanted very badly to see that put right.

"Then listen to me! I am anxious for you. I would like to see you living the life you ought to live, at home in Withysham with your daughter and in time, perhaps, with a new husband. Oh, I know you—I know there's something wild in you that makes you different from most other women, but all the same, you're not . . . forgive me, but you're not a young girl anymore. You have a daughter who is growing up and a fine house to call your own, and both of them need your attention. Are you taking the best possible care of Meg?"

I wasn't. But I wanted to. In that moment, sitting in that dimly lit room more than four hundred miles from home, with the sounds of someone else's wedding revelry drifting down from above, I was nearly drowning in homesickness. Yes, I did want to give up, to go away, to set out at once for the south, for Withysham, for safety, and for Meg.

"At heart, I agree with all you say," I told him. "But still, Edward has been murdered, and he was on an errand which had in it the seeds of harm to Elizabeth. I can't just—walk away."

"You can and you should. You should leave it to those whose business it rightfully is. Ursula, murder has been done, and where there's murder, there's danger. You're in more than one kind of danger, as a matter of fact. Why were you here alone with Dormbois?"

"I wanted information from him, of course! Nothing else, I promise you."

"I daresay, but Dormbois has a reputation as far as women are concerned. He's not safe company for you."

"No," I agreed, and I couldn't keep the feeling out of my voice. "I would accept that."

"Then go home, for the love of heaven, and leave me to do the investigating!"

"I can't," I said. "For one thing, Queen Mary expects me to stay at least another week . . ."

"You could make an excuse and finish your visit early!"

"I daresay, but you're not the only one who has been ill. Dale has, as well. We can't leave until she's stronger. That will take a further week in any case. That being so, I may as well use the time. I would like, if I can, at least to find out whether that list reached Mary or not. If Rokeby managed to get hold of the first version, could he also get hold of the present one? So that we can compare it with the copy you have with you and see if they're the same or if the list is now different? If it is, then it's probably the version Edward was carrying. It could be that by finding that out, we shall also find a clue to Edward's murderer."

"I can't think how," said Rob huffily.

"Nor can I, yet, but one never knows. Can Rokeby do it, though?"

"Oh yes," said Rob in weary tones. "I expect so."

"Well, will you ask him?"

He gazed at me in an exasperated fashion. "Is there a remote chance that if I obtain a copy of Mary's present list for you, and you see that it won't lead any further you may agree to go home and leave the proper authorities to deal with Edward's death?"

"Possibly. It depends on what emerges. Rob, I may be here without the consent of Queen Elizabeth or Cecil, but I still feel I am working on their behalf."

"Very well. I'll see what I can do. See here, Ursula, have you even informed his family yet that Edward is dead?"

"No. First of all I thought it would be best if I carried the news myself, and then, when I saw that that would mean delay, I wasn't sure how to find a messenger. I don't want to lose Brockley's company. Have you been corresponding with Mattie while you're here? Could I send a letter with your courier? I'd like to write to Mattie, too. She's looking after Meg for me—oh, I suppose you know that. You don't mind that Meg is at Thamesbank, do you? I had to leave her somewhere, and it couldn't be with Aunt Tabitha."

"No, I understand that. I feel," said Rob, "that in view of last year, it was bold of you to take her to Thamesbank, but I don't quarrel with little girls. Meg is welcome in my house as always, naturally. You may certainly use my courier—it will be Barker—for any letters to the south, if you can get them written within two days. He's setting off the day after tomorrow. That is, if you really can't or won't leave for the south at once."

"Much depends on how quickly Dale recovers," I said mildly.

Rob had disturbed me. He had made me understand how much, at heart, I did want to go home. It was true that I was in danger here, of more than one kind. I had never wanted to set out in the first place, after all!

But I also knew that I hoped very much that tracing the fortunes of Edward's wretched list would, somehow, lead me farther on the road to tracing his murderer, and that until I had either followed that road to the end or knew the end to be unattainable, I could *not* go home. I didn't say that to Henderson, however.

For the moment, he was—*just*—willing to help me. I had, as it were, put a slender rope across the chasm between us.

It was hardly the moment to lean out, knife in hand, and slash it.

I went back to the wedding feast. Darnley reappeared after a while, his fair hair looking damp and flat to his head, as though someone had dunked it in cold water, and his complexion somewhat pallid. Mary Stuart was all smiles to see him, though, and danced with him. Then came the bedding, and I helped to undress Mary Sempill, as she now was, and place her tenderly in the decorated bed, and I joined in the raucous jokes when her bridegroom was brought into the room and bundled in with her and the bed curtains were drawn around the pair.

I hope they had a happy wedding night. My own night was frightful. Rob's talk of danger had gone deep with me. As I lay in my bed, my recurrent nightmare came again. I dreamed that I was awake and watching as the bed curtains were drawn stealthily back to reveal a shadowy figure that stood menacingly over me, and that the faint starlight from the window was gleaming on a raised and naked blade. I woke with a scream to find myself safe and alone but soaked in sweat and shaking and wishing I had not let Dale and Brockley sleep together, for I needed Dale's reassuring company and she wasn't there to give it . . .

It took me a long time to get back to sleep and I woke in the morning heavy-headed. However, I had letters to write, so I pulled myself together and got on with them. One was to Mattie, with a second one enclosed, for Meg. The third, however, was to one of the people I had met in East Anglia the previous year. Sybil Jester's husband had been arrested for treachery and her daughter had been expecting a child out of wedlock. Sybil had been allowed to take over her husband's business, but I had worried in case there was too much gossip to make it comfortable for her. I had liked Sybil very much and wanted news of her. It had occurred to me, once or twice, that she was the kind of woman, educated and gentle in her manners, who would make a good companion for me and for Meg at any time when I was away. Rob had jolted my conscience. I had been slow in making proper arrangements for Meg so that she could have an uninterrupted life at Withysham. It was time to amend that.

My fourth letter was to Malton at Withysham, assuring him that I was well and asking if all was in order at home. The fifth, and the hardest, was to my family at Faldene to tell them that Edward Faldene would never return to his home; that Helene was a widow and her children fatherless; that my uncle and aunt had lost a son. I told them of the inquiry and its unsatisfactory outcome and said that I was staying on for a while in the hope of learning more. I gave them my condolences. There was nothing else to say.

Then I sent Brockley to find Henderson and give him the letters, but it transpired that Henderson had gone hunting with Darnley and the queen and wouldn't return until late afternoon. Darnley had clearly not had the violent hangover he deserved, I thought sourly.

Brockley was followed, however, by a page bearing an invitation from Queen Mary. There was to be a small supper party that evening, with cards and music to follow, and she would welcome my presence.

The page, a bright young lad who obviously enjoyed rolling great names off his tongue, was able to tell me who else would be there. Apparently, the guest list was headed by a half brother of the queen (whose father had clearly been much more prolific outside the marital bedchamber than in it) whom I had not yet met, one John Stewart, who was betrothed to the Earl of Bothwell's sister, Lady Janet Hepburn.

"Both she and the Earl of Bothwell will be there," said the page. "So also will David Riccio, Sir Brian Dormbois, and of course, Henry Lord Darnley with Master Rob Henderson, a member of his suite. The queen wishes to honor those guests presently at her court."

That explained my own invitation. I must certainly go. It would give me a chance to hand my letters to Rob and find out if he had been able to set Rokeby to work. And Dormbois would be there too and there was always the chance that he might after all decide to tell me what he knew and not expect to be—well, paid for it.

Looking back, I can see now that even after my nightmare, and even after the fit of conscience that made me write to my friend Sybil Jester, I still did not understand how deeply my talk with Rob Henderson had crystallized my private fears and longings. The image of the midnight intruder with the drawn blade had terrified me but I still didn't know how much, nor did I yet understand the fear and fascination with which Dormbois filled me, both at the same time. I didn't even fully recognize how intensely I had *not* wanted to travel to Scotland or how badly I now wished to go home.

I knew none of these things until, in the course of the afternoon before the supper party, I came down with the worst attack of migraine I had had for over a year.

14

Mouse Dipped in Honey

It started during the afternoon. Our rooms included a small parlor, and Dale and I were sewing in company. I have a liking for embroidery and I was making an edging to go onto the neckline of my silver-gray dress. Dale was repairing the embroidery on the black dress that had become so battered-looking after its sojourn in my saddlebags.

I noticed that I had a slight headache, and remarking that the afternoon was depressingly gray, and wouldn't it be lovely when spring really came, I moved my seat to where the light from the window was better. Even that simple movement turned the throb over my left eye from mild to vicious, and before I had been in the better light for more than a minute, it had become too bright. My eyes narrowed, and suddenly the pain was like a band of iron around my head, with a blacksmith's hammer crashing rhythmically on to it just above my left eyebrow.

I put down my work. "Dale, I think I've a migraine coming on. I had better lie down. Will you make me a draft? You did bring the ingredients with you?"

"Yes, ma'am, of course. I always have them by me." Dale laid down her own work and looked at me with concern. "You do look pale. I'll help you to bed and then get the draft ready."

"I've got to be all right for this evening," I said.

"I hope you will be, indeed I do. What brought this on? I wonder."

I didn't answer, but presently, as I lay in the soothing shadow of shuttered windows and closed bed curtains, sipping the drink that Dale had made to the recipe invented by my ancient hanger-on, Gladys, I searched my mind to see what the answer should be, for I knew that this malady only came on me in times of doubt and conflict. When I wanted to do one thing but knew I must do the opposite; when I wished to take such and such a path but was faced with obstacles I did not know how to surmount; when living in a way that made me unhappy and unable to see a road out; those were the times when migraine struck.

Now, grimly, I contemplated the fact that Rob had frightened me and that I did not want to go to this accursed supper party. I faced the truth that Dormbois to some extent intrigued and drew me and that this was a reason for staying as far away from him as possible. Above all, I faced, and shrank from, the fact that to pursue any inquiry whatsoever into Edward's death could bring me near to the unknown assassin whose shadowy shape had loomed over me in last night's horrid fantasy.

"You're being a fool, Ursula," I castigated myself. "If Dormbois does decide to tell you anything, let him whisper it in your ear in the supper room. You have already said you will do without his information unless he gives it freely. He can't force you to slip away alone with him. If he asks, say no. He can't misbehave with you in a room full of people including the Queen of Scotland! And if Rob Henderson hands you a piece of paper, no one will think anything of it. He isn't likely to shout, *Oh, Ursula, here's Queen Mary's secret list of English supporters, the one Edward Faldene was going to update* at the top of his voice! He'll pass it to you quietly, saying it's a letter from home or something harmless like that. It won't bring you into danger. And you want to give him your own letters. You *must* go to the supper! Collapsing with a headache! What a feeble thing to do; what a pathetic excuse! Hiding behind migraine because you've lost your nerve, that's all it is! You've let Rob make you timid. Shame on you!"

I lectured myself harshly, trying to drive the headache away.

It got worse.

I lay there, longing to be at home again, thinking of the hundreds of miles between me and Withysham. Dale came to see if the medicine had worked and saw with concern that it had not and that I hadn't been able to finish it.

"I couldn't swallow the rest," I said faintly. "It wouldn't go down."

"Ma'am," she said, "I'm going to fetch Roger. If

there's something on your mind, well, maybe he can clear it. He has before."

It was generous of her and I knew it. Also, it might be a good idea. Brockley understood my migraines. It was quite true that at least once in the past his advice had helped me out of a deep uncertainty and brought about a cure. Perhaps he could work the miracle again.

He didn't, for the very good reason that when I saw him standing anxiously by my side, I wasn't able to explain my dilemma to him properly. I couldn't bring myself to say: "Brockley, I need to go to the queen's supper party this evening, because if I do, I may learn something useful about Edward, and I can hand my letters to Rob Henderson in person. However, poking into Edward's death may well be dangerous and I'm too frightened."

So I stared up at him and said all the wrong things, such as: "Dale was kind to fetch you, Brockley, but you can't help. I've got to get to this supper party somehow or other this evening and that's the end of it. I must just get up and *make* myself go. I might as well get up now. Ask Dale to come here and get me dressed."

"But, madam, you can rest for at least two hours yet, surely."

"Just do as I say!"

He went. Dale came back, and at my insistence, helped me out of bed. The pain, which was just barely endurable when I lay still, at once broke over me like a giant wave, crashing into my skull and knocking me off balance so that I reeled, clutching at my head, and collapsed back onto the edge of the mattress. "Oh God. I can't. I can't! If only I could be sick . . ."

Dale tilted me backward and swung my legs back onto the bed and then produced a basin. I gazed at it wistfully, but although I could feel nausea twisting in my guts, nothing happened. I retched vainly, and the agony crashed in on me once more, so that I flopped back onto the pillow, grabbing at my temples again, trying to squeeze out the pain like juice from a cider apple. I heard myself whimpering in anguish.

"*Roger!*" Dale's voice was really alarmed. "Come here—the mistress is that ill!"

She pulled the covers over me and stood there biting her lips until Brockley reappeared. He stood looking down on me and then said: "This is just migraine, madam? You're not feverish?"

"No." I tried to shake my head but stopped immediately. "No. It's migraine pure and simple."

Brockley stood there, frowning a little, and through the haze of pain I saw the frown slowly intensify, until he looked as though he were trying to calculate a difficult sum in his head—such as ninety-two yards of brocade at twenty-three shillings a yard plus forty-seven yards of Sicilian silk at seventeen shillings a yard with a 5 percent discount for cash. The mere thought of arithmetic, however, made my head hammer more furiously than ever and I stopped thinking about it. Brockley spoke.

"Been sick yet, madam?" he inquired.

He used his most casual and countrified voice, which usually meant he was concentrating on something else and had forgotten to keep up the manner of the perfect manservant. "No," I said, or groaned. "I wish I could, but I can't. It won't come. If it did, I might feel better. As it is, I can't move. I hardly dare lift my head. Oh, God, it's torment!"

"I don't like to see you in such pain," Brockley said. "And if you really must get well enough to go to the supper this evening . . ."

"Don't talk about supper," I said, unreasonably. "Food would kill me."

"It might bring on the crisis," said Brockley seriously. "Or you could try salted water."

He might well be right, and to reject the experiment was completely illogical, but the thought of trying to swallow anything at all was so intolerable that all I could do was gasp: "No!"

"But it might work, madam."

"Some cures are worse than the illness. No!"

There was another silence. Then, in his most expressionless voice, Brockley said: "I have heard that a mouse, dipped in honey to make it palatable and swallowed whole, is a certain cure."

"What?" If I could have sat up and shouted with outrage, I would have done. This was physically impossible, but from where I lay, I demanded feebly: "*What* did you say?"

"A mouse, madam, dipped in honey. I think you'd have to hold it by the tail and . . ."

"Brockley, have you gone mad?"

"They have mousetraps in the kitchen and plenty of honey. I expect I could get one for you. Or maybe if you just imagined it . . ."

"Stop it, Brockley, stop it!"

"Another cure that I've heard of, madam, is a mixture of bull's blood and mashed spiders . . ."

"Roger, what on earth are you talking about?" cried Dale, appalled, and she turned away, with her hands to her mouth.

". . . or some authorities say crushed maggots . . ."

"Brockley, be *quiet!*" I put my hands over my ears.

"Think of it, madam," said Brockley, raising his voice slightly so that my hands were no protection, "think what it would look like, and smell like and taste like . . ."

"When I'm well enough," I said, "I'll kill you, personally . . ."

". . . and what it would feel like, slipping down your gullet. Or there's a third nostrum I've heard about. You take the guts of a cat . . ."

"I'll have *your* guts for lute strings! I'll . . . Dale, Dale, quick, the basin . . . !"

What followed completely eclipsed Darnley's performance in the anteroom on the evening of the Sempill wedding. It went on a long time, and before it was over Brockley was apologizing anxiously for his drastic treatment and praying aloud that it would do me no harm. When at last the paroxysms ceased, I sank back once again, stomach muscles aching and limbs as weak as if the bones had dissolved. But the huge breakers of pain had ceased. Like an ebbing tide, in a series of small and steadily weakening waves, the agony was receding.

"Close the curtains and leave me," I said, with my eyes shut. "I'll sleep awhile. An hour before the supper begins, come and wake me, Dale. I shall be all right."

When the moment came, although my fears were still with me, the physical enemy had been defeated. I was shaky but free of pain, and I hoped it would not come back. Brockley was waiting to see how I was when with Dale in attendance I emerged from my bedchamber; he eyed me questioningly, and I smiled at him.

"I think I have to thank you. But I hope you'll never do that again."

"I had the feeling, madam, that to be there this evening was important to you. I did what seemed necessary, but I'm sorry it came so hard to you."

"You're forgiven. You won't have to provide me with new lute strings this time."

Dale, out of kindness for me, had fetched him to help me. As I said, it was generous of her. Now, once again, she sensed the secret understanding between Brockley and myself, the exchange of private laughter, the intimacy of our minds. Once again, I saw it in her face before she looked away.

Quickly, I changed the subject to something businesslike. I had not gone into detail about that unpleasant confrontation in the anteroom, but I had told Brockley and Dale that according to Dormbois, someone had laid information about Edward's quarrel in Master Furness's tavern.

Now I said: "Brockley, there is one person we haven't so far thought of talking to and that's Master Furness, the landlord of the tavern where Edward and Ericks had their disagreement. Do you think you could find the place and see if you can learn any more? You could go while I'm at the supper."

"Do you think there could be more to learn, madam?"

"I don't know, Brockley. I'm casting a line at a river where I can't see any fish—and hoping something will take the bait. Will you go?"

Brockley's rare smile showed. "I shall enjoy it, I expect."

"Don't get drunk, will you?"

"Now when did I ever?" said Brockley in mock horror.

Once more, Dale looked away. We had just done it again.

15

Blind Faith

I would feel weak for some time, I knew, and I also knew that to make sure that the pain didn't return, I shouldn't hurry too much or eat anything highly spiced for the time being, either. I let Dale take her time over fastening laces and buttons and allowed her to brush my hair rhythmically for a long time. It would soothe me, she said.

Finally, I sat with closed eyes while she piled my hair intricately at the back of my head and bound it in a silver net. When she had finished, my mirror told me that although I was pale, I was well groomed, but all these leisurely preparations meant that I was the last arrival at the supper party, which was being held in Queen Mary's private apartments.

The supper room was aromatic with scented candles, warmed by a good fire, and adorned with red and green wall hangings. In shape, it was narrow and intimate. The eight people already in it made it seem crowded.

It became notorious later, that room, for not much more than a year later, nobles jealous of David Riccio's friendship with Queen Mary burst into another of her supper parties there, at which Riccio was present, dragged him out, and stabbed him to death. Far away in England, I heard the news and heard where the killing had happened and shuddered. It must have been a kind of rape, as the gentle innocence of music and polite conversation were torn apart by coarse violence and Riccio's terrified screams. On that dreadful night, before the murderers burst in, the scene was probably similar to the one that met me when I made my late and apologetic entrance, and nothing could have been more delightful.

Indeed, it was positively domestic. Gatherings very like it were no doubt going on, at that moment, all over the land, in manor houses and town houses, and on a smaller scale in cottages where neighbors were making a little music and encouraging a courtship or two, and the visiting housewives had brought pies or dishes of stew to help the hostess out.

There was Queen Mary, in a dark gown as usual, seated at a card table and playing a hand with Bothwell, John Stewart (whom I identified from his resemblance to the queen's other half brothers), and his betrothed, Lady Janet Hepburn, her dark, vigorous handsomeness wonderfully set off by a gown of crimson damask. A tall triple candlestick on the table lit up their game, and by the hearth on the other side of the room, for all the world as though Holyrood didn't contain manservants enough to form an army and maidservants enough to do the chores for one, Rob Henderson was on his knees with a pair of bellows, encouraging the fire.

To complete this civilized picture, Sir Brian Dormbois was standing by a spinet, turning the music while Darnley played a gentle melody, and David Riccio, seated on a stool close to the queen, accompanied him on a lute.

A page announced me. I came forward, murmuring an apology for my lateness, but Queen Mary, looking up from her cards and giving me her lovely smile, said: "No need for apologies, Madame de la Roche, or can I just say Ursula? There is no formality this evening; this is just a party of friends. The supper will not be served yet, though there is wine on the little table near the fire, if you wish for some."

An echo of nausea clenched at my stomach and I said: "I think not at present, ma'am."

"As you will. Do you play any musical instrument, Ursula? The spinet or perhaps the lute?"

I told her that I could play both and she called to Rob, "Master Henderson, there is a spare lute there on the settle by the hearth. Let Ursula have it. Would you play it for us presently, chérie? And then perhaps you would enjoy a hand of cards."

I said yes to all this, and as Henderson rose and went to the settle, I joined him. Casually, and not in the tones of one who cared whether or not we were overheard, I said: "Rob, I have some letters to give you for Barker. Is he still leaving tomorrow?"

"Yes." He held out his hand and I gave him the

packet, which I had tied with a length of twine. "I've something for you, too," he said, also casually, and in turn passed a package to me. It seemed to consist of several sheets of paper folded together to make a small, thick pad, sealed at one side with wax. Moving so that my back was to the rest of the room and my wide farthingale could mask what I did, I took it and slipped it into my hidden pouch. "The list?" I asked, and this time I did not speak aloud but mouthed the words instead.

Rob picked up the lute and pointed to a scratch mark on the edge. "Yes. Mine and a copy of the one the queen now possesses. Rokeby says there was no sign of any other, either older or newer. He has copied the one filed among her papers as the present working list." He spoke softly. Then, stepping back, he added more loudly: "It won't affect the music, and I think you'll find it's tuned."

It was as easy as that.

The evening went pleasantly on. The music smoothed away the unease left by the migraine. I played the lute, once by myself and once along with Darnley. We chose English tunes that were not familiar either to Mary, with her French upbringing, or to the Scottish guests, and I was pleased to see that the melodies were well received.

Then Bothwell gave up his place to me and I played cards with Mary, John Stewart, and Janet Hepburn, and saw the gentle, playful fashion in which Mary encouraged the two of them to admire each other's skill in the game. They were a dignified couple and no doubt behind their forthcoming marriage lay any amount of careful calculation about the value of their respective possessions and prospects and the advantages to be gained by their two families in the intricate pattern of feud and alliance that formed Scottish society. But they did seem to like each other, and Mary, clearly, wished to cast a gloss of romance over them.

She was kind to me, too, making light of my mistakes—this particular game was unfamiliar to me—and asking after Dale, whose illness had been reported to her. To be in her presence was to be warmed and comforted by a feeling that one mattered.

When supper was served, I ventured a little food and drink. I knew I must choose plain items but I was beginning to feel hungry, which was a sign that my illness had truly passed. Mary had meant it when she said the evening was informal, for the servants who had brought it in left us to help ourselves. As I stood by the table, selecting hot chicken drumsticks, I found Dormbois at my side.

"And have you changed your mind in any way, my charming Madame de la Roche?" he whispered.

"I have not, I thank you, Sir Brian. Will you tell me who led the authorities to Adam Ericks?"

"Would it win your sweet love if I did?"

I sighed. "No, Sir Brian. It wouldn't."

"Alack. Alas," said Dormbois, aping the air of a strolling player, and glancing at him, I saw that the ice-green eyes were dancing. "How can ye be sae hard of heart?" he inquired, exaggerating his accent. "Will ye no' tak pity on a poor, rough Scots laddie?"

Here in the crowded supper room, I felt safe enough to exchange banter. "It isn't difficult," I told him. "My heart may be hard by nature. Have you thought of that?"

"Aye, I've given it some thought and I canna believe it." He dropped the histrionic air. "Or would be it be," he inquired, "that you are a truly honest woman and would hold out for marriage? Well, now, I might be prepared to consider that. Do you no' have property in the south? So you said, when we talked before, and I hear you have served at the court of Queen Elizabeth. We're in the same level of society. A match between us would be fair and equal."

"But not a match I wish for, Sir Brian." I seized on a possible means of repelling him. "Sir Brian, I think I should tell you that I have a dubious background. I was brought up by my mother's family because, well, my mother wasn't married. And she never told me or anyone else who my father was."

"But you were made welcome at the English court and have been made welcome here; you were wed to a man of position in France and you have a good house in England. And in yourself, you are . . . well, put it this way, lassie, I dinna care who your father was." He looked at me with eyes suddenly narrowed and full of genuine and sympathetic inquiry. "Do you, though? Is it a trouble to you?"

I shook my head. "I rarely think about it. I suppose I would like to know, but I suspect that the truth is commonplace enough. I think he was a court gallant, but a married one. If I knew who he was, I might well be disappointed in him. I have never inquired, though I suppose I could have done—I mean, I could have asked questions of older people at court, who might remember something useful. But I never have. And now," I said, "if you will excuse me, I think I'll take a bowl of that wholesome smelling pottage. If you could let me get near enough to it . . ."

He was preventing me from moving along the table. He didn't stir.

"I wonder what would change your mind towards me?" he said softly.

"Nothing, I assure you," I said. I waited, looking pointedly at the pottage and avoiding his eyes. I was finding his physical nearness uncomfortable, not because it was unattractive but because it wasn't. There was no doubt that Dormbois had it, that indefinable thing that calls to the opposite sex like a deep calling to a deep and will not listen to cries of protest from the rational mind or even the moral sense. It can be defied but it can't be silenced. At a range of a mere six inches, it was deafening. I wanted to back away, and the only thing that stopped me was resentment. I knew very well that he was as conscious of his power as I was and was trading on it. I would have liked to kick him, hard.

I would have liked to dissolve into his arms, too. I stood rigid.

"Are you really interested in that pottage?" Dormbois was inquiring. "Dull stuff, I call it. And why no sauce for your chicken? There's a fine hot sauce here that has a name for warming up other parts of a lad or a lass than just their tongues and their gizzards."

"Then I assuredly don't want to put it on my chicken,

and besides, it might not be good for me. I had a headache this afternoon."

"No, no, lassie," said Dormbois insinuatingly. "Head-aches are what a woman suffers *after* the honey-moon."

"Sir Brian, please let me pass."

He stepped back. "My time will come, lassie. You'll see."

I edged by, warily, but he didn't try to touch me or hinder me further. I filled my pottage bowl and with-drew, quickly, to Queen Mary's side. I had discovered that even with a whole crowd of other people in the same room I didn't after all feel safe anywhere near to Dormbois. I went to Queen Mary as to a refuge.

After supper, Dormbois and Bothwell joined Lord John and Lady Janet at the card table, while Darnley, Henderson, and Riccio took turns at providing music and Mary beckoned me to sit beside her.

"I have given my Maries some time off this evening. Will you take their place for a while and talk to me? I am surrounded by people here, as one always is at any court," said Mary. "But sometimes I am lonely. Scotland is so wild a place, compared to France. Did you know, Ursula, that there were even schemes to abduct me when first I came here? Some of my nobles would like to make themselves king."

"I had heard that, ma'am. I was very shocked."

"Nowhere near as shocked as I was, I assure you," said Mary sadly. "There was bloodshed and I was com-pelled, once, to attend an execution in person. Only thus, my brother James said, could I make it plain that I had no knowledge of or will toward the marriage which others would have forced on me, but the executioner was clumsy and . . . oh, I wept to see such butchery."

Her voice shook and so did her hands, as the memory came back. I opened my mouth to say something calming but she controlled herself without my help and said: "But this is no kind of talk for a happy supper party. Tell me, Ursula, how does my land of England fare? How were last year's harvests and do the people flourish? I think of them as my people, you know."

I was practiced at dissembling but I found this difficult. My mother had served Anne Boleyn and loved her. To us she was as true a queen as any, and Elizabeth her lawful issue and our true queen as well, which meant that Mary had no business to think of the English as her people. With an effort, I said: "England is prospering, I think. Of course, the climate is milder, farther south."

"Oh yes. How I long to set foot there myself. I have many friends there and I keep in touch with them, but I often wonder—will I ever see them face-to-face as their acknowledged queen?"

I sincerely hoped not, and for several reasons, some of them quite unconnected with religion or legitimacy. She was so very young and somehow so innocent. So *unwary*, I thought. Elizabeth, though still quite young in body, had a mind that I think was mature when she was born, and she was well aware of the world and its perils, and that makes for good government. She would never have talked as confidingly as this to anyone she had not known long enough and well enough to be sure she could trust them, and probably not even then.

Instinctively, I tried to make use of Mary's simplicity.

"How do you keep in touch with your English supporters, ma'am?" I asked ingenuously.

"Oh, Ursula, and you the widow of Matthew de la Roche, who toiled so long and honestly for me? There are priests, in my employ, who travel in England in other guises. They go from one Catholic house to another, holding mass, hearing confession, ministering to the faithful—and with them they carry, always, my kind good wishes and assurances that those who have honored me with their friendship are never forgotten and one day, if God wills, may be rewarded."

"Isn't that dangerous for them?" I asked. "In England, they would be considered lawbreakers."

"You think I am sending good men into peril?" Mary's smooth white brow wrinkled. "Perhaps. But I send no one against his will, and after all, in the end, to die for the faith is the noblest of deaths."

It was also apt to be one of the nastiest. I was about to suggest as much, but Mary's golden brown eyes had begun to sparkle, and she had more to say. "One day, it will happen! One day, God will show the way, and I will ride to London, leading my army, sleeping in the fields as we journey, perhaps, as the men do, sharing their hardships, gathering my people to me. When God wills."

"What of Queen Elizabeth?" I asked. "If all this comes to pass, what of her? She is loved, you know."

"I would not harm her," said Mary. "Oh, Ursula, of course not. If ever God leads me to the throne of England, she shall be my beloved sister. She shall live in dignity, privately, as King Henry's fourth wife Anne of Cleves did when theirs was declared no marriage. Or I will find her some noble husband among the great men of Europe or, if she truly does not wish to marry, then a refuge in some French abbey."

I tried to envisage Elizabeth in any of these roles, and my mind reeled. A warning stab of pain struck above my left eye, as exasperation rose up in me. Here it was again, the rose-tinted innocence I had glimpsed in my own family at Faldene, and the thing that most of all had come between myself and Matthew. It was a malady of sentimental, blind faith which was simply unable to confront the horrors that would come about before England could become a Catholic land ruled by Mary.

I looked at my hostess's charming young face and her bright eyes, and thought of Elizabeth's face, that watchful shield that guarded her thoughts and her dreams— and, yes, her fears too—from the world around her. Elizabeth, I thought savagely, understood executions too and not merely as a weeping bystander. Her mother had died under the ax before Elizabeth was three, and her young stepmother had died under it when she was eight, as though King Henry actually wished his daughter to understand the matter thoroughly. Later, when her sister Mary Tudor was on the throne, Elizabeth had feared death on the scaffold for herself. A prisoner in the Tower, she had for a time not known when she woke each day whether she would see the evening.

I had to keep my pretense up somehow. "I am sure, ma'am, that you would never harm a living soul if you could avoid it," I said sweetly. I heard the false note in my voice, but Mary, innocent, devout Mary, didn't.

"Of course, I would not! But all this may well be far

in the future. Again, we are being too serious. Davy! The music you are playing is too melancholy; you are sending our thoughts into solemn paths. Play us something merry! And then it will be time to end this gathering and all go to our beds."

I would be thankful, I thought, as my head began to throb in good earnest, when I got to mine.

16

Don't Ask Who: Ask Why

Scotland was indeed a wild place. Even at Holyrood, the queen's principal home, things occurred that on the whole did *not* happen at Elizabeth's court. When the supper was over and I took my leave, I was not even out of earshot of Queen Mary, who was still talking to Janet Hepburn in the supper chamber, indeed had only walked down one short flight of stairs, before a pair of hands stretched suddenly out of a dark doorway at the foot of the staircase and grabbed me.

They jerked me out of the light of the flambeaux that lit the stairs and the hallway into which they led, dragged me through the doorway, and pushed me roughly up against a stretch of cold stone wall. I opened my mouth to cry out but a hand came down across it and the cry was muffled out of existence.

"That manservant of yourn has been snooping at Furness's Tavern and asking questions," said Ericks's voice furiously in my ear. "I went in there tonight and Furness told me. Just what do ye think ye're about, my lass? Tell me that!"

A lady leaving a private supper party held by Elizabeth could usually expect to get back to her own quarters without being attacked en route. I would have liked to say so but since Ericks's hand was still over my mouth, I was in no position either to answer his question or tell him what I thought of the way he had asked it.

I waited. The hand, cautiously, eased its pressure. "I want an answer," Ericks whispered. "But no caterwauling, now, or God help ye . . ."

I managed to grunt in an affirmative tone and the hand dropped to press against my left shoulder and keep me pinned against the wall, which ground into my back. His other hand had my right upper arm in a savage grip. "Verra well. Now, answer me. What's that man o' yours after?"

He was strong and he was causing me considerable discomfort but at least he wasn't threatening me with a blade. I was dealing with an angry man but not, I thought, a murderous one. I could almost have sympathy for Adam Ericks. He might be innocent, after all, and if so, he had something to complain about. After Mary's cloying simplicity, the Ericks rudeness even had something refreshing about it.

"Information," I said quietly. "Anything that might lead me to the man who killed my cousin. Edward Faldene *was* my cousin. It is a matter of family feeling. Surely you can understand that?"

"Ye ask that of a Scot? We'll hunt down ony man

that offends one of our clan, hunt him across the world and through the ages if need be."

"Then you do understand. I want to find out who killed my cousin. I have learned that Master Furness was fetched to the inquiry because someone laid anonymous information about the quarrel Edward had with you. I wanted to know who the informant was and I wondered if the tavern keeper knew—or could guess. I think it possible that whoever did the informing may also have done the murder and be looking for a scapegoat. I sent my man to talk to Master Furness. That's all."

"Laid information . . . ? I didnae know that." Ericks's grip slackened a fraction. "A scapegoat, eh? So someone's tryin' to point a finger at me; is that it?"

"It could be." I tried to move but it was still impossible and the attempt made his grasp on me tighten again.

"May the lord have maircy on them if ever I catch them, whoever they are. Layin' snares for an innocent man. I've no time for papists, and that means you as well, my lady. Ye're another of Faldene's papist kin, are ye not?" The mere thought made him so angry that he shook me, like a dog with a rat, rattling my teeth and knocking the back of my head against the wall. Fortunately, due to Dale's ministrations, my head was well protected by my piled and netted hair.

"I said this at the inquiry and I'll say to ye again now," Ericks growled. "I might tak a drink or two and get angry and tear a papistical thing like a cross off a man's throat or plant a fist in his face, but that's one thing, and creepin' in at a window in the middle o' the night with a blade an' doin' murder on a man asleep is another. That's an insult in itself, to be washed oot wi' blood!"

"If my cousin's killer is ever found," I said, "then as far as I'm concerned, you are welcome to fill a whole washtub with his blood. Please do. Now, will you let me go? Before someone comes through here—or comes to look for me?"

The grasping hands relaxed and fell to his sides. "Aye. Verra well." He paused. Then he said: "Ye keep askin' who killed him. Strikes me, ye ought to be askin' why."

When I left the supper room, my headache had been trying to return, but the encounter with Ericks had the odd effect of dispersing it. Feeling enlivened once more, and patting my skirt to make sure that the documents Henderson had given me were still safely there, I went to see if Brockley had come back, found that he had, and summoned both him and Dale to my chamber so that we could all talk. "Did you learn anything, Brockley, and if so, what?"

"The landlord, Master Furness, had little to tell me, madam, except one thing. He repeated what Lady Simone's butler said. There were strangers in his tavern that night who egged the quarrel on. I can't see how anyone could plan it in advance, but it seems to me more likely than ever that someone meaning harm to Master Faldene might just have snatched a chance to put the blame somewhere else."

"Yes. That *is* interesting," I said thoughtfully. "Thank

you, Brockley. Now, then. Listen. I have here a copy of
a document which Master Henderson has with him. It
is the original list of Queen Mary's English supporters—
a version supplied to her some years ago. I also have a
copy of the list she now has. If my cousin ever did get his
list to her, then the version now in her possession should
differ from the original—it should contain up-to-date
changes. It may even be the very document he gave her.
I want to compare the two. If they're not the same, then
probably Edward did deliver his list. I want to know
because . . ."

"Because it's possible that Master Faldene was
killed for some reason connected with the list,
madam?"

"Yes. But if he delivered it safely, then that probably
isn't the reason."

"Everyone," Brockley said slowly, "has kept asking
who. But if we knew for certain why, we'd very likely
know who, straightaway."

"Yes, exactly!" I said in surprise, because he had virtually repeated Ericks's remark. And of course, they
were both right. I saw it now. It was the moment for
telling them of my encounter with Ericks. Brockley, of
course, was scandalized and wanted to rush away then
and there to teach Ericks some manners, but I
peremptorily stopped him.

"No, Brockley! He did me no harm, and if someone
has tried to put false blame on him, he has every right
to be angry. In fact, you and he both think the same way
and it is good sense. *Why* was Edward killed? That's
what we need to get at."

"It seems to me, madam," Brockley said grimly,

"that it's a very pressing need, a great fear or a great hatred, that would cause a man to kill in such a fashion. The reason ought to be as big as a mountain."

"Yes. Yes, I agree." I frowned. I was considering the matter from this angle for the first time. I had been so overwhelmed by the simple fact that Edward had been murdered that I hadn't considered the extraordinarily vicious, stealthy, and elaborate manner of it as important. "But in that case . . ." I began slowly.

I stopped, groping after an idea that refused to clarify. Brockley, his intelligent forehead wrinkling just like mine, said: "Are you thinking, madam, that he may have been killed and the list taken, just to stop it from being delivered? That could make sense. There are plenty of Protestants in Scotland who wouldn't think the queen's claim to England was lawful and wouldn't want to encourage their queen to invade England."

The idea found its way into speech at last. "But she had a list already." I rubbed my upper arm, where Ericks's finger marks would soon be showing up as bruises. "How could it be worth killing Edward just for an amended version? Anyone who knew enough to know he was carrying it very likely knew about the first one as well. Anyway, how *did* anyone know he was carrying it? There are a lot of questions here that need answering. Well, the two lists I have here should tell us whether he delivered his message to the queen or not. Let's settle that first. Sit down, both of you. Which of you is best at reading aloud?"

They were both literate, but Dale said: "I can read receipts and put labels on pots of unguent and scent, and make shift to write a letter or read one, but Roger's the one who had real schooling."

"Very well. Then, Brockley, I want you to read one of these lists out while I check it against the other. I'd like to do it now, before we go to bed. We'll need to light some more candles."

Dale lit them while I brought out the package that Rob had given me and unsealed it. There were indeed two lists, on slightly different paper, each running to three pages. They consisted of names, individuals in some cases and families in others, with details of where they lived and what they had offered to help Mary Stuart turn herself into the Queen of England: money (and how much), men and horses (and how many), and arms (what kind). Each had a note in Rob's handwriting at the top of the first page. One said laconically: *My Old List.* The other said *M's Present List.* There was also a separate note, which said, *I've taken a look myself. The two aren't the same but the changes don't look recent. But I know you'll want to see for yourself. Rob.*

I regarded the lists with pleasure. In so many of my past adventures, I had been the one who stole into other people's studies and private chambers, picking locks in the process, to examine their personal papers. I had hated it, for I was always afraid of being caught, and besides, it felt so tasteless. This time, for once, someone else had done it for me.

"Read out the old list," I said, passing it to Brockley.

I sat on the side of my bed, with the queen's version in my hand while Brockley pulled a table near the window seat, arranged a bank of candles on it, and sat down with Dale at his side. He began to read.

It was interesting. Some of the names, of course, were no surprise—those of powerful Catholic families whose allegiance I could have foretold. Others were unknown to me. But one family was mentioned whom I knew and had liked and was sorry to find in such circumstances, and others I knew slightly and was surprised to find so treacherous.

The one I was holding, the list purloined for me by Master Rokeby, had indeed been annotated in places. A few names had been crossed out, and notes, in a variety of hands, had been scribbled against them. Two or three men had died. Another had lost his wealth and so his offer of money was void. Another had married his daughter to a man who was decidedly not sympathetic; it was not advisable to rely on him now. Most of the annotations were dated, though, and Rob was right, none of the dates were recent. They could not be connected with Edward's list but presumably reflected information that had drifted in over the years.

"Thank you, Brockley," I said when we had finished. I lowered the papers in my hand to my lap and sat gazing down at the last sheet, wondering what line of inquiry to follow next.

An entry that had passed me by with no more than a private nod of recognition when Brockley was reading suddenly leapt at me, as though it had bounded from the page.

John and Euphemia Thursby of St. Margaret's, Northumbria. Have offered a dozen horses from their stables and twelve men from the

St. Margaret's tenantry, and what money can be
spared when the time comes.

A pity, I thought. A great pity. To be expected, of
course. They were Catholics living in the Catholic
stronghold of Northumberland and had connections
in Scotland. It was perfectly natural.

Was it?

"What is it, ma'am?" Dale asked anxiously. "Why,
ma'am, your face has gone so . . . so fixed. Are you all
right? Is it your head again?"

"No, Dale. No. I'm just . . . wondering something."

"Wondering what, madam?" Brockley asked.

"That's the trouble, Brockley. I hardly know. It's
so . . . tenuous. Like morning mist. There's nothing
solid there. And yet . . ."

In my head, fragments of the conversation I had
had with the Thursbys on the day I arrived at St. Margaret's were reciting themselves, with all their nuances
of voice. I could see the faces of John and Euphemia,
red-cheeked and bright-eyed, Robin and Robina
Goodfellow, as I had thought of them then. I could see
St. Margaret's itself: comfortable, well cared for,
beloved.

*"The fact is that we love St. Margaret's too much and can't
help but hope we will never lose it."* That had been John
Thursby.

"It would break my heart if we did." That was
Euphemia.

*"Yes, well, that's as may be. But if it's ever God's will that
our religion be restored in England, well, as Madame de la
Roche says, it's a sacrifice we might have to make."*

Another voice chimed in my mind, that of Lady Simone Dougal, speaking of her husband and the English abbey he had once inherited.

"On his last visit, he was approached by some emissary or other of Queen Elizabeth and asked if he would give an oath that he would back Elizabeth if ever there should be a war between England and Scotland. They told him that he might lose the former abbey if a Catholic ruler ever took the throne. He didn't believe that. He said he was sure that our Queen Mary would never reward faithful followers by taking their homes away from them, and that this was nothing but a ploy, a cruel pretense of Elizabeth's."

Elizabeth and her agents were quite capable of such a ploy. And might not the Thursbys believe it? They clearly loved their home and would grieve bitterly if they lost it, and though John Thursby sounded like someone prepared to endure a situation that was right but sad, he hadn't sounded at all like someone prepared to offer horses, men, and money to bring that situation into being.

And there was more.

". . . our daughter, our dearest Jane . . ." Euphemia, with anguish in her voice. *". . . we were held up on the road by armed men—under the command of this young noble. Our daughter was taken from us."* And she had died, their beloved daughter Jane. And then John Thursby, saying: *"Of homesickness and ague in that vile, cold castle, and probably of ill usage too. She had a black eye when we saw her . . . She was dead in six months . . . God have mercy on her soul, and a curse on the soul of the man who seized her."*

I had asked if this sort of thing was a commonplace in Scotland and John Thursby had said ominously that

Scotland was very different from England. *"It is a wild place,"* he had said, *"with little rule of law."*

The Thursbys, once, a few years ago, had been willing to support Queen Mary in any invasion of England. But since then, they had learned to love St. Margaret's, which might be lost to them under a Catholic government, and they had utterly lost their daughter, to a lawless, undisciplined Scottish noble. How likely were the Thursbys, now, to want, really to want, Mary, Queen of Scots, as a ruler in England?

Mistress Thursby's voice spoke again in my head. *"We breed horses and people come to buy our stock at times, and now and then, of course, groups of traveling players come by, or a stray peddler or merchant . . ."*

This was foolishness, I said to myself. I couldn't build a theory—an accusation—out of a common-place remark like that, something anyone might say. Peddlers roamed about everywhere. It was true that the peddler who had been one of the messengers who had been used as a go-between for Matthew, Edward, and the Scottish court had eventually been caught, and of course, he might have stayed with the Thursbys on his travels. But there was a huge gap between a casual remark about stray peddlers, and the idea that the Thursbys, knowing that one particular stray peddler was a spy's courier, had betrayed him. And that Edward had somehow discovered this and might report it.

"Our steward is not here just now. He is a Scotsman with family over the border—as indeed we ourselves have—and went off yesterday, to see a kinsman who's been ill or had an accident or some such thing." That had been Euphemia.

Dormbois had confirmed it. The kinsman in question had been his land agent, the worse for wear after breaking his leg. And Dormbois apparently lived close to Edinburgh.

Quite a useful excuse, though no doubt another could have been found, if the Thursbys wanted to send a man to Scotland, for an innocent-seeming purpose.

When all the time their real purpose was to send a man to dispose of Edward before he could let Queen Mary know that they, the Thursbys, were no longer to be trusted. That messengers who passed through St. Margaret's were liable to be betrayed. The Thursbys might have formed a habit of going through the belongings of Queen Mary's messengers and found that Edward had them down as unreliable on his list; even had them down as betrayers of other messengers.

I tried to put myself in Edward's place. I was my cousin, traveling north, knowing—from some source or other—that the Thursbys were no longer friends to my cause. When had they changed their minds? I wondered. The peddler's betrayal had been recent. Perhaps their decision to betray Mary's cause had been recent too. These things can burn slowly and then spring suddenly to life. Very well. I am Edward, aware of their duplicity—but I don't realize that they are actually inspecting my baggage or that they wish to get rid of me because they know that *I* intend to betray *them* to Mary Stuart. I am of course aware that they might have reported me to the English authorities. Had Edward ever meant to return to England? He might have hoped to smuggle his family to Scotland instead.

So, I am Edward, bound for Scotland and perhaps intending to stay there, but the Thursbys have decided to dispose of me. They wouldn't, of course, want to do this on their own premises . . .

It's all supposition, I said to myself, while Dale and Brockley sat watching the expressions on my face come and go. It's a house built on sand, a theory made of bits and pieces, like a patchwork coverlet.

Yet it made sense. It created a *pattern*. Too much of a pattern to be dismissed as just imagination. It was something that must be examined.

Go through it again. The Thursbys loved St. Margaret's and feared to lose it. They had loved their daughter and Scottish savagery had taken her from them. So they'd changed sides and betrayed the peddler and then—yes—it *did* make sense, had become afraid that if the news reached Scotland, there might be reprisals. I remembered the defensive walls around St. Margaret's. Raids across the border were nothing new.

Their steward, Hamish Fraser, had undoubtedly been near Edinburgh at the right time.

Over my left eye, another warning hammer blow made me narrow my eyes against the candlelight. I knew why. I didn't want to believe this of the Thursbys. I had liked them so much. I put the papers quickly back into my skirt pouch and slowly, unwillingly, through the thudding in my skull, I told Brockley and Dale of my theory and its reasons.

"I think," I said, "that we shall have to go back to St. Margaret's and see the Thursbys. At once, if you can manage it so soon, Dale. I want to see them again, to learn, if I can, whether this idea of mine is even possible. I don't know how I'll do it. I shall have to talk to them . . . trail a lure, as it were . . . and see what happens." I rubbed my forehead and Dale's eyes became alert.

"I am well enough to travel if need be, ma'am," she said, "the weather's not so cold now, but I think that you need a good night's rest. I can tell that your head's getting bad again. There's quite a lot left of that poppy draft that the queen sent me, bless her, and one only needs a small dose. You'd better have some."

17

Trailing a Lure

The sleeping draft was an unappetizing muddy brown and I didn't like the look of it much. However, it dissolved out of sight when mixed with red wine, and it worked quickly. I took it when I was in bed and fell asleep within ten minutes. I had a good night's sleep. In the morning, I was capable of traveling.

We therefore set out for St. Margaret's the very next day, a Thursday. I sent polite excuses to Queen Mary and had us on our way before noon. We didn't travel hastily, and I pretended that this was out of consideration for Dale, for I knew quite well that she was still not strong, but although I wouldn't admit it, it was really out of consideration for myself. I was much improved but I didn't want another attack of migraine.

The weather was clear and dry and there were no delays. We reached St. Margaret's without incident on the Saturday, just as the daylight was settling toward dusk.

It looked so welcoming that it made me homesick.

It hadn't reminded me of Withysham when first I saw it, but now I realized that there were indeed resemblances. Both had protective gray walls (though at Withysham they lacked battlements because they were there to defend Benedictine serenity not from besiegers but from the temptations of the world). Both had low, recessed doors with pointed arches, and the last time I had seen my own home, candlelight had been gleaming from the slender leaded windows, just as it was doing from the windows of St. Margaret's now. Tears sprang to my eyes, of sheer longing for Withysham and Meg, and when Euphemia Thursby hurried out to see who the new arrivals were, she found me sitting on my horse—or rather, the horse I had borrowed in the first place from St. Margaret's—and dismally blowing my nose.

"Oh, dear, this cold weather. I know; it makes my nose run too. My dear Madame de la Roche! Do get down and come in, all of you. We have lots of company just now but the more, the merrier, we always say."

"You have other guests?" I asked, as Brockley dismounted and came to help me and Dale to alight.

"Yes, but it doesn't matter," said Euphemia, chatty as always. "You can have the room I meant you to have before, except that you insisted on rushing away the same day. The one overlooking the cloister garden. The Bycrofts always have the one in the corner tower when they stay overnight, and Uncle Hugh likes a room on the ground floor because his joints ache now that he's getting on in life and stairs are a trouble to him. And Father Ninian prefers the tiny top-floor room above the Bycrofts because it's just right for a priest's cell, and the stairs lead down to a door that's only a few yards from the chapel."

"The Bycrofts are here?"

"Yes, because of Father Ninian. He's a priest who visits us now and then. He stays either with us or the Bycrofts and we always get together so that he can say mass for us all at once. You will join us tomorrow, of course."

"Of course. You have a houseful, I see." I hesitated and then said carefully: "I hope we shan't be a nuisance. We're on our way south but neither Dale nor I have been too well lately and I did hope we could rest a couple of days here . . ."

"Oh, by all means! Think nothing of it. I see you've brought our horses back in good condition. We have the ones you left here, also in good condition, sound and healthy. Now, do come inside."

"Yes, and at once!" John Thursby, short, rubicund, and perky as a pixie, had come out to join us, but was shifting restlessly from foot to foot and had crossed his arms in order to rub warmth into his elbows. "No one's the better for standing in a cold wind. There's a fine fire in the parlor and there'll be mulled wine and raisin cakes on the instant, and in the kitchen, they'll find something for your servants. Our steward is back, heaven be praised. Hamish Fraser watches over every detail of our household. We have a little joke that if anyone in it were to lock themselves into a room at the far end of the house from Hamish, and cough, the moment they came out they would meet the maidservant he had sent to them with a licorice and horehound cough mixture. When he is here, the household is all it should be."

We went indoors with them, while Brockley helped the St. Margaret's servants to bring our saddlebags in. The horses were now in the care of their own grooms and for once he didn't feel obliged to look after them himself.

Could my theory possibly be right? I thought once more of Edward lying in that bloodstained bed, eyes staring and mouth distorted. Could such a crime have been hatched here? Could this happy, busy house be the seedbed of murder? Was it conceivable that either of the jolly, talkative Thursbys could have dispatched their steward to Scotland in order to . . . ?

It seemed like madness. "Mulled wine and raisin cakes by a good fire sound most inviting," I said.

Nevertheless, when we went inside and I realized that we were being greeted by Hamish Fraser, the steward, I studied him with curiosity. Dormbois had spoken of him disparagingly as an indoor man, but although he wasn't weather-beaten, he was a stocky fellow who looked tough enough to me. He had one of those boyish faces which are not as boyish as they seem, with round, steady blue eyes and the corners of the mouth tucked in. He might well be capable of killing someone, I thought. But were the Thursbys capable of ordering such a thing?

Wanting to keep Brockley and Dale near me, I asked Euphemia if there was a bedchamber near mine where they could sleep. "Indeed, yes," said Euphemia, beaming. "There's a small chamber leading from yours—it looks out from the other side of the house, over the stableyard. I'll show you up myself. One of the apple trees is close by. I wish you could have seen it in bloom, but of course, it's too early in the year for that. It's a sight to delight the heart when the blossom's out."

"St. Margaret's is so big," she added, as she led the way upstairs. "There's always room for a few more. It's a house for a big family. We had other babes beside Jane and our son, but babes are so tender we lost all but those two. Our son married well and he said that if he could inherit the stud, Jane could have this house as her dower. We hoped that one day she and her husband would fill it with their children, but . . ."

"Well, let's not speak of that," said her husband, who was following us. "There's nothing to be done about it now."

They made sure that we had all we needed and then left us. I washed my face and hands quickly and Dale tidied my hair. Then, calling Brockley to come in from the adjoining room, I told them both to go downstairs and make sure that they had something to eat and drink.

"That we will do, madam," Brockley said. He considered me questioningly and then repeated a question that he had already asked at least three times on the journey.

"Madam, what exactly do you mean to do here? You keep saying things like *I'm going to trail a lure,* but just how are you to go about it? I think Fran and I should know—so that we say and do nothing that might interfere with you by accident. What does *trailing a lure* mean? You can hardly smile at the Thursbys across the dinner table and ask them if they sent their steward to Edinburgh to murder your cousin!"

"No, of course not! I'm not going to talk about Edward at all. No, what I want to know is whether, perhaps, the Thursbys really did inform on that unfortunate peddler and, also, I shall try to learn if the tooth-drawer ever stayed here. And I shall try to find out just how far the Thursbys would go to protect their ownership of St. Margaret's. After all, they think I'm a Catholic like Edward. Perhaps I can get them to confide in me a little. I can—well—raise topics of conversation and see what emerges. So can you. Try and find out what kind of man Hamish is."

When I went down to join the company, I found the Bycroft family in the parlor. Mistress Bycroft was in a window seat, away from the fire, her coifed head bent over a book, but her grave, bearded husband was sitting in the inglenook, with a daughter on either side of him, talking quietly to a younger, plainly dressed man opposite. The fifteen-year-old Bycroft son was at a small table, playing chess with an elderly man in a dark blue gown. They all turned as I came in.

"Madame de la Roche!" Mistress Bycroft exclaimed, and laying her book aside, came to meet me with outstretched hands. "Euphemia told us you had come. A welcome addition to our company. I well remember the edifying conversation we had with you when you stayed at our house. You know my family, of course." Both the male Bycrofts rose and bowed and the daughters, slipping off the seat, respectfully curtsied. "And this is Father Ninian, who will say mass for us all tomorrow."

The plainly clad younger man to whom Master Bycroft had been talking also rose and bowed. The elderly man, with the air of one who likes to finish one task before beginning on another, put his opponent in check before rising stiffly to do the same.

"The mass won't be said for quite all of us," he observed. "I have great affection for my niece Euphemia but I follow the Reformed religion and do not attend Catholic rites. But that is by the way. I too am happy to make your acquaintance, Madame de la Roche. I always enjoy seeing a new face. I am Hugh Stannard, brother of Mistress Thursby's mother."

From a lined face, a pair of bright blue eyes looked into mine and in them I saw keen intelligence and also a frank appreciation, but of a pleasanter sort than that of Dormbois. "When I have finished my game with Dickon here, madam," said Hugh Stannard, "will you come and talk to me?"

I spent much of the evening doing what I had told Brockley and Dale I meant to do—trailing lures, as a falconer does when training a hawk to fly from its perch to his fist. The falconer fastens a morsel of meat on the end of a cord and whirls it in the air or drags it invitingly across the ground, hoping that the bird will rouse, fluff its feathers with interest, fix its gaze on the bait, and fly. In similar fashion, I offered topics of conversation. My hawks, as it were, sat solidly on their perches, with plumage sleeked, and refused to take wing.

I did not of course waste time on trailing lures for Hugh Stannard. I talked to him for a while, as he had asked, but we discussed such harmless subjects as chess (at home he had an ivory chess set from China) and gardens (at home, he had a knot garden where he grew phlox and gillyflowers and roses chosen for their scent, and a herb garden bordered by lavender).

He also, rather embarrassingly, asked me about my family and who my father had been, which obliged me to explain that I didn't know; that my mother had been at court as lady-in-waiting to Queen Anne Boleyn, had had a lover whom she would not name because he was married, but who had fathered me.

"My mother was sent home to her family," I said simply. "And that's where we lived, until she died, and later on, I married Gerald Blanchard." There was no need to go into detail about my runaway match with Gerald, I decided.

Stannard was interested and sympathetic, guessing more than I told him, I think, about the grudging shelter that the Faldenes had given my mother and myself. However, when supper was served, and we were gathered around the table, I praised anew the beauties of St. Margaret's, and described Withysham in detail and said I wondered if I should admit it but I would do almost anything to protect my ownership of my home. That was my first lure.

Mistress Thursby sighed and agreed that the love of one's home was a powerful force. But no such repossessions had taken place in the time of Queen Mary Tudor and she hoped that if ever we came under the rule of Queen Mary Stuart, things would be the same.

Father Ninian rather obtusely observed that Mary Tudor's reign had been short. During a lengthier reign, many matters might be dealt with that had gone unheeded before. Mistress Thursby looked depressed, but neither she nor her husband displayed anything that resembled embarrassment or anxiety. They didn't exchange any conspiratorial glances. Mistress Bycroft, whose Christian name I now learned was Catherine, said predictably that it was best to do what was right and let God look after the outcome. Master Henry Bycroft gravely agreed.

Since I was the widow of Matthew de la Roche, I might reasonably claim some knowledge of his messengers, and so I spoke openly of the arrest of the peddler and the tooth-drawer. I drew a wary breath and then, offering my second lure, asked in what I hoped were not overcasual tones, if the Thursbys had ever met the tooth-drawer.

"He was a most competent man," I said, crossing my fingers in a fold of my skirt, and trusting to luck that the fellow hadn't been a complete butcher. "Aunt Tabitha was upset over losing him. When he failed to arrive, that last time, she was suffering from recurring toothache, and was most anxious to see him. In the end she had to go to a local man who was less experienced and caused her a great deal of pain."

Aunt Tabitha, whose small, even teeth were in very good condition for her age, would have been interested to hear it, and the local tooth-drawer, who was justly proud of his skill, would have been heartily insulted. I hoped that neither of them would ever learn of my slanders.

Unexpectedly, Catherine Bycroft said that she thought she knew the man, that he had once spent a night with them and had tended one of their maidservants.

"Though I can't be sure that it was the same one," she said. "All manner of travelers stay at Bycroft and at St. Margaret's too. As you know, madam, inns grow scanty the farther north one goes."

"Indeed," Euphemia agreed. "So many people pause here for a night, we might almost be innkeepers ourselves!"

"We can't remember all who stay," John Thursby agreed placidly.

After supper, we returned to the parlor and from a lidded settle, Euphemia produced a couple of guitars, on which the Bycroft daughters, who proved to be quite accomplished players, entertained us. When they had finished, I started a new topic, this time on the question of loyalty to one's sovereign.

"I didn't always agree with my husband on this matter." It was a moment, I decided, for a little more openness about myself. "I don't know how much Edward ever told you about me, but before I married Matthew I was for a time one of Elizabeth's Ladies of the Presence Chamber. Indeed, we met at Elizabeth's court. He came there once as a guest of one of her lords. I always felt that having taken her pay, I owed her some kind of loyalty, and indeed, it seems to me that all Elizabeth's subjects owe her that. I told Matthew, more than once, that I didn't like the notion of encouraging them to intrigue on behalf of another ruler."

"But, my dear madam, naturally one owes loyalty to one's true king or queen. The point is that Queen Mary Stuart *is* the true Queen of England," Mistress Bycroft said. "It is as I said before. One must do what is right and leave the rest to God."

"We did know that you once served at Elizabeth's court," said John Thursby, "though not from Edward. He really said very little about you. But our steward, Hamish, was at the inquiry into Edward's death and you declared your connection with Elizabeth then, did you not?"

"Yes, I did." So Hamish had been interested enough in Edward to turn up at the inquiry. But it had been a much-publicized occasion. This was hardly significant news.

Father Ninian remarked that he was tired and must be up betimes in the morning, and Uncle Hugh, yawning, said that he too wanted his bed. Candlesticks with fresh candles in them were standing ready on a shelf, and Euphemia, bidding priest and uncle good night, lit one for each of them and handed them over. The priest left the room briskly and Hugh Stannard, whose feet were clad in loose, soft slippers, shuffled after him. As I watched them go, I remarked that I too was weary from my journey.

"My woman will be sitting up for me, too, and she is even more tired than I am. I should retire," I said. "What time is tomorrow's mass?"

"At six of the clock," said Euphemia.

"I will be there," I said.

I thanked the Bycroft daughters for their music and Euphemia, wishing me sound sleep and pleasant dreams, gave me my own bedtime light. "Good night, all," I said, and withdrew.

Outside the parlor, there was a wide stone-flagged

passage with windows looking into the cloisters. The leaded panes reflected the flame of my candle, mingled in ghostly fashion with the outlines of the cloister pillars beyond. I walked away along the passage, letting my shoes ring on the floor, went around a corner and stopped. Removing my shoes, I tiptoed back. It was a risk, for someone might have been about to leave the parlor just as I got back to the door, but as I halted outside it, I could hear the sound of conversation from within and no one was speaking in the tone of imminent departure.

I set my candle down on the sill of a passage window and pressed my ear to the parlor door, in time to hear Master Thursby observe that it was a pity that Sorrel Jennet wasn't in foal this year, but it was always useful to have such a fast mare under the saddle, and if the Bycrofts were agreeable, he would try her this summer with their stallion instead of his own. Master Bycroft replied that Norseman did indeed have a good breeding record and a fine turn of speed as well. "If there's a foal, it could prove excellently fleet of foot."

Euphemia said something I couldn't hear though I doubted if it would be anything relevant. Then I drew quickly back from the door. Along the passage to my left, just at the corner, there had been, surely, a rustle of movement.

No, I was mistaken. No one came on along the passage. I shrugged. The conversation inside the parlor was useless anyway. I retrieved my candle and, still carrying my shoes, made my way softly back to the corner, intending to go up the staircase that lay beyond it.

But as I did so, a shape moved into my path and Uncle Hugh said shortly: "In here, if you please."

He opened a door behind him and in the same instant shot out a hand and gripped my elbow, drawing me toward it. I resisted. "Master Stannard? I don't quite understand . . ."

"Don't be a fool, woman," said Stannard, in a low and irritable voice. "I'm fifty-two years old, I've had four mistresses and two wives and in the end one simply gets tired of it all, especially when it doesn't even result in children! You are a most charming lady and a pleasure to look at but this is not an attempt at seduction. I had only been in my room for a moment before I heard your feet approaching and then stop. So I looked out and I saw you taking your shoes off. You crept back the way you had come and I was curious enough to take my own slippers off and follow you, damning these cold flagstones every step of the way, I may tell you. When I looked round the corner, you were listening at the parlor door. Now will you come into my room? I want to put something on my feet again and I want to talk to you in private!"

He pulled at my elbow once more, quite roughly, and I gave way. His room was lit by only a single candle and the glow of a fire, which was now burning low. Closing the door, Stannard took my candle and used it to light several more before motioning me to a settle.

He found his slippers and put them on. Then he sat down on the edge of his bed, facing me, and said abruptly: "You've been making conversational gambits all evening, like a chess player tempting an opponent with a sacrificial pawn. And I know who you are. My home is in Surrey, near the Sussex border. I know all the principal families in both Surrey and Sussex, including the Blanchards. I know Luke Blanchard well. Your first husband was his son Gerald and it was after Gerald's death that you joined Elizabeth's court. I also know, though the Thursbys don't, that you have worked, most unusually for a woman, as an agent for Elizabeth and for Sir William Cecil. Luke Blanchard told me that too."

"He isn't supposed to know it."

"Well, he does know it, as do a good many other people. Did you marry De la Roche for love or was that another task you undertook to infiltrate Mary Stuart's network of—shall we say—well-wishers?"

"No. It was love."

"How sweetly romantic," said the elderly, chess-playing cynic in front of me. "Now, why were you pushing out pawns all through supper and why were you listening at that door?"

"Why do you want to know?"

"Because I don't want any harm to come to my niece, Euphemia. I have no daughters of my own but I have always looked on her in that light. I care very little for matters of religion or politics but I do care for her. If you are looking for evidence that she or her husband are traitors . . ."

Choosing my words, I said: "You could say that I was looking for evidence that they are not."

"What do you mean? Why should you come here seeking such a thing? What were you about this evening?"

"I came north for the reason that I gave on my first visit here. My cousin's family feared that he was running into danger. They wouldn't tell me much about its nature but they sent me to bring him back if I could. The danger got to him first. Now I am on my way home. But . . ."

"Wait. You say that your family sent you north. Not Cecil?"

"No, not Cecil. Master Stannard, I cannot discuss this with you. Please understand that."

"And I can't compel you because you're Cecil's employee and anyone who touched you would regret it. Say no more!"

There was a silence. The candles flickered in a chilly draft and the fading fire had left the room cold. Stannard noticed. He rubbed his hands together and then got up to feed the fire. Having done so, he came back to his place and sat staring at me as though trying to read my mind.

For my part, I was thinking rapidly. To Brockley and Dale I had used the metaphor of a falconer but Hugh Stannard thought in terms of chess. So did I now, as I took a conscious decision to push forward another, significant pawn.

"Unless, of course," I said, "you were to murder me and both my servants. Perhaps by intercepting us on the road home, so as not to foul your own doorstep."

"What on earth are you babbling about?" Again, Stannard sounded irritable. "Murder, indeed! If you won't talk to me, then I'll talk to you. From your choice of gambits over supper and after, I had the impression that you were wondering whether John and Euphemia had informed on those unlucky messengers your husband sent through England—the tooth-drawer and the peddler. At least, you brought them and the fact that they had been arrested into the conversation and you talked very earnestly about being willing to do almost anything to protect your ownership of your own home, as though you wondered whether my niece and her husband might feel the same about theirs."

"It had crossed my mind," I said. "But if so, then they are on Elizabeth's side, and as you seem to realize, so am I."

"But why do you want to know?"

Why indeed? Because I wondered if here was a motive for the murder of my cousin. Decidedly not something to be suggested to Euphemia Thursby's loving uncle. I checked for a few seconds while my mind scurried around possible answers like a mouse that has smelled a cat, and then said, as steadily as I could: "I can't give you a clear-cut answer. Habit, I think. Once an agent, always an agent. It is necessary for Cecil to know as much as he can about who he can and can't trust and how far. That's all."

"Ah. Habit. Always a weak point. I've been a soldier in my day and it's useful to learn the enemy's habits. If the man you wish to capture always takes *that* route on a certain journey; if the enemy commander relies on a certain tactic . . . so agents form habits as well, do they? Well, well."

"I think we understand each other now," I said. "And I would like to return to my own room. My woman is waiting up for me."

He rose and opened the door for me. "I love Euphemia," he said as I went out. "She is a dear, sweet, *innocent* woman. She has never harmed a soul. I will not tell the Thursbys who you are—or that you are not a Catholic—if I can help it. But if necessary, I will fight for Euphemia. Remember that."

"I don't want the innocent harmed, either," I said. I looked into those steady blue eyes. "Believe me, Master Stannard."

18

The Clandestine Departure

I had spoken to Stannard with as much cool authority as I could muster but I went to my room in a chastened mood. I had not been as clever as I thought and it looked as though too many people knew too much about me. The Thursbys and Bycrofts had perhaps been deceived, but I had underestimated Hugh Stannard completely. He had seen straight through my casual conversation to the purpose behind it and I could only hope that he would keep his knowledge to himself.

I would have felt better about it if my efforts had met with more success, but what had I learned, after all? The peddler might have stayed at St. Margaret's; the tooth-drawer had probably stayed with the Bycrofts. The Thursbys might have known about it if he had, but I had watched their faces and I had seen nothing to suggest that talk of peddlers and tooth-drawers had any guilty significance for them. I was no further on.

I slept poorly, and in the morning I found that I had underestimated someone else besides Uncle Hugh, and that was the priest, Father Ninian. Before breakfast, I attended the mass (I met Uncle Hugh as I was going along the passage on my way there and ignored his knowing smile with difficulty) but afterward, as we were about to leave the chapel, the priest came up to me and asked if he could have a word. Surprised, I agreed.

The chapel, though small, was well appointed. There were painted and gilded statues in niches, some beautiful medieval stained glass, a richly embroidered altar cloth on which devout ladies had once expended much time and silken thread, and some benches, too, for the comfort of worshipers. We sat down on one of them, and the priest came straight to the point.

"Madame de la Roche, from the tenor of your talk yesterday, at supper and after, I think you are suffering from a troubled spirit. You spoke of owing loyalty to Queen Elizabeth because you had served her, and also because she is queen of your country. It sounded as if your sense of human honor and loyalty has come into conflict with your sense of your duty to God. Am I right?"

Keeping up my deception, I said: "Yes, Father. I suppose you could say that."

"I understand." He had a south of England accent, and although his hair was dark and his shapely face was browned by riding in the wind, his eyes were light. Calling him *Father* made me uncomfortable; he was too young for that. "It does you credit, my daughter," he said. "It is not wrong to feel that if you have worked for someone and taken their wages—eaten their salt, as the saying used to be—then you owe them something. And naturally, subjects do owe loyalty to their sovereign. These, I think, are the things you were trying to say last night?"

"Yes, Father. And there was more I could have said."

"Indeed? And what was that?"

"There are many people who would fight for Elizabeth and for the Reformed religion. Any attempt to change either the queen or the religion could lead England into civil war. How can that be justified, even for the sake of bringing England back to the fold of the true Church?"

"My daughter, this is where you are confused. I sense that to you such an attempt would be an attack on your true queen, your accredited sovereign. But Mistress Bycroft put her finger on the principal point. Your confusion lies in the fact that although Elizabeth sits on the throne and wears the crown, although she has been anointed as queen, she is not your rightful ruler. Her presence on the throne is an attack on the true queen! It is indeed the duty of true subjects to resist it—by placing their loyalty behind Queen Mary Stuart, who will reign with the blessing and approval of the Church."

"But . . . I have met Queen Mary," I said. "She is gentle and kind. Would she truly want to reign over England—once she understood that it really would mean war?"

"She will listen to her spiritual advisers. I think Mistress Catherine Bycroft put it very well yesterday evening, when she said one must do what is right and leave the rest to God."

"Even if it means—a battlefield?"

"If that is God's will."

I was angry. To hide it from him, I lowered my eyes. I said in a trembling voice: "When I was a young girl, when Queen Mary Tudor ruled, she . . . she began to root out heresy."

"Yes, I remember. I was only a child at the time but yes, I recall those days."

"I never saw a burning but my uncle and aunt did and they . . . they described it to me. It horrified me! If such things were to happen in England again . . ."

"Mary Stuart is not willing that they should. She believes that the flock should be led, not driven," said Father Ninian calmly. "But if the Church were to insist . . . you speak of being horrified, my child, but the pains of hell would be ten thousand times more horrible. Those who died at the stake were saved from it. They are now in heaven, their souls purged by fire of the errors they committed on earth, and if you could ask them, they would say now that they are grateful."

I sat still, not letting my hands, lying in my lap, clench as they wanted to do, keeping my eyes downcast, concealing with all my might the cold sickness with which his words had filled me.

"Be at peace," he said soothingly. "There is no need to torment yourself. Put your faith in God and His Church; follow where they lead you; do not rack your brain with questions. It is a mistake to question, a mistake to think too much."

I said: "You spoke just now of what Queen Mary believes. Have you met her?"

"Yes indeed, my daughter."

"I know that she has priests and other people in her employ who travel through England bearing her goodwill to those who support her, and seeking out those who will offer practical help when the time comes. You must be one of them."

He didn't reply. I took a deep breath. "What can I do," I said, forcing myself to look up and smile into his eyes, "but wish you well and pray for you? Thank you for talking to me, Father. You have cleared my mind. I think I understand now. I have a little money with me, in my room. May I give you a donation for your cause? It will be modest, I'm afraid—but even modest donations add up, I suppose?"

Money is one of the great solvents. One of the things it dissolves, sometimes quite magically, is suspicion. If you are willing to give money to a cause, then your credentials as a supporter are assured.

"I would be most grateful, daughter. Be sure that the money will be well used. I do gather donations, and I keep the most careful account of them. They are wisely invested on the Continent. Your husband used to see to it for us at one time. Now—we have found someone else."

He didn't entirely trust me and my promised donation clearly hadn't dissolved *all* his doubts. I had better keep my word and let him have one, I supposed. Promises ought to be kept. One donation was neither here nor there; it wouldn't alter the outcome of any future war.

I knelt for his blessing and went away, in turmoil of mind, caught between the millstones of a piety too blind to recoil from starting a war, and a love of one's home, which I understood but which might have led to murder in the night. I found them both unbearable. I wanted to leave it all and go back to Withysham.

But I couldn't. I had seen Edward's deathbed.

After dinner, Hugh Stannard, who had been seated some way from me, came to my side and said quietly: "We had an unhappy conversation yesterday evening, but I think at the end of it, you understood me. Yesterday, when we first met, we had a pleasanter talk together. Could we renew that, do you think? Will you have a game of chess or backgammon and talk to me . . . Mistress Blanchard?"

I wasn't certain what he meant by this, but agreed, and it turned out that he meant exactly what he said. We sat in the parlor and played a game of chess, found out that although I could play, I was nowhere near a good enough opponent for Stannard, and turned to backgammon instead.

While we played, we conversed. We talked, again, of gardens. I described the herb garden that I had restored at Withysham and had also done much to enhance at Blanchepierre, in the Loire Valley, during the brief time I spent there with Matthew. Stannard spoke of new varieties of roses that he had cultivated. He became animated, even merry, as he told me about attempts that had gone sadly wrong.

"If there were such a thing as an ugly rose, that

would have been it! And the other experiment I made that year was charming to look at but had no scent." He laughed freely and could afford to do so because he had lost few teeth and those that remained were still white. Yesterday's talk of tooth-drawers had made me very conscious of such things.

Our talk drifted on to literature, to poetry, and to the Latin I was studying with my daughter and the Greek I hoped we would both learn in due course. At the end, he said suddenly: "You enjoy speaking of these subjects, do you not? How in the world did you get into your extraordinary line of business, mistress?"

"Money," I said succinctly. "I needed it to clothe myself suitably for my place at court, and to support my daughter. It happened, almost by chance, that Sir William Cecil offered me a way to earn it."

"I see. But are you still in need of it? Surely not."

"No. But . . ."

"Quite. Habit," said Stannard. "But you could form other habits—as a student of Latin and Greek and a lover of herb and knot gardens, perhaps?"

"I was trying to do that when my family summoned me and sent me after Edward."

"So although I suspect that your family have not always been kind to you, you were willing to help them? Now of that, I approve. That was good-hearted of you. Evidently you did not make this journey altogether of your own free will. I hope you will soon reach your home again and resume your own private life. You will be happier." He smiled. "You are good company, and very pleasant to behold, and if you have no known father, you are none the worse for it. It would make a difference to some men but not to me. If I were not so much older than you, and if I didn't know myself unable to give a woman children, which is after all what most women desire, I would offer you my hand."

I blinked at him.

"Oh yes," he said. "But as things are—I wish you well. And I urge you simply to leave all these secrets and all this probing, to let others protect the interests of the queen and Cecil, and to settle into the peace of private life. Your cousin's wife, in Sussex, will be awaiting your return, will she not? She will want to know all you can tell her of her husband's death and his burial. Unhappy news, but still, she will want it."

"I have written, in some detail."

"But nevertheless, she will need you."

"I will go home," I said, "as soon as I can."

Which might as well be tomorrow, I thought, as I prepared for bed that night. I had learned nothing. I had a theory; I had suspicions; I could not see how to confirm any of them. I was so uncertain that I didn't even want to put my ideas into writing and send them to Rob Henderson. He had authority, which I had not, and might be able to launch an investigation, but I did not want to turn such heavy cannon onto people who might indeed be as innocent as Hugh Stannard evidently believed.

Well, innocent of murdering Edward, anyway. They had probably harbored traitorous messengers, but then so had the Faldenes, my own family, and the messengers had been sent out originally by my own husband!

Though the Thursbys might have betrayed the said messengers. The sides in this secret war were becoming appallingly muddled.

As I got into bed, I felt another warning twinge of pain above my left eye. I wanted no more of this, I said to myself. I would go home, as Hugh Stannard had advised, give what comfort I could to my aunt and uncle and Helene (since they didn't like me, I wouldn't be able to do much for them but at least I could try), and leave the moral muddles, the deceptions, and the betrayals to others.

The hovering headache faded after I had lain quietly for a while with closed eyes. I had slept so ill the night before that this time, once I was asleep, I went deep. I dreamed vividly, and not of Edward, but of Withysham, of walking through the herb garden and breathing the scent of mint and lemon balm. When someone shook my shoulder and began calling urgently to me to wake up, I didn't want to and resisted. The sun was just coming out from behind a cloud, and the downland near my home was splendid in the green and gold of grass and buttercup. Then my eyes opened and the sunlight, after all, was a candle, held by Dale, who was shaking me with her other hand. She had pulled back the bed curtains and I could see that the room was still dark.

"Wha . . . what's the matter, Dale? What time is it?"

"Not much past four of the clock, ma'am, and I'm sorry to disturb you but Roger says to come. Something's going on down in the stable yard under our window."

I was out of bed at once and Dale, setting the candle down, picked up my loose gown and threw it around

my shoulders. Seizing the candle again, she lit my way
through to the little adjoining room where she and
Brockley had been sleeping. Brockley was by the window, his silhouette showing dimly against a faint gray-
ness outside. The casement was open a little, and a
cold wind blew in, making the candle flame stream.

"I heard a horse whinny and it woke me," he said in
a low voice. Brockley was always alert to any disturbance involving horses. At heart, he was still more
groom than manservant. Still speaking low, he said:
"Put out the light, Fran. It mustn't show. Madam,
please to come over here."

I did so. I heard the clop and scrape of restless
hooves and the murmur of voices before I even reached
the window. When I peered out, I saw that John
Thursby and Henry Bycroft were both in the yard,
John holding up a lantern and Henry at the head of a
saddled horse while a third man tightened the saddle
girths. They were all just outside the stable door, which
was quite close, but because of the apple tree, which
was also close though fortunately not between me and
the stable, the Brockleys' window was in deep shadow
from the point of view of anyone below. Cautiously, I
pushed the casement wider and leaned right out, strain-
ing my ears.

". . . I know it's a long way and it's a bad time of year
but I told you; your pay will take that into account. We
trust you." Thursby was talking to the man who was
adjusting the girths. In the still, cold air before dawn,
his voice floated up to me with reasonable clarity.

"You're on my best mare and I don't want her
foundered, so it's a matter of not too fast but fast

enough." Thursby, as voluble as his wife, was fussing. "Ninian won't leave until after breakfast; you'll have a fair start. Just as well. He's traveling as a clerk on his master's business so he'll not linger. He only stayed here yesterday because it was Sunday. You've to get to London ahead of him if you can."

Bycroft, whose voice was deeper, rumbled something that sounded like: "Not so loud." He said something else as well, but the horse chose that moment to snort and stamp and I couldn't make out the words.

"The house is asleep," said Thursby, though more softly. "Here's the letter, Paul, and the token to help you deliver it. Keep them with you at all times till you've done our errand."

With the girths now satisfactory, the man who had been tightening them turned and took something that his master was holding out to him and I recognized him as Paul Bisselthwaite, one of the Thursby grooms, the one, in fact, who was good at doctoring horses as long as he was paid extra. He was evidently being paid extra for a different kind of service now. He spoke to Thursby in a quiet voice, which again I couldn't hear, but I could make out Thursby's reply.

"Of course the token will work. There was only a difficulty that once, when you had to deal with a new servant. Cecil's people didn't give trouble at other times, did they? Not that it mattered even when they did; you persisted and got in to see him just the same. Of course you did. You're a good man. I said we trust you."

I had begun to shiver, and not just from cold. The Thursbys were sending a messenger to Cecil and were making sure that he got to southern England ahead of

Father Ninian. It wasn't hard to interpret. They *had* been betraying the messengers who kept Mary Stuart in touch with her English and Continental adherents. At least, John Thursby had. I didn't know about his wife. The Bycrofts were obviously involved as well, which was surprising, but there was Henry Bycroft in the stable yard, to prove it.

I still did not know if the Thursbys—or the Bycrofts, come to that—had had Edward murdered to keep their activities private, but the motive was there: no doubt of it. Thursby was holding the lantern up in order to watch Paul stow what he had been given inside his jacket. The light fell on the red Thursby cheeks and gappy smile but cast John's eyes into shade. He didn't look like Robin Goodfellow now, but like an evil goblin.

I drew back, slowly, carefully, and inched the window shut. "Did you hear any of that, Brockley?"

"No, madam. I was standing behind you. What's happening?"

I said carefully: "They are sending word to Cecil— about something. I'm going back to bed now. But make sure I'm not late for breakfast, Dale. It could be important."

I went back to bed and lay there in turmoil. Should I warn Father Ninian or not? I detested and feared him, for he was working to destroy Elizabeth, to bring about the ruin of the England I loved, but then, so had Matthew been. I had in the past saved Matthew from being caught, and although Ninian was a stranger to me, should I not also save him? Even if he was not thought worth a traitor's death, he might still find himself imprisoned for years in a Tower dungeon once Cecil got hold of him, and before he was finally locked up, he would be questioned. I knew what that would mean.

As a true subject of Queen Elizabeth, it was my duty to let him be taken. I should admire the Thursbys and the Bycrofts for what they were doing. I did not know what motives the Bycrofts had but they might well have their reasons. The Thursbys certainly had reasons, and normally would have had my sympathy. I too served Elizabeth, and in my time, I too had sent men to their deaths. I too loved my home and I had been saddened, as well, by their story of their kidnapped daughter. Why should they love Scotland? Why should they not do all they could to halt the ambitions of her queen?

But there was still Edward, my objectionable cousin who was nevertheless my cousin, and who had died so horribly.

Yes, there was still Edward. Then I fell asleep and woke an hour later to find that the migraine that had threatened me again last night had kept its abominable promise. I could scarcely lift my head from my pillow. I had feared that our hasty journey to the Thursbys would make Dale relapse, but I had done the relapsing instead. In the intensity of the pain, Father Ninian's plight was wiped from my mind. By the time the onslaught had climaxed and the tide of agony had gone out, leaving me as wobbly as a newborn foal, Father Ninian had set out and was on his way to his betrayal.

I told the Brockleys then what I had heard in the night. Brockley considered the matter thoughtfully. "The illness came to stop you from warning him, I fancy, madam," he said. "The queen and Cecil wouldn't have wanted you to. You always keep faith with them, even when they haven't kept it with you. I've noticed that."

"I sometimes feel like a pawn on Elizabeth's private chessboard," I agreed bitterly. "But if these people had my cousin murdered, then I am not prepared to be a pawn, even for her."

"So—what now, madam?"

"As soon as I feel strong enough," I said, "which at the moment I don't, we must set off again. We must pretend to our good hosts that we are going home, but in fact, we must go back to Scotland. I'm ready now to report what I know to Rob Henderson. He may be able to find out the rest of the truth."

I would leave it to Rob to question the Thursbys and Hamish Fraser and arrest them if he felt it right. If this were the answer to Edward's death, then Rob could have the credit for finding it. Perhaps that would mend the breach between us.

19

The Uncouth Wooing

We left St. Margaret's the next day, a Tuesday, once more riding our own horses. We announced that we were off to London, waved good-bye, rode away, and as soon as we were well out of sight, turned north instead of south and made for Edinburgh. The weather stayed dry and we were there by midday on Thursday, which gave us time to look for lodgings. I didn't wish to go back to Holyrood, nor did I think it right to lodge with the Keiths or Macnabs or even in the place where we had stayed before, because they all had links to the Thursbys. It would be best, I thought, if the Thursbys didn't learn where I was. Brockley had duly tried to find out what he could about Hamish Fraser, and he said that Hamish was regarded by his fellow servants as a thoroughly dutiful steward. I didn't want him creeping in at my window with a thoroughly dutiful blade in his hand.

We found lodgings in the house of a merchant. It

was as plainly furnished as most houses in Edinburgh seemed to be, except for Lady Simone Dougal's, but the fires were good and our room had both a box bed and a four-poster. The Brockleys could have the box bed, I said.

I had to send Brockley to Holyrood anyway, because I wanted to see Rob Henderson. He came back, however, with a long face. "The queen's gone to Stirling, madam, and Lord Darnley's with her and Master Henderson, being part of his suite . . ."

"Has gone to Stirling too, I suppose," I said. "Yes, I see." The three of us were all together in our hired chamber, Dale, who was tired, resting on the box bed, with the door to it open, while I sat on the window seat, where I had been passing the time with a little embroidery until Brockley's return. I had put it down on my lap while I listened to Brockley's report and now, studying his face, it struck me that Brockley looked almost as tired as Dale. For the first time ever, I thought: *he's growing older.* When I first met him, over four years ago now, his hair had been brown and wiry, with only a few silver threads at the temples. Now the silver had scattered itself all through the brown, and his hairline had receded still farther from his high forehead.

"Brockley," I said on impulse, "how old are you?"

If the question surprised him, he didn't show it. "I shall be forty-eight years old in May. Fran will be the same age in August."

"Sit down," I said, indicating a settle. "You look exhausted. I'm sorry, Brockley. I've been driving you too hard as well as Dale."

"I'm fit enough, madam," said Brockley, slightly aggrieved. "I wouldn't like to join an army and go on campaign, I admit that, but I can still do whatever you're likely to want of me."

All servants grew nervous when their employers began to imply that they were past their best but neither Dale nor Brockley had anything to fear from me. I looked from Brockley, now seated on the settle, with one brown-hosed ankle over the other knee, to Dale, propped on her elbow on the box bed, and thought: it's true what everyone has been telling me. I should give up this way of life and give my servants an easier time. And for their sakes and mine, I should find another husband.

I only wished that something in me didn't shrink from the prospect. It wasn't only because my bereaved heart had not yet healed from Matthew's loss—or even, I sometimes thought, from the earlier loss of Gerald. There was something else. Meg's birth had been difficult, and since then, I had had two failures, one of which had almost killed me. I did not want to face that battlefield again. There is a widespread belief that all women so passionately desire babies that they are indifferent to the dangers. It isn't true. I was anything but indifferent.

"I will always look after you two," I said gently. And then, of course, I added: "How far away is Stirling, I wonder?"

Our landlord's name was Master Alexander Muir. He was a widower, though he had several children at home. He was a well-fed, well-dressed man, and he made his living by importing furs from Norway and Sweden (a benefit to us because we had warm fur rugs for our beds). Later that afternoon, he invited me to his firelit parlor for what he called a welcoming dram, by which he meant a glass of the amber-colored spirit that the Scots call whiskey. During my time in Scotland, I got used to it, and I grant you that nothing warms you better on a cold day, but it was so fiery that I always coughed at the first mouthful. Having got over this stage, I seized the chance to ask him if he knew how to get to Stirling.

"Stirling? It's away up at the head of the firth, thirty miles and a bit, as the crow flies. It's a guid place for trade. I've a hoose there and I have my captains put in there as often as not. It'd tak ye no more nor a day to get there on horseback, or ye micht go by water . . ."

I opened my mouth to ask for more details, but before I could speak, a brisk hammering on the street door interrupted us. Master Muir looked annoyed. "Now who might that be? I'm expecting nae callers this afternoon. On Thursdays after dining, I work in ma coontin' hoose, always, and mostly I'm still there at this hoor . . ."

A maidservant appeared at the parlor door and said something. She spoke broad Scots, and as so often, I couldn't understand it, but Master Muir at once rose to his feet and said: "Well, bring him in, then!" The maid-servant bobbed and disappeared, coming back a moment later with, to my surprise and disquiet, Sir Brian Dormbois.

Dormbois acknowledged Master Muir with a nod

and made straight for me, hands outstretched. "Madame de la Roche! I heard you were back in Edinburgh, for your man called at Holyrood today, did he not, inquiring for Master Henderson. One of my own men was by and realized who he was. But why are you here and not at Holyrood? The queen has received you; there'd be no difficulty . . ."

"Madame de la Roche?" said Master Muir, eyeing me with doubt. "I understood that ye were Mistress Blanchard."

"I've been married twice," I said. "I sometimes use my first husband's name when I wish for privacy. I am in Edinburgh on a very private matter, which is also why I didn't seek shelter at Holyrood."

"This lady is known to and approved by Her Majesty Queen Mary," said Dormbois brusquely. "And now, Master Muir, I wish to speak with her alone."

Whereupon, Alexander Muir, substantial merchant (in every sense of the word), paterfamilias, and no doubt a prominent citizen of Edinburgh, quitted his own parlor like a meek lamb.

"You've just ordered him out of a room in his own house!" I said in amazement.

"He respects my reputation," said Dormbois. "I am known to have a short temper, a ready fist, and a sharp blade always to hand. I also buy furs from him, and there's no respect like that of a merchant for a good customer." Dormbois favored me with one of his spectacular grins.

"Would you assault a man for staying put in his own private parlor?"

"Aye, if necessary. But enough of that. May I sit?"

"Please do. It *is* Master Muir's parlor, not mine."

He sat down on a settle near me. "These lodgings are not too bad, I'm glad to see," he remarked. "As comfortable as anywhere in Edinburgh, I fancy."

"Yes, indeed."

A silence fell. Outside, although sunset was more than an hour away, the sky was dimming with the approach of rain. The parlor faced north and was shadowy enough at the best of times; now it was so dark that only the firelight let me see Dormbois's face. His eyes were fixed on me with a searching look, which I found so disturbing that when at length I felt that the silence had lasted long enough, I said: "What is it?"

"I'm wondering what words to use to ask a question and what you'll say in answer."

"Should you not just ask the question and see?" I said uneasily.

He gazed at me for a few more silent moments and then said: "God knows . . ." and stopped.

"God knows what, Sir Brian?"

"What's going on in your mind and why I feel like this! About a woman like you! You've a tongue like the edge of a saw . . ."

Matthew had called me Saltspoon because he said my conversation had so much salt on it. In my head, I heard him whisper it as he had so often done in the darkness and intimacy of the night, and I was shaken to the depths of me. *Matthew. Oh, Matthew . . . !*

Not for a sackful of gold would I have shared the darling secret of that pet name with Dormbois, who now said harshly: "You're not listening!"

"I'm sorry. Please go on. I've a tongue like the edge of a saw . . . ?"

"Aye. You have. You can speak words to tear the spirit, and all said as sweet as if you were asking a guest to sit down and take a dram, while you help him off with his boots."

"If you tried to drink whiskey while someone was pulling your boots off, I think you might spill it."

"Hell and damnation! You're doing it again! And every time you do it, my heart turns somersaults and I can scarcely keep my hands off you and I don't know whether it's to throttle or to . . . hold you to me till you melt right into me and we're one for the rest of our lives. Will you wed wi' me, Madame de la Roche?"

"Will I . . . ?"

"I'm offering you my hand in marriage and my name. You'll be Lady Brian Dormbois, of Roderix Fort, and I'll not keep you from your home in the south, either. We can go there each winter and keep Christmas there, if that's what you'd like. I'll treat your daughter as mine and find her a nobleman to marry when the time comes. There's something else that I need to tell you, to show my good faith, but I hope it'll not make a difference. I'm no longer Catholic. So far I've kept up a pretense of it at court, so as not to upset the queen, though I'm open about it outside of the court and she'll find out sooner or later. That will all just have to take its course. A year or more ago, I heard a sermon by John Knox that changed my mind. It has its advantages," he said, his grin taking on a ferocious tinge. "The queen's brother Moray is ardent for the Reformed faith as are many of the lords of her council. Do you mind on the hawking party, when you saw me come from the house, wrangling with my secretary, Father Bell?"

"Yes. You said he was reminding you of letters to be written, or something of that kind."

"Aye. So I said, but the truth is, he was at me about my religion and my falling away, as he put it. He canna accept what I've done. He's good to the Catholic folk on my land and he's a good secretary so I keep him on, but there are times I get gey tired of listening to him, and more than once I've threatened to cast him off. He can marry us, though, if ye wish it, and minister to you with the mass and the like, once we are wed. I'll not hinder your way of worship, never fear it. I'm no' so extreme as Master Knox. I've not mentioned before that I was at the inquiry into your cousin's death, since I've so far wanted you to think I was of your persuasion. But do you mind, at the inquiry, one of his friends pulled him down from the pulpit when he tried to take command?"

"Yes," I said. "I thought, when we first met, that I'd seen you somewhere before. That was you, wasn't it?"

"Aye. Knox can go too far, I grant you. He hates having a woman on the throne, too. I've no objection mysel'. To my mind, there's a magic in women that can water a land, and make it prosper, if they use it right."

I sat there blinking. Not knowing what to make of my silence, he added: "The time might come when I'd be glad of a home in the south, in Elizabeth's country, maybe. It remains to be seen which way Scotland will go in the end, to the Romans or the Lutherans. But that's a small thing and not why I'm seeking you in marriage. I've plenty to offer in return, to even up the balance, anyhow. I can give you jewels and fine clothes and good horses, all you could wish. I want you in my bed, Ursula de la Roche. Now, how do you answer?"

I said all the right things. It was a serious proposal and this was no time for clever replies. I said that I recognized that he had paid me a compliment and that I thanked him for it and did not underestimate the benefits he was offering. I pointed out that although it was true that I had a Sussex manor house, and came of a family with a tradition of court service, I nevertheless had no noble connections, such as he had. I reminded him that I was only a natural child, with no known father.

He began to brush this aside as unimportant but I hastened on, saying I had had no idea of the depth of his feelings and apologizing for having accidentally inspired them. I had not meant to do so. I was sorry to give him pain.

But, I said earnestly, I couldn't marry him. I wasn't ready yet to marry again, and I wanted to go back to my home and stay there. I didn't want a life divided between homes more than four hundred miles apart.

"I feared ye'd say that," he said. "Ye wouldna wed me even to learn who'd pointed the finger at Erichs, though ye say ye're after the blood of whoever killed your cousin. But what if I name the man who ordered the killing? Not the name of the fellow who did the deed, no—but I know who ordered it."

The room had now become very dark indeed, except for the flicker of the firelight. The rain had begun, pattering at first and then blowing against the window as a north wind began to gust. "And," I said, "you'll tell me if I agree to marry you?"

"Aye. Another inducement. It could count as an extra emerald pendant, maybe?"

"I have no need of it. I think I already know who it was," I said.

He let out his breath in a long sigh. "I might have guessed that you would. Yes, I see."

"I'm sorry. I'm really very sorry. I hope you find some more suitable lady—a Scottish lady—who can share your life with you. Sir Brian, I think you should go now."

A little to my surprise, without further demur, he went, walking obediently out into the rain.

At that moment I felt genuinely sorry for him.

"I know, Dale," I said as we trotted along a stretch of track flanked by heathery hillside, traveling northwest, bending our heads against a keen wind and hoping that we were on the right road for Stirling. We had occasionally passed other riders and people trudging sturdily on foot, but not many, and just here, the road was empty apart from ourselves. "But I promise," I said, "once I have seen Master Henderson, we'll leave for home. I'll let him finish the investigating and bring my cousin's killers to justice—if there is any, in this country."

"And then we'll go home, ma'am?"

"Yes. We will. We'll be riding south in a few days now, and we won't hurry. We'll go by easy stages. We'll be home for the best of the spring. After that, I don't intend to go traveling anymore. Now what are you shaking your head for?"

"I'm sorry, ma'am. I didn't mean to shake my head. I didn't mean anything by it."

"You mean," I said resignedly, "that you don't believe me. That you are quite certain that I shan't be at home five minutes before I'll be off again on another mad adventure." I looked at Brockley, who was jogging on the other side of me, wearing a very large hat and looking unusually broad of chest. "And you," I said, "are wearing your old helmet under that hat, and your old breastplate under your jacket. I didn't even know you had them with you!"

"Stuffed into my shoulder bag, madam, from the outset," said Brockley. "I've always heard that the north was wild. Now that we're seemingly on the track of your cousin's killers, I felt it was a good time to put them on. As for Fran's doubts—forgive me, but they're hardly to be wondered at. In view of the past."

"I was younger then. I'm beginning to feel more staid as time goes on and I realize that I often ask too much of you, both of you. When we reach Withysham, we'll stay there."

"I should like to. The sooner we're back at Withysham, the happier I'll be. As steward, I shall find plenty of work waiting for me," Brockley said. "There always is in spring."

"Yes, I know." The three of us began to discuss Withysham, spring sowing, and an idea I had had for buying a new ram to improve our sheep flock. I spoke of my plan to find a tutor who could instruct Meg and myself in Greek, and a lady who could act as a companion for me. As we rode and talked, I scanned the terrain, wondering how many miles we still had to cover. We should

be riding parallel to the firth, which ought to be somewhere over to the right, but the road was low-lying
and the distance was hidden by folds of heathery hillside.

The firth was surely there, though, for now and then
seagulls glided over from that direction, and the mew-
ing of gulls mingled with the croak of a pair of ravens
disturbed by our hoofbeats. Despite the cold, I wished
that we were using the firth, that we had hired a boat and
were going by water instead, but Brockley had been
worried about leaving the horses in a strange livery stable ("You never know how careless they'll be if you're
not there to keep an eye on things, madam") and I
myself had wanted to set out southward, straight after
leaving Stirling, rather than return to Edinburgh to collect our mounts.

I was however finding the ride unusually arduous.
We were burdened with our luggage, which meant
bulging saddle- and shoulder bags, and also, I had been
sleeping badly again, to the point that on the previous
evening, Dale had given me another small dose of the
poppy draft.

Queen Mary had provided a generous amount and
we still had enough for several doses. I had therefore
slept well enough the night before, but the fact is that
although sick headaches do no lasting harm, they can
leave you unsteady for a while, and my two attacks had
been vicious. Despite the eight drugged hours just
behind me, I was feeling as weary as I knew the Brockleys were. My grip on my saddle pommels wasn't as
secure as usual.

Brockley was also glancing about him while he

talked, as if he too wanted to make out where the firth was. Then, in the midst of suggesting that the Withysham vicar ought to know Greek and might be able to recommend a tutor or even teach it himself, he suddenly stiffened and broke off, twisting in his saddle to look behind him. "There are riders behind us, madam, coming at a gallop. They're catching up fast."

"Perhaps they'll know whether we're really on the Stirling road. Better draw over to the side, though, in case they're on urgent business and don't slow down."

"Madam, there's something . . ."

His hand was on his sword hilt. "Careful!" I said. "There are at least a dozen of them. They'll probably go straight past us . . ."

But Brockley had understood what I had not: that the approaching horsemen had their eyes on us. As they raced toward us, they divided, so as to sweep around us on both sides, bringing us perforce to a frightened halt inside a circle of fierce, bearded riders armed with swords and pikes and bestriding small shaggy mounts with thick manes and tails, which swirled in the wind. They sat still for a moment, and then one of them, who was riding a silver-gray pony with a dark mane and tail, rode forward, pulling off the hat that shadowed his face so that I could see him clearly.

"Sir Brian Dormbois!"

"Mistress Ursula Blanchard—or Madame de la Roche, whichever you prefer. I give you good morning."

"I don't understand . . . we're on our way to Stirling, to where the queen is." Mentioning the queen sounded more impressive than merely saying that I wanted to see Rob Henderson. "Have you come to escort us? But who told you we were going?"

"Your landlord, sweetheart," Dormbois informed me, smile broad and molars glittering. "I spoke with him this morning, no mair nor half an hour after you left him. But you'll no' be getting to Stirling this day. The hospitality of Roderix Fort awaits you and the place is no great distance away. Be pleased to come with us, my lady."

20

Roderix Fort

I shouted: *"No!"* at Brockley as he drew his sword and rode forward. I could see what he was trying to do, which was to make a target of just one man and cleave a way out of the circle for us. Once out, we could indeed have stood a chance. The horses we had chosen for our ride to Scotland were built for stamina rather than speed but they still had longer legs than the hairy ponies that our assailants were riding. We might well have outdistanced them. Sir Brian had promised me "good horses," but by the look of it, we had very different ideas of what a good horse was.

But there were too many of them and it was too dangerous. Brockley ignored my cry of warning and a pike took him in the chest, hurling him out of his saddle. Dale screamed. Dormbois seized my horse's bridle, wrenching the reins from my grasp and whisking them over my horse's head. I struck at him with my riding whip, but he caught my arm, twisted the whip out of my hand, and threw it away. I heard him shout to his men to bring the tirewoman, saw Dale, her shoulder bag bumping from side to side, throw herself off her horse and go to Brockley, heard her despairing shriek of "*Roger!*" as someone scooped her up and put her in front of his saddle.

I glimpsed Brockley lying curled up on the ground, knees protecting his chest and belly and arms over his head as the horses milled close to him. Dale's loose mount, reins and stirrups flapping, actually leapt over him before bolting away over the heather and vanishing behind a rise. I remembered with thankfulness that Brockley was wearing a breastplate. Then we were galloping, galloping, leaving Brockley behind, racing westward. I thought wildly of the dagger I carried in my hidden pouch, but Dormbois was now out of arm's reach, and besides, I was outnumbered just as much as Brockley had been. "Where are we going?" I shouted at Dormbois as we tore along, my horse's head stretched out at the end of the reins, which the Scotsman was using as a tow rope.

He half turned his head to answer. "Roderix Fort! I told you! Where else?" he shouted.

A few minutes later we came to a fork and swerved to the right, taking a narrow uphill path. The ponies breasted it with energy, snorting and scrambling, and I glimpsed my gelding's eyes, white-ringed with fright as it was dragged relentlessly up the slope. Dale was on the pony alongside me, weeping bitterly and still vainly struggling. The man holding her had shoved her bag to one side so that he could hold her tightly against him, and the encircling arm that kept her in place astride the pony's withers looked as thick and strong as an iron girder.

We reached the crest of the slope and tore down the far side. I glimpsed small fields, divided by low stone walls, stretching away to either side, and here and there stooping figures with spades and hoes, who straightened up to stare as we went by. At the foot of the hill we sped through a cluster of hovels that huddled in the valley as though seeking protection from the wind. Poultry scattered before us and women with heavy boots below their thick skirts and shawls over their heads appeared in their doorways to watch us go by.

Another slope rose ahead of us, crowned with a building like a dark finger pointing to the gray sky. The path swept uphill again, this time on a zigzag. Sheep grazing on the hillside raised their heads as we approached and two of them hastily got out of our way, bleating. I saw that the dark building was a tower, and that between us and it was a stout gray wall with a wide gateway in it, standing open.

Without slowing down, we galloped through the entrance into an open grassy space where more sheep were grazing. Running, plaid-draped figures came from nowhere and I was dimly aware that behind us they were closing the gate. A track led across the grass to another wall and another gate, which two more plaid-clad men were in the process of opening. They had just got the second leaf back when we reached it and they stood back to let us through. They were youngish men, stocky, tough, and martial. If this was Roderix Fort, it was very much a fort.

Once through the second gate, we pulled up at last in a muddy, unpaved courtyard with outbuildings set untidily here and there against the outer wall. An open stable door had horse-droppings and wisps of straw in front of it and a stablehand, carrying a bucket of oats toward it from what looked like a granary, stopped to look at us. Another building, round with a high slate roof, had a smoking chimney and gave off a smell of cooking meat. The tower was in front of us, a tall, square, battlemented keep, built of the same harsh gray stone as the walls. Steps went up to a main entrance; the ground floor, as at Bycroft, was surely a medieval-style undercroft for animals or storage.

Dormbois was out of his saddle and lifting me out of mine. "I've grooms for the horses. Come with me. Fraser, be bringing the tirewoman and for God's sake stop her greeting and howling like that. She's here to serve her mistress, not harrow us all by wailing like a soul demented."

"Why shouldn't she wail?" I shouted at him. "That was her husband you left lying in a heap on the ground! He's probably dead!"

"Not he, more's the pity. I thocht he was, but I looked back and saw him get up. He'll mak trouble for me, I daresay, though I daresay too that I'll manage," retorted Dormbois. "Though how he could get up again after that spear thrust, I wouldna know. He's a tougher mannie than he looked, that one!"

The breastplate had done its work, then. With luck, I thought gratefully, Brockley was not only alive but not too badly hurt. And he was free. I could only hope that he would be able to raise the alarm and bring help, although how he would know where to bring it was another matter.

"Dale!" As the man holding her got down and heaved her and her bag to the ground after him, I caught her hand. "It's all right. Brockley's all right! He had armor under his jacket. Stop crying! It's all right!"

"Aye, haul your noise!" said the man called Fraser, marching forward beside us, as Dormbois dragged me toward the steps. I saw that he had a limp and realized that this was probably the brother of Hamish Fraser, the steward of St. Margaret's and quite possibly the man who had stuck a blade in my cousin. Shuddering, I pulled Dale close to me and farther away from him. I wanted nothing to do with any Fraser.

Dale's wails subsided but her tears continued to flow. We were hustled in at the main door and through a wide, chilly hall with an empty hearth and scarcely any furnishings beyond a couple of settles, one long table in the center, and a profusion of stags' antlers on the stone walls. The flagged floor was innocent even of rushes, let alone rugs, and there wasn't a cushion to be seen. A pile of fleeces on one of the settles and the fact that logs were stacked in an alcove by the fireplace were the only hints of comfort.

The cheerless hall even seemed to annoy Dormbois. "Can you idle loons not even light a fire when you know the laird's coming?" he bellowed as he haled us across the floor, and once again figures came running from nowhere and presumably set about transferring firewood to the hearth. I didn't have time to watch. A flight of spiral stairs came down into the far corner of the hall and Dormbois ran me and Dale straight to it.

Up and up we went, stumbling now and then on the narrow, wedge-shaped steps. The only light came through occasional arrow slits and the staircase smelled of damp stone. We passed narrow arched doorways at successively high levels, until at last, Sir Brian thrust one of the doors open and propelled us through it. Breathless, we came to a halt in what appeared to be a parlor of sorts. Or perhaps the medieval term *solar* would be better, for the room and its contents were very old-fashioned, with narrow, deep-set windows and a disused loom in one corner. Even the lute lying on one of the window seats was of a pattern that had been out-of-date when I was a child.

One wall was handsomely paneled though, and here at last was a hearth that actually had a fire in it and a sheepskin rug in front. I went to stand there, holding out my hands to the warmth, and Dale, miserably, came with me. She pulled her shoulder bag off and automatically helped me slip mine off as well. We put them down on the fleece. Dormbois had stopped in the middle of the room.

"It'll be rough and ready by southron standards, I daresay, but we'll set that right in time. You'll say what you want and it'll be bought. Edinburgh's been getting a gentler place since Her Majesty came from France and there's plenty of pretty furnishings to be got there. You'll appoint your parlor as you will." He nodded, as though congratulating himself on these kindly plans. "I see that at least the fire in here's been lit as I ordered. There'll be wine and food presently and I'll send someone with hot water and towels."

To listen to him, you would have thought that we

were willing guests and he the perfect host. I looked at him in bewildered disbelief.

"The fire's been lit as you ordered?" I echoed.

"Yes, indeed. I wouldna give you a cold welcome, lassie."

"But when did you order it? You were in Edinburgh yesterday!"

"I sent a rider off last night," said Dormbois casually. "I took my men and went to fetch you from that lodging this morning but you'd gone. To Stirling, Master Muir said, after I'd stuck a dagger under his nose to get some sense from him. Well, that was easy enough. I'd only to catch you up on the road."

"And now?"

"Here you are in my home, Roderix Fort. All's ready. It'll all be done decent. Father Bell's ready to wed us; I thocht that would please you best."

"So that's what this is about. Forced marriage." Beside me, Dale let out a sob. I rested a hand on her shoulder in an attempt to calm her. I wished I had someone to keep me calm as well. I was very angry and also very frightened. In fact, I was wishing I had tried to close with Hugh Stannard's semi-proposal of marriage. I was no longer aware of Dormbois's attractions. He had left Brockley, my dear faithful Brockley, Dale's husband, lying on the ground, to die for all Dormbois cared. He was an enemy now.

"Please understand," I said. "I meant what I said yesterday. I have no wish to remarry. I . . ."

"Grief passes, lassie. I don't dislike it that you still have such feeling for your dead husband. It shows a good heart and maybe one day, you'll mourn as much for me. But that's just it. Life's short and the dead don't come back. It's good to weep awhile but not too long."

"Sir Brian, please listen! Yesterday, I said no, and I meant no. I cannot and I will not marry you. I ask you to remember that marriage vows taken under duress are not lawful. If you drag me to the altar with a knife in my ribs, I might give my wedding promises but they would mean nothing. Nor would any honorable priest agree to proceed with the ceremony."

"Father Bell will," Dormbois assured me. "He may argue with me over doctrine but he knows far how he can go. I'm his landlord. He comes up here every day but he lives in one of those cottages at the foot of the hill. I can turn him out and put him into the road in the clothes he's wearing. But it'll not come to that. He'll obey, once you agree. Though he won't have to worry that ye're taking vows at knifepoint. What a notion! You've hurt my feelings," said Dormbois, in tones that verged on the plaintive. "What do you take me for? I came to you yesterday with an honest proposal of marriage and I'm still the same honest lover. If you refuse to wed, then you refuse. So be it."

I stared at him, and he gave me that glittering smile. I saw it now as diabolical.

"I can wait," he said. "At least, I can wait for the wedding vows. But love's hard to keep reined in."

"Love!"

"Aye, love, my lass. As you'll learn before long, but when it comes to the point," he added in soothing tones, "it'll no' be so bad. Ever watched a falconer straighten out tangled tail feathers on a hawk? He has to hold them in hot water and it doesnae hurt the bird, but it feels the heat coming up and could harm itself struggling if it were let, so a good man holds the hawk firm and strong so it canna fight, and so the job is done easy and painless. I'll hold you firm and strong tonight, sweetheart, and I think there'll be peace between us before the dawn."

"Oh, ma'am, what are you going to do?"

"God knows, Dale. I don't."

Dormbois had left us alone in the parlor. A little investigation had shown that it was actually part of a suite. It had three doors. One led to a privy and one, alarmingly, opened into a bedchamber that contained a lady's toilet stand and an ominously wide bed, hung with green velvet, made up with linen sheets, and piled with glossy fur rugs.

The third door was the one that gave onto the stairs and this was bolted on the outside. There were windows, all of them looking down onto a sheer drop of something like ninety feet. When I pushed the parlor window open and leaned out, I realized that I could see the firth. There was a lantern bracket next to the window. Presumably Roderix Fort stood so tall that it was also used as a lighthouse. When the visibility was good enough, that would be. In the west, I could see the gray skirts of more approaching rain. I stared wistfully at the world outside. Bleak and lonely though it was, it was still the world of freedom.

"If we had a rope," I said, "we could tie it to that lantern holder and escape. You haven't got a rope in your shoulder bag, have you, Dale?"

"No, ma'am, what would I want with a rope?" Poor Dale was quite unable to see that I was trying to lighten the air with a feeble joke. "I've just a shawl and some shoes and my linen and our medicines! My only proper changes of clothes were in the saddlebags and the horse ran away! I just can't abide not having a change of clothes, ma'am."

"We can ask if someone could go to find your horse. If so, you might get your saddlebags back. I know one thing I'm going to do, Dale, or rather, not do."

"Ma'am?"

"I'm not going to remain Dormbois's captive, whatever happens. I've no doubt," I said grimly, "that he's capable of forcing me into bed and even into marriage, but I will still, sooner or later, escape. As I once did from Matthew, at the beginning. And then we'll go home to England. It doesn't matter even if I have been married at knifepoint or whatever. I've no wish to wed anyone else, and besides, I can probably get an annulment on grounds of duress. The queen will help. Whatever happens, we will somehow get out of here. But it ought to be as soon as possible, before that man gets me with child. Is there any vinegar among the medicines?"

"No, ma'am. But when they feed us, I can ask for some!" At the thought of doing something useful, Dale brightened a little. "I have a sponge in my shoulder bag. I can cut it up for you, ma'am."

"That should hold off the danger for a while," I agreed. "If I can't hold Dormbois off." I stiffened. "Someone's coming up the stairs!"

I turned to face the door, bracing myself in case of a

new threat, but it proved to be a servant lad with a tray. There seemed to be no women servants in Roderix. The man Fraser came protectively with him, as though Dormbois feared that I might have wrenched a leg off the table and stationed myself behind the door, ready to knock out the first man to enter. Fraser closed the door behind them and stood with his back to it while the lad set out the food and drink on the table.

"You *are* Jamie Fraser, aren't you?" I said. "Your brother's Hamish Fraser of St. Margaret's. I know the Thursbys."

I found it hard to mention the names either of Hamish or the Thursbys, but in this situation I needed to form what links I could. There was always the hope of bribing or suborning my captor's servants.

Jamie was older than Hamish but similar in looks to his brother, with the same stocky body and deceptively boyish face. His blue eyes, however, were hard and blank as he stared back at me.

"Aye. Jamie Fraser's the name."

"I thought you were the bailiff—the land agent," I said. "Sir Brian has spoken of you. But here you are indoors."

"Aye. I've taken over from the old steward that was due for his pension. I've a limp, as ye've no doot seen. Broke ma leg a few months back and it's no' a pairfect mend."

"That was unlucky," I said. "I know that when your brother came to see you, there was some idea of inviting him to replace you, but it came to nothing. Has someone been found to take over from you after all?"

"Kind of you to take sich an interest, mistress," said

Fraser. He sounded as though he wasn't sure whether he was being sarcastic or not. I wasn't sure, either. "True enough, Sir Brian's found someone. And ye're right; this is no place for Hamish. He doesna like Scotland. It's his homeland but he doesna like it! I sent word when I was laid up and wondering if I'd ever walk again, asking him to come and see me, but I had to send twice before he'd do it, and when he was here, we couldn't even get him to go out round Sir Brian's lands and tak a look at them. He stuck under this roof like a delicate maiden, the whole time he was here."

"Really?" I said. "He didn't strike me," I added, "as a particularly delicate or . . . foolishly fastidious fellow."

"Can't always go by looks, lassie. Hamish doesna care to soil his hands or tire his legs and that's the truth. He . . ."

"Ma'am," said Dale, who was inspecting the viands, "we have good meat and bread here and salt too, but no pepper and no vinegar." She addressed the lad. "Can you fetch pepper and vinegar for us?"

The boy looked blank but Fraser said something to him in broad Scots, in an impatient tone, and he nodded and scurried out. We heard him hastening away down the stairs.

I looked at Fraser thoughtfully, and tried a long shot, knowing that it probably wouldn't hit its target, but all the same, determined to try.

"I have some money, Fraser. How much do you want for leaving a good long coil of rope here in this room by—well, by accident?"

Dale immediately understood what I was after and looked ready to faint at the idea of swarming down the outside of the tower on a rope. I didn't like the notion much myself. I was almost relieved when Fraser said coldly: "I'm no' for sale, lassie. Sir Brian's a good laird and he'll mak a good husband too if ye've the sense to give him the chance."

"You obviously admire him," I said gloomily. "And you love Roderix Fort, too, from what you say."

"So will ye, one day."

I doubted it. If Dormbois's first wife had died in childbed, his second, according to him, had died simply because of the starkness of her husband's stone tower. I could understand it, all too well.

My silence seemed to spur Fraser into words. "I tell ye, my father was bailiff here before me and his father before him and I'd live nowhere else. My brother has no sense. The place we were offering him was the best in the world to my way of thinking but wud he have any part of it? Not he. Wouldna stay above four days and scarce poked his nose out of doors once all that time."

"I expect it was cold," I said.

"No colder than Northumberland, from all I've heard! But four miserable days, they were all he'd give me. Got here at twilight, saying he was tired because he'd been riding hard for two days—they breed good horses at St. Margaret's, I grant you. He took the laird by surprise! Sir Brian was hoping that he'd come for the second time of asking, and himself came back from Edinburgh a-purpose to see him if so, and was here the next midday and found Hamish here already. But four clear days, that was all Hamish would stay. When Sir Brian rode back to Holyrood, my brother rode off with him, wanting to see the big city and buy gewgaws for his wife." He grinned, briefly. "They left at dawn and Hamish said they'd be in Edinburgh the same day and he'd spend the whole of the next one in the town because it would be the fourteenth and that was the feast of some popish saint or other, to do with love . . ."

"St. Valentine," I said.

". . . and his wife would like it if he bought her something on that date. Popish saints!" said Fraser with a snort. It looked as though some of Dormbois's adherents had been far ahead of him on the road to the Protestant faith.

The boy reappeared with the pepper and vinegar. He put them on the table and then he and Fraser took themselves off. I pulled the table over toward a window seat and signed to Dale to join me.

"Thank you for getting the vinegar," I said. "I'll be prepared before Dormbois comes back."

"Ma'am, whatever happens, even if you get hold of some rope, I can't climb down the tower on it—I can't!"

"I don't think I can, either," I admitted, as I took some cold meat. "This looks good and the bread seems fresh. We'd break our necks, as like as not. I think . . ."

In the act of breaking a piece of bread, I froze.

"What is it, ma'am?"

"Dale!"

"Ma'am, what *is* it?"

"Just a minute!" I looked about me, saw nothing in the form of writing materials, and began to count on my fingers. "I'm wondering . . . Dale, from what Fraser said, Hamish must have left here on the thirteenth of February. He was in Edinburgh on the fourteenth, St. Valentine's Day."

"Yes, ma'am. The day of the inquiry. We know he attended that."

"Yes, but that isn't what I mean. His brother said just now that Hamish was here for four clear days before that and arrived at dusk on the fifth day, counting backward. Four clear days before the thirteenth would be the twelfth, eleventh, tenth, and ninth, so he must have arrived on the evening of the eighth. Edward was killed on the night of . . ." I counted on my fingers again. ". . . yes, of the eighth! Hamish can't have been here *and* in Edinburgh murdering my cousin! If what Fraser is saying is true, we've got it all wrong. It can't have been Hamish Fraser, and in that case, the Thursbys are very likely innocent too."

I didn't mind being wrong. I had liked the Thursbys. They had almost certainly been responsible for betraying enemy agents, but not, it now seemed, for murdering my cousin. I could hardly blame them for the first, and concerning the second, I could only be relieved.

But if they and Hamish Fraser were innocent of the murder, then who was guilty? The only person who might have the answer was Dormbois.

21

The Price of a Name

The washing water should have come before the food but followed it half an hour later instead and wasn't all that hot, either. There was no doubt that the hospitality of Roderix Fort was on the rough-and-ready side.

Still, there were warm towels to go with it, and the saddlebags from my horse were brought up at the same time. Having washed and tidied ourselves, Dale and I unpacked. We had lost her saddlebags but we had a good many things safely with us: facecloths, a hairbrush, my clean stockings and underlinen, and our medicines, including the remainder of the queen's poppy draft and the ingredients for the dose that sometimes relieved my headaches. A sick headache would have been quite welcome just then but migraine is a wayward visitor who never comes when it might actually be useful.

Dale's shoulder bag yielded the sponge she had

mentioned and three or four spare vials. These we filled with vinegar, and with the small dagger that I carried in my hidden pouch, we cut up the sponge. Then we stowed the vinegar and the sponge pieces back in the bag in readiness.

Shortly after that, Dormbois came to the parlor once again, to ask us how we did.

I had made up my mind. I had little to lose, after all. I had thought of some wild and desperate expedients, but just as I didn't think I could climb down a ninety-foot tower on a rope even if I had a rope, I didn't think either that I could stab Dormbois with my dagger during the night. To do that, I would need a mentality like that of the man who killed Edward. I hadn't, and didn't wish to have, either.

Not that it made much difference, because there were in any case some powerful arguments against it. Even if I succeeded, which certainly couldn't be guaranteed, how would we get out of the fort? And if we did, the body would soon be found and we would be hunted down . . .

No. The dagger was not the answer, any more than it had been on the ride to Roderix Fort. It was just possible, though, that I might be able to negotiate. At least I could try, and if it cost me a night . . .

Oh, Gerald. Oh, Matthew. My two dear lost ones. What would you have me do?

They could not answer. I thought then and think now that they would have wanted me to resist, not by risking my own life in an attempt at midnight murder, but at least by struggling until I could struggle no more. I don't think they would have wanted me to—sell myself.

But it would come to the same thing in the end whether I resisted or not, and meanwhile, I might gain some information.

And so, my decision taken, I greeted Sir Brian Dormbois calmly. Yes, we had washed and eaten—"Though not in that order. Your servants seem to be trying hard but their training leaves much to be desired."

"You'll tak them in hand, maybe? Marguerite tried for a while and would have done well, if she'd lived long enough. She had a good way with servants," Dormbois said.

"You're assuming that I will live here from now on," I said.

"And so you will, and it'll not be the terrible fate you imagine," Dormbois informed me reassuringly. "As you'll find out."

"Sir Brian," I said, "I want to make a bargain with you."

That interested him. He sat down on a settle and looked up at me inquiringly. "We Scots have a reputation for liking a bargain. What's on offer?"

"I will give you one night of my life," I said. "One night. Willingly, with no resistance; indeed with co-operation. One night—in return for the name of the man who ordered the death of my cousin Edward Faldene."

"I thocht ye knew it."

"I have realized that I was wrong."

"One willing, complaisant night, as the price of a name?"

"Yes," I said as steadily as I could. I couldn't believe now that I had ever been drawn to this man. I wasn't sure that yielding to him wouldn't prove as impossible as stabbing him. But I would have to try. "And after that," I said. "My freedom."

"No, no, lassie, that's too hard a bargain! I want you for a lifetime and all you're offering is a single night!"

"A happy night, worth having," I said. "Otherwise," I told him, "I'll fight with all the strength I have. Don't mistake me, Sir Brian. I'll destroy your pleasure. It seems plain enough that you'll use force if you have to, but you say you don't want to, and if that's so, then you have a conscience of sorts, and I'll wake it up! By God, I shall! I'll make you hate yourself. When my strength gives out—oh yes, I know it will—then I'll lie like a log of wood, like a corpse. I'll sicken you of yourself. If you keep me here, I'll sicken you of me. I'll moan and whine and pine till you can't stand the sound of my voice or the sight of my face. But I'll give you one kind night—for the sake of that name."

Dormbois came to his feet. His eyes were sparkling as if the sun were on them. "By God, lassie, how I like you! I'll have a wager with you! I'll tak the bargain. One night from you, one name from me, and then you and your woman can walk out of my gate free as air—if that's what you then want. After a night with me, in friendly style, and who's to say you'll want to walk anywhere? That's the heart of my wager. I'm gambling on myself to be man enough tonight to win you."

I said: "We had horses. We should ride out of the gate, not walk."

"Och no!" He shook his head. "No, no, if it comes to it, I'll keep the horses. To remember you by, if nothing else."

I had been going to ask that a search be made for Dale's horse. I thought better of it.

Dormbois, meanwhile, had crossed the room and opened a cupboard in the paneling. I hadn't realized it was there, for the knob of the cupboard perfectly matched the wood behind. Inside, was a shelf with a row of about a dozen tall, narrow goblets on it. He took four of them out and brought them to the table. I looked at them in some surprise, for I had never seen anything like them before. They were beautiful, but most unusual. The stems were short and most of the height was taken up by the cups, which had the proportions, roughly, of a daffodil trumpet, and were fluted in much the same way. They weren't daffodil color, however, but were made of rich brown earthenware, glazed to a high polish and delicately edged with gold around their fluted tops.

"These are a tradition in my family," Dormbois said. "On any grand occasion, before any great undertaking or if there are oaths to swear, we drink to the enterprise, whatever it is, in these. One moment." He went to the door of the stairs, put his head out, and bellowed: "Fraser!"

There was an answering call from below and Dormbois, a hand cupped around his mouth, shouted: "Come up here and bring wine for four! In a jug! The goblets are here!"

There was an interval while Fraser was fetching the wine. Trying to preserve an atmosphere of civility and dignity, I sat down and made conversation about whatever harmless subjects came into my head. I asked which crops grew in this climate—oats and barley were the answers, of course—and whether there were any books or embroidery materials with which Dale and I could pass the time. All ours had been in the saddlebags of Dale's runaway horse. There were books somewhere, Dormbois said. Marguerite had liked poetry. He'd find them for us.

When Fraser arrived with a jug of red wine, he seemed to know what this little ritual was all about. He filled the four goblets, which used up all the wine, and each of us, Fraser himself included, took one.

"To a bargain!" pronounced Dormbois. "A bargain between Sir Brian Dormbois of Roderix Fort, and Madame Ursula de la Roche, also known as Mistress Ursula Blanchard, of Withysham. That's right, is it not, my lady?"

"Yes."

"You are our witness, Fraser, and this is the bargain," Dormbois declared, holding his goblet high. "That tonight, she will be as my bride, bonny and buxom as ever she was to the husbands who went before me. And that tomorrow, I shall tell her a certain name which she desires to know, and then, if she still wishes it, set her free to walk unmolested out of Roderix Fort, with her tirewoman. Though I shall strive my best to see that she does not so wish, for her place here as my bride is assured forever, if she will only choose it. Drink!"

We drank, with some difficulty, owing to the narrowness of the goblets. One's nose got in the way. The dark, narrow shape made the wine look like ink, as well. It was good wine, though. Dormbois had a worthwhile cellar. There were gleams of refinement in his peculiar nature and his equally peculiar home.

Such a pity, I thought, that the barbarian in him took over so easily, and at all the wrong moments.

That night, I sold myself, body and spirit alike. To my life's end, I shall remember that night with bitterness.

I was carrying out my part of a bargain. I kept that in mind throughout. It was for me to smile, to look willing, to respond, to welcome, and all of it was false. I longed so much for Matthew. It was nearly a year since I had parted from him, and things had not been quite right between us then. Now he was gone and this reminder of what we had had together broke my heart. I wanted to weep. And must not.

In fact, once we were in the dark, with the candles out and the bed curtains closed around us, a few tears did escape me. I tried, in the dark, to pretend that the man I was embracing was Matthew but it was no use. I was conscious, all the time, of Dormbois's own shape and texture. The bones and muscle of his body and limbs were different; the texture of his skin was different; his smell was different, sour compared to Matthew's smell.

He was different too from that other memory, farther back, of Gerald. Nothing at all was familiar or comforting. I was left with only one recourse, to do as whores do, and pretend.

One of the troubles between Matthew and me was that because we had such different beliefs, he had secrets that he kept from me. Gerald and I, though, had talked of anything and everything. Among the things that Gerald had told me (though not from personal experience) was that even with a whore, some men still want to give pleasure. They want her to enjoy it. Whores mostly don't; they do it as a job and spend the time thinking about something else. When enjoyment is demanded, they act.

Dormbois wanted enjoyment from me. He began with prolonged, unhurried nuzzlings and caresses that made his wishes amply plain and so . . . I acted. Having known the real thing, I knew how to create the semblance. At least, that is how it was the first time. But the second time . . .

The second time is the worst of my memories of that night.

After that first union, Dormbois slept. I did not, but lay beside him open-eyed and wretched, waiting for him to wake up again, knowing that he would, and to me that time seemed endless. Then, while the night was still deep, he stirred and turned over, reaching drowsily out to me and his caresses began once more.

And this time, against my will, treacherous as quick-sand, my wayward body answered him. I fought it. Inside my head, I screamed to it to be silent, to be unfeeling, to refuse its own needs, its own instincts. It would not. It had been almost a year since I parted from Matthew. I was still young, and more hungry than I knew.

That second time, I did not have to act. Against my own will, I gave the reality and not the semblance. Then he fell asleep once more, and as the gray dawn began to seep through a chink in the bed curtains, I cried silently but in good earnest, the tears mingling with the sweat of my own unwanted passion.

There was only one part of that night that I can recall

without shame, and that was earlier, after our first love-making, if it can be called that. Before he fell asleep he talked to me for a little while, I think trying to build some kind of friendly bridge between us. He said: "You were interested, were you not, by those brown goblets? You'd expect goblets used for ceremony to be of gold or silver or jewel-studded, maybe?"

I responded politely. "I suppose so. I've never seen goblets made of earthenware before."

"They're not English. They're Roman—modern Roman, that would be, nothing to do with Nero or Julius Caesar. My father's father—his name was François Dormbois—liked to travel. My da took after him—which is how he came to Scotland. But when he was young, before he was wed, Grandda's itchy feet took him the other way, south, to Rome. He wanted to see the pope. He was of good family, and on the way he'd look for lodgings in the houses of good families when he could, but one night he found the dark coming down on him and nowhere to lodge but in a little village place. He knocked on doors and found beds for him and his man, with a potter."

"Go on," I said, becoming intrigued despite myself, and finding that I preferred this version of Dormbois, telling a story with his mind on telling it well, rather than on impressing me.

"Aye, well. The pottery adjoined the house and had a kiln in a kind of shed behind it. In the night, Grandda smelled smoke and woke up, and just as well, for something had gone awry with the kiln and it was afire and the shed as well. He roused the house with shouting, and they all woke up and went rushing to the well for water, and the fire was put out. I never knew him but he told the tale to my da and Da told it to me. Seems there was little danger to life, for the buildings were only one story and everyone could have got out of windows if they'd had to. Grandda said he wasnae any great hero, just for smelling smoke and giving the alarm.

"But the potter was grateful, because the fire would have taken the workshop next, and destroyed the wheel and the work he was doing and all the things that were made and ready for them that had ordered them. Grandda was good with his hands and didnae think it shame for a nobly born man to use them, though some think in that fashion. He stayed on awhile to help rebuild the shed and the kiln, and the potter made him these goblets and fired them in the new kiln as soon as it was ready. He made them to a new pattern, just for Grandda, so that no one else in the world would have anything the same, and he even used some of a little store of gold leaf that he kept handy for special orders, which was generous of him for he wasnae wealthy. It was the best thanks he could offer.

"So I grew up," said Dormbois, "with those goblets as part of my life. My grandda and my da both had affection for them, and as I told ye, they became something to drink from on special occasions. They're a bit awkward for common use, as ye may have noticed."

"Yes, I did," I said, and he laughed and so did I, and just for a moment we were two human beings sharing a moment of harmless amusement that had nothing to do with male and female.

But it didn't last. He slept, and then woke, and our

second joining had no easy conversation afterward. He slept again, and I wept.

I did drift into slumber eventually, but not for long. Soon, too soon, it was time to rise. Hoping that my face didn't reveal my nighttime tears, I gave my companion good morning. He sat up. Below his mustache, his chin was gray with stubble, and his black hair was tangled. He grinned at me. "And how did I do, my sweet bird?"

"You were excellent," I told him.

"So were you." He eyed me glitteringly, and, with resignation, I saw that he was going to pounce on me again.

"One moment. I need the privy," I said, and fled from the bedchamber into the parlor where Dale had spent the night on a truckle bed. "New sponge," I muttered to her as I went past, and then waited in the privy until she had handed in a fresh piece of vinegar-soaked sponge. The one I had donned the night before, I tossed down the privy chute. Then, I arranged a pleasant smile on my face and went back to bed.

After a night that had been all but sleepless, I had no energy left either to respond or to pretend a response beyond a few sighs and murmurs. When it was over, I lay quiet on the pillow and said: "I have fulfilled my promise. Will you now fulfill yours? Who ordered my cousin's death—and why?"

"Strewth, woman, can you no' wait until we're up and dressed? You havenae told me whether or no you're willing to stay with me or whether you intend to walk out o' Roderix this morning."

"I haven't yet decided," I said ruthlessly. I was lying but wanted to keep an advantage over him until I had the information I had bought so dearly.

"I'll tell you one thing. It isn't a name you'll like to hear."

"I still want to know what it is."

"Verra well." He too lay back on the pillow, linking his hands behind his head. He turned his head so as to look at me and smiled.

"Master Rob Henderson," he said.

I said in bewilderment: "Why? Why would Henderson do such a thing?"

Dormbois shrugged. "He's Cecil's creature, is he no'? Edward Faldene was carrying news to Queen Mary which Cecil didnae want her to have; that's what I heard."

"From whom?"

"Ah. Well now, that was not in the bargain. You have the name you wanted. I'll not reveal to a living soul how I know, but Rob Henderson it was, and that's the truth. I said you wouldnae like it."

"It's time to get up," I said.

He called Dale to me and then went to dress in the parlor, shouting down the stairs for someone to bring him fresh garments and leaving me to dress in private. I told Dale what he had said.

"Do you believe him, ma'am?" she asked.

"Yes. Yes, I do." I puckered my brow, thinking. "The reason *must* concern that list. I'm sure now that it never reached Queen Mary. I fancy that Henderson ordered Edward's death on account of it, though I still don't quite understand why. But I suppose whoever did the killing took the list and either handed it to Master Henderson or destroyed it."

"The list that Master Henderson gave you, madam, that he said was a copy of an old one . . ."

"Oh, it was. If he's got the new one, he wasn't likely to admit it to me!" I said grimly. I was still trying to think. "I must say," I said, "that I'd like to know how on earth anyone found out that Edward was carrying the thing in the first place or what was in it, and I do *not* see why they couldn't just have taken it without murdering Edward, but . . . yes, I believe Dormbois. It would be such a pointless and unlikely lie! Oh, dear God, if only he keeps his word and lets us leave here today. I want to go home!"

Since I had my saddlebags, I had spare clothes and was able to put on a fresh gown. Tidy and miserable, I went out to the parlor at last to find that breakfast, in the form of ale, buttermilk, porridge, salt, and what looked like fresh bread, had been brought upstairs. Dormbois, who was already eating, was fully dressed as well, in a businesslike doublet and hose of black woolen cloth, though, since he was a man of position, the slashings on the doublet sleeves were of satin, patterned in silver and pale blue.

The outfit wasn't new, for I could see the dull patch on the doublet where it had been sponged, probably to get rid of wine or gravy stains. It was typical, somehow, of the Scottish nobility: a mixture of the luxurious and the scruffy.

The morning had turned bright, the best I had seen since I came to Scotland, and a shaft of warm sunlight slanted across the room. As we sat down at the table,

Dormbois looked at me questioningly across it, lifting his dark brows.

"You promised that if I chose, I should go free this morning," I said. "Will you keep your word? For I still wish to go free, to go home. I am sorry."

He looked at Dale and jerked his head. "Tak your breakfast into the other room, woman," he said, and Dale, looking frightened of him, gathered up a beaker of buttermilk and a bowl of porridge and hastily departed.

As the door closed behind her, Dormbois said: "Will nothing change your mind?" in a voice so grave and sad that I actually found it touching.

"I said, I am sorry," I told him. "But I can't stay. I can't. I'm homesick, for one thing. As Marguerite was, I think. Would you want me to die as she did?"

"You are a stronger woman than Marguerite. Ursula, can nothing at all persuade you? If I were to go down on one knee . . ."

"No," I said, putting out a hand to check him as he slid from his seat and began to kneel. "Please don't. It won't make any difference."

"Would this make a difference?"

He caught hold of me and pulled me against him. I endured his kiss with my lips closed. He put me back from him and his eyes were angry. "So it was all acting, in the night, was it? The performance that women of the night put on for their buyers?"

I searched his eyes, trying to find in them some trace of understanding or even guilt and seeing nothing but a hard brightness. "It was more dignified than the alternative," I said. "Wasn't it?"

He didn't answer. I said: "Will you keep your word?"

Dormbois sighed, taking his seat again. Then he nodded. "Aye. I had the feeling all along that that would be the way of it. Obstinacy's your middle name, lassie." He picked up his porridge spoon. "I'm a man of my word. You go on foot for I'm not minded to make it easy for you, but yes, you can go. Fill up with a good breakfast, now. It's a long walk to Stirling, though there are hamlets on the way. I'll see you have bread and meat to take with you and water flasks."

I could hardly believe it, but he appeared to have given in. Perhaps, I thought, I had not proved such a delightful bed partner as I supposed. Perhaps he was wondering if a different lady might indeed prove a better wife. To my own astonishment, I felt almost indignant.

But Dale, when I went to tell her what was afoot, was full of thankfulness. "I only hope we can find Roger, ma'am. If he wasn't much hurt, he'll have made for Stirling, I suppose. Maybe we'll find him there."

"We'll find him, anyway," I reassured her. "We won't set off for home until we have."

I didn't want to waste time, partly for fear that Dormbois would change his mind, but there was no sign of that. He left us to finish breakfast in private, telling me to call him when we were ready to go. We made all the haste we could. The food was filling, though the porridge, like yesterday's washing water, wasn't as hot as I would have liked, probably because it had had to be brought across the courtyard from the round building I had seen on the way in, which must be the kitchen. The appointments of Roderix Fort really were medieval.

After breakfast we packed our shoulder bags, stuffing in the things from my saddlebags as best we could, and slung them on over our cloaks. I called for Dormbois and he came to escort us downstairs.

At the door, we were each given a basket containing food and a leather water flask. Dormbois walked with us across the courtyard and the grassy outer enclosure. Both the inner and the outer gates must have been barred the previous night, for they had to be unbolted and opened for us, by gatekeepers who seemed to be constantly on duty. Once the main gate was open, I kissed Dormbois good-bye. It seemed fair, and I was grateful to him for releasing me with such good grace. Together, Dale and I set off down the zigzag path toward the hovels in the valley.

At least the morning was fine, even warm. "We'd better go at a steady pace," I said to Dale. "We'll only tire ourselves if we try to hurry. Someone in those cottages may know how far it is to the next hamlet toward Stirling. I wish I'd thought to ask Dormbois. Dale? What is it?"

She had stopped and was looking over her shoulder. "I think, ma'am," she said tightly, "that if you want to ask him anything, you'll still have a chance. Look."

I spun around. Half a dozen riders were spilling out of the gates of Roderix, and in the lead was Dormbois. I knew him by his steed, the silver-gray pony with the dark mane and tail. I looked desperately around for somewhere we could flee to, which would offer shelter, but there was nowhere. We did start to run, but the riders, regardless of the steep slope and the sharp bends of the zigzags, were galloping down the hill, and in a moment they had encircled us.

"What's this?" I demanded, just as one of the riders leaned out of his saddle and seized hold of Dale. She shrieked and flailed at him with her basket, but just as when we were captured the first time, her captor hauled her up before his pommel as though she weighed nothing. "You promised!" I shouted furiously at Dormbois.

"I promised you should walk unmolested out of the gate of Roderix Fort," Dormbois informed me coolly. "And so you did. I never promised not to come after you; I never promised not to bring you back. I've come to tak you home, my sweet."

He reached down for me. I backed away but immediately bumped into the shoulder of another pony. Dormbois pushed his own mount up closer, dropped his reins, twitched my basket out of my hand, tossed it away with the remark that I wouldnae be needing that now; there was food aplenty in Roderix, and then caught me around the body with both hands and lifted. The strength of these men was terrifying. Like Dale, I was hoisted from the ground to the pony as though I were thistledown. Though I knew it to be useless, I still instinctively resisted, twisting around, pushing at his chest, trying to break his grip and slip off again.

He had not put on a cloak. On this warm spring morning, his doublet was enough. As I turned and thrust my hands against him, my nose was only an inch from the buttons down the front.

They were covered in black velvet and on each, a crisscross pattern had been worked, in tiny stitches of silver thread.

And one of them was missing.

22

No Sense of Honor

The shock turned my muscles to water. I stopped struggling. I think my body instinctively adopted stillness as a protection, like a red deer calf in the long grass when a fox is prowling. I let myself be borne unresisting back up the hill and through the gates. Dormbois dismounted before the main steps and lifted me down, and I let him lead me in. Dale had given in, as well. Pale and wet-eyed, her pockmarks as visible as black spots on rose leaves, she walked silently at my side.

But when we had once more been taken up to the parlor and thrust inside, I found the courage to face Dormbois and say: "If you have any feeling for me at all, if your protestations of passion and your endearments in the night were anything more than empty words, then leave me in peace for a while. Dale will look after me."

"If I strike you as rough or dishonorable, lassie,"

said Dormbois, "then you can take it that my protestations and endearments were a muckle more than empty words. What I feel for you is too strong for dainty wooing in a garden full o' roses. I'll leave you awhile, to think and calm your spirits. You'll find occupation here; I had it put ready, since you asked for it yesterday and maybe it's best you should have something to do to quiet yourselves. And in that chest there, you'll find dresses and linen that belonged to Marguerite. Tak what you fancy. She and you weren't much different in size and I daresay your woman here can tak in or let out as needed. I'll leave you now and send wine."

He bowed and I thought that I even glimpsed something hangdog about him. So did Dale, for as soon as he had gone, she said: "You've a hold over him, ma'am. I can see it. You might talk us out of this in the end. He's got it bad. You've got that power over men. I think sometimes you don't know it." On the last two sentences, her voice dropped and she looked away, as though she were talking to herself rather than to me. I knew she was thinking of Brockley.

Quickly, I said: "Dale, where's that button we found on the floor of my cousin's room? Do we have it with us?"

"Yes, ma'am. I dropped it in among the medicines."

"Bring it here."

When she did so, I laid it in my palm and stared at it. There was no mistake. I looked at Dale. "When he seized me today, I had all too good a view of the buttons on Dormbois's doublet. One is missing. This one."

"What?" Dale's blue eyes bulged. "But . . ."

"Yes. Which means," I said, "that if Dormbois was

telling the truth when he said that Rob Henderson gave the order, it was Dormbois himself to whom the order was given! It was Dormbois who was in Edward's room that night."

Fuming, I began to pace around the room, further outrageous thoughts surfacing in my mind. "And what, I wonder, was it all about when he promised to find out more about Adam Ericks for me? A ploy to keep me thinking Ericks was guilty while dangling a bait to make me interested in himself? I think it was! He's been playing me, Dale, like a fish on a line! My God!"

"Madam?"

"And I've just thought of something else!" I was frightened and raging, both at once. "When I first met him at Holyrood, Dormbois led me to believe he wasn't in the city when Edward was . . . was killed. But he was! Do you remember what Jamie Fraser said? That Sir Brian came back from Edinburgh on purpose to see him—Hamish, that is—and was here the midday, after Hamish arrived. Hamish Fraser got to Roderix on the eve of Edward's death, so Dormbois must have arrived the day after. Oh yes, he was in Edinburgh on that night . . . and I know what he was doing!"

I went on thinking aloud, still pacing. "No doubt either he or Henderson was the man who put the authorities on to Adam Ericks. I daresay that it was men in their employ who urged Ericks and Edward into quarreling in that tavern. They probably had Edward under surveillance and saw their chance of setting up a scapegoat for his murder."

Unexpectedly, Dale said: "Were there any stains on the doublet with the missing button, ma'am?"

"It's been cleaned—sponged, I expect. I noticed it at breakfast. I thought that food stains had been removed. But it needn't," I said grimly, "have been just food."

"Oh, ma'am!"

"Quite. Oh, ma'am, indeed! And last night . . ."

The memory of the previous night poured over me in a flood. I swayed on my feet and sat down on the nearest settle. "Last night, I lay with that man. I . . . oh, God, Dale, what have I done?"

Dale, tearful Dale who tired so easily and hated riding and so often declared that she couldn't abide this or that; Dale who grieved because sometimes her husband and I were closer friends than she could bear, had a core of strength and sheer common sense that showed itself at the most unexpected moments.

"What you've done, ma'am," she said in a common-sense voice, "is to get part of the way to the truth. You know about Master Henderson's part in it as well. So it didn't go for nothing. You just put last night out of your mind, now. God willing, no harm will come of it. The vinegar always worked when you used it before."

"Bless you, Dale," I said. "I'll try."

"The thing is, ma'am," said Dale, becoming positively brisk, "we're prisoners here and we've got to get out. Well, I'm ready. Even if we do have to knot the sheets together and let us ourselves down from that lamp bracket out there."

"Dale!" I got up again and hugged her. "My dear Fran. My very dear Fran. No one ever had such a good friend. But I shan't ask you to climb down any knotted sheets. We'd probably both break our necks and anyway, we'd still have two walls and gates between us and freedom. We could hardly try it in daylight and they bar the gates at night. But escape we must, somehow. You're right there. Let me think."

Dale said: "I wish they'd bring that wine. You could do with it, ma'am, and so could I."

I looked listlessly around the room. It had been made ready for our return, the floor swept and a fire lit. It also contained a few things, including a backgammon set and a workbox, which hadn't been there before. There was the chest that Dormbois had mentioned as well. I moved over to it and looked inside. Dresses and linen, as he had said, all of fine quality, and also some lengths of unused material. All were carefully folded and laid in dried lavender; Marguerite had no doubt had women attendants who had seen to that after she was gone. I pictured them, smoothing the lovely fabrics and maybe crying over them before they closed the chest. I hoped that Dormbois had let them take a few things for themselves, as mementos.

There was a jewel box in the chest as well, but I was in no mood to ooh and aah over jewelry. Closing the chest, I looked at the other things that had been provided for us. I wasn't in the mood for backgammon, either, but I opened the workbox, which was made of sandalwood and was no doubt an import from some Far Eastern land. It contained needles, a little pair of shears, a good supply of silken and woolen thread in a choice of colors, and some folded papers, which when I opened them out turned out to be designs for embroidery.

"We certainly have occupation," I said dryly. "We can amuse ourselves until tonight, but tonight . . ."

"You're due, ma'am!" said Dale. "Tomorrow, for sure. Tell him it's started. That'll gain you some time. Oh, dear heaven, the linen squares were in my saddle-bags that we've lost . . . oh, well, there's linen in that chest. Let's cut some of it up."

We were engaged on this when at last the wine arrived, brought by Dormbois himself, who was not alone, but was accompanied by a short, dark-gowned man with a red face, whom I had seen before, although for a moment I couldn't remember where. Dormbois, however, informed me.

"I've brought Father Bell to you," he said in irritable tones. "He came to me and said he had heard there were ladies of his faith here in Roderix and should he no' minister to them? Well, I said I'd not hinder you in matters of worship. Father Bell, this is Madame Ursula de la Roche." He used my French title, ignoring my English one. "And this is her woman, of the same faith, nae doot. And here's the wine I promised, ladies, to put some heart into you."

He then sat down on a window seat and Father Bell regarded him with annoyance. "Sir, before I offer the consolations of the mass, which I wish to do, I must hear the confessions of these ladies." Dale, who had a real loathing for what she called popish practices, bristled at my side, but I put a hand on her arm and gripped hard, keeping her quiet. From his voice, the priest wasn't a Scot but more likely a well-educated Northumbrian. A man bred at Roderix Fort might have an unquestioning loyalty to Dormbois, but with luck, this man had not. "The confessional is secret," he said to Dormbois. "I must ask you not to remain within hearing."

"No, I cannot confess while Sir Brian can over-hear," I agreed smoothly. Dormbois stared at me, and I watched while it dawned on him just how embarrassing he would find such a confession.

"What are you about, cutting up that linen?" he demanded.

"Preparing to deal with the nature of women, Sir Brian. Forgive me for mentioning this before you, Father Bell. My nature, I'm afraid, has now manifested itself."

Dormbois looked at me hard, as though trying to work out whether or not I was lying, but I simply stared back at him. "Don't be too long over it," he said to Father Bell, and withdrew. The priest watched him go and cocked his head to listen as Dormbois's footsteps receded down the stairs.

Then, in a whisper, he said: "Madam. You have a manservant called Roger Brockley?"

"What? Yes, yes!"

"He's my husband!" Dale gasped. "Is he all right?"

From within his robe, Bell drew out a small cylinder of paper and handed it to me. "This is from him. He needs your instructions. He is in my cottage. He turned to me as a man of God, hoping I wouldn't fail him. He said that if I tried any double-dealing with him, he would kill me. He need not have worried. Sir Brian," said the priest grimly, "is an apostate. I fear him, but I have little wish to help him in his present activities. Your man says that you ladies are prisoners against your will. He would be here himself, only he says Dormbois would recognize him. I supplied Master Brockley with writing materials."

I unrolled the cylinder. Dale pressed close, to read it over my shoulder.

What a blessing, I thought, that Brockley was literate. He had learned his letters as a child and still wrote the hand he had been taught then, which was slow, simple, and legible.

And what it said was startling.

> Mistress Blanchard:
>
> I caught Fran's horse and have your belongings safely. I rode the horse to Stirling but the queen and Darnley were away on a hunting trip and Master Henderson too and not expected back for three days. By chance, I met Adam Ericks at Stirling Castle. He is there with his master. He is very angry. He says he has recognized one of the men who urged him on to quarrel in the tavern and that this man serves Rene of Elbeouf and therefore is under the command of Sir Brian Dormbois.
>
> This fellow told him (I think Ericks asks questions with fists and sword) that Dormbois ordered him to keep watch on Master Faldene when he arrived in Edinburgh, and see whom he met and where he went. He was given two companions to help him, strangers, not Scotsmen but English. Ericks now thinks it was Dormbois who told the authorities to seek out the tavern keeper and thus Dormbois who has tried to point him out as a murderer by night. Ericks also says you are surely at Roderix Fort and has told me where it is.
>
> I am desperate with anxiety for both you and my wife. Are you still safe? How should I go about res-

cuing you? Do I go back to Stirling and wait for the
queen's return, or is there aught I can do here, and
at once? I require your instructions.

    I send you my duty as your servant and my
hearty love to Fran. Tell her that I swear before God
that we will be together again soon.

R.B.

I looked at Father Bell. "You realize that I have been
brought here with a view to a forced marriage?"

"Yes, madam, so it is being said among the people in
the cottages. These things happen in this wild place."

"Will you help me?"

"As far as I can. I brought you the letter, did I not?"

"Then tell Brockley that we are both well. And tell
him also—tell him—please take heed of this and repeat
my words exactly . . ."

"Trust me, madam."

"Tell him to seek help from Queen Mary as soon as
he can but to avoid Master Henderson at all costs. Have
you got that? And tell him—these very words, mark
you—that *the button belongs to Sir Brian Dormbois.*"

"Ask help of Queen Mary as soon as may be but
avoid Master Henderson at all costs. And the button
belongs to Sir Brian Dormbois. I won't ask you the
meaning. There is more to this than appears on the
surface, it would seem."

"There is. But if you get that message safely to
Brockley, I hope that rescue will come before long."

After that, I made a confession of sorts, because Father
Bell expected it. I had done the same thing when I lived
in France with Matthew. Elizabeth was sometimes impa-

tient with the fuss that people made over the difference between the old religion and the new. It was nothing but a dispute about trifles, she said. I was inclined to agree.

In any case, since I had so little belief in a beneficent God, it scarcely mattered which rituals I took part in, for I usually felt that I was only paying lip service. I therefore went through the form of confession, though with caution, for I did not want to involve this decent man too deeply in the business of my cousin's violent death.

I did not mention the bargain I had made with Dormbois; only that I had been constrained to spend the night with him, had given in to preserve a sense of dignity, but felt it still to be a sin. I said I might have to do the same again before I was freed, and would prefer not to hear mass until after my release. I also soothed Dale's tension by explaining that she was in fact of the Reformed faith and would not confess.

After that, we all shared the wine, and when I had let Dale read the letter for herself and gaze awhile at Brockley's writing, we thought it wise to burn it in our hearth. Father Bell once more repeated the message I had given him for Brockley. Then Dormbois returned.

"Oh, ma'am," Dale whispered as soon as Dormbois had escorted the priest downstairs. "There's hope now. I feel there's hope."

"So do I," I said, and at that point a vague ache in the lower abdomen, which had been pulling at my attention for a good half hour, increased to a pitch that was unmistakable. "And there's one thing," I said cheerfully. "I think I really do need those linen squares now. What a mercy. I can keep Dormbois at bay for a while without bothering to lie."

* * *

Dinner was brought to us in the parlor, and after that, we examined some of Marguerite's gowns. They were of very good quality. They were all too small either for Dale or for me, but not by much. Since it would indeed help to pass the time, we each chose a gown and started to let out seams.

And then came the confrontation that I had known I must face sooner or later. Dormbois came back to talk to me.

"I am sorry for deceiving you." He stood in front of me, feet apart, a brown fur-edged jacket swinging from his wide shoulders. But the front of it was open and I could still see those buttons, and the space where the missing one had been. I pushed my needle into my work and sat with my hands clasped, wondering frantically what Brockley was doing now.

"At least," said Dormbois, "I find you calm and occupied. It gives me hope that you are thinking now with a clearer mind."

"I am thinking only of the work I am doing," I said in a trembling voice. And then added: "Needlework interests me. That is a well-cut doublet you are wearing. Did an Edinburgh tailor make it for you?"

"No. Marguerite made it, embroidery and all," said Dormbois. "New it is not, but I am fond of it. Like the earthenware goblets, it is something that no one else has copied. Never mind my doublet. I didnae come for small talk. I hoped that there would be no need for the violence this morning, that I'd win you in those sweet hours we had together. I'm sorry I didnae succeed.

Now, pay heed. I'll not trouble you at night until nature's run her course, but don't think to hold me off longer. You'll do better to make terms with the future, Ursula. Why not? It's live with me as my concubine, or else as my wife. As my wife, you'll be a highly respected lady and no one'll think the worse of you because your husband won you by capture. Many a girl that lacks your magic'll envy you and maybe go to some auld witch for a love potion to get some fellow to care for her as much. What's the use of saying you don't want to marry again? The time has to come and it's against nature to defy it."

I said nothing. I had put my theory to the test but the last faint hope that he was not guilty had gone. There was no possibility that someone else, wearing a doublet like his, had been in Edward's room that night. It had been Dormbois and no other. Dale, seated apart and still stitching industriously, had understood too. She let out an inadvertent snort and Dormbois glared at her.

"Make that woman of yours know her place," he said to me. "It's no' for the likes of her to comment. Listen, lassie. You're no fool but a woman of the world, with a daughter. What of her?"

I was jolted into speech. "Meg? She's safe in Sussex!"

"Aye, but reputations travel. One day she'll be old enough to wed, but who'll wed a maiden whose mother is living with a Scottish laird, and they've half a dozen children and no bond of marriage? When the first bairn is coming, I think you'll gladly take me for your lawful husband."

I went on staring at him and he grew impatient. "Why the big wide eyes? It's a natural thing between a man and a woman. As well you know. How else did your Meg come into being?"

In my mind, a door opened, narrowly. Peering through the chink I could see a faint hope. As well as a vista of fear.

"If it's children you want," I said, "you would do best to find another lady. I had great trouble to bring Meg into the world. Since then I have miscarried once and had one stillbirth, which almost killed me. It isn't only grief for Matthew that makes me unwilling to marry again. I want to live, Sir Brian. Force me into bearing your bairn as you call it, and you might find yourself mourning for me as you did for your first wife. She died in childbed, did she not?"

"You keep comparing yourself to Jeannie and Marguerite, but you are nothing like either of them. Jeannie was too young. You're a woman grown. Most women have their bairns safe enough, or none of us would be here. Some trouble they have, but that's the payment for the sin of Eve. You may have suffered, but you didn't die, did you? Now what's going through that elusive mind of yours? Something is. I see it in your eyes."

I was thinking about Elizabeth. Elizabeth feared marriage because she feared to give herself into a man's power. She had told me as much. But thinking now of her slender, fragile form, I found myself suddenly wondering if the danger of childbearing was part of that fear as well.

After returning from France, I had gathered from her other ladies that the council had once tried to urge her toward marriage by begging her to imagine the comfort and delight that beholding an imp of her own would bring, whereupon she had lost her temper with them and with tears of rage in her eyes shouted at them to be silent. The ladies knew about it because some of them were the wives of council members and their husbands had told them. Everyone, man and woman alike, assumed that the tears were born of temper but had they, perhaps, been caused by terror? Elizabeth feared death more than most, for she had experienced the shadow of the ax, and childbearing had killed two of her stepmothers. I remembered my own perilous confinement in France and I understood.

But Dormbois didn't. "I'll leave you now. You need time to settle and to think. Sweetheart . . ."

I ground my teeth.

". . . sweetheart, don't let it come to force. It didn't last night; don't let it be so next time, either. I want to love you, nothing more. Breeding bairns, that's part of it, but that comes later. For now, it's my sweet lady in my arms that I want and I've all the world to offer her. Only, I'm not a man to say no to. So—think well, my dear."

He was gone. I put my face into my hands and Dale said: "Oh, dear Lord, this is terrible. What are we to do?"

"We've a few days," I said. "Five—I sometimes go on for six. I doubt if that will help, though. Brockley said the queen would be gone for three days. Does that include yesterday or not? Not that it matters. She'll have to start by ordering my release and then Dormbois will say no, and she'll have to mount a siege. If she thinks I'm worth the effort, that is! Oh, I could kill Dormbois! Dear heaven, has he *no* sense of honor?"

23

Loading the Dice

I shared the big bed with Dale that night and I slept, because I was too worn-out to do anything else. My cramps had passed by then. In the morning, Dormbois did not appear. Breakfast was brought. Then Dale and I went on altering Marguerite's clothes.

As we worked, we talked. I wondered if the letters I had sent through Henderson had been received at Faldene, by Mattie at Thamesbank and Sybil Jester in Cambridge, and whether any replies would ever reach me. "Am I truly cut off from the world in this place?" I said to Dale. "Surely, Queen Mary will try to set me free, and if she doesn't, well, when Cecil and Queen Elizabeth find out, they will make representations . . ."

"I hope so, ma'am," said Dale unhappily.

"I know," I said. "But we're so far from home!"

Dinner came: mutton stew with dumplings and bread, and a kind of tart made of thick pastry and filled with cherries preserved in wine. The flavors were pleasant but much more of this heavy fare with no exercise, I thought, and Dale and I would both have upset stomachs.

When the dishes had been removed, I suggested that we should walk about the room, but when we were doing so, our attention was caught by voices below, and we went to look out of the window.

Two visitors were crossing the courtyard from the gate, escorted by two of Dormbois's plaid-draped soldiers. One of them was Father Bell. The other was Brockley.

Ten minutes later, Fraser appeared to say that I was wanted in the hall. "And ye're woman had best come too, this being a place of men otherwise."

He was polite enough to let us go down first. We arrived in the comfortless hall to find Dormbois there, with the visitors. The two men who had brought them in were standing back, but with an air of being on guard. All the faces were serious, to the point of grimness. Brockley was holding a piece of rolled parchment.

"Ah. Madame de la Roche. Come here." Dormbois beckoned me. "This concerns you." He looked at Brockley. "Speak your piece, man."

"I come as a herald," said Brockley. His plain brown clothes were splashed with mud from much riding and his face was both tired and unshaven, but he held himself with great dignity. Brockley had presence and knew how to use it.

"Madam, I have of course asked for your release and that of my wife," he said. His eyes went briefly to Dale, and he smiled at her before continuing. "This was refused, which I expected. But I did not come principally for that purpose, but as an emissary from someone else."

There was a pause while he unrolled the parchment. He cleared his throat and read. "Master Adam Ericks, descended through his mother from the Gordons, a swordsman serving Patrick Lord Lindsay in arms, sends me as his second. He has a lawful quarrel with Sir Brian Dormbois in that he accuses Sir Brian of having tried to lay on him the blame for the bloody and dishonorable murder of Master Edward Faldene in Edinburgh on the night of February the eighth in the Year of Our Lord 1565.

"He wishes to clear his name by combat. The combat to be sword against sword, the time and place to be chosen by Sir Brian Dormbois. In the event that Master Ericks prevails, Sir Brian, if living, must publicly clear the name of Ericks; if not living, then someone appointed by him must do so in his stead. Also, in the event that Master Ericks prevails, Madame de la Roche, otherwise known as Mistress Ursula Blanchard, and her tirewoman, Frances Brockley, otherwise known as Frances Dale, at present held in captivity by the said Sir Brian Dormbois, are to be set free that they may return to their home. On this understanding, I, Roger Brockley, agree to act as herald and second."

"I have said," Dormbois declared, "that I havenae attempted to blame Master Ericks for anything whatsoever. I've scarcely heard of the man. He apparently claims that I laid information with the authorities concerning the quarrel in the tavern between Ericks and Faldene. I did not. I also said, before you came down to the hall, madam, that I saw no reason why I should accept this challenge, since this man Ericks is no more than a man-at-arms whereas I am nobly born. However . . ."

"Master Ericks," said Brockley, "bade me to say, if this point were raised, that he is third cousin to George Lord Gordon—whose brother, though he was executed for treason, once aspired to the hand of Queen Mary herself. Master Ericks holds the rank of captain rather than that of a plain man-at-arms. His challenge is not beneath a Dormbois."

"Having heard that," said Dormbois, "I granted the point, but saw no reason why you, madam, should be involved. However, Master Brockley had more to say. Speak again, herald," he added ironically.

"I was bidden to explain," said Brockley calmly, "that if the challenge is rejected, Sir Brian should consider what Her Majesty Queen Mary will do when she learns that Madame de la Roche is a captive. Her Majesty may well order the release of Madame de la Roche herself, and back the order with force.

"Ericks also states that he means to have satisfaction and will make opportunity to waylay you and force you to fight him—perhaps when tired and unprepared. He reminds you that he has a reputation as a swordsman and that to refuse his challenge might suggest that you feared it."

"That being so," said Dormbois, "I have agreed, on one of two conditions. One is that the clause concerning the release of Madame de la Roche is omitted. The tirewoman may leave whenever she wishes. I can replace her. The other alternative is that the clause may stand, but if I prevail, unless I am too sore wounded, the lady shall wed with me, then and there, with Father Bell to officiate; and if I am too much hurt to take the vows of marriage at once, then we wed as soon as I am healed."

Brockley's eyes met mine in anguish. "I would offer to fight for your freedom myself, madam, except that I am many years older than Sir Brian and am only a mediocre swordsman."

"And I would not accept you as a champion, for your own safety," I said.

"Master Ericks knows the swordsman's trade, madam. He is the best hope I can bring you."

"Aye. This is a strong place. Even Queen Mary's forces might not find it easy to take." Dormbois grinned. "And I might have the lady away to France before ever a siege was in place. Well, Ursula de la Roche? The decision is yours. Which of the conditions will you accept? If not one, then it has to be the other. I must fight. No man calls me craven."

"I see," I said.

I did see. I stood there, staring at the floor in order to hide the desperation in my eyes, and wondered: do I do this? Do I gamble on Adam Ericks and the righteousness of his cause and be prepared to say "I will" to Dormbois if after all Ericks loses?

There was no question of omitting the clause concerning my release. The chance of that had to be included. But if Ericks lost . . .

I even wondered for an insane moment whether the prospect of marriage to Dormbois was altogether impossible. I remembered that conversation in the night, when he had told me the history of his brown earthenware goblets. Just for a moment there, I had glimpsed another Dormbois, the human being behind the posturings of the male animal, the possible friend hidden within the domineering nobleman.

But my mind, groping for solace, for hope, checked and stumbled on a name. *Edward.*

The image of Edward's dead face and the blood-stained walls came back to me yet again, drifting between me and the floor, a vision so horrid that I blinked to drive it away, concentrating on the floor itself. It was innocent of rugs, even of rushes, and certainly of any sweet, flea-dispelling rosemary or rue. It was clean, though, made of dark oak planks, which must have had to be brought from a distance. I hadn't seen an oak tree for miles. The color of the planks was much the same as the color of those curious earthenware goblets . . .

And then I saw the answer. Its outlines were blurred, and even now, before I could see them plainly, I knew that this would be a difficult plan to carry out. It might easily fail. It would be difficult to make sure that . . . What if this happened? Or that? How could I make certain . . . ?

I couldn't. I could only try. Even if I failed and Ericks failed, the future still existed, with opportunities of further ploys. I would not, not, *not,* remain with Dormbois, even if I were fifty times his wife. My heart began to pound.

I must pretend. I must allay all suspicion and pretend with all my might, like a mummer or a strolling player. With my eyes still downcast, I said slowly: "If Adam Ericks loses, I will wed you, Sir Brian."

"Oh, ma'am," said Dale despairingly, when we were once more in the parlor, "how could you? How could you?"

"Sit down, Dale."

"Ma'am, I can't go on with altering these gowns; I've no heart for anything."

"Just listen. This way, if Ericks wins, I go free. If he loses . . ."

"But, ma'am, if he *does* lose . . ."

"Then I take vows, which as far as I am concerned are null and void."

"But they wouldn't be, ma'am! Bell is a proper priest! All your property would belong to Dormbois, ma'am! Withysham would be his!"

"I daresay," I said. "But married or not, I will still make every effort to escape. He will no doubt try to keep me mewed up in Roderix, but a chance will come eventually, or else I'll create one as I did when we had to escape from Withysham, when I was first married to Matthew. If I have to, I'll let him think I've given in, until he trusts me and relaxes his grip. I swear I'll do it. I *will* escape, and I'll get across the English border and get home, and once I'm back in Withysham, if he wants to claim either it or me, he'll have to venture more than four hundred miles into a foreign land, and at the end of the journey, I'll be waiting to charge him with the murder of my cousin Edward. I trust that with the help of Queen Elizabeth, I can get the marriage set aside, anyway. I will never acknowledge it as valid, Dale. I will *not*. Look, you at least can go home if you wish. He said you were free to go."

"And leave you, ma'am?"

"I said, I'll escape somehow. Your place is with your husband. I'll send you to him. You need have no conflict of loyalties."

Dale looked at me gratefully and also miserably.

"In times gone by," I said, "when trial by battle was commonplace, I daresay a guilty conscience weighed down many a sword arm, but of course, Dormbois has only a rudimentary conscience, if any at all. There's only one thing to do, if I can."

"And what's that, ma'am?"

"Load the dice," I said. "Now, listen . . ."

24

The Price of Freedom

"But, ma'am," said Dale, when I had finished, "for those men, it'll be a matter of honor!"

I was exasperated. "Dormbois has no more sense of honor than one of the rats in his own granary! As for Ericks, well, it's his misfortune. I need to escape from Dormbois's clutches and that's more important to me than the honor of Adam Ericks! And if your eyes pop out any farther, Dale, they'll fall on the floor."

"Oh, ma'am!" Poor Dale wrung her hands. "I can't abide this place and these people; I'd sell my soul to get out of it and get you away, too. But this'll never work! It's that difficult . . ."

"You said yesterday that I had a hold over him. If that's true—well, I doubt if it's much of a hold," I said. "But it might be just good enough—just barely good enough—to let me command him for those few moments. If I can be dignified enough, regal enough . . ."

* * *

One thing I had learned from Elizabeth, by observation, was that if you want to create an impression of power, you should start by dressing for it. For public appearances, for receiving ambassadors and presiding at state banquets, Elizabeth always made sure that she looked like a monarch. For these occasions, on went the stays that reduced her waist to a scarcely believable slenderness; on went the gleaming silks and brocades; on went the ruby and diamond pendants and earrings and the glistening ropes of pearls; onto her pale, slim fingers went a fortune in gemstones and gold.

"We'd better see what Marguerite's wardrobe can do for me," I said. "Black velvet for preference—I *am* in mourning and I shan't let Dormbois forget it. But it must be as impressive as possible. There's a jewel box at the bottom of that chest. It's time to look at it."

"But, ma'am, I just don't see how . . ."

"Nor do I, quite. I have got to insist on this little ceremony and somehow I must control the way it's carried out. It may all be snatched out of my hands. But by God, I *will* try!"

"You're right, ma'am. No one would see it. But how do we make sure that . . . ?"

"That's the tricky bit, Dale. I don't know that I *can* make sure. One of the problems is making certain it isn't a case of too much or not enough. I once saw a man at a fair, walking along a rope, twenty feet above the ground, just balancing. This is nearly as bad!"

"Like this, Dale. The positioning must be just so or I shall get confused. I think we'd better run through it again. You're Ericks, now. If necessary, I shall ask you to . . ."

"Ma'am, I can hear hammering, but I can't see what they're doing. I think it's coming from the outer bailey."

"Well, I don't suppose they're setting up a gallows. If my champion loses, Dormbois is going to marry me, not bury me."

"I'll use this black velvet gown and this long rope of pearls. And the ruff with the silver lace edging, and the black velvet cap with the pearl edging."

"There's a rope of amethysts too, ma'am."

"Yes, I'll wear that too," I said, trying it on with the help of a small mirror that had been lying on the toilet table in the bedchamber. "Dormbois must be a man of means to afford such clothes and jewels for his wife. What a pity his morals don't match his income. Why on earth does he go on living in this dreadful keep with a kitchen on the other side of the courtyard?"

"I think something in him prefers it, ma'am. This keep is in his blood, so to speak."

"I hope," I said grimly, "that before long, his blood will be spattered in the keep instead."

"Ma'am, when you talk like that, you give me the shivers."

"I know. I'm sorry, Dale."

Ericks and Brockley had promised to arrive in the morning at ten of the clock. Dale and I would be summoned down to the hall when they arrived. I don't think I would have slept that night, except that I took a small dose of Queen Mary's sleeping draft, which soothed me into slumber quite quickly. I knew that in order to face the morrow, I must rest. I must not have what Elizabeth called a white night. We both suffered from them sometimes. I endured mine by lying awake, just waiting for the dawn. Elizabeth usually got through hers by waking up her ladies of the bedchamber and making them read to her or play chess with her, but I never troubled Dale in such a way.

The morning was sunlit. I rose, nervous but reasonably refreshed, washed as best I could in the usual tepid water, and sat in a loose gown, once Marguerite's, while Dale carefully brushed and pinned my hair. When breakfast came, I forced down the porridge and a piece of bread and drank some buttermilk, knowing that I needed the strength it would give me. When the serving boy brought it, I said to him: "When you come back for it, bring another tray with you. I shall need it later." He was well trained and didn't ask why, and when he returned, he had the tray.

"We've surmounted the first obstacle," I said to Dale. "Now for the rest. You had better get me dressed. Then we'll pack up our belongings and put them by the door and set the tray."

Watching from the window, we saw Adam Ericks enter the courtyard, carrying a very businesslike claymore. Father Bell and Brockley were with him. We watched as Dormbois's men escorted them into the keep, and a few minutes later, Jamie Fraser came to summon us downstairs.

"Bring the tray, Dale," I said, rising to my feet.

"What's that for, mistress?" Fraser asked. "Those're the master's special goblets."

"Indeed they are. They're needed. I'd ask you to carry them but with your limp, I should think the stairs are difficult enough for you already. Dale will do it instead. Come, Dale!" I said imperiously and without giving Fraser any more time to argue, I led the way.

The hall was crowded. The principals were there: Dormbois, also equipped with a claymore—Ericks, Brockley, and Father Bell. All were dressed much alike, in brown or black. Ranged around the walls were Dormbois's men, his servants, and his garrison, all of them armed. There was also a piper, with bagpipes.

I had Dale for support, but never in my life had I felt quite so lonely. I stepped off the staircase and halted, wondering how on earth, or in the name of heaven, I could dominate a situation like this. The crowd of masculine faces was intimidating, alien. The idea of commanding them, like a general controlling an army, felt not just unnatural but impossible. I wondered if Queen Elizabeth, taking charge of her council for the first time, had felt as nonplussed as I did, and I could well understand why Mary Stuart surrounded herself with Maries.

Poor Dale, I knew, would do her best, but I could feel her trembling. I wished my friend Mattie could have been with me. Or no, perhaps not Mattie, for she was Rob's wife and that relationship was tarnished for me now. My mind went once more to that admirable woman Sybil Jester, whom I had briefly known the previous year, in Cambridge, and whom I had left dealing with so many difficulties, such as a pregnant daughter and a business that might fail under the onslaught of tittle-tattle that she herself had not deserved. Sybil was not beautiful but she had a calm good sense and a serene good humor, and a maturity of mind that would have been like a wall at my back, if only she had been here.

Dormbois was moving forward, about to greet me and no doubt to tell me what to do next. As confidently as I could, I raised a hand to forestall him. Within my head, I was murmuring a prayer, though not one that Father Bell would approve. I was actually asking the deity why, when the forces of light and virtue needed such a small piece of help as this, it wasn't forthcoming.

If Dormbois and Ericks had known my plans in advance and set out to wreck them, they couldn't have placed themselves more effectively. I had remembered correctly that the table was in the center of the room. Ericks and Brockley were standing together on the far side of it. From my point of view, they were to my right and Dormbois, who was closer and on the same side of the table as myself, was on my left.

And I needed Dormbois to be on my right.

Well, I must do my best. I had known that this could happen. Since the scene before me was not to my liking, I must find from somewhere the strength of mind, the power, to change it. I had a rough and ready scheme in my mind if only I could carry it off. I walked forward, slowly, in measured fashion, my head high. Dale came behind me, carrying the tray. She was shaking so much that the goblets were rattling. I was relieved to reach the table, so that I could sign to her to set the tray down on it. Raising my chin more proudly still, I rapped on the table and spoke one word. Spoke, not shouted. But I drew a deep breath first and put it behind that single word, to make it resonate. "Gentlemen!"

It won their attention. Dormbois had been about to speak but he stopped. All eyes were on me.

I paused, and with my gaze, I gathered them all in. Then I let my voice ring out again. "This is a most serious and solemn occasion!" I was myself surprised by the clarity and steadiness of my words. "I am aware that there are certain customs in this house that are observed at times like these. I have taken the liberty, Sir Brian, of bringing the wherewithal for such an observance here with me. Do you not, on such occasions, drink ceremonially to the hope of a satisfactory outcome, in your grandfather's earthenware goblets?"

"I do," said Dormbois. He came up to the table and looked at the tray. "I see you've brocht three goblets."

"Yes. For you, for Master Ericks, and for myself since I am concerned in this, as much as either of you. Will you send for wine, sir, and drink according to the Dormbois custom? Not too much," I added. I allowed myself a thin smile and shared it with the silent onlookers. One or two of them smiled faintly in return. It seemed that most of them understood my English. "The champions' minds must not be clouded."

Dormbois gave an order and a servant hurried away. There was another pause. The door to the courtyard was open, giving a view of the sunlit world outside. Curious, that Dormbois and Ericks should be so eager to offend the spring sunshine with human blood. I supposed that the duel would take place out there. No one had said.

The servant came back with a jug of wine and I beckoned to him and pointed to the goblets, standing back to let him pour. I saw that he was careful only to half fill them, which was all to the good. While he was still filling the last one, I announced: "There is one more thing!" and once more all attention was on me. "Master Adam Ericks, come round the table to me, please! You are my champion and I wish to present you with my favor, as ladies did in times gone by!"

I could see Brockley watching me, a slight frown on his high forehead. He was wondering what I was about. So was Dormbois, who now tried to interrupt.

"Och, enough of this flummery! This is no tournament from the days o' King Arthur! Favors, indeed! Forget this nonsense, and let us drink to a good outcome and get to the business and be done with it!"

My inside turned over with fright but my voice was calm and dignified as I said: "Grant me this small thing, I beg you, sir. It will take only a moment. Master Ericks . . . ?"

"Flummery!" barked Dormbois, and marched forward to catch up a goblet. I turned toward him, however, with a cool smile and moved into his path. "Why so impatient, Sir Brian?" I asked him and let a trace of amusement enter my voice. "You are not nervous, surely?"

This produced a reaction from the onlookers, in the form of a couple of indignant exclamations but also some faint chuckles and fleeting grins. Dormbois stood still, looking furious.

Adam Ericks, who had no objection to flouting him, came around the right-hand end of the table and I turned to meet him. He was my hope and yet, with that dark face of his, and carrying that claymore, he was a remarkably menacing spectacle, quite disturbing enough to explain why, as he came up to me, I should take a step or two backward and bump into Dormbois, causing him, too, to take a couple of steps back.

I murmured an apology, smiled at Ericks, and drew a silk handkerchief from my sleeve. "You can put it inside your shirt, Master Ericks. It will not inconvenience you. Even a brooch could be knocked awry and jab a pin into you but this is harmless. May it bring you good fortune. My hopes and my prayers go with it, my champion."

I gave him the favor. He thanked me and thrust it into the sleeve of his shirt, and then, unexpectedly, took hold of me and kissed me. "I'll not fail you, mistress, not if God knows His business."

I hoped his optimism would be justified. Reaching out without looking, I took up the goblet nearest to me and gave it to him. My heart was pounding like a hammer in the grasp of a mad blacksmith and I don't know how I kept my hand steady as I picked up a goblet for myself. Turning back to Dormbois, I said: "Let us have the toast!"

Dormbois took up the remaining goblet. "You had best propose the toast yourself, lassie," he said dryly.

"I will. Hear me, all of you! These are the terms! That Sir Brian Dormbois and Master Adam Ericks shall engage in a duel to clear the good name of Master Ericks, who has been suspected of the murder of my cousin Edward Faldene. If Sir Brian should prevail, then Master Ericks, whether living or dead, remains under suspicion and I will marry Sir Brian. If Master Ericks prevails, then Master Ericks shall be declared innocent and I and my two servants are free to go, forthwith, with all our belongings and this time we will not be brought back."

"You make yersel' verra plain," Dormbois remarked.

"We agreed it yesterday, did we not? What harm in making it public?" I said in an undertone. I raised my voice again. "For my part, I call on all in this hall to witness once again that I accept the terms! Sir Brian, Master Ericks, do you do likewise?"

"I said so yesterday," Dormbois growled. "Aye, I consent."

"Master Ericks?"

"Aye, mistress."

"Then," I said loudly, "here's to a good outcome of this contest! May the right be defended!"

We drank.

As I had surmised, the duel was to take place outside. We went out in procession, led by the piper, following the skirl of his bagpipes across the courtyard and through the gate to the grassy outer bailey.

Here, I found the explanation for the hammering that we had heard yesterday. An arena had been marked out with short poles driven into the ground at the four corners and ropes slung between, a few feet from the ground. A platform had been carpentered together as well and a chair placed upon it, and here I was invited to seat myself.

I was to watch, apparently, from the place of honor. The platform, I noticed, was well away from the outer gate, but beside the gate three saddled horses were tethered, Brockley's, mine, and Dale's. They didn't like the bagpipes and were tossing their heads and fidgeting against their tethers.

Dale stood beside me and Brockley found a moment to come up to the platform. "The horses are ready, madam, as you see. Fran tells me all your gear is packed."

"Yes, it is."

"If all goes well, best order someone else to fetch it down. None of us should go back inside. These folk aren't to be trusted."

"Dormbois certainly isn't," I muttered. "Thank you, Brockley. For everything."

There was no time for anything further. The piper, who had been playing all this while from a position behind me, now fell silent (obviously to the relief of the horses) and Father Bell, who seemed to have constituted himself master of ceremonies, was calling the contestants and their seconds out into the arena. Brockley rested a hand momentarily on my shoulder, and then stepped off the platform and went to Ericks's side.

Dormbois and Ericks both took off their doublets. As they did so, I noticed, with a lurch of the heart, that Dormbois, in order to shed his doublet quickly, had only had a couple of its buttons done up, and that beneath it, he had no shirt, but had stripped to fight bare-chested.

The sponge marks on his black wool doublet, I thought, might well have been to remove the marks of wine or gravy after all. It had niggled at my mind once or twice that blood was difficult to remove unless you soaked the stained fabric in salt water and the doublet had not given that impression.

But Dormbois could have worn it, lightly buttoned, in order to creep into Edward's room. Clad in black, he would not be easily visible to inquisitive eyes as he climbed out of the alley and swarmed along the wall. But once in the room—the truth was revealing itself now before my inner eye—he had shed the doublet, pulling off a loose button in the process, and no doubt on that occasion too, he had worn no shirt beneath it. Afterward, he had pulled out the sheet to wipe Edward's blood from his body and put his doublet on again, over more or less clean skin. He had had blood on his shoes, which had left a trail but neither shirt nor doublet had been spoiled with it.

In the arena, Fraser and Brockley had taken the discarded clothing and withdrawn with it to opposite corners, ducking under the ropes in order to stand just outside. Father Bell ordered the principals forward and placed them a few feet apart.

They stood still, their right hands on the hilts of their claymores. The sunlight was warm now and I saw

Dormbois brush his left hand across his forehead, as though the heat were troubling him.

Father Bell's right hand was upheld, as though he were about to pronounce a blessing but he was not. He dropped it, not in the manner of a benediction but as though he were cleaving the air between the opponents with the edge of his hand, and that was the signal to begin. He stepped backward quickly, getting out of the way, and the contestants drew and clashed.

I had seen swordfights before, both in earnest and in sport, but I had never seen anything like this. I don't think I had realized until then just how deadly serious this was, how dangerous for the participants. I had, I supposed, expected that they would protect themselves with some sort of armor, but they had done nothing of the kind. This was a crude business, weapon against weapon with neither helmets nor body armor; in Dormbois's case without even clothing on his upper half while Ericks had only a loose shirt. They had no defense at all beyond their skill.

I knew enough to see at once that both men were expert. For a full five minutes they circled each other, striking and clashing, using both hands to wield the heavy swords and neither coming within inches of the other. One hit would finish it, I thought, with my stomach heaving. These were no slender, elegant rapiers with which it was possible to draw blood but still not do serious harm. A single slash from one of those murderous blades with the speed and weight of a trained fighter behind it and that would be the end of it; very likely, the end of a life.

Very well then, so be it, but let it be Dormbois's life

and not that of Ericks. Please. Please. The chair I had been given had wooden arms. I sat with my fingers clutching the ends of them, watching Dormbois, watching him . . . watching him . . .

It was going to go wrong, I thought. Marginally, he was the faster and the stronger. There hadn't been enough time afterall to tilt the balance. That brush of the hand across his forehead had been only due to the warmth of the sun; it had meant nothing . . .

Then, jumping back out of range of Ericks's blade, he did it again, shaking his head as though to clear his eyes.

After that, the conflict was not prolonged. Rigid in my chair, I watched it happen, watched his speed and strength fade, as the poppy draft which had been waiting in the bottom of the earthenware goblet, took effect, weighing down his arms and legs and slowing his responses. It had been so difficult to make sure that he picked up the goblet that contained the drug. So difficult. But now it was difficult for him to raise the heavy sword, impossible for him to parry quickly or strike with force. Once, twice, he struck blows that faltered as though his sword were suddenly too heavy, and then a sweeping stroke from Adam Ericks took him in the side, and he fell.

He went down on his back. Ericks was after him at once, sword upraised, but he did not swing it down. He stood still and spoke. Dormbois tried to rise and could not. He said something to Ericks in reply. Ericks lowered his blade and stood back, wiping the sweat out of his eyes and leaning on his sword like a tired gardener on a rake handle.

Brockley and Fraser and Father Bell ran to Dormbois, followed by a couple of the Roderix men, one of them carrying a bag. Brockley looked around for me and beckoned; rising, I left the platform and went to them, accompanied by Dale.

Dormbois was lying still. His face was a terrible color. The bag I had seen contained medical aids, and his two men, crouching at his side, were easing a bandage under him so as to bind a pad into a place. A pool of blood was spreading beneath him. He groaned as the bandage was edged into place, and before the pad went on I saw white splinters of bone where the sword had smashed into his ribs.

He looked at me with bitterness. "What did ye do, lassie? How did ye do it? Was it witchcraft? What was amiss with my wine?"

If I hadn't been wearing his dead wife's black velvet cap with pearl edging, I think my hair would have stood on end with terror. Was my escape to be jeopardized even now?

"No witchcraft, Sir Brian," I said, making sure that his men, and also Fraser, who was eyeing me suspiciously, could hear me plainly. "I have no such powers. And you saw for yourself that your man brought the wine and poured it. I never touched it. Do right by me, Sir Brian, and keep your word and let me go free. It was no witchery that lost you the battle, and the wine was honest." Well, so it was, till it got into the goblet.

"It was hubris," I said sententiously. "Or the hand of God." I looked down into his eyes. They were drowning in sleep but it had not quite overtaken him. He could still hear me. I knelt beside him and spoke for his ears only. "You lost a button from your black and silver doublet," I said, "on the floor of Edward Faldene's chamber."

"What are you saying?" Fraser caught my arm and pulled me to my feet again.

"Leave her," said Dormbois. "*Leave* her, I said! Fraser . . ."

"Sir?" said Fraser.

"Let her go, with her things and her people. I command it. She's ill luck for me."

I glanced at Fraser. "My belongings are packed and waiting in the room where I was kept," I said. "Will you have them brought down?"

"Aye. Since that's the laird's bidding. The sooner ye're oot of this place, the better," said Fraser sourly. He gave me another nasty look, but he turned away and barked out orders. A couple of serving men went back through the courtyard door and the men who had been tending Dormbois's wound went to fetch a stretcher— it looked like an old door—which had been lying ready and lifted Dormbois onto it. His head lolled and this time he didn't groan. I think he had slipped out of consciousness.

Dormbois had ordered our release, but Dormbois was as near to dead as made no difference. We were still in danger. I hadn't liked that word *witchcraft*. Brockley hadn't, either. "We'd better get to the horses, madam. Come, Fran. Let's mount."

There was a murmur from among some of the garrison, who by this time had crowded around, and for a perilous moment, some of them moved to block our way. Surprisingly, it was Fraser who stopped them.

"The laird's given his orders and he's no' dead, not yet. They're to go, as was sworn yesterday in the hall of this keep, and again this morning, and good riddance in my view. Let them pass!"

Brockley, facing the crowd boldly, said: "Master Fraser is right. You all heard, in the hall, what had been agreed. Is our gear being brought? If not, we will leave without it. Get to the horses, madam, Fran."

"Your gear is coming," said Fraser. "And the outer gate is open as a sign of good faith. The sooner the pack of ye are through it, the happier we'll be."

And yes, our baggage was being brought. The servants who brought it scowled at us, but they carried our belongings to the horses, put the saddlebags in place, and even helped us to put our shoulder bags on and mount. Brockley's bag was already slung across his saddle. He heaved it onto his back.

Father Bell came to wish us Godspeed. His good wishes included Adam Ericks, who had a pony tied outside the gate and evidently proposed to leave with us. From Dormbois's men there were no friendly looks to bid us a good journey and the muttering continued, but Fraser, whatever his private feelings, was a somewhat more honest man than his master and they respected his authority. Nor had we given Dormbois's men time to brood on such matters as witchcraft or double-dealing and ferment themselves into defying orders. I think it was a near thing, but in the end, they let us go without hindrance.

This time, we went free. Genuinely.

* * *

We parted from Ericks when he turned west for Stirling while we turned south for the border. "Tell me, madam," said Brockley as we jogged along, afterward, "how did you do it? You did something. I know it."

"I used the poppy draft that Queen Mary provided for Dale," I said. "There was quite a lot of it left. Sir Brian has a custom of drinking to important occasions, in special goblets. There's a story attached to them, but the point is, they're made of dark brown earthenware, almost the same color as the draft, and they're very deep and narrow. I thought that if a little were in the bottom of a goblet, it wouldn't be visible. It wasn't, either, at least not after I'd diluted it with a little water. It was difficult to estimate the dose—I had to use enough to make a difference but I daren't use too much or it would be quite obvious that he'd been drugged."

"We experimented last night," said Dale. "The mistress needed her sleep anyway, so she took a small dose herself and I watched to see how long it took to work. I think we got Dormbois's dose more or less right."

"He guessed, even so," I said. "But not until it was too late! The hardest part was making sure that he drank from the drugged goblet! I'd put the draft in the one on the right but when Dale carried the tray in, Dormbois was on my left and Ericks on my right! I could have torn my hair out. I dared not even take the tray from Dale and turn it round. I had to be as remote from it as possible. I dared not touch it."

"But you thought of that in advance, ma'am, and thought of the trick with the favor!" said Dale, laughing.

"Though my heart turned over when Dormbois tried to interfere and almost picked up the wrong goblet! If you hadn't made that suggestion that he was nervous, I think he would have spoiled everything at that moment! *And* . . ." Dale was clearly lost in admiration, "when Master Ericks came up to you, you moved away to your left, so that the goblet there was nearest when you reached out to pick one up and hand it to Ericks. I felt faint, ma'am, wondering how you'd manage but you did! You pushed Dormbois back at the same time."

"I know. I trod on his foot as well as pushing him," I said.

"What on earth would you have done if Ericks *had* picked up the wrong goblet?" Brockley asked.

"Jogged his elbow and spilled it, I suppose," I said.

After a pause, Brockley said: "Did Master Ericks know about the . . . drug, madam?"

"No, of course not."

"I don't think he would be very pleased if he did know. His sense of honor . . ."

"Brockley, I wasn't going to risk having to marry the man who murdered my cousin by crawling in at a window and stabbing Edward in his sleep. Not even to save Adam Ericks's honor!"

Brockley sighed. "I understood your message about the button, madam. Dormbois murdered Master Faldene, I take it?"

"Yes."

"But why?"

I said: "You're not going to like this, Brockley. Master Henderson ordered it."

"Master . . . how do you know, madam?"

I said: "You won't like the answer to that, either, Brockley."

"Madam!"

"Leave it," I said. "Let us never speak of it again. Dale will tell you when you're alone. I don't ask her to have secrets from you."

"Dear God!" said Brockley.

I said, determinedly: "How far is it to the English border?"

25

Face-to-Face

It took us five weeks to reach southern England. The weather turned wet, changing tracks to rivers, flooding fords, converting once solid ground to quagmires and delaying us, and then both Dale and I caught cold on the way. We fell ill virtually together, Dale on one day and myself on the next, and spent a fortnight of shared misery, confined indoors in a Midlands hostelry. It was lucky that I still had enough money with me to pay the innkeeper for the extra time and the stabling for our horses.

I was very worried about Dale, with whom colds so easily turned serious. She developed a cough, which I did not, and took much longer to recover than I did. Brockley, who remained well (and prudently slept over the stables rather than with Dale), went out to buy horehound medicine and a balsam to put in boiling water so that she could inhale the aromatic steam. We got her well in the end, but she had lost a great deal of strength, and when we set off again, we could only do a few miles a day.

Brockley's manner to me, throughout the whole ride, was odd; not disapproving exactly, more a mixture of the distant and the anxious. But only during the later part of the journey did he actually comment, and then it was oblique. He did not mention Dormbois's name, or speak of Roderix Fort, but as he rode at my side one misty morning, he said: "Madam, you may think me impertinent, but you know me well enough to know that I only have your welfare in mind."

"Yes, Brockley?"

"The way you are living isn't right, madam, for you, or for Fran. I do ask you, with all my heart, to find a more settled manner of living. I urge you to marry again."

He didn't add *and it would be easier for me,* but the implication was there and I knew it. Brockley loved me. Dale by now must have told him (even if he hadn't guessed) that in Roderix Fort I had been with Dormbois as I would never be with Brockley himself. He was a conventional man and he could accept the thought of me with a lawful husband, but Dormbois had not been that, and the thought of that night must stick in his gullet. It was hard for him.

I said: "I know," and he nodded, understanding that I also knew the things he hadn't actually said.

It was the last week of April before, at last, we came in sight of the chimneys of Thamesbank, where I had left Meg. I intended to collect her but not to sleep under Thamesbank's roof. I didn't want to hurt Mattie's feelings, but this was Rob Henderson's house and accept its hospitality now I could not and would not. I saw to it that we timed our arrival at Thamesbank for mid-morning, so that we could easily pack Meg's things and be on our way to Withysham the same day.

But before we had dismounted, Mattie came out to greet us, and though she was smiling bravely, I knew at once that something was wrong. The smile was a mere pretense. She reached up a hand to clasp mine and hers was shaking.

"Mattie, what is it?"

"You'd better get down. You . . ."

"Mattie! What's *wrong*? Meg? Is Meg all right? Tell me!" Giving Brockley no time to alight and offer his help, I was already scrambling out of the saddle.

"Meg is perfectly well and is at her lessons," said Mattie. "You shall see her in a moment. This is nothing to do with Meg. Please come inside. You too, Dale, and Brockley, leave the horses to our grooms. You know very well they're reliable. Come."

Bewildered, we did as she said. Thamesbank was a large and beautiful house close to the river, with a wide stretch of grass running down to the water and a landing stage and boats of its own. We had come to the landward side, but as soon as we were indoors, in the big main hall where the family dined, with the minstrels' gallery above and windows looking out to both the front gate and the river, I saw that an unfamiliar barge was drawn up at the stage.

"You have visitors?" I said to Mattie.

"They've been here since yesterday," said Mattie. "They're waiting for you."

"For me?"

"Ursula . . ." Mattie took my hands and drew me away to a window seat, out of anyone else's hearing. We sat down and she looked gravely into my eyes. "My dearest Ursula. I love you, and I love Meg. But I also love Rob. I don't know what to say to you. Rob came home a few days ago. He expected to find that you had been here long before him and was surprised and worried that you had not."

"I was ill on the way and so was Dale. Mattie . . ."

"Yes, we know that now. Word reached Cecil three days ago—one of the innkeepers on your route is . . ."

"One of Cecil's agents. Is that what you mean?"

"Shh. Listen. Ursula, we know everything that happened in Scotland. I know that your cousin was murdered and by whom—which means that I know what part my Rob had in it. What *am* I to say to you? To me, he is still my Rob and always will be. But . . ."

"I don't blame *you,* Mattie. How could I? You have been a good friend, a blessing. No one could have been kinder to Meg. Only, now . . ."

"I know. Oh, Ursula . . ."

"It means," I said, "that I can't stay a night with you because . . . because . . . well, I've come to fetch Meg and take her home. I'll have to go to Faldene, of course, and . . ."

I was upset and nervous, almost rambling. Mattie put a finger on my lips.

"Ursula, I said that I had guests who were waiting for you. They come from the court. It was they who told us that you were on your way and were making for Thamesbank and would arrive soon. Sir William Cecil sent them, with orders to bring you to court at once. If you hadn't appeared by tomorrow, they were to set out to meet you. They haven't actually come to arrest you, but . . ."

"I went to Scotland illegally," I said tiredly. "I daresay that a man called Christopher Rokeby informed them of that. But . . ."

I broke off, hearing voices. The door of the hall opened and in came three men. One of them I instantly recognized. He was middle-aged, his hair by this time almost entirely gray, but he looked as tough as ever and he was a man whom Cecil trusted absolutely. So, indeed, did Brockley and I. He had been with us for a while in France and Brockley had made friends with him.

"John Ryder," I said.

"Mistress Blanchard." He bowed, but his face was unsmiling. "We are relieved to see you safely here. You will wish to take a glass of wine with Mistress Henderson and greet your daughter and I will allow that. But after that, you and your people must come with us. We have orders to bring you with all speed to Hampton Court, where the queen and Sir William await you. And I regret to say," added Ryder, sounding as though he really were regretful, "that you have no choice in the matter."

I said: "But I *must* go to Faldene. My cousin Edward was murdered and I ought to see his family and . . ."

"Your letter, sent in March by Master Henderson's man Barker, was duly delivered," said Ryder. "They know of Master Faldene's death. They can wait a little longer for you to come in person. Mistress Henderson, I suggest you send for the wine and fetch

Mistress Blanchard's daughter to her. But we must leave before midday."

So, a brief hour with Meg. Long enough to hug her, to exclaim that she had grown again, to ask after her studies in Latin and hear her play a melody on the lute. I asked her the name of it and she said: "It is 'Leicester's Dance,' Mama. The music master here says it is the most popular dance at court, and has been named after the Earl of Leicester."

"Robin Dudley," said Mattie, who was watching in the background. "He was made Earl of Leicester in the autumn."

"Yes, I know. So he is still—very much a favorite?" I was speaking to Mattie.

"It would seem so. But that's of no interest to you, Meg," Mattie added hastily. "These court affairs won't matter to you for a good many years yet. I only wish . . ."

She stopped. Knowing that she wanted to speak to me privately, I kissed Meg and told her to fetch her latest piece of embroidery, so that I could see it before I left. Then I looked at Mattie.

"I only wish I could share her future with you," she said. "I wish that together we could see her grow up and go to court and marry. I see that that may not now be possible. But need we quite cease to be friends, Ursula?"

"No. No, Mattie, of course not. After I get home— when I'm released!—I will write to you. I promise," I said.

Presently, having admired the embroidery, it was

time once more to hug Meg, assure her that I would come back for her as soon as I could, and then, with the best grace possible—because, as I had found at Roderix Fort, if you are being forced to do something, it is more dignified to look as if you are willing—I went out to the barge, Brockley and Dale in attendance, and embarked for Hampton Court.

It wasn't far. The day was one of brisk wind, with alternate sun and cloud. The river went from sparkling to iron gray and back again to sparkling as we journeyed, and I was glad I had a thick cloak to keep the breeze off. I told myself that I was shivering because the breeze was so cold. It was better than admitting that I was frightened.

Hampton Court is a beautiful palace, standing serenely by the river, built of rosy brick with gray stone edgings, its rooms spacious, its tapestried and ornamental ceilings a wonder to the eye. It has ghosts, though. It is also the palace where Kate Howard, King Henry's young, frivolous fifth wife, was arrested. She glimpsed him at the far end of a gallery and ran screaming toward him, only to be dragged back by the guards. Some say that sometimes, in that gallery, at dusk, those screams still echo, and although I have never heard them myself, I always feel uneasy there, as though there were a shadow on my spirit.

I was now, for the first time, coming to court as something nearer to a prisoner of the queen than one of her servants. As I disembarked and walked into that beautiful palace, my feet felt as though they were weighted with lead.

I was taken to a small room overlooking the wide

grounds, and there I waited, with Brockley and Dale, with Ryder to keep an eye on us. We were there for the best part of an hour, before I was called into an adjoining room. Cecil was there. With him was Rob Henderson.

I made a correctly deep curtsy to Cecil, and a very shallow one to Rob. He held out a hand to raise me, but I pretended I hadn't seen it and straightened up unaided. Wordlessly, he stepped back.

"Be seated," said Cecil. He was already sitting down. Like Uncle Herbert, Cecil suffered from gout and did not like to stand for too long. He studied me gravely. He had a neat fair beard, serious, intelligent blue eyes, and a deep line between his eyes. "Ursula," he said, "you had no business to go to Scotland without asking the queen's consent. I think you know that."

"It was a family matter," I said. "And Edward . . . I couldn't ask permission without stating my business. Because then I would have had to explain Edward's and his was treason. I can say that now, since he's dead, and anyway, I think you know. But I went to try to stop him from committing treason. It can't be wrong to try to stop someone from doing that! And," I said, suddenly ceasing to be afraid because I was very angry and anger drives out fear better than anything else, "I hoped to bring him back alive. I didn't go to Scotland to murder him! As you did, Rob!"

Henderson said soberly: "I had to. At least, I *could* have arrested him and brought him back to the Tower. Would you have preferred that, Ursula? You know what would have happened to him next. And even men in prison have been known to smuggle information out.

Instead, I stopped his mouth for good, and he died quickly. Does that make me a monster?"

"I don't know," I said. I stared at him. I was seeing the Rob Henderson I knew: the handsome, fair-haired man who had so often helped and supported me in my difficult and dangerous work, the beloved husband of my dear Mattie. But he had, so to speak, put the dagger into the hand that killed my cousin Edward and something in me cried out against that. I had once got my own uncle Herbert arrested for treason and I had always felt uncomfortable even about that, though I had little enough reason to love him and I had at the time been trying to do my duty as a loyal subject of Queen Elizabeth. This dead-of-night assassination was far worse. Rob had been my friend, but that friendship was poisoned now, beyond all recovery. I said blankly: "But I don't understand how anyone knew what Edward was doing, anyway."

Cecil said quietly: "Your cousin Edward dismissed a valet he believed was spying on him. His family told you that, I think. Well, Edward was quite right, but what he didn't realize was that the valet wasn't—and isn't—the only servant at Faldene who was in our pay. A copy of the document that Edward was carrying to Scotland was made and sent to us just before he set off with it. Master Henderson here was already preparing to join Henry Lord Darnley and accompany him to Scotland. When the news arrived, he was given a second task to perform, that of seeing that neither Edward nor his document reached their destination. And then, just as Master Henderson had finished his packing, further news arrived—that you were going after your cousin as well."

I remembered the hovering maidservant when I was at Faldene.

"I told Mattie that I was going north to retrieve some jewelry that had been sold by mistake," I remarked. "I felt at the time that she didn't believe me."

"She knew what Edward was doing," Rob said. "The news that he was going to Scotland was sent to Thames-bank first and then, because I wasn't there, Mattie herself dispatched it on to me at court. When you arrived, also bound on an errand to the north, she guessed that there might be a connection. She was worried about you. She wrote to me to say so."

"You didn't send after me to bring me back," I said, puzzled now as well as angry.

"It was considered but I argued against that," said Rob. "*I* argued against it, Ursula. I didn't want you to realize that we knew what your cousin was about. Because if you did, you might also, when you heard of his death, begin to suspect that we had arranged it. Believe it or not, Ursula, I knew how much that would distress you. I urged that you be left alone, allowed to make your journey—and bring back the sad news to Faldene's family."

"I see," I said. "But once I reached Scotland, I would be likely enough to find out that you were there."

"That wouldn't have mattered, as long as you didn't come to realize that I wasn't just there to watch over Darnley," said Rob. "Dear heaven, I'm so sorry you found out what my other errand was! When I agreed to ask Christopher Rokeby to obtain Mary Stuart's original list for you, I did it because I wanted you to believe I knew no more of Edward's death than you did. I didn't even risk just forging a second version of the list for you to compare with mine, because you are so damned astute. I've known you to recognize a forgery before now, from very small clues. And if I'd refused outright, you were quite capable of trying to get at it yourself—I know you!"

"I'm sorry I put Master Rokeby in danger," I said stiffly.

"You didn't. That *would* have stopped me from taking the risk. Rokeby has a set of lockpicks, a fund dedicated to the purpose of bribery, and he happens to know that one of the clerks in William Maitland's secretariat is the real father of the only son and heir of a particularly short-tempered Scottish noble. Rokeby can usually get his hands on any document he wants without running much if any risk. He and I played the comedy out, sweetheart, right to the end. He was in on the secret, yes. Ursula, all that was part of trying to hide the truth from you, to look innocent in your eyes. Mattie loves you. I value you more than you know. But you . . ." His voice took on an exasperated tinge. "I've told you before. You're just like my dog Pokenose. You have to find out everything!"

"Sir William Cecil," I said coldly, "has on occasion paid me to do precisely that."

"You have a talent for it," said Cecil, and at last he smiled. "You have not been arrested, Ursula. You are not going to be taken to the Tower. But you are being warned. For your own safety—from us as well as from others!—never act alone in this way again."

"I overtook you on the road north," Rob said. "I

raced you to Scotland, and then went straight to Dormbois. I really did have Darnley to watch. I was supposed to be encouraging a match between him and Mary Stuart. I had work to do, as well as wanting to keep in the shadows as far as Faldene was concerned. I made Dormbois my deputy, as it were. He has been in our pay since John Knox converted him, a year ago now. And Dormbois—doesn't mind too much what he does."

"As I well know," I said. "And Edward was murdered in the night because he was carrying a list of Mary's English supporters—an updated list. When she already has one, even if it is a little older."

"Ursula." Cecil's voice was calm. "Edward was carrying more than a list. He was also carrying the names of those who were on the original list, but who have since changed sides and are working for us. Dormbois is not the only man who seems to be hers, but is really ours."

"Yes," I said. "I realized that something like that was happening."

Cecil nodded. "She and her supporters are building up a network of supporters in England—but we are creating a network, too. Ours consists of her apparent supporters, who will keep us informed of what she is doing, of every move she makes. Dormbois's own name was on that list. The Thursbys—you stayed with the Thursbys, did you not?—are on it too. So are the Bycrofts."

"Those two families were the ones I found out about," I said.

"Pokenose!" Rob put in.

"The Thursbys," said Cecil with slight amusement,

"are afraid of having their home repossessed by the Church if a Catholic ruler took over the English throne. My agents have worked quite hard to encourage that fear to the point where the Thursbys agreed to work for Elizabeth. The Bycrofts needed money and could simply be bought."

"Just like that?" I had wondered a good deal about the motives of the Bycrofts. "But—they're so pious!"

"They overdo it," Rob said. I knew from the glint of humor in his voice and eyes that he was trying to win me back as a friend, but I couldn't respond. "They are so very anxious to appear committed to the Catholic religion," he said. "There are many others. If their names were ever to reach Mary Stuart or her lords, our network would be lost."

"And Edward found out," said Cecil. "Though it isn't clear how."

"We have spies in his home at Faldene," said Rob quietly. "Perhaps other places too harbor servants who listen at doors and read their masters' letters. Bycroft and St. Margaret's, for instance."

John Thursby's voice spoke in my mind. *Hamish Fraser watches over every detail of our household. We have a little joke that if anyone in it were to lock themselves into a room at the far end of the house from Hamish, and cough, the moment they came out, they would meet the maidservant he had sent to them with a licorice and horehound cough mixture.* I had been relieved to know Hamish Fraser innocent of murder. But perhaps he was guilty of other things instead.

"I know nothing of the other households concerned," I said, "but if you don't want Mary to learn that the Bycrofts and the Thursbys have changed their allegiance, I recommend a sharp look at the Thursby steward, Hamish Fraser. I can't be sure, but he could be the source of Edward's information."

"Thank you, Ursula. We shall investigate," Cecil said. "We shall make a point of it."

"And another point that must be made," said Rob Henderson, "is that Edward Faldene assuredly carried most of those names in his head. We could have stolen the list—Dormbois did—but silencing Edward Faldene was essential as well. And as I said, it was surer, from our point of view, and kinder from his, simply to kill him."

"Do you understand?" asked Cecil.

"Yes. I understand." Without warning, I was close to tears. "I understand completely and it only makes it worse. You have to protect Elizabeth . . ."

"Yes." Henderson was nodding.

". . . you *do* have to protect Elizabeth. She is England. Yet it seems that everyone else is turned into nothing; people are bought, or threatened, or killed . . . we're all nothing but pawns on her chessboard and all as expendable as Edward, if it came to the point."

"Not you," said Rob. "You are no traitor. Listen, Ursula. You think we are ruthless? What of yourself? You encompassed Dormbois's death, did you not? I know all that happened in Roderix Fort, my dear. I arrived there less than two hours after you left it, dispatched by Queen Mary with an armed escort to demand your release and bring you back to Stirling. When Brockley went back to Roderix with Ericks, he had the good sense to leave word for the queen. He left it with one of her Maries. Dormbois is dead now, but he was still alive when I got there and he regained his senses for a while. He told me everything. He realized that he couldn't live long. He had nothing to lose. He had a conscience of a sort, you know."

"Really?" I said.

"Yes. Really. He let you buy my name from him and it was on his mind. At the time he didn't think it mattered. You were his prisoner in Roderix and he didn't anticipate that you'd ever escape him and talk. He didn't know you! He was mad for you, you know. I stayed with him till he died, five days later, and he said as much to me, over and over. Frankly, Ursula, you are a menace, unattached as you are, riding round the countryside and making men like Dormbois fall in love with you. I wish you would marry and settle down!"

"I agree, though I wouldn't put it quite so roughly," Cecil remarked.

"Dormbois," said Rob, "also told me that he believed you had somehow tricked him into drinking drugged wine and watched him fight and lose. He said he didn't blame Adam Ericks. He reckoned it was a fair duel as far as Ericks was concerned, but he was as sure as he could be that somehow or other, you had cheated."

"Of course I cheated," I said. "I had to escape marriage to Dormbois so I had to make sure that Ericks won, even if it wasn't in a fair fight. I probably helped to save Ericks's neck—if he was in any real danger of arrest for murdering Edward. Was he?"

"Not after John Knox stood up at that inquiry and spoke for him! Any real chance of making him a scapegoat vanished at that moment and that, by the way, was no scheme of mine. Dormbois's men saw a chance of finding someone to take the blame and seized it, and when they told him what they'd done, Dormbois was more than happy to go along with them. I knew nothing of it until I read the report of the inquiry. Even those of my men who were in Furness's tavern didn't quite grasp why Dormbois's men were so eager to encourage the fight. I got an admission out of Dormbois while I was with him in Roderix."

"So it *was* Dormbois who told the authorities about the quarrel in the tavern? That was the substance of Ericks's challenge to him."

"I know. And Ericks was quite right. Oh, he didn't issue that challenge out of pure chivalry! He really was outraged by the smear on his name. Your Brockley just worked on that." Rob grinned. "I feel sorry for Ericks, I really do. First a false accusation and then an assisted victory against a drugged opponent! But I did make sure that the accusation wouldn't rise up against him at some later date. Once Dormbois was dead and beyond the reach of any law, I let it be known that there was no case against Ericks. The mystery remains officially unsolved."

There was a silence. Then, with dignity, I said: "I understand everything you have told me, Rob. I understand why you—did what you did, to Edward. But I can't forgive it. I hope you in turn can understand that. I am sorry. Mattie will mind it, I think."

"I am sorry, too," Rob said. "Believe me, should we in the future need to work together again, what you have said will make no difference."

"I hope it won't arise," I told him. I looked at Cecil.

"I want no more secret missions," I said. "Now . . . may I see the queen? Or am I in the outer darkness as far as she is concerned?"

"No," said Cecil. "She wishes to see you, as it happens. She asked me to bring you to her when we had talked. If you are ready, we can go now."

26

Ancient Truths

"You have been very foolish, Ursula," said Queen Elizabeth. "What have you to say for yourself?"

She must have been waiting for me, for Cecil took me to her without any delay at all, passing straight through an anteroom crowded with courtiers and ladies. I recognized most of them but no one greeted me. My unlawful expedition to Scotland was evidently known, and they probably all expected that my interview with Elizabeth would end with me being marched off to the Tower under guard.

She was alone, however, with no guards to be seen. She was seated regally, ruffed and bejeweled, in a gilded chair, embroidered skirts spread wide, very much the queen receiving an erring underling, and her first words were ominous, yet her voice was kind.

Cecil bowed and stood back. I knelt. "Ma'am. I am sorry. I did not want to displease you. My family begged me for my help and all I wished to do was bring my cousin back to them safely, and bring him back also to a sense of his loyalty and his duty to yourself."

"Well said. I will forgive you, Ursula. Just this once."

There was a pause.

Elizabeth looked much as she had done when I last saw her. She was no longer a young girl. She was over thirty now, and the first trace of hardening was there in the pale triangular face. The armor of jewelry and embroidered satins, dramatic ruff, and spreading far-thingale no longer protected a timid young girl but a seasoned ruler. Yet just now, she was for some reason uncertain. She was looking at me as though she wasn't sure what to say next. I looked back at her question-ingly.

"What are you thinking, Ursula?" she asked abruptly. "You have seen my cousin Mary Stuart now. How does she compare with me?"

"She is beautiful and accomplished, ma'am, but . . ."

"But?"

Elizabeth used people as pawns. But she had done that to me before and it had made no difference then. She was England, and our safety and prosperity depended on her. Besides, although she was as power-ful as her father had been, she was also a woman, and therefore vulnerable in ways that he never was. When I answered her, I spoke from the heart, to a degree that surprised me. "But no more so than you, ma'am, and my loyalty, my love, are for you."

Elizabeth's face did not change. "And what of Henry Lord Darnley? Did you see them together?"

"Yes. I understand that Master Henderson was in

Scotland firstly to encourage a match, but I am not sure that there was a strong attraction on either side."

"Are you not? Well, news has reached us that is later than yours. It seems that Darnley has fallen ill with measles—so childish, and how typical of him!" said Elizabeth with a sudden snort—"and that Mary is personally nursing him, and all is now enchantment on both sides. I fancy they'll marry."

"You wish for the marriage, ma'am?"

"On balance, yes," said Elizabeth. "At the moment."

I asked no more questions. Darnley, I supposed, was another pawn on Elizabeth's chessboard and perhaps she hadn't quite decided what use she ought to make of him.

Her attention came back to me. "You declare your love and loyalty and yet you still broke my laws and went to Scotland without my consent. Oh, no need to repeat that it was a family matter." She raised a hand to make sure I didn't. "I understand family matters. Now. I want to hear from you the whole story—or as much of it as you can tell me without indelicacy."

She listened attentively to my careful and embarrassed account. She showed particular interest in my description of how I had taken command in the hall at Roderix Fort and presided over the drinking of the drugged toast and asked me to go through it a second time.

"I understand how you felt," she said. "I too felt it, at the beginning, when I was still at heart the Princess Elizabeth, Queen Mary's prisoner. You had to overcome not only that hall full of men, but yourself, did you not? You had to find strength where you did not think it existed;

cease to be a woman and become simply a mind implanted in a body, and take command of the other minds in the room. I am right, am I not?"

"Yes, ma'am. Yes. That is just what it was like."

"Well, well. Continue."

I did as she asked. At the end, there was a pause.

It was a long pause, during which she did not look at me, but at Cecil, and they gazed at each other, long and hard, as though exchanging a wordless message. The atmosphere in the room altered. It grew tense, as though that silent message were on the verge of being spoken aloud, but was being held back. And then, curiously, it grew warm, almost intimate. At last, Elizabeth spoke.

"Well, Cecil. Do you agree?" she said. "Is it time to tell her?"

"I think so, ma'am. I think that Ursula's loyalty is unquestionable now. It has been amply demonstrated time and again, and since Matthew de la Roche is dead . . ."

"Yes, quite. Nothing could be said while he was alive."

My astonished gaze went from one of them to the other. I had no idea what they were talking about.

"This matter was under discussion between us as soon as we heard the news of your husband's death," Elizabeth said. "A grief to you, Ursula, but it left me with a freedom I had not had before. However, Cecil and I thought it best to wait until you had got over your first mourning. And then, just as the time had almost arrived, you were off to Scotland! I wish now that I had spoken sooner."

"I don't understand."

"Of course you don't," said Elizabeth. "But let me tell you that you dispelled my last doubts just now, when you talked of that moment when you entered the hall at Roderix Fort and took control. It was as though I were listening to myself describing how I took control at my first council meeting. I shall never forget it. Ursula, your mother . . . served at court . . . before, and for a while after, my own birth. That is so, is it not?"

"Yes, ma'am." My mother had in fact served Anne Boleyn, Elizabeth's own mother. I never knew Elizabeth to speak of her own mother but once, although I had reason to believe that she thought of her often.

"And then," said Elizabeth, "she was sent home, in disgrace, with child by a court gallant she would not name. She said he was married."

"That is true, ma'am."

"Not entirely," Elizabeth said. "Your father was a married man, yes. But your mother was not sent away. She asked permission to leave the court, admitting her condition and saying that she was not willing to cause trouble, and that her family would care for her. She had a personal maid, however, who did not leave the court, but found employment with another lady-in-waiting. The maid knew who your father was. Cecil?"

"She kept her mouth shut," said Cecil, "and she went on working at court as a tirewoman for more than a quarter of a century, until she died, about a year before you came to court, Ursula. You were in Antwerp then, with Gerald Blanchard. After her death, a memorandum was found among her things."

"She had held her tongue," said Elizabeth, "but she

wrote her knowledge down. Perhaps she had a muddled idea that one day it might matter; or perhaps the burden of the secret was simply too great. We do not know."

"The memorandum was discovered by the lady-in-waiting who then employed her," Cecil said, "and, wisely, she brought it to me. She too is dead now, and she was always discreet. No one knows of this but the queen and myself. I have never even told my wife."

"But . . ." I was beginning, with amazement, to understand.

"You must often have wondered who your father was," Cecil said to me. "Have you not?"

"Yes. Yes, of course. Even more, lately—my daughter so much resembles her own father that at times I have wondered if I in any way resemble mine. But . . ."

"I think you do," said Elizabeth with a smile. "We couldn't of course be sure at first that the memorandum was anything more than a flight of imagination. But it was one reason why you were accepted as one of my ladies. Then you came to court. And after that . . . time and again . . . I saw. It was there. A turn of the head. A way of standing, of speaking, a nuance in the voice. I had almost made up my mind to tell you, when you became entangled with Matthew de la Roche, who was a Catholic and supported Mary Stuart. We—Cecil and I—decided that we couldn't tell you then. But now, we can."

"Ma'am?"

"What you did in that hall at Roderix Fort," said Elizabeth, "was very difficult. I know! Oh, how well I know! I fancy that you only achieved what you did at

Roderix because you have inherited in your blood-stream the ability to do it. Just as I have. Your father, Ursula, was also my father. You are the natural daughter of King Henry the Eighth, and therefore, half sister to me. Which means," said Queen Elizabeth briskly, while I still stood in front her, blinking and trying to think of something to say, "that in future, when it is a question of family matters, remember that your nearest adult relative, my dear Ursula, is myself."

I found my tongue. I had after all had a reason for asking to see Elizabeth, and I had not yet raised it.

"Ma'am," I said, "I asked to see you before I knew that you had already requested this meeting. Now, I know that it is doubly important. If I am really your half sister . . ."

"You are. There can be no doubt of it."

"Then I will say at once that I realize and accept that I have no dynastic significance. I also promise, before you ask me, never to trade on this; never, in fact, to tell anyone. But sometimes, such things do become known, or are guessed at, and in that case, I might be courted, as someone who . . . who matters to you . . . to whom you might listen . . ."

"What are you trying to say, Ursula?" asked Cecil, the line between his eyes deepening.

"I wish to stop being an agent," I said. "I wish to give up this life of adventure and danger. I would like to leave the court altogether and withdraw into private life. May I do so?"

"I am heartily of the opinion that you should. I always have been," said Cecil. "I have used you—as a pawn, as you would no doubt say—but always I . . ."

"We," said Elizabeth.

". . . always we have had a conscience about it. It would be best if you could marry."

"I have thought of that," I said. "And several people apart from yourself have advised me to do precisely that. They are probably right. If I have doubts, they are because, dearly as I love my daughter Meg, her birth cost me dear, and when I tried to bring Matthew's child into the world, the child was born dead and I nearly lost my own life. For me, marriage has its perils."

"These things are in God's hands," said Cecil.

"That's what you have on occasion told *me*," said Elizabeth. "I don't agree with you. I prefer to keep them in mine. I understand how Ursula feels."

Cecil shook his head disapprovingly. "I still think that Ursula should have a husband. She has an estate. For a woman, that is a heavy responsibility without a man, and besides, Ursula, you will be troubled by suitors. Haven't your recent experiences taught you that?"

"They have," I said. "And I have in fact made my decision."

I had made it between the Midlands and Thamesbank, at the moment when Brockley himself said that I should marry again. It only remained to see if the man in question would respond.

"I have a man in mind," I said, "if you will give your consent, ma'am. If so, perhaps Sir William would make the approach on my behalf. I think the gentleman in question may be willing but I am not sure."

"Who is he?" Elizabeth asked.

* * *

I stayed at Hampton Court for a fortnight, during which time it was made clear to the court at large that I was no longer out of favor. It was a pleasant time, or would have been, except that I was longing so much for Meg and for my home. Brockley and Dale were thankful that I was not in the serious trouble they had feared. They were less thankful, though, when I told them that the queen and Cecil were interesting themselves in my marital future and that Cecil had actually written a letter on my behalf.

"I advised marriage, madam," Brockley said, "but this . . . I can't feel that this is ideal. Not after Master de la Roche."

"No, indeed. We were thinking of a proper love match, ma'am, an affair of the heart," Dale said sentimentally.

I told them to mind their own business.

At the end of the two weeks, I sent a courier to Withysham to announce that I was on my way home and traveled to Thamesbank by hired barge. Rob Henderson offered to escort me, but I said that I would prefer it if he did not. I was civil. Once again, I chose to keep my dignity. But my feelings had not changed. With my head, I could understand why he had had my cousin killed but my heart, my viscera, would not listen. This man had had a blood relation of mine slaughtered and I could not forgive him. I could not bear to be close to him for long, or to exchange more than the most conventional remarks with him.

At Thamesbank, Mattie met me, holding Meg by the hand, and we went into the house together for a goblet of wine before I traveled on. Dale and Brockley were

with me and our horses, of course, had been left at
Thamesbank. We could, and would, ride on the same
day. I still could not bring myself to stay a night under
Rob's roof, even in his absence. I would take wine there
only for Mattie's sake.

With Meg out of hearing, because she had gone
with Dale to the nursery to see Mattie's infant daughter, Elizabeth, I looked at my friend across the goblets
and said: "Mattie, you told me that you know what
happened in Scotland. What Rob did."

"Yes, Ursula. I know more or less all of it—that's
quite true."

"I can't . . ." I stopped, and then began again.
"Nothing will ever make me less than fond of you,
Mattie. Nothing. And you're right to be loyal to Rob.
But for me . . ." I stopped again. Mattie looked at me
sadly and I saw the glitter of tears in her eyes.

"You mean that nothing will ever be the same again.
I know. Believe me, you and Meg will always, always,
be welcome here, but if you don't choose to come . . .
well . . ."

"I'll write to you now and then, Mattie, and tell you
how Meg does. If when she is older, she chooses to
visit you, I won't stop her. Will that do?"

"It will have to, won't it?" Mattie looked at me
wryly and sipped her wine. "What plans have you
made now, Ursula?"

I told her of my future intentions and she wished
me happiness. We embraced before we parted, but it
was a deeper and more final parting than any we had
had before and would probably last longer. Then I
rode away.

Before going to my own home, I went to Faldene to see my uncle and aunt and Helene. I was careful in what I said. I did not harrow them with a full description of Edward's deathbed, and I told them that he had been murdered by one of Mary Stuart's Protestant nobles.

It was almost true, as far as it went. They didn't ask many questions. For the most part, they listened and cried. Helene wept so much that I found myself embracing her with a real desire to give comfort and then doing the same to Aunt Tabitha, for the years were telling on her seriously now. Her hands had become stringy and marked with liver spots, and the fine dry skin of her face was showing wrinkles and looked as though it had worn thin with time.

I had always been so afraid of her but now she was a sad figure, a woman past her best years, trying to grapple with the knowledge that a son she had loved and been proud of would never come home again. It was much the same with Uncle Herbert, though he would not let me embrace him. I would never love them, and they would never love me, but they respected me now, and I could pity them.

I once more collected Meg, who had stayed in the kitchen with Brockley and Dale, and at last, we went home to Withysham.

Never in my life had I been so glad to see it. It was so dear, so familiar, and yet it felt as though I had been away from it for a hundred years. At the front door, Brockley helped me out of the saddle, and Malton came down the steps to welcome us. My ancient hanger-on Gladys, a shawl over her head and her terrible fanged grin joyously splitting her nutcracker of a face, came hobbling after him, and it was Gladys, no respecter of anyone's status, who got in before him and informed me that I had visitors awaiting me.

"That was for me to say, Gladys," said Malton reproachfully, and was then forestalled again because before he had time to tell me who the visitors were, one of them came hurrying out to join us. At the sight of her, I uttered a cry of joy.

"Sybil!"

It was indeed Sybil Jester, the friend I had made in Cambridge the previous year. Sybil's features always made me think that when she was small, someone had put her chin on a table and a heavy weight on the top of her head and then pressed. Her nose was too broad, her lips a little too thick, and her dark eyes were deep-set behind heavy cheekbones. But they were eyes full of serenity and good temper and her welcoming embrace was full of genuine liking.

"You wrote to me from Scotland," said Sybil. "And hinted that if things were difficult in Cambridge, there might be a place for me here. Your letter was so kind, so affectionate, that I thought . . . I hoped . . ."

"So did I. I'm so glad to see you. What of your daughter, though?"

"She had a son," said Sybil. "The child has been adopted by his father's family and they found a match for Ambrosia. He is a schoolmaster in Norwich and runs a school for merchants' sons. I think they are well suited. The wedding was last month. As for me, I tried to settle down in Cambridge and go on with the business my husband left but . . ."

"It was difficult?"

"Impossible!" said Sybil. "I felt like a freak in a trav-eling fair. People would come into the pie shop just to stare at me. I tried to ignore it, to live it down, but . . . well, I've farmed it out to a manager. And then, I decided, because your letter was so kind, that I would come to you. I am not empty-handed, of course. I still have the income from the shop."

"Mistress Jester arrived a week ago," said Malton, "and has been helping to prepare for your return."

"I haven't interfered," said Sybil anxiously. "But I have made myself useful."

"She has brushed tapestries and aired bedding and polished candlesticks," said Malton, beaming. "You'll find everything in the best of order, madam."

"My dear Sybil," I said. "You're more than welcome and there is much you can do in Withysham. With you to look after her, I need never send Meg away from home again. Consider yourself part of my household from now on."

"But there's someone else here, madam," said Malton. "He arrived yesterday—I believe as a result of correspondence which he has had—he says—with Sir William Cecil on your behalf."

Behind me, I felt both Brockley and Dale stiffen. But I couldn't afford to worry about that now. I had sug-gested the match myself and there was much to be said for it. If it lacked passion . . . well, I had had my fill of passion, and more than my fill. Now, I wanted security and I also wanted safety from the perils of childbirth. Here was a chance to combine the two. With a gesture, I invited Malton to precede me inside and announce me. My second guest was in the main parlor, playing chess against himself. He rose at once as I entered.

"I thought it best not to rush impetuously out to greet you. I hope I did right. I feel quite shy, which is remarkable, at my age. I have come," said Hugh Stannard, rose grower, chess player, cynic, and elderly uncle to Mistress Euphemia Thursby, "to tell you in person that after receiving Sir William Cecil's unexpected but most welcome letter, I could not stay away. Since meeting you at St. Margaret's, I have scarcely been able to get you out of my mind. But what made you ask Sir William to write to me?"

I love Euphemia. She is a dear, sweet, innocent woman. She has never harmed a soul . . . if necessary, I will fight for Euphemia.

"You were ready to fight for Euphemia. I thought perhaps I could trust you. I thought that if you meant what you said at our last meeting, you might—make me a good husband."

"My dear Ursula, I can with the greatest pleasure offer you every kindness and a position in society and all manner of worldly goods. I am also as sure as I can be that our marriage will not result in children, and in this respect I would not deceive you, but Sir William assured me that since you have a daughter already, this is not a drawback in your eyes. If you hold by what you apparently told Sir William and the queen, and are truly of a mind to grant me your hand, it would please me very well."

THE FUGITIVE QUEEN

FIONA BUCKLEY

Turn the page for a preview of
The Fugitive Queen. . . .

1

A DOWRY FOR A WAYWARD MAID

I married Hugh Stannard in 1565, the seventh year of Queen Elizabeth's reign. I was thirty-one, a little younger than the queen herself, and Hugh was more than twenty years my senior, but this suited me very well. I had had enough of passion. I had felt passion for both of my previous husbands, and it had brought me more suffering than joy.

Well, it was true that my dear first husband, Gerald Blanchard, had given me my daughter, Meg, who was a blessing to me. But I had nearly lost my life in bearing her, and I had lost Gerald himself to smallpox while Meg was still small. Now my second husband, Matthew de la Roche, was dead of the plague, and although I had been deeply in love with him, we had never had any peace or lasting happiness together. I bore him a stillborn son, whose birth brought me even nearer to the grave than Meg had, so that I learned to fear childbearing. And also, I was loyal to Queen Elizabeth of England while he had continually plotted against her on behalf of Mary Stuart, who was queen of Scotland and in the eyes of ardent Catholics such as Matthew should have been queen of England, too.

If I were tired of passion, I was even more tired of conspiracy. For many years I had served Elizabeth as a Lady of the Presence Chamber, but I had been more than that. I had also worked for her as a spy, seeking out plots against her. For a while, I found the excitement exhilarating. It had called to me in a voice like the cry of the wild geese, winging across the sky. When I heard the geese, something in me always longed to bound up into the air and follow them. In the same way, I had responded to the summons of adventure.

But my work divided me from Matthew, and willy nilly, it caused me to send men to their deaths. It put me in mortal danger, too, once or twice. I continually worried and frightened my two good servants, Fran Dale, my tirewoman, and Roger Brockley, my steward; I more than once risked leaving Meg alone without either mother or father; and when my adventuring finally brought me perilously close to being forced into a disastrous third marriage, I knew I had had enough.

In Hugh Stannard, I found a refuge from conflict combined with freedom from the perils of childbirth. He was a widower and hadn't spent his widowhood like a monk, which meant that he had had every chance of siring children yet he had never succeeded in doing so. With him, I could be fairly sure that I would not have to face pregnancy again. He was also a decent, honest man, interested in chess and gardens, an uncomplicated Protestant and a trustworthy subject of the queen. Life as Hugh's wife might be dull, I thought, but it would be quiet. I was glad to settle for that. I could do without excitement. I could even do without happiness, as long as I could have some peace.

I hoped that we would make a good partnership. I would retire from court and conspiracy alike. Hugh and I would live together in amity, dividing our time between our two homes, my Withysham in Sussex and his Hawkswood in Surrey. I would educate my daughter; cultivate my herb garden; enjoy the society of my recently acquired woman companion, Sybil

Jester; let Fran and Roger enjoy each other's society, too. They were married, though Fran was still usually known as Dale, out of habit.

And so, in businesslike fashion, I ceased to be Ursula Blanchard and became instead Mistress Hugh Stannard, and if for a while I secretly grieved for Matthew, and cried in private because I had not been with him to comfort him at the end as once I had comforted Gerald, I did so only when I was alone.

And time erodes sorrow. Presently, my private fits of weeping ceased. Then I found that I had entered into more happiness than I would ever have believed possible. Hugh's lovemaking, if not frequent, was perfectly satisfactory, and his temperament was a pleasing mixture of the competent and the generous. He took a kindly interest in Meg, and it was Hugh who achieved what I had not, and found a tutor, Dr. Lambert, who could teach her Greek as well as Latin. Then, in the third year of our marriage, he was perfectly ready to welcome Penelope Mason, the daughter of my former acquaintance Ann Mason, into our home.

I was pleased. Years ago, I had uncovered a conspiracy that was brewing in the Mason household, although the Masons themselves were not involved. It was an unpleasant business, though, and keeping up any kind of friendship with the family seemed impossible afterward. Ann Mason's letter delighted me.

I was less delighted, however, when, after Pen had been with us for a month and I was exchanging messages with the court prior to taking her there, Hugh observed that, romantically speaking, she was susceptible. "You should urge the matter of her court appointment on," he said to me, "and get her away from here. I think she's falling for the tutor."

"For *Lambert?*" I said in astonishment. Dr. Henry Lambert was about Hugh's own age, and his hair was already completely silver. "He's too old to interest a young girl, surely!" I said.

"Don't you believe it," said Hugh. "He's a fine-looking man, and since Pen is studying Greek with Meg, she sees him every day. It won't do. Even if he were younger, it wouldn't do. He has no property beyond a cottage in the town of Guildford. And he's Protestant. Her mother wouldn't like that." Hugh had Catholic relatives and was tolerant of their creed. "Get her to court and under the eye of the queen, fast."

I did as he said. My happiness with Hugh was based as much as anything on his reliability. He was a clearheaded man and I trusted his judgment. It wasn't Hugh's fault that Pen's sojourn at court was less than successful. I certainly didn't blame him for that.

In all our life together, Hugh and I quarrelled only once, and that was for the most improbable of reasons.

Pen had been at court for only two months, when the letter came from Sir William Cecil to tell us that, having been removed from Dr. Lambert the tutor, she had now fallen in love with Master Rowan the interpreter and was causing embarrassment and would we come to court to deal with her.

"Oh, really!" grumbled Hugh. "And riding makes all my joints ache. I don't *want* to travel to Richmond. It's all of twenty-five miles. Why can't this Master Rowan fend her off without our help?"

I wondered, too. Between them, Master Rowan, Queen Elizabeth, Sir William Cecil, and the mistress in charge of the Maids of Honor really should have been able to call Pen to order. However, a summons from Cecil could not be ignored. Dutifully, we set out for Richmond Palace.

I had always liked Richmond. Of all Elizabeth's homes, it seemed to me the most charming, with its gardens and wind-chimes, its delicately designed towers and its gracious rooms, so many of which looked out on the Thames. On days like this, when the sun was out and the gardens were full of scent and color, and the Thames sparkled under a mild breeze, it was at its most beguiling. I would have enjoyed this visit, my first in years, if only we hadn't had to cope with Pen.

Cecil had arranged lodgings in the palace for us, and Pen was sent to us there. She stood miserably in front of us, and

Hugh and I, enthroned side by side on a broad window seat, probably looked and sounded like a pair of judges as we took her to task over her behavior.

Penelope obviously felt both frightened and embarrassed. First of all she turned very red and indignantly denied the charge. Confronted by the evidence in the form of Cecil's letter to me and also the sonnet in her handwriting (it was technically rather good, as a matter of fact; Pen was a clever girl), she did the only thing left for her to do and burst into tears. Hugh, without speaking and with a most unsympathetic expression on his face, took a napkin from his sleeve and handed it to her.

Gazing at her as she snuffled into the napkin, I sighed. It is no light responsibility, taking charge of someone else's daughter.

As her mother had said, Pen was not a beauty. To be truthful, she was almost plain. Her forehead bulged too much and her chin was too square. Her hair, demurely folded into waves under a white cap with silver embroidery, was no more than mousey. Her best features were her dark gray eyes, which were beautifully set, and her complexion, which, when not swollen with tears, was clear and pale. She held herself well, too, had good taste in dress, and she was intelligent, as that confounded sonnet demonstrated. I was sorry for her now but I hardened my heart. Pen was not going to spoil her reputation through girlish inexperience or waste herself on the wrong man if I could save her, and I meant to do that for her sake as well as to please her mother.

"Dry your eyes," I said firmly. "And listen. You have fallen in love—well, it happens. Few of us, though, marry our first loves, and most of us realize later what a good thing that is . . ."

"*You* married your first love," said Pen mutinously.

"And what would you know about that?" Hugh enquired. Soberly clad in a dark formal gown, his blue eyes icy with annoyance, my husband looked particularly judgmental. He also looked tired, I thought. We had taken two days over the ride from Hawkswood, and his mare was an ambler, thus providing a very smooth and easy pace, but the rheumatic pains in his joints had troubled him badly. It gave me an extra reason to be angry with Pen.

"I heard about it when I was with you at Hawkswood," she said in a resentful voice. "Dale told me. You ran off with your cousin Mary's betrothed. *You* pleased yourself. Why can't I?"

"That is enough. You will not address either of us in this pert fashion," said Hugh.

"I should say," I observed, thinking that Dale had talked too much and that I would have to raise the matter with her, "that my circumstances and yours, Pen, are not the same. I was not living as a welcome guest with my aunt and uncle, as you were at Hawkswood, but was there on sufferance and being treated as a dogsbody. No one was going to arrange a marriage for me. I had to make a future for myself."

"There's no need to justify yourself, my dear," said Hugh.

"One moment," I said. "I've a reason for talking like this. Pen, I ran away with Gerald Blanchard, but he was a suitable choice for me and he cared for me as I did for him. It was mutual. Master Rowan, on the other hand, is married already, with a family of children. He has no interest in you. You have been annoying him." I rapped the last two sentences out with deliberate brutality, and Hugh, on the point of intervening again, raised his eyebrows and didn't.

"We noticed at Hawkswood," I said, "that you were gazing after Dr. Lambert, too. It is clear that you need to be watched. We understand that the queen has released you from your duties for the time being, and returned you to our charge. For the moment, you will remain here in our rooms. I will send Dale to bear you company though not to gossip with you. Master Stannard and I are to have an audience with the queen, in which your future will be further discussed, I daresay."

"Oh, no!" It came out in a wail. "It's not . . . you're not going to tell the queen!"

"My dear girl," said Hugh impatiently, "she already knows. Mistress Stannard has just told you that she has released you to our care, and your deplorable behavior is the reason why. I suspect that most of the court knows! It's hard to keep any kind of secret here, and maybe it's time you began to understand that."

Dale was waiting in an outer room. Sybil Jester was not with her, having remained at Hawkswood to look after Meg, who was too young as yet for court. On returning to Dale, I eyed her severely. "You're to go in and keep an eye on Pen. You'd better both settle to some embroidery until we come back. And Dale . . ."

"Yes, ma'am?" said Dale, scanning my face with her large, light blue eyes and realizing that in some way or other she must have offended.

"In future," I said, "will you please not gossip to Pen about me! It seems that you told her how my first marriage arose. It's given her some very wrong ideas about the kind of behavior I will overlook!"

"Oh, ma'am! I'm sorry! I never expected . . . I didn't mean to gossip; I can't abide tittle-tattle. Only, nearly everyone that knows you knows about you and Master Blanchard and . . ."

"I know." I melted, and smiled at her. I sometimes had to take Dale to task, but I was at heart very fond of her and she of me. "It's just that Pen is so young. Be careful what you say to her, that's all. Only improving conversation, if you please!"

"Have a competition to see how many psalms each of you knows by heart," said Hugh, his normal sense of humor reasserting itself. "Meanwhile, we must attend upon Her Majesty."

"You almost frighten me sometimes," Hugh said as, having found a page to guide us, we made our way through the palace toward Elizabeth's apartments. "I thought for a moment that you were going to be too soft with Penelope. And then you descend on her like a stooping falcon. *Master Rowan has no interest in you. You've been annoying him.* It was more effective than if you'd thrown cold water over her. It will do her good, as of course you knew. But how you take me aback at times! You are so gentle, so compliant at home, that sometimes I forget what you've seen and done in your life—and what depths you have, and what skills."

"I didn't like doing it," I said somberly. "It was necessary, that's all. I used shock tactics because I thought they might succeed, and I did it because I'm very annoyed with her—but also worried about her. We're about to face the queen, and I daresay she'll tell us that our ward is in disgrace and must be removed."

"Elizabeth is fond of you. She owes you much."

"She won't like *this*," I said.

The walk to Elizabeth's rooms took us through the lively bustle that pervaded all her palaces. Elizabeth was a human magnet who drew people to her. The wide passages and lofty galleries, the tapestried anterooms and winding staircases of Richmond were crowded. Pageboys and servants hurried hither and thither, and the Lord Steward's chief officials, carrying white staves as symbols of office, went hither and thither as well in more measured fashion, transmitting orders and inspecting the work of underlings, ready at any moment to pounce on the pageboy overheard being less than respectful or the maidservant caught dusting too carelessly, spilling the goblets on her tray or getting out of her betters' path too slowly.

And, of course, there were the courtiers: queen's ladies and council members; the ever-present but ever-changing group of foreign emissaries (all moving as often as not in a cloud of their own clerks, secretaries, or interpreters, such as Master Rowan); and numerous hopeful young men who had come to court to make their careers. By right of well-born or sometimes merely rich and influential fathers, they had the entrée to the public rooms of the palaces, and came there daily at their own expense, hoping to be noticed by the queen or one of her great men, and thus obtain employment, or a patron for their poetry and music. The court was a world to itself and as busy as an antheap full of well-dressed ants.

We found the queen in a thronged gallery. It had deep window bays, almost small rooms in their own right, and she was standing in one of them, talking to a couple of her councillors. We caught her eye as we came to the entrance to the bay, and with a faint nod she let us know that in a moment she would beckon us in. While we waited, lingering where she could see us, I looked with interest at the little groups of men and women strolling or standing all about us.

I absorbed, as I always did, the byplay of it all, especially the cheerful smiles and studiedly confident stance of people who were not quite as richly dressed as those to whom they were talking but were trying to give the impression of belonging to some worthwhile inner circle—because to be an outsider is humiliating and, besides, life is so perverse that it is easier to attract a patron if people think you already have one. Those who understood the signs could tell at a glance who really mattered and who did not.

A rich variety of perfumes scented the air, and the whole gallery was full of murmuring voices and rustling silks. As my gaze moved round, I noticed a well-made man with a face both weather-beaten and intelligent, and a doublet cut differently from the doublets of the English courtiers, in earnest conversation with a dark-complexioned individual who had an agreeable smile and very good clothes that I thought were in the Spanish style. I had been away from court affairs for so long that my memory of faces was rusty, yet I thought I had seen the weather-beaten man somewhere before and I was almost certain of his companion's identity. As I watched, I saw the probable-Spaniard attempt to detach himself, and then check politely as the other man laid a hand on his arm.

If I were looking about me, trying to recognize people, there were also those who recognized me. A tall and splendid figure in a mulberry taffeta doublet, the queen's friend Robin Dudley, now ennobled as the Earl of Leicester, bore down on us. When we had exchanged greetings, I indicated the pair I had noticed and said, "Who are those two? Is one of them the Spanish ambassador? I'm sure I remember him—de Silva, isn't it?"

"Dear Ursula," said Dudley, his own gypsy-brown face lighting up with amusement, "you never change. You arrive at court after a long absence and instantly tease out the important threads in the complex tapestry of political life. The dark man is indeed de Silva. He is a charming and, fortunately, a sensible man. It's just as well, because the fellow who is talking to him and won't let him get away is Lord Herries, emissary from Mary Stuart. He came to England with her."

"I *thought* I'd seen him before as well. It must have been when I was in Scotland a few years ago."

"No doubt. Ah. Her Majesty is beckoning to us. Come."

"Beckoning to *us?*" queried Hugh.

"Yes. I am concerned in the matter, as it happens." Dudley saw my face and laughed. "No, no, Ursula. Your naughty Penelope hasn't been making eyes at me, not that it would have done her any good if she had. I have a reputation," said Dudley, "for being irresponsible, but I'm not *that* irresponsible. The queen prefers me to concentrate on her. Follow me."

As we joined the queen, Cecil also arrived. Every time I saw him, I thought that he had aged since the last time. On this occasion, the gap was nearly three years long and the change was very noticeable. There was far more gray in his fair beard, and the line between his alert blue eyes was now a deep furrow. Like Hugh, I thought, Cecil was tired.

Elizabeth was informally dressed and had now seated herself in casual fashion on a broad window seat. From these subtle signals, I gathered that Hugh and I were not going to receive a blistering public condemnation for Pen's foolishness but I knew that we wouldn't escape quite unscathed, and nor did we.

"My Cecil! Ursula! And Master Stannard! Sweet Robin, you are welcome." As we made our courtesies, Elizabeth gave each of us in turn her hand to kiss. Then she fixed her golden-brown eyes on my face and came to the point at once. "You know what this is about, of course. The girl Penelope Mason cannot remain at court. We understand that you know why."

"Yes, ma'am," I said sadly. Elizabeth too looked older. Her pale, shield-shaped face had settled into mature lines; her mouth was less vulnerable. She was no longer the young girl she was when I first met her.

"We expect the Maids of Honor to be lively," she said, "even if they sing and dance in their rooms and irritate people in neighboring apartments. After all, they are young. We even expect them to flirt a little. We watch them for their own protection but allow them some latitude. Not to this extent, however. This blatant pursuit of a married man—sonnets pinned into his cloak, no less!—Such things will not do. We understand that the girl's mother wants to find a match for her. We would recommend that this is done without loss of time—before she has a chance to misbehave again, perhaps disastrously for herself. And now," said Elizabeth, turning to Dudley, "my lord of Leicester has something to say."

Hugh and I looked at Dudley, puzzled. He smiled. "One of the problems the girl has is lack of dowry," he said. "We have enquired from her and from her mother what her portion is likely to be, and there is little to spare for her."

"The rents of one small sublet farm and the tiny hamlet that goes with it," said Cecil, speaking for the first time. "Not enough to attract a court gentleman unless he were to fall deeply in love with her—and that doesn't seem likely."

"No," I agreed regretfully, thinking of Pen's unremarkable looks. "With Pen—no, it isn't very likely."

"I, however," said Dudley, "am willing to help."

Hugh and I continued to gaze at him, but now it was with astonishment. Dudley was a very wealthy man and could be generous; he gambled a good deal but had a reputation for paying his debts on time. He was not, however, known as a philanthropist, and I had never heard before that he went about providing dowries for plain young women who had no connection with him.

"I have a parcel of land in the north of England, about fifteen miles from the castle of Bolton," he said smoothly. "It's on the edge of a wild place called Saddleworth Moor. I was left it by a former employee who had no family of his own to will it to. It's a fair-sized stretch of land, with arable fields, a big flock of sheep, and both meadowland and hill grazing for them. They're valuable. The wool is good. It all amounts to a very respectable piece of property, or so I understand. I have had reports of it, although I haven't seen it myself. I have little time or, to be honest, inclination to travel north and inspect it personally. In fact, in many ways, it's a nuisance to me. I am willing, as it were, to donate it to a good cause. It might well help to attract a husband for the girl."

"We understand that her mother would prefer a husband with Catholic beliefs," observed Cecil. "Provided, of course, that he has a loyal reputation and attends Anglican services at least once a month, as the law states. There are many Catholic adherents in northern England. A suitable man might be easier to find there. Mistress Penelope should perhaps go to see her dowry lands in Yorkshire."

He finished on an odd, thoughtful intonation. I recognized it. I'd heard him use it before. I looked at Dudley. "The place is near Bolton, you say, my lord?"

"Reasonably near," Dudley agreed suavely.

As soon as the word *Bolton* was spoken, I had come alert. That was where Mary Stuart was being held. Something was coming; I knew it. There was more to this than just making arrangements to marry off a wayward Maid of Honor.

"Mary Stuart of Scotland is at Bolton," said Elizabeth, echoing the words that were already in my head. "You met her, did you not, Ursula, when you went to Scotland a few years ago?"

"I . . . yes, ma'am. I did."

"And I believe she liked you? You were her guest at Holyrood in Edinburgh for a while?"

"Yes, ma'am," I said with caution.

"No doubt she finds life strange and limited at Bolton, compared with life as a queen," said Elizabeth gravely. "Her representative, Lord Herries, is at Richmond now and would like us to receive her here, but my good Cecil is much against the idea of bringing her to London."

"She has a charge of murder hanging over her. She is not a fit person to associate with the queen of England until her name is cleared," said Cecil, his voice now quite colorless. The words *over my dead body* were not spoken aloud but hung in the air like an overripe ham from a ceiling hook.

"We think," said Elizabeth, smiling sweetly, "that it would be an excellent idea, Ursula, if my lord of Leicester's generous gift could be signed over to Pen at once, and if you took the wench north to inspect it. You could look for a husband for her in that district—and while you are about it, you could visit Mary Stuart. We can arrange that Sir Francis Knollys, who has charge of her, will admit you, though I shall tell him only that you and she have met before, and that since you chance to be in the district because you are accompanying Mistress Penelope, I wish you to present my compliments to my cousin."

"I see," I said uncertainly. "Or—do I?"

"Not yet, but I am about to explain," said Elizabeth. "In fact, Ursula, I want you to pass a confidential message to Mary Stuart, from one queen to another. I said confidential—it's more than that. It's personal—on an unofficial level, if you understand me."

I did. There are strange rules in the world of diplomacy. A message passed on by an official personage may be confidential, but it is not personal. *Personal* means a far greater degree of secrecy. *Personal* means that no one will ever acknowledge that the message was ever passed at all.

"I know of it," said Cecil in a low voice, "and so does Leicester here . . ."

"Because I trust your discretion as I trust my own," said Elizabeth. "And the same applies to you and your husband, Ursula. But I wish the matter to be known to no one else, not even to Knollys. He is official. And the task might make him uneasy," Elizabeth added. "He might even dilute the message without meaning to. A mere tone of voice can make a difference sometimes. I know that you, Ursula, won't do that."

"Either that or he might approve of it too much and imagine himself to be Mary's champion," Cecil remarked. "We put him in charge of her, thinking he would be immune to her charms, but we understand that he finds much in her to admire! That won't do, either."

"Quite. She is not to have champions among my subjects. By all accounts, she is remarkably good at acquiring sympathizers and has enough of them as it is. So, you will be my mouthpiece instead, Ursula," said Elizabeth. "Cecil advises it, and I have agreed."

I glanced at Hugh, but he was looking at the queen. His face told me nothing. "The message has to be by word of mouth, I take it, ma'am?" I said. "Nothing written down?"

"Exactly," said Elizabeth. Her eyes met mine again and held them. "There will be an enquiry," she said. "Into the facts of how Henry Lord Darnley, the husband of my royal cousin Mary Stuart, met his death. We have received an emissary from James Stewart, Earl of Moray, her half-brother and at present the Regent of Scotland, requesting us to hold such an enquiry, and we can scarcely refuse him."

"The request is reasonable, in the circumstances," said Cecil.

"But . . ." Elizabeth's gaze was still fixed on mine. "There is a difficulty. Any such enquiry could well turn into something very like a trial. Representatives sent by Moray will attend and may demand that Mary give evidence herself and allow herself to be questioned. This must not happen. It mustn't happen because Mary is an anointed queen and if one monarch is treated like a subject and questioned like a felon, then it can happen to any monarch—especially to one who permitted such a thing to be done in the first place. That is the message you are to take privily to Mary, Ursula. Tell her from me, her cousin, that the enquiry will probably have to proceed but that she must on no account whatsover agree to testify in person or to be questioned. That is all."

She smiled. "We will not demand an answer now, this moment, Ursula. Think about it." Her gaze moved to Hugh. "You must think about it, too. You and your wife must discuss it. Ursula can give me your answer tomorrow."